THE HUNTED

BLACK CARBON #1

A.J. SCUDIERE

The Hunted - Black Carbon #1

Copyright © 2019 by AJ Scudiere

FIRST EDITION

PRAISE FOR A.J. SCUDIERE

"There are really just 2 types of readers—those who are fans of AJ Scudiere, and those who will be."
　-Bill Salina, Reviewer, Amazon

For *The Shadow Constant*:

"The Shadow Constant by A.J. Scudiere was one of those novels I got wrapped up in quickly and had a hard time putting down."
　-Thomas Duff, Reviewer, Amazon

For *Phoenix*:

"It's not a book you read and forget; this is a book you read and think about, again and again . . . everything that has happened in this book could be true. That's why it sticks in your mind and keeps coming back for rethought."
　-Jo Ann Hakola, The Book Faerie

1

J oule could hear the dogs in the distance, and she broke into a run. Just barely in earshot, they rustled the underbrush in the woods behind the houses.

The approaching clouds had brought them out early tonight, and she hadn't calculated correctly. Breath huffing, arms pumping, she ran down the street and hung a sharp righthand turn. Her feet pounded the pavement as she heard the first deep bark—faint, but within range.

She had another turn to make, then the tenth of a mile up her dead-end street before she could close the door behind her. They lived in the last house, and right now she wished they didn't. Her breath was coming hard, but she didn't slow down. The sky was darkening rapidly, and that would only make things worse.

Her house was less than two-tenths of a mile from the place she'd been raiding, but she couldn't cut through the woods— not with the cloud cover rapidly coming in. So she was taking the long way because, although it was not safe at all, it was safer than the alternative.

She could almost hear her mother, worrying at the window.

But her parents were smart enough to close the curtains anyway... even though she wasn't home. At least, she hoped they were. If they didn't do it, the dogs would get them, too.

Joule listened to the slap of her sneakers on the pavement, thinking it would keep her focused. It didn't stop her from seeing the blur of movement behind the Dunford house. The Dunfords were dead, the house empty. Still running, she counted. *Just the one dog. So far.*

She might be able to take on one of them, but they never traveled alone. She could only see one, but she was certain there were at least three others—if not ten—right behind him.

She could see the roof of her house over the slight hill and found some stamina to pick up her pace again. Halfway down the street, she passed a mental checkpoint. She could see her whole house from there.

But she could also see the lone dog that had braved his way out into the street.

He stood between her and her home, pacing on soft paws. His eyes seemed to glow, reflecting light almost like a cat's. Though he changed direction, he never stopped staring at her.

It was over.

She wasn't going to make it.

The dog had seen her.

She had seen victims of the dog packs before. She'd seen a few of her neighbors—or the pieces left of them—after they had stayed out too late. Their sense of smell sucked, but once the dogs saw you, they were relentless. Smart. Operating almost from a hive-mind. No one had ever survived an encounter to tell whether that was really the case.

Though she didn't let the dog see her eyes flick, she gauged the distance to a tall tree she had picked out. There was no telling if it would work. She had no idea if they could climb up behind her. No evidence that they were or weren't strong enough to topple a tree. But she was relatively tall for her age, and if she gave a determined jump, she could grab the lowest branch and scramble up. She only had to make it until morning.

The Cranston house had bank notices pasted all over it. It was definitely abandoned, so she'd picked up two small computer units when she was there. Now they felt heavy in her hand, like a decision that would change everything.

She hefted the bigger one at the dog. Though she missed his head—where she'd been aiming—Joule managed a glancing blow off its side. Still, it was a mistake.

The whining yelp the helldog let out summoned its friends. Though Joule was bolting for the tree, it was still too far away.

Two dogs appeared in the road before her, cutting her off before she was even halfway there. Running home had been her only real plan. Now, she turned on a dime, heading the other way, and spotting three more dogs emerging from behind the house.

For a moment, she stopped moving. They had her on three sides. She'd seen what they did to the people they caught, and she could only pray death would be quick, though she knew it would not be painless.

But they move in packs, she reminded herself. Thus, they'd likely been together before spotting her. The chances they had managed to surround her—when they'd only just now been willing to step out into the darkening twilight—was low.

She had to bank on it. It was her only chance.

With a lightning-fast dash, Joule bolted through the empty space. One house stood there, and she prayed it wasn't locked. The inhabitants were gone. The wife was dead by the dogs, the husband and daughter disappeared. But whether they'd moved away or if the dogs had gotten them, too, Joule didn't know.

The knob turned under her hand, the only good luck of the darker-than-usual afternoon, and she stumbled harshly through. Turning, she slammed the heavy door shut, feeling the weight of a dog pounding against it as she slid the bolt shut.

She might be inside, but she likely had less than a minute.

The dogs knew she was in here. She was their prey, and once spotted, they would not give up. She'd seen more than ample evidence of the dogs having broken into houses— ramming down doors, hurling themselves against windows, however many tries were necessary to get through—just because they'd spotted someone inside.

Hearing the first dog make an attempt at the window on the porch, Joule dashed upstairs. She was looking for something specific.

In the hallway, she passed a shotgun carelessly left leaning against the wall. These people had tried. They hadn't known the dogs were hard to kill with bullets and axes and baseball bats. As she passed, she caught a whiff of food rotting from the kitchen. No, they had not left willingly.

The window behind her shattered, and she heard the scrape of nails on hardwood floor. One dog, two, three... too many to count. They were inside the house and behind her, racing up the stairs.

Joule looked up and spotted what she'd been looking for.

2

"Close the curtains!" Kaya commanded harshly, grinding the words out to her husband, who stared out the window, waiting for their daughter to come home.

Her heart would be breaking, if it hadn't frozen solid. A little while ago, as the cloud cover had come over the neighborhood, she'd become worried. Now she would be in full panic, but she'd shut that part of herself down.

Joule had gone over several streets to check out one of the growing number of empty houses. She would see if anything of value had been left behind. She'd gone out later in the day, but until just moments ago, the day had been sunny and the light kept the dogs at bay. They usually just came out at night. In fact, the dogs operated with such regularity that most of the residents of Rowena Heights went on about their days as though they were normal.

People merely closed up shop early. Pulling all the curtains, shutting the windows, and dramatically lowering the noise levels within the house right before dark seemed to do the trick well enough. The Mazurs did the same, and their usual pattern had worked very well... until now.

Most days now, dinner was early. Evenings were for reading. Voices were kept low and all was fine. The family had taken to using clothes pins to keep the gap in their curtains tightly shut. Kaya smacked them into Nate's hand now, whispering, "Close the curtains."

Her husband just stood there, staring at her, and she could almost hear him saying he would go out and find Joule. But she couldn't lose him, too. Still, he stood before her, jaw clenched, open hand still cupping the clothespins, but doing nothing.

She listened to the sound of the curtain rings, dragging across the pole at the top, as Cage stepped in and did what the rest of them couldn't do: *Close the curtains and shut his sister out.*

If he didn't do it, the dogs would see them.

If the dogs saw them, they would beat the doors until the wood broke, or come through the windows and get all three of the remaining members of the Mazur family.

So it was the hardest thing she'd ever done, but Kaya went through the house and bolted each of the three doors.

Just as she did every night.

But tonight, her daughter—her oldest by only two minutes —was still outside.

She could only hope that Joule had stayed in the house she was checking out. Joule would know that her family realized the danger of the darkening sky and locked all the doors and closed the windows. Kaya crossed her fingers that her daughter had taken the necessary precautions and was safe. But neither Kaya nor Nate, nor her brother Cage, had received any message to that end.

That made Kaya think her daughter had headed home. If Joule was safe, she would have turned the phone off. None of them had considered pinging her or calling or anything that would make the phone beep. Even just the light could attract the dogs' attention. If Joule was hiding, then messaging might kill her.

Kaya looked to the two men—her husband, who was almost the same age as her, and her son Cage, literally the same age as Joule.

"Each of us takes a door," she said, her voice soft in the tone that she generally used in the evenings. Anything more would indicate something was wrong. It *was* terribly wrong, of course. One of her children was outside and there was nothing she could do about it except kill herself, too. So she pretended that she knew Joule was safe, and she used her evening voice.

Once the curtains had been closed, if someone stubbed a toe and yelled, the dogs would know they were inside. Turn the TV up too high? The dogs would know. The family had learned to sleep a quiet sleep—but not tonight.

Both Nate and Cage nodded at her and headed off for the other doors. Turning her back, Kaya slid down the wall until she was sitting at the base of it. Not the warmest place in the house, but she didn't care.

The slightest noise and she would gladly throw the door open wide. If the dogs wanted to get in, all they needed to do was learn how to knock like a human.

She stayed there for an hour, numb in her position and her thoughts. When she looked at her watch, the face glowing dull in the dim light—all the beeps and whistles disabled—Kaya realized it was over. Either Joule had found a safe place or she was dead.

There were no other options that Kaya knew of. No one had ever survived the dogs.

It had started with the neighborhood cats disappearing. First the feral ones, then the house pets. There had been an increase in the number of "missing pet" signs. Then the small dogs had gone missing. Pet owners had started using leashes and not letting their dogs out at night.

But the bigger pets began to disappear, too. When her neighbors' three pit bulls had vanished, the neighborhood realized that there was truly a problem: Something was stalking the night and eating the animals.

They first thought it was a cougar—the marks on the local deer that they had found, or the pieces of them, were indicative of a slashing attack. But it wasn't a cougar, nor a bobcat. Not a coyote pack.

No, it was the dogs.

People had begun to see them at the edges of their property at night.

One of the families had seen the pack. The dogs had tried to bust into the house overnight. The human occupants had spent the entire time frantically screaming. Two police officers had come. But there was nothing the police could accomplish. Both officers had died in the street, shooting at the dogs, trying to save the family.

The next time the police came, they'd wisely stayed in their cruiser. But the windows—bulletproof windows—had not withstood the tenacity of the relentless dogs. With four officers down, the force sent a third car, but only after it had grown light the next day.

Luckily, two of the family members had escaped to a tornado shelter and the dogs seemed to have lost track of them. They'd weathered the night through the screams and sirens. In the morning light, the dogs had disappeared.

And, finally, someone could tell what was really happening.

It seemed to only be happening in their local area. A group of "concerned neighbors" had formed, and Nate and Kaya had attended meetings twice before realizing the group couldn't accomplish much at all. They wanted to talk more than act.

They wanted to erect signs—as though vicious dogs would pay attention to their "we're watching you" posts.

Kaya had found another group that wanted to kill. This gathering was mostly younger, mostly male, and mostly idiots. Despite the police officers losing their lives to the dogs, these guys believed *they* could accomplish eradication, one dog at a time, despite having no information about what the dogs were or how to kill them. Kaya hadn't even given them her name. That had been two months ago, and she couldn't find any evidence of that group now. Maybe they were dead?

The groups had not been having much effect, because over the past several months, reports showed the dogs' range getting bigger. And why not? House pets were a feast, and the dogs were running unchecked. Though Kaya regretted it deeply now, she and Nate had decided not to move.

Curie, Nebraska—the town where they'd been before here —had had its own problems. There were legitimate reasons why they'd left. However, those were small in comparison to what they faced now, with the dogs. Kaya wished she could go back, but Curie didn't exist anymore. Wildfires had rushed through and burned the plains after the harvest season, fueled by the dried stalks left in the fields. Everything had burned to the ground. Grain silos, filled with corn dust, had gone up almost like rockets. Then the floods had come. Most families had chosen not to rebuild.

Lincoln was suffering massive fires every several months. In other parts of the country, flooding had taken the coastal towns and cities near the Mississippi. The big rivers' dams had suffered to the point where they had broken, and several towns were now fully underwater.

Kaya and Nate had thought the dogs were manageable, so they decided to stay where they were.

Now, sitting with her back against the door, her heart

broken, Kaya regretted that decision with everything she had. They might never find Joule.

As she thought about what the dogs might do to her seventeen-year-old daughter, Kaya broke down into silent sobs, tears dripping down her face as she sat in a cold huddle and waited for a knock that did not come.

3

Cage sat with his back to the door. The bolt had been turned—both of them—but he was ready to leap up and throw the door open, if Joule should knock on the other side.

His mind wandered. It was easier to think about how his parents were handling this than to handle it himself. His father, though emotional, had always been the more even-keel parent. Nate Mazur felt his emotions deeply, talked about them, and hugged his children often. He told his wife he loved her on a daily basis, and handled crises as though they were, in fact, crises.

Cage's mother, Kaya, was more extreme. Nate would be sitting at his door, crying and mourning the loss of his daughter, wanting to throw the door open and run into the night to find her, even if it meant his own death. Kaya was the parent who raged emotionally or found a way to freeze her blood and run things as they needed to be run—from a logical perspective. She'd turned fully logical tonight.

Killing themselves wouldn't save Joule, she said. "Besides,

Joule is smart." She'd stared them down, daring them to say otherwise. They didn't. Kaya was holding it together on the belief that her teenage daughter would somehow be the first to defeat the dogs. Or that she had managed to see the storm coming and got under cover before it mattered. Cage held tightly to that same belief.

Tonight, he was grateful that his mother had demanded the curtains be closed. It was the only reasonable response. Joule was alive. Or she was not. They could not save her. What they could do was save themselves, and Kaya had demanded it. If she had not said it, he would have. He was grateful he'd not been forced to grab his father and hold him back from running into the dark night. He couldn't lose two family members on the same day.

However, Cage had something neither of them had: the firm belief that if something happened to his twin sister, he would know.

He had shared a womb with her, and most everything else ever since. Had anyone at school asked who his best friend was, he would not have said Joule. But he knew in his heart, that was the answer. She was smart enough to keep up with him, and smarter still to run ahead and force him to keep up with her.

They had moved houses and towns together, repeatedly. Just the two of them, the only children in this family. They followed their parents' jobs. And they'd all come here when they realized that Curie wasn't the Camelot it had been hailed as. They'd landed here in Rowena Heights.

High school seniors now, he and Joule had been accepted to several colleges. Their most recent discussions had been: Did they want to go together? Or was it time to split up and go in different directions?

Right now, with his back against the door, he would agree to anything his sister said.

The family had talked about moving again, months ago when the dogs had begun showing up. They had all agreed: the dogs could be managed. The disasters in other parts of the country, maybe not. They'd taken their chances on closing the curtains and reading in the evenings. Their days were perfectly normal. In fact, they were so normal that the rest of the country wasn't yet declaring the dogs an emergency.

Besides, there were too many other, larger emergencies the country had to deal with: Tornado damage in the billions in the fly-over states. Fires. Massive rains destroying city systems, even if the town didn't flood. Sink holes. Earthquakes. High winds. Blizzards... No, the dogs weren't even on FEMA's radar.

Staying had seemed the best decision. They hadn't counted on the dogs getting bolder, or on the cloud cover allowing the dogs to come out early.

Cage told himself his sister was the smartest person he knew. That was saying a lot. His parents were brilliant. Hence, all the moving around. In Curie, Nebraska, he'd met Nobel Prize-winning scientists. He'd hung out with a man who was so brilliant, he was murdered for his ideas. Yet, when it came down to it: Who was the smartest? Who was the fastest thinker? He would have said his sister.

And he didn't have the feeling that he had lost her. So he dozed against the door off and on during the night.

When the morning came, his mother began moving around. He could only assume the sound had woken him, though if he was asked, he couldn't say he had been asleep.

Cage was still waiting for a knock at his door.

Kaya was up and peeking outside. The clouds were still present, but the light was now bright enough that she made a decision to throw the curtains wide and look down the street.

Moving from his position—hoping it wasn't a mistake and that his sister wasn't just on the other side, about to knock—

Cage joined his mother. His back resting against the front door, Nate still slept with his head tilted down to his chin, his neck at an odd angle. They didn't want to wake him if he'd finally found sleep. It had come hard for all of them, but maybe hardest for Nate. He'd been ravaged by the inability to go out and save his child.

How long? Cage wondered. How long before they went out and looked for her? How much did they look before they decided it was a loss?

He didn't know.

He didn't want to know.

So he stood next to his mother, peering down the empty street.

When movement caught their eye at the same time, they jerked. Kaya's hands flew to press at the glass of the large front window. But it was only the neighbor, pulling his car out of the driveway and heading off for work.

The Pearsons didn't know that Joule had been out all night. They had likely closed their curtains early, all their family members intact, and spent the night as they usually did. Now, they were heading off for work, just as normal.

But it was too much for the Mazurs. Kaya, still being quiet so as not to disturb Nate, motioned to Cage. In a whisper, she said, "I'm going out."

He shook his head at his mother. "Not by yourself. I'm coming with you."

"No." She shook her head sadly, and he could tell she was pushing through the words. "If I find anything, I don't want you to see it."

He shrugged. "I wouldn't want you to see it, either. You're her mother. You carried us."

Silent tears rolled down Kaya's face, indicating what she expected to find. But that was the only crack in her ice-blood armor. "If anything happens, wake Dad up."

"No!" Cage demanded in a fierce whisper. If there was ever a time to deny his mother, it was now. "We'll wake Dad up now. Tell him to hold down the fort. But you and I are going out together."

4

J oule clutched her phone, turning down the volume
even as the screen came to life. She had to tell her
family she was okay, but she couldn't see beyond the
roof. Though she was certain it was now light enough
to turn on the phone, she still held her breath. It wouldn't do to
have the phone bleep if any of the dogs remained in the house
below her.

It took an agonizingly long time for the phone to load, even
though she knew it was as fast as it always was. Once it was up,
she tapped out a note to her family and waited.

Immediately, two messages came back, one from Cage and
one from her dad.

Her dad simply said, "Oh thank god baby." He didn't even
use his standard full words and proper punctuation. Joule
smiled at the screen, thinking just how worried her dad must
have been.

Cage replied with, "Where? Mom and I are out."

Tapping a message back to them, she explained which
house she'd ducked into at the last moment. She'd been so
close to home, but it hadn't mattered.

Though the day was far enough along that the dogs should be gone, Joule couldn't make promises. She hadn't expected them to be out as early as they were yesterday. So clearly, their understanding of the dogs' behavior was off.

The building had been dark when she'd come in, and she'd seen her way by the glow of streetlamps filtering through curtains that had remained opened since the family left. So it was entirely possible a dog or two was still in the house.

No one knew where they went during the day. They appeared at the dark and disappeared at the light. If you saw them in the dark, you were done. No one saw them during the light. So no one knew where they stayed or how much they slept. Joule had only recently learned what they ate and how they hunted it.

She heard the front door open and listened carefully, not quite willing to come out. Voices she knew and loved, voices that sounded like her own, hollered out as they tromped through the house. Joule figured the goal was the opposite of that at night: make as much noise as they possibly could, in the hopes of scaring away any remaining dogs.

When she heard the footsteps get close, she yelled, "I'm here! Up here!"

Crawling over to the hole in the rough plank floor, she saw the strings. Both had pull knobs on them. One belonged up here, to help get out of the attic. The other was supposed to hang down, just overhead, in the hallway below. She called out as the attic door swung down, extending the staircase that more closely resembled an escape ladder.

When she'd raced up here, she'd pulled the string up with her, so the dogs couldn't jump up and grab it. She was afraid if they did, the door would swing down for them—like it had for her, on well-oiled hinges—and would offer them an easy path up into her hiding place.

She was halfway down the stairs on tentative feet, still

hungry and nervous, when Cage shot up the remaining two steps, grabbed her, and leapt down. She was in too tight an embrace to protest. In a heartbeat, she felt her mother's arms around both of them. Only then did Joule let herself cry.

She heard the synthetic sound her mother's phone used to mimic an actual old-style shutter go off. She realized her mother had taken a picture of the three of them, or maybe just her, and was sending it to her father.

"Where's Daddy?"

"At the house. Guarding the door and waiting for you to come home." Her mother rubbed her head as though to prove she was real, and for once, Joule didn't mind the overly-parental gesture. "I tried to come out by myself, but Cage insisted."

Joule felt her arm snake around her brother and squeeze tighter just one last time before she stepped backward onto her own feet. "I'm hungry."

Her mother laughed, the sound golden in the dim light of the abandoned home. "Of course, you're hungry." Kaya liked to joke about the kids eating more than they weighed.

"I got a cool computer system," Joule volunteered, "but I threw it away when I realized it was weighing me down." For a moment she wondered if she would have been fast enough to make it all the way home if she hadn't tried to run with her pockets full. It didn't matter; she'd survived, and she would take that as a win.

"Oh, what kind?" Kaya asked. They were all trying to make the meeting as normal as possible, and not the aftermath of the first time they thought they'd lost one of their own.

Joule rambled her way through what she'd seen. Honestly, she couldn't even think now about what she'd grabbed. "I don't remember. Just that it seemed like a good idea at the time. But I also got—" pushing her hand down into the deep pocket of her jacket, she pulled out a wad of nylon. "These bungee cords and this webbing. I wasn't the first one who'd looked through their abandoned things."

The three of them headed out the front door and down the steps. Only her mother thought to turn around and pull the door closed behind them.

None of them commented on the deep gouges in the hardwood floor.

The dirt rubbed on the wall.

Or how high up the scratches had reached underneath the attic door.

5

Kaya was frustrated. She wanted to put her foot down and be a demanding parent, though it wasn't her usual style.

Nate had taken the day off yesterday and so had she. Today, they had both gone in to work. No one at either office balked at missed days anymore. In fact, she'd had days when the place cleared out and no one questioned it. Everyone knew about the dogs, though no one talked much about it.

However, since her excuse for missing the whole day before was that her daughter had gotten stuck outside, everyone wanted to be sure Joule was okay. Kaya had brought the kids to the office more than once, and everyone loved them. "She was smart enough to find a good shelter," was all Kaya told them.

It was too much to say how she herself had stayed up all night, her heart pounding. They didn't ask that kind of thing. When one coworker hadn't shown up for three days and wasn't answering his phone, another had gone by his house but hadn't found anything. Kaya was hoping he'd gotten out but had no idea where "out" might be. She certainly hadn't found it for her family.

So when everyone said, "Oh! Thank God she's safe," Kaya didn't comment on the fact that Joule had seen the dogs. That she had run from them. That her daughter was the first person she knew who had actually escaped. She didn't want to bring that kind of attention to Joule.

Kaya didn't like the way yesterday had gone down, or that her family was still voting to stay in Rowena Heights. Kaya was certain they should get out. If the other night had shown them anything, it was that the dogs were painfully unsafe.

"But other people don't have houses." Cage had pointed out that the markets in other places were painfully high—to the point where they couldn't afford an apartment—or painfully low, because most of the houses had been destroyed by winds, tornadoes, earthquakes and more.

Nate, on her side originally, had been swayed by the kids. "He's right. I don't think we can talk about moving. Where is better? We both have jobs here."

"We can't go back to Curie," Joule had argued. That shocked Kaya the most. Joule was the one who had seen the dogs. She was the one who had run from them, had closed the door and felt the weight of the dogs pounding on the other side. Yet her daughter still wasn't voting to move.

"Curie is burned to the ground," Cage said, joining his sister. "Lincoln isn't far behind it. Or Omaha. I mean, they're breathing ash all the time." He was right. The wildfires were taking out houses and making the air borderline-unlivable for those who still had homes.

"We could go back to Charleston, but a lot of the houses are old. With the earthquakes, they're cracking down the middle. The construction crews can't keep up. I don't want to escape the dogs and die because a house collapses on me."

Joule surprised her mother again. The argument was solid, valid. Instead of traumatizing her daughter for life, the brush with violent death had seemed to make her think she was immortal.

Kaya thought that might be even more dangerous.

"There's got to be somewhere," Kaya said.

Cage was clearly in alignment with his sister. That was one thing Kaya had always loved—until the twins ganged up on her. She appreciated that her children liked each other. But damn they were obnoxious and smart, and she was losing this battle.

"Joule's right" Cage said now.

"There's somewhere… But *where is it*? I think we should have this argument again, but when we're not just getting in the car and driving into a floodplain or a fire zone, or a supercell tornado area. Once we have a destination in mind."

Kaya had found no comeback, nor had Nate. The two of them had climbed into their cars today and gone to work. Joule and Cage had gone back to school with notes for their missing day, though the school had stopped reporting truancy.

The children told her they had a plan for the afternoon. Kaya wasn't all that keen on the idea, but the goal was to find safe houses throughout the neighborhood. Joule's attic idea seemed to have worked… at least for one night.

Kaya wasn't so certain that the dogs wouldn't figure it out. The marks on the walls had been terrifying in their accuracy. Several marks had hit the ceiling right underneath where her daughter was. They had known their prey—*her daughter*—was just above them.

If nothing else, at least Joule had been smart enough to pull the cord to the attic stairs up with her. She'd looped it around the board when she yanked the stairs up behind her. Had she not done that, she might not have survived. Kaya always felt her organs freeze when she thought about that. Had Joule not picked the right house, had it not had an attic with stair access, had she not thought to—

Kaya shut the thoughts down. Joule *was* okay. She'd survived. The children would be okay. It became a steady mantra.

Unfortunately, even Kaya couldn't find a safe place to move. Though she'd looked several times today when she caught a moment, she'd still found nothing. They'd had to shelve the argument.

She back-calculated what she knew about the dogs. It had been about a year and a half since they had first showed up. That was when the cats started disappearing. Though it was possible the dogs had been around before then, that was the earliest she could be sure of. It was the first sign that they had been out there waiting. *Hunting.*

If her math was right, then in a year and a half they had gone from hiding and picking off only the tiniest animals to standing down humans. They now operated in packs that took down police officers, crashed through the windows of cars, broke into homes, and were rumored to fight groups of people. Not big packs of people—the humans hadn't organized well enough yet to do that—but they had all learned the dogs could withstand a shotgun blast, and even a handful of bullets before beginning to slow down.

When she found another spare moment away from her experiments, Kaya logged in again and continued her search for someplace safer to move because, deep in her heart, she knew the dogs were getting worse.

6

Five days later, nothing had changed except that Kaya's frustration level had ratcheted up. There *was* no safer place to move.

The Earth was basically fighting back against the humans inhabiting it. As one of those humans, Kaya Mazur was desperately trying to keep herself and her kids alive. It was frustrating as all hell that living with the dogs seemed like the best option.

In the past, Nate had to stop her on more than one occasion from yelling at her TV. They would watch a congressional hearing, and some scientist would testify, "We predict X amount of damage in the next ten years."

Of course, Congress would answer back, "But what if you're wrong? What if it isn't in ten years? What if it takes twenty?"

But Kaya would holler at the TV. "That's exactly the problem! What if they're *wrong*? What if it doesn't take ten years? What if it only takes five? What if it only takes *two*?"

In the end, it hadn't taken ten years. The scientists *had been wrong*. They had dramatically overestimated how long it would take once the damage really began occurring. They'd missed that, once it started, it wouldn't come in linear increases but in exponential waves.

Three blizzards had howled through the eastern US this year alone, leaving in their wake a massive toll. Lives had been lost. Homes were lost. Jobs were lost and more. It was no longer shocking to anyone that sea level rise had decimated Miami and caused more problems in Florida than could be counted. But what the experts hadn't factored in was how the added water would change the Gulf and how that would affect everything up the Mississippi River. Sea level rise had altered every port city in the US.

As she searched for places to move her family, Kaya encountered flooding, fires, earthquakes, and more—all on the rise. The dogs, at least, only came out at night. It had been the family's mistake that they had let Joule out on her own.

There were easier ways to avoid the dogs than there were to fight tornadoes, blizzards, and floods. So Kaya had walked in the door that night with a scowl on her face.

"And how was your day?" Cage asked, his sarcasm reflecting off her expression.

The think tank she'd come here to join had been working on the mechanics of windmills for alternative fuel sources and pumps for natural gas. Since hiring on for the job, it had gone from a dream plan to a survival mode/last ditch effort. Everything at her job had ratcheted up since she'd started. The stress was so much higher, but so were her paychecks and her hours.

She wanted to cut back. She wanted to spend time with her children. But the fact was, she had to fix the world for her children to live in. "It was the same as every other day. How was school?"

"I got a one-hundred-and-five on my Latin test," he said. But that was no surprise to Kaya. "I think Joule did, too."

"You had lab today, didn't you?" she asked, as she thumbed through the mail. How was there still junk mail? Who was killing all these poor trees to tell her that her car warranty was about to expire? She looked up just in time to catch Cage's absent nod. That was a bad sign. "Did you jury rig the experimental setup again?"

"Maybe a little."

He and his sister were no longer allowed to be lab partners in Mrs. Winston's class, something that always made Kaya cringe. She'd never gotten the full details of the event that had warranted that split, but the words "explosion" and "evacuation" had been thrown around. They'd let her children keep attending the school and the class, so Kaya assumed it wasn't *that bad* and didn't ask any more questions.

She sighed. "Did you get suspended?"

"Nope," he replied as Joule walked into the room.

"Did your brother get suspended for jury rigging the physics lab?" she asked her daughter instead.

"Nope," Joule replied, "and neither did I."

"Oh, dear god." Kaya focused back on the mail, looking for anything that could be attended to and finished, unlike her children.

"You got a minute?" Joule asked her. She held a blueprint-like document rolled up in her hand, making her mother wonder.

"Sure." She set her purse into its usual messy spot. Kaya had other things in her life that she did well, but home organization was not one of them. "What do you have?"

Joule rolled out the document on the table with Cage helping. Using pencils and tiny toys, he weighted down the corners. *That, in and of itself, is telling*, Kaya thought. Her children still had LEGOs, her daughter loved funny-faced erasers, and her son had found tiny, squishy toy animals for stress relief that he carried in his pocket everywhere. They were still kids. But now those toys anchored blueprints that Kaya could see represented their neighborhood.

"These houses." Joule pointed to green highlighter checks on some buildings and orange highlighter x's on others. "These are the ones that have attic access—like the one that I found. I think it's important that we remember these locations in case we need them in the future."

Joule didn't say if they needed them because they were caught out late and it was dark—their fault—or if she thought the dogs would evolve and the daylight might no longer be protection enough.

"How many still have neighbors living in them?" Kaya asked. A reasonable portion of the neighborhood had disappeared. She didn't like to think about how many had been eaten and how many had been smart enough to leave.

"That's the blue." Joule pointed out as she traced a finger around the outside of the homes that still had people living in them.

"Do we tell them about the attic access?" Kaya asked, knowing her kids understood she meant *should they tell them how valuable it might be*?

Normally, her own answer would have been *Yes*, just go tell them it was an option. But she'd tried to do that before, when her family first noticed it was the darkness that brought the dogs out. Some of the neighbors had been rude, saying they'd already figured that out. Kaya had expected as much, but was hoping to open a line of communication. Several had rebuffed her, suggesting she was crazy and that they just started going to bed early for almost no reason. The denial was shocking.

In her more generous moments, she understood that the anger and denial were forms of self-preservation. People were reacting to the dogs and the horrific consequences of minor errors. In her less generous moments, Kaya imagined just shrugging at them when they asked if she'd seen their beloved dog Taffy. Now, she was simply reluctant to knock on doors and share information.

"So we have three houses on our street with probable safe spaces." Kaya told the kids. "That's good to know. But how long do we have before the dogs figure out how to get into the attics?"

"We don't know," Cage replied with an easy shrug that belied the severity of the situation. "They seem to be evolving relatively quickly—at least in their actions. No one's ever caught one to see what they look like. So there's not a good way to predict when they'll get to that point."

Kaya started to open her mouth. Then she closed it, not wanting to give the kids any ideas. "So what's our alternative? What if the attics don't work?"

"Well." Cage smiled and used a tone that almost said *I'm glad you asked*. What he actually said next was, "Come outside. We'll show you."

7

C age led his mother into the backyard, knowing his sister would follow. The two of them stood in the middle of the open space, an area they had once talked about for a puppy. Now, they looked around.

His mother put her hands on her hips, and clearly she'd had a shittier day than she'd lead on by her tone earlier. This more matched her facial expression when she'd come in the door. "Faraday Carson Mazur, what did you do?"

"Hey," he replied. "Don't full-name me." They'd always called him "Cage." His two physicist parents had thought it was funny to have a kid named *Faraday* and call him *Cage* when he was an infant. However, it had stuck, and Cage wasn't a bad name to go by. Every now and then, when he told someone his first name was actually Faraday, they grinned. That's when Cage knew he had found his people.

"All right," Kaya said, looking back and forth between the two kids, because clearly they had both been involved. "What did you do?"

Cage waved his hand across the open space of the backyard.

"Look at the trees. Which ones can you climb to escape the dogs?"

His mother looked back and forth and he watched her thinking. Eventually, she answered. "None of them."

"Right. Why not?"

One by one, she pointed to each tree, listing its problems. "That one is so bushy that even if I got up into it the dogs would follow me right up. It's *too* easy to climb." She pointed again. "That one's got a nice clean trunk, but it's not very tall. It's young and probably wouldn't hold my weight." She turned and pointed to the far corner, where the biggest trees grew. "The ones that are tall enough... well, I don't think I could get up into them. The problem is, if the dogs can't reach the bottom branches, probably neither can I."

"Exactly," Joule said from behind them. Cage turned, and he and Kaya both realized why it had taken her a few extra minutes to come out. Joule had half a gummy worm hanging out of her mouth.

As Cage watched, his mother opened her mouth—probably to suggest that gummy worms weren't a good afternoon snack —but Joule beat her to it. "I just ate a handful of carrots. And I've only got two worms. Also, that's exactly the problem with the trees."

Nice redirect, Sis. "Well," he offered in his best infomercial announcer voice. "Do you have problems getting away from dogs? Trees not going to hold your weight? Are the low branches too high up? Well, let us introduce the *Dog Ladder 2000.*"

Kaya raised one eyebrow at him, but at least a little of the sourness left her expression. "Go on."

"Right now," he continued in his usual voice. "What we have are ladders hanging from the trees. We've got them on a pully system. So, come on." He motioned, and they all walked to the far side of one of the larger trees.

He and Joule had hung it on the other side, thinking that if they had need of it, it would be because they couldn't get to the house. Thus, the ladder should be on the far side. "See? We can climb up into the tree and pull the ladder up behind us."

With a motion to his sister, Joule—who had a tail of a gummy worm still hanging out of her mouth—went right up the ladder. At the top, she turned and pulled it up.

"There are two modifications we want," she hollered down to their mom. "The first is that it needs to come up right behind you, not wait until you hit the top. It would suck to be halfway up, or three quarters up, and then a dog gets on the bottom rungs and pulls it down. And you with it.

"The other problem is that we don't want to leave them hanging down all the time. I'm sure the dogs will destroy them, and it may very well give them ideas to climb trees. So what we actually need is a ladder that we can pull down only when we need them."

She was nodding to her brother, and Cage continued to describe the modifications they had talked about earlier. "It has to work all the time, every time. Because if you yank on it and it doesn't come down ... well, that's not going to be okay."

What he didn't say was, *If the ladder didn't come down, you were dead.* If you had decided your best chance was to climb a tree, then not only were dogs chasing you, but they were close. A runner wasn't going to have time to pick another tree, and Cage didn't know how many trees he could put ladders in.

Kaya was nodding. "I wonder if there's maybe a way to have it on you and then throw the ladder up into the tree..."

Cage nodded. "We thought about that. Firefighters have hook ladders that they throw. But those are dependent on having an orthogonal top on a roof. The trees just don't have flat edges to hook. Even if you had a branch you could catch the ladder on, you would be climbing in midair, rather than braced as you went up the trunk. Also, there are a number of other branches in the way. I would assume that would mean getting it up correctly in the first place would be difficult."

Joule, swallowing the tail of her gummy worm, added in, "I can't imagine throwing a ladder when I was stressed."

Cage didn't comment, but he took her statement at face value. His sister knew what it was to run from the dogs. If she didn't think she could throw a ladder into a tree, he wasn't going to press it.

"Well, okay," Kaya said. "I think they're all really good ideas. I think you're right and it just needs a little more work. Once we get it figured out, maybe we should talk to the neighbors about it."

Joule rolled her eyes and Cage seconded the thought, if not the action. Some of the neighbors were asshats.

"It's really good work guys," his mother said. "And we're never going to lose track of a family member again. I'm so sorry, Joule."

Joule swiped her hand as if to wave her mother off. Not to dismiss the situation or the ensuing trauma, but to convey the idea that it wasn't her parents' fault. Cage knew they each felt individually guilty about Joule being out when the clouds had come in. No one had known that the dogs coming out at dusk didn't necessarily mean "as the sun set" but "as the darkness came." But he understood his parents' guilt, because he felt it, too.

"Still, it's a good start," Kaya told them as the kids dismissed her and she turned to walk into the house.

Cage caught his sister's eyes behind their mother's back. There was more work to be done. Just not things he was going to tell his mother about. Not yet.

K aya worked from home the next day. The children were out of school for teacher training. It was weird, she thought, the way things continued on as though they were normal.

There was no FEMA funding to deal with the dogs. The government agencies were stretched far too thin, busy cleaning up after actual natural disasters. There was nothing left to help with the dogs. Rowena Heights was in one of the nicer parts of the city, and their city didn't have tornadoes. They didn't have flooding or earthquakes, at least not the big ones.

This neighborhood had been sought-after when they first moved in. It had taken both Kaya's and Nate's salaries to qualify for the mortgage on the initial value of the house. Then, as the disasters started encroaching on other areas of the US, and considering what was going on now... Kaya wasn't sure what it was worth. She hadn't looked it up and wouldn't trust a number she got anyway. No one wanted to move where the dogs were.

"We're heading out." Cage's voice pulled her from her irritated reverie. He had a backpack slung over one shoulder and held a brown paper bag in his hand. When she motioned to it with her eyes, he said, "Lunch," and shook the bag a little bit, as though to demonstrate there was something inside it. Not that she had doubted her son would take extra food with him wherever he went.

Her eyes flicked next to Joule and the compound bow she wore slung over one shoulder. The cross strap on her chest indicated she was also wearing the accompanying quiver.

When she and Nate had first bought the kids bow and arrow sets, Kaya thought it was for fun. Cage had put his set down relatively soon. But Joule had stayed outside and practiced day in and day out. Now, she could hit a bullseye from a distance farther than the bow and arrow was supposed to range.

Three years ago, the bow and arrow had been a toy. Now Kaya was glad her daughter was wearing it. Guns didn't work— not easily. The bow and arrow probably wouldn't kill a dog, either. But it was broad daylight, and if anything happened, she could only hope it would slow the dogs down. She wasn't keen on her kids carrying guns into the woods. Then again, she was no longer keen on any of her loved ones going into the woods —period.

Standing up, she hugged each of them tightly. She would have kissed them on their foreheads, but they had grown tall enough to kiss her on hers. So she didn't try. She wanted to wrap them in packing materials and keep them safe, but now that would mean keeping them from living life. She had to trust them on their own, the way she trusted Nate.

She was taking a gamble every time she let them out of her sight. But it was broad daylight, they were together, and there wasn't much more she could ask. "Be safe."

They weren't even snarky in response anymore. Cage looked her in the eye and said a clear, "Yes."

Joule replied, "We're on it."

So she watched her only children head out the front door,

turn right across the lawn and head into the woods on the side of the property. Several years ago, she would have enjoyed watching her kids romp off to play in the woods. Today, it just filled her with trepidation.

She thought by now—her children were seventeen years old—that she wouldn't have taken the day off just because they were out of school. But she wasn't ready to let them go. They'd discussed colleges, but the colleges were having the same problems as everywhere else. Kaya had her fingers crossed the twins would still decide to go together.

It was difficult to get in the way of their education, because she could only hope things would get better. People would figure out what they needed to do and begin to patch the Earth, and when they did, her children's education would give them an edge. *If they can just live through it.*

With everyone out of the house, she logged out of her work program. Work could wait. Her job gave her too many hours, and she logged too many more trying to find solutions to everyday problems. Not today.

Kaya pulled up another screen and dove into other research.

She was a physicist. She sorted out weights and balances on pumps. She was working out the nature of the mechanics of windmills. Her husband—also a physicist—was in a different sub-field than she was, but they spoke the same language.

The dogs, though... they were not a problem of physics. Kaya had never before wished so strongly that she'd gone into biology.

She tapped on her keys and pulled up an image. Then she began the research she hadn't told anyone about.

9

J oule led the way into the woods with Cage just a few feet behind her. He'd tucked their brown bag lunch into the backpack before they crossed the small creek that marked the border between lawn and forest.

She had the bow and arrow in her hands now, no longer leaving it slung over her shoulder. Cage was keeping his hands free. It was what they agreed upon before they coming out. Though the brown bag had, in fact, contained peanut butter and honey sandwiches, a handful of carrots, gummy worms, and Reese's Peanut Butter Cups, another double-bagged Ziploc inside the backpack contained pieces of raw meat.

They had not told their mother that they had taken it. Yesterday afternoon, Cage had nicked a frozen chicken leg and shaved a thin piece of each of the four steaks in the freezer. Joule still hoped no one noticed either loss. They'd snuck the meat into the back of the fridge to thaw and no one had called them on it yet.

They'd walked a little way in silence before Cage spoke. "So, what a little internet search told me is that a coyote—a lone

one—can have a ten-square-mile range. The number is much bigger for a full pack; they can cover up to sixty square miles.

"If we consider that range as an actual square, then we're looking at just over three miles distance on the side." He paused before adding, "That's not too far, and we could possibly find one. If it was a lone coyote."

Joule shook her head. "The pack analogy makes more sense, and we don't know that they're like coyotes. But if they are, sixty square miles in a compact arrangement would come out to..." she thought for a moment. "About seven-point-seven miles on each side of the square."

The woods didn't go that far back, and their parents would notice if they walked seven miles out and seven miles back. The sun would notice if they stayed out that long. The chances of getting caught out at dusk would be too high, and the ladders weren't ready yet.

Joule wasn't even sure she wanted to get that far from home on foot. Where would she find a house that she knew for sure had solid attic access?

"Right?" Cage was still following the coyote analogy. "You're assuming seven miles on the side of the square, *if* we started at a corner. I am assuming we're probably closer to the middle of the square. So only three and a half miles in any direction gets us to the edge of the territory."

"Yeah, but we have to walk in the *right* direction. And what really decides what the center of the coyote territory is?" Joule asked these questions as she swung her bow from side to side. She did not pull back on the string, although she was tense and ready to. She did not trust the woods to stay silent during the day. Using her own voice, she talked over her fear. "Is the center where they hunt? Or maybe where they sleep?"

"That is something the internet was not quite so willing to give up," Cage replied, and she trusted he was watching her back even as he talked. "But I would assume it's where they sleep. That's the point they have to return to each night. So—unless they just sleep wherever they find themselves when the daylight hits—then the epicenter should be where they sleep."

"So what do you think about *how* they sleep?" she asked.

This was their plan: find the dogs and use their unconsciousness as an opportunity to learn everything they could. It was a ridiculous plan. Joule knew that they might walk ten miles today, and if they got lucky, stumble onto a dog. Or they might find a den and not even recognize what it was. If the dogs reacted, they might be toast. Or more likely, nothing would happen

She'd seen deer in the yard—back when there had been herds of deer roaming the area. More than once, she'd watched one walk into the woods from her yard. A deer on the lawn was obvious. By stepping into the woods, the front end of the deer would completely disappear. Joule could still see the white tail flick, but she could not find the head, even though it had to be at the other end of the tail. The deer would pass the edge of the bushes and, even in the winter, when she would think she could see through bare branches just fine. The deer knew how to simply *disappear* into the underbrush.

She could only imagine it was possible the dogs had a similar level of camouflage.

Cage was still answering her question. "I'm guessing they sleep with some kind of shelter. What do you think?"

"I think it is entirely plausible that they sleep directly on the ground. They just curl up, in groups or even a dog pile, and go to sleep."

"Really?" Cage asked. "You think they do this and no one has seen them?"

"Exactly," she said, shaking her head, still not looking at her brother, but scanning the underbrush that hadn't quite started filling in its spring growth. "No one sees them because no one *can* see them. But I think they might be right there."

When he offered her a carrot from the backpack, she took it. Then she continued with her theory. "No one has seen them in the daylight, Cage. So we really have no idea what color or *colors* they are. My guess is that they're very well-camouflaged. We know that they're reasonably dark. And from what I saw the other night, it looks like they have rough fur in shades of brown —kind of like a brindle that a boxer might have had."

Joule noticed she used the past tense regarding pet dogs. No one around here had them anymore. Stepping cautiously through the woods, she continued, still not turning and looking at her brother. "I would imagine they are here in the woods, asleep. It's also plausible that they're so well camouflaged that we wouldn't know we were on them until we stepped on one."

Behind her, the crunch of leaves stilled for a moment, and she could imagine her brother looking all around them— checking out the ground, checking for changes in the patterns of leaves. Clearly, he'd been thinking the dogs would be more hidden. That they would have to go looking for them. That the two of them would spot a den and decide whether or not to look inside. Joule thought that very well might not be the case.

The dogs were vicious, but they also appeared to be hardy. Hardy animals could sleep on the ground. Hell, deer did it, and they were prey animals.

The two of them walked in silence after that, stepping softly through the woods, not speaking. Now, the only noises came when they broke twigs and stopped cold, freezing in place for a moment. They would stand back to back and watch for move-ment in the underbrush.

Joule had paid close attention to the path they had come in on, knowing they might need to get out quickly. She looked at trees now and thought about having to climb up them to escape. Would it work? Could she get up high enough? The trunks had few low hanging branches, but she thought with the right motivation she could get up there.

According to her watch, it was thirty minutes later when she paused. Turning to Cage, she said, "Look. Look at that."

The bright red and true black didn't belong in the forest with her.

"It smells," she commented as they got closer for a better look. It smelled bad.

As Cage approached the object, she held court with the bow and a single notched arrow as he leaned over and picked up a nearby stick to poke at it.

"Well," he said, "that's asstastic."

"What is it?"

He continued to poke at it for a moment, but at last he stood up and looked at her. His hands on his hips and quirk in his eyebrow, he said, "It's a human foot."

10

L eaning over, Cage looked at the foot again. Then, knowing his sister had his back and was watching the woods around him, he examined it a little more closely.

He pulled off the backpack and reached inside. Grabbing one of the plastic grocery store bags he'd stuffed in there, he made a grimace and immediately grabbed for another. His idea had been to use the bags to take things home to study. Now he considered using them like a latex glove.

Double-bagging his hand, he leaned over and picked up the shoe with the foot still inside. A bone protruded where the leg would have been. It went from looking like a perfectly normal shoe near the toe to looking skeletal about halfway up the tibia.

Joule turned, her gaze just shy of a real glare. "Don't pick that up."

He turned, still holding the foot in his hand. "I'm double bagged, it's okay."

"That's not what I'm worried about," she replied. Arrow notched into the string, ready to pull back and let fly as she swung back and forth, Joule scanned the woods. "It's not that you might get sick from holding it or that it might squish in your hand. It's that the dogs ate somebody and dragged them out here. You are clearly holding their *food*."

Cage looked down at the foot in his hand. *Well, when she said it that way* ... For a moment, he examined it a little closer, wondering if he could recognize the shoe, the size, anything that might explain who it had once belonged to. But he didn't.

Holding it out toward her, Cage asked her if she recognized any features of the foot or maybe the shoe itself.

"I don't know," his sister replied after a brief glance that clearly bothered her. "I don't think any of our friends has feet that big. I'm trying to think who in the neighborhood it might have been. Looks like a man's shoe—maybe a big guy."

That matched Cage's initial assessment, though he could have added some of his teenaged friends had bigger feet than they were built for, but he left it at that. Joule was right, he didn't want to be holding dog food. So, with a toss, he chucked the foot into the distance.

The two of them, automatically in sync, stood there silently waiting to see if his move had roused any waiting dogs. After a few moments, when nothing stirred, he turned to talk to her. "Well, we know they don't have a good sense of smell. So, I'm not that worried about it."

Joule nodded her agreement. That was something the Mazur family had figured out early on. If they closed the curtains, if they didn't flash any lights inside or make loud noises, the dogs didn't try to come in. Without visual or auditory alerts, they didn't seem to know they had prey inside the house. The family had decided that had to be true, because once the dogs did know a person was inside, almost nothing stopped them from eventually finding a weak point and bashing their way in. So they didn't have the sense of smell of coyotes, wolves, or even a standard house pet.

Stepping carefully, they walked away from the severed foot.

Cage had thrown it off to the side—not in their way going forward, and not something they would stumble on coming back. But they would both be keeping their eyes open for more body parts.

If the local systems had been working better, he would have insisted on bagging it and calling it in. The police or forensic center might have been able to identify which missing person it belonged to. Cage was no medical examiner, but he was pretty certain that the person who'd once been attached to the foot was now dead.

But each time the police had come to help, they'd tried to fight rather than hide, and they'd died. At one point, animal control had been called in, but they had fewer weapons and fared worse than the police did. The packs were relentless. It hadn't taken long before the local law enforcement's position was to advise everyone, including their officers, to stay inside at night. The police chief had even publicly said she wouldn't send her officers into an area with poison gas, and she couldn't in good faith send them out on complaints of dogs anymore.

"I'm assuming the foot means we're getting close to where they sleep, or at least where they stop and eat. They dragged it this far for a reason, and I can only hope we can find a den, or a sleeping pile of dogs, somewhere around here."

"Do you think they're really *dogs*?" Joule asked her brother.

Cage shrugged. "They look more like dogs than wolves. More like dogs than coyotes."

But Joule had a good point. They looked like mongrels with thick jaws and wide heads. Their chests were barrel shaped and muscular. But, where many dogs had thinner legs, these dogs had thick appendages and long claws. And he'd seen the damage they could do. When he thought about it, people just called them "the dogs" or even "helldogs," but no one had analyzed them. Not that he knew of.

No one who'd gotten a good enough look had lived to see

what they looked like—except his sister. But from what Cage could tell, they were at least as different from dogs as they were from wolves or coyotes. Which messed up all of his math for their little sojourn today. With a heavy sigh, he asked Joule what she thought.

"I think they are dogs... something about the eyes, and the way they barked and..." she used her hand to mimic the snout in front of her face. "The way they snapped. It just made me think of dogs. At least, that's what I'm remembering from seeing them. But their heads are huge and they have claws, not regular dog nails."

Joule also had to know that it was entirely plausible she'd been run down by a pack of angry boxers and simply inflated the memories to helldogs in her mind.

However, the damage Cage had seen them do—the aftermath from attacks his parents had tried to shield him from—said these weren't *just dogs*. The cuts and deep bite wounds weren't anything he could imagine coming from even the wildest of feral canines.

They talked a little more, but in another fifteen minutes, she said, "We've been out for too long. We have to go back."

He wouldn't argue with her. She didn't deserve that. A guy gained a lot of respect for his sister when he'd spent the whole night thinking she was likely dead, even though now it was clear she wasn't. "We can turn around and head straight home. Or we can loop, and make the turn here. Take a different path back."

Cage voted to loop so they didn't retrace steps. He wanted to cover as much territory as possible. When Joule had no issue with this, they took a sharp turn to the left.

They walked all new paths—headed in the right direction, Cage knew, because of the GPS he was carrying—but nothing appeared. They'd been out for hours, and they were finally coming back toward the house. Pulling the GPS out of his pocket again, he checked their trajectory. They were less than a mile from the house now and he started to feel some of the tension drain.

Though he'd not actually thought they would get caught outside at dusk, it was nice to know they'd made it with plenty of time to spare. It was nice to know they wouldn't worry their mother. He'd thought about bringing a regular compass, but the GPS allowed him to mark the coordinates where they had made their turns. Of course, he'd marked where they'd found the foot.

Even close to home, they remembered not to get too lax. Joules stayed out in front, the bow still pulled taut. Though she'd left the house with the bow slung over her shoulder, it hadn't left her hands the whole time they'd been walking. He suspected the casual look had been for their mom's benefit.

Now, she held one hand out to him, her eyes still trained forward. "How about that sandwich?"

He handed over her half, thinking he'd been hungry for a while but wondering when she would ask. So the two of them walked the last leg of the little loop through the woods, munching on sandwiches, a little more comfortable now that they were so close and hadn't seen anything.

Or maybe Joule was right, and they *had* seen it, but the dogs had been so well-camouflaged, the pair had walked right by and not known it. At least there had been no incidents along their walk.

He was halfway through the sandwich, Joule not as far along with hers, when he heard the noise.

Placing a hand on her shoulder, Cage let the sandwich dangle at his side, before thinking better of it. He was grateful again that the dogs had a poor sense of smell.

He didn't even whisper, just moved her shoulder, directing her to where he the sound came from. As they watched, in the distance through the trees, one of the dogs trotted by.

11

K aya perked up as her children suddenly burst through the front door.

"How was it?" she asked brightly. The two had acted as though they had been going out to play in the woods today but, at seventeen, that story didn't hold water. She suspected they were looking for something specific, but she had no real idea what it was. Given recent events, she was highly suspicious that it was related to the dogs.

"Well," Joule began, setting her bow down. Kaya now noticed that she'd been clenching it tightly in her hand. Though she set it aside, she seemed reluctant to leave it. "It was eventful."

That made Kaya spring up from her seat. Though, as she looked at her screen, she realized she didn't want to leave her own research up or be so obvious. She tried to surreptitiously tap a button and change tabs to a different picture. She only wound up on another tab with a similar image and she clicked again and again until her screensaver was up.

Then, she jumped up and threw her arms around her daughter and said, "Oh, tell me."

Joule sank into the embrace—not the most normal reaction for her very independent, sometimes to the point of prickliness, daughter. The past few days had changed her, made her a little more aware of her family and the need to hold them tight. While Kaya appreciated Joule's new affection, she hated the reason. Now Joule was hugging her and saying she'd seen something. As she stroked her daughter's hair, Kaya pushed, "Tell me."

But it was Cage who spoke up. "We saw a dog. It went past us."

Kaya stilled. *Surely she'd heard him wrong.* The dogs weren't out during the daytime. Confusion and disbelief warred in her expression.

"It was alive, walking around... with a human foot in its mouth." Her son added the last as though it were a funny afterthought.

Kaya almost barfed, but she got herself together enough to ask, "What the ever loving fuck?"

She and Nate had never been the kind to censor themselves in front of their children. The children had been taught there were words they could say at home, words they could say with their friends, and words their friends' parents would kick them out for having taught to their own children.

Now Kaya shakily ushered the kids over to the table, where she plopped down into her chair and saw that the two kids weren't as stable as they had originally seemed.

It was Cage who kept talking. Joule had not yet removed the quiver from her back, and Kaya was not going to point it out.

"It walked right by. We found the human foot," Cage said, as though there were a perfectly reasonable explanation, "on the walk out, and we tossed it aside."

Kaya put her hands over her mouth to cover where it had completely fallen open in shock and fear. She whispered the words, "Do you know whose foot it is? *Was*?"

Both kids shrugged and this time Joule spoke. Though Kaya didn't like the words, she was glad her daughter was communicating. "It was some high-end, red and black sneaker. Had some ballplayer's name on it. I think. And it was at least a size twelve."

Kaya was nodding, not recognizing the shoe or the size as someone she knew who'd gone missing, and honestly, she felt grateful for that. "So you *picked up the foot* and tossed it aside?"

"Not really." Cage shook his head as though she were being silly. Of course she was. She was having a conversation with her kids about finding a severed human foot in the woods. Instead of discussing calling the police and opening a murder investigation, instead of asking them to lead a detective to it, she was instead worried that they'd seen a dog. Shaking her head, she focused on her son's words.

"I double-bagged my hand. I just picked it up because we were trying to figure out whose foot it was. When we couldn't, I tossed off to the side of the trail. It was... what?" He looked to his sister. "Probably a few hours later the dog walked by in front of us carrying that foot."

Kaya didn't ask if maybe it was the other foot.

"He didn't see us, or hear us," Joule added to the conversation. "Since I don't think they can smell us, we just stayed still and quiet. He trotted by." She motioned with her hand as though the dog were at a tea party, but she still hadn't taken off the quiver.

"That's good," Kaya agreed. But it wasn't. It was shit. It was pure shit.

It was good that the dog hadn't seen them. It was good that Joule was an excellent shot with her bow and arrow. It was good that the arrows were made of sturdy metal that might pierce a dog well enough to slow it down. *Might.*

Kaya was immensely bothered that those were the good points.

She looked to both of the children, stark terror in her eyes and her heart. She should have hidden it, but she couldn't. She'd thought the world had tilted on its axis when they discovered the first people missing and discovered that it was the dogs.

Now, she felt it tilt again, and though everything her children said added up, she had to ask. "So the dogs are out during the day now?"

12

J oule sat up in the tree and surveyed the neighborhood, first with bare eyes, and then through the binoculars she'd brought up with her.

The weekend had gone by with lots of work and several hundred dollars spent. The Mazur family had hit up a home store, and her parents had readily paid for the things she and Cage loaded into the cart. They'd looked like they belonged on a TV show called *Apocalypse 101*. She would have laughed if it wasn't so close to true.

Joule was also suffering a serious case of senior-itis. She knew many high school seniors claimed to have the malady, and she thought it made sense. Unless she flat out failed more than one class, graduation was guaranteed, including honors. As long as she showed up half the time, she wouldn't fail. Normally, she was an enthusiastic student, but she'd ground her way through a project due on Monday. She didn't need a presentation on Oedipus Rex.

What she did need was a college education, and dropping her GPA at the last minute of her senior year would not look good. So she'd readied her presentation, and she'd done it well enough, but she and her brother and her father had spent the bulk of the weekend on the ladders. They talked about nylon rope, but eventually engineered it with webbing. The flat, tape-like shape made the webbing less likely to get tangled.

They'd discussed wood size—thinner boards weren't solid enough to hold them, while thicker boards added to what was already becoming a weight problem. With two-by-fours, the problem was the arm strength a person needed to pull twenty planks up behind them, considering any friction and possibly tired arms from a frantic climb or a more frantic escape. Even worse, the ladder might give a dog just enough purchase to get up.

In the end, they used more-expensive but slightly lighter polymer planking. Making the ladders out of flat pieces allowed the design to zip up like blinds, taking up very little space, once pulled up tight. They considered using ship anchors to tie the cords down but, on the first test run, the cleats had epically failed the speed test.

Instead, they used finger hooks and cross handles. If you needed the ladder, one need only yank it out and let it go. The ladder would zip down. Another cord dangled about two thirds of the way, so that once a climber got there, they could pull the ladder up behind as they climbed. This would limit susceptibility to a well-placed jump, at least as long as the dog wasn't right underneath.

They'd made a prototype and tested it until her arms hurt, but Joule's heart felt light. As she sat up here on the first warmish afternoon of the season, she felt a weight come off her shoulders.

This afternoon, there were three functioning ladders in her yard. One front, one back, and one out in the woods. The family had knocked on doors—deciding this was too important to let a few angry answers dissuade them—and asked a few neighbors if they wanted any. They'd then added two more down the street. A feeling of safety settled into her chest, loosening the ties that had held tight this week.

She'd been repeatedly jolted awake at night, with no memory of what her dream had been, only knowing that she'd been petrified, and that she was grateful to be awake—to touch her sheets, to know she was inside the house and she was safe. She would sit for a moment and hope she hadn't made enough noise to attract the dogs. But so far, none had banged on the windows. And she felt better, stronger. Tonight, she intended to sleep through.

While she and Cage and their father had made the ladders, her mother had installed attic access in the upstairs hallway. Their own home had not had the pull-down stairs. They had only a square frame in the top of one of the closets.

Joule had analyzed it and found it beyond lacking. Trying to get anyone—let alone the whole family contorted up through that frame was not a survivable scenario, Joule thought. Now they had attic access, and that was another thing that would help them all sleep better.

This morning, there had been handsaws, plywood, and plaster dust everywhere. Her mother understood all things physical: She knew exactly how the hinges worked, the weight they could bear, the best angle to place them at, and so on. But Kaya Mazur was no carpenter.

"How are you doing up there?" Joule's father called up. Setting aside her binoculars, she looked down at him from where she was tucked into the crook of two branches.

"I'm good." It had been her answer all week, but he hadn't pushed and she'd been grateful.

"What do you see?"

"Nothing of value." She'd hoped to spot a pack of dogs, but it hadn't happened. They'd not seen another one since "the foot sighting," nor any other evidence of daytime activity.

Joule wasn't sure if that made her feel better or worse. If

they were out, she wanted to see them and know where they were. If the one had been a fluke, it would take days, or months, of data to convince her that was the case. Also, she was standing behind her theory that the dogs were well enough camouflaged to be moving through the woods unseen.

Her dad knocked on the tree's trunk. He might have climbed up behind her, but she'd pulled the ladder up after her, realizing that—as the person in the tree—she had solid decision-making power about who could join her and who couldn't. *Interesting.*

"Come on down, Sugar Plum," he said after a moment, using an old nickname that she hadn't heard in a while. "Your mom has decided to gather the family. She wants to have a talk."

That wasn't ominous at all... But what Joule said was, "Look out below!" and waited until her dad was out of the way before she let the ripcord go. Turning around and climbing down was the hardest part. She jumped the last few feet to the ground, and then zipped the ladder back up into the tree. Keeping tension on it, she hooked the handgrip into the metal fingers, satisfied the next person could grab it and release the stairs when necessary.

Nate put a gentle arm around her shoulders as they crossed the wide yard. Joule looked over her shoulder at the woods one more time. Just to be sure.

Right before he opened the door, her father stopped and looked at her. "You haven't talked about what you saw. But your mom has decided that it's time you do."

Joule nodded. She didn't like talking about the night she'd run and huddled in the attic while the dogs clawed and growled in the hallway below her. They'd known she was there. She couldn't even turn her phone on to write messages to her family. And she hadn't said anything about that since.

But now, it was time to tell what she'd seen.

13

J oule wanted to drag her feet as she headed into the house, but she didn't do it. It was past time to get this over with.

Honestly, she was somewhat surprised the police hadn't shown up and asked her about her night out. Then again, the police force was only taking reports. They had sworn off handling the dogs, saying first that they couldn't risk their officers and second that it was animal control's job. Animal control said it was a police issue. Both agencies claimed that too many of their workers had gone missing to cover more than the basic city services until they could hire more qualified candidates. So the Mazurs hadn't bothered to file a report about Joule's attack.

Joule had noticed—when they were knocking on neighbors' doors to offer to build ladders in their trees or suggest that they had usable attic access to escape the dogs—that her mother had carefully skirted the issue that Joule had seen the pack of dogs and lived to tell about it.

As much as it had freaked her out to see the dog walking by yesterday, she was grateful that now Cage had seen one up close, too. Maybe that was why her parents had decided it was time to talk.

Her mother started by asking the kids if they wanted a soda. That was a pretty telling hallmark that this wasn't going to be a pleasant conversation. Her mom did not hand out sodas freely.

Joule took her up on it. "Coke, please." How often would she get this chance?

As she sat down, her father organized an odd collection of things on the table while her mother pulled drinks from the fridge. Joule frowned when she saw her dad was gathering art pencils and a sketchbook and she glanced sideways at it, wondering what was going on. But his return look told her nothing.

It was Nate who started the conversation. "I think it's time that your mom and I know as much about these dogs as we can. It's possible other people are doing the same things we are doing: fortifying their houses and making plans. It's also possible that they saw the dogs but they're not telling anyone, either."

Oh. Joule hadn't considered that possibility. She'd thought she was special, but maybe she wasn't. Maybe *everyone* else had seen the dogs.

"Let's create some kind of composite drawing and figure out what they really look like," her father continued.

That was when they all turned and looked at her. Despite Cage having seen one, Joule was still the one with the most knowledge. She looked to her brother, and he offered a small nod back, though she had no idea if that meant *Go ahead, you can do this,* or *Yeah, I've got your back.*

"They're big," she started.

"Weight?" her mother asked, but that wasn't something Joule usually thought about. She didn't have a comparison.

"Bigger than a German Shepherd."

Kaya opened her laptop and began typing. "So, maybe sixty

or so pounds? That's the average weight of a German Shepherd."

"Probably seventy then," Joule replied, realizing that this was how it would go. It would be more like a police interrogation and not a monologue about what she had seen and her general impression of the dogs.

"What did their ears look like?"

"Pointy. Like a German Shepherd. Or fox or wolf." Joule noticed this time, Cage nodding along beside her.

As her mother turned to look at her brother, Joule listened to another surprising question. "Are you sure the dog that you saw yesterday wasn't just a regular house dog, or even a feral dog?"

Cage and Joule looked at each other. It was a thought that hadn't crossed her mind before, but she replied, "It looked exactly like the dogs I saw the other night."

It hadn't occurred to her that all the house dogs might not actually be gone, that some might actually still be around. But Cage replied, and turned her attention away. "It didn't look like a regular feral dog. Like Joule said, it was too big and it carried its weight in all the wrong places to be a pet."

"Okay." Kaya nodded at them. "Then both of you agree: pointy ears?"

Cage nodded.

"What does the face look like? What dog should we start with to model this dog's face?"

"Boxer." Cage's answer was both instant and emphatic. Joule nodded along, glad to have the backup.

"So, squarish snout?

"Less square than a boxer." Joule found it was easier to chime in when everyone wasn't staring at her, wanting her to dig into the scariest night of her life. So she kept going. "These dogs' snouts protrude a little more than a boxer's does. Same general shape, but bigger. The jaws are scary."

Kaya was making notes when Joule had another thought. "Their jaws are *thick*. And their faces are wide."

Her mother offered a quick sketch and Joules and Cage offered a few changes. "More here, less here." "The eyes should be bigger." "The nose smaller."

"Body?" Kaya asked next.

"Thick and lean. Fur looks short and wiry. I didn't touch it!" Joule added, grateful that was the case.

Her mother's eyebrows quirked, and Joule imagined again that she must be glad her daughter had not gotten close enough to touch.

"They're barrel chested." Cage motioned with his hands, up his chest toward his head. "Their necks are thick." He was pointing to the drawing her mother was making.

Kaya's drawing was almost elegant, Joule thought, but these dogs were not. They were thick, lean killing machines.

"Legs?"

"Meaty."

"Big haunches." Joule and Cage answered in overlapping voices.

"Huge feet," Joule said. "Think of the biggest puppy dog paw you can, and then make it angry and give it claws."

She watched as her mother's face pulled into a strange expression, but it clearly indicated her horror at the thought. Still, she sketched a little bit more, took a few pointers from the kids, and then looked up. "Tail?"

"Thick."

"Bushy?"

"No, meaty."

Their mother added a few more dark strokes and turned the art tablet around, showing them the drawing. "So, basically like this? I'm no artist. But you get the idea."

Joule nodded. Her mother *was* an artist. Maybe not one who would ever have her work displayed in the Met, but her mother had some serious sketching skills. "Yes, very much like that."

Nate looked at each of them around the table in turn. He'd been relatively quiet the whole time, but now he said something Joule had not seen coming. "These dogs are killers. They hunt in packs, and they're getting smarter every day. I think we have two options: We either move or capture one."

14

"That's not disturbing at all," Kaya said to her husband as they stood in their large backyard. When they'd bought the house, they had thought the cow farms that abutted the back edge of the property were quaint and cool.

The owners of the farm were of the "gentlemen farmer" variety. The herds small, the land large, the occasional stray cow in their yard a humorous occurrence rather than a nuisance. Only once or twice had she even smelled the cows.

Having moved from a cute little neighborhood in Curie, they had been swayed by the place and the deal—and they now owned more than five acres. Given the age of the house and the size of the land, the property came with its own special zoning. They were allowed to have farm animals, and they were allowed to shoot guns on their property. This was the first time she'd considered taking advantage of any of it.

Realizing the kids were seventeen, and because Nate had argued in favor of it, they were now all standing out in the backyard, passing the gun around. Kaya did not like guns. She only agreed to this because she saw no other option. They had a rifle and a nine millimeter, and they all wore ear protection as they took turns firing at the target.

She'd thought about drawing a dog on the hay bale she'd set up in an attempt to curb stray bullets, but instead she'd drawn a standard bull's eye. Tomorrow, they could fire at something that moved, although it appeared only her children would be doing that. She and Nate had proved to be complete marksmanship disasters who should never pick up a gun in either of their lifetimes.

Nate had been literally hit or miss—with either a bullseye or a stray bullet. Kaya, on the other hand, mostly hit the target, but her aim was completely for shit.

As she'd been ready to give up on the first option for their plan, Nate had turned to her and said, "I think we should let the kids take a try."

Her rebuttal had been swift and fierce. "I don't want them to have a gun in their hands!"

"They're seventeen," Nate argued softly. She hated when he did that. It meant he was confident of his argument. "They'll be eighteen in a handful of months. At that point, they'll have the option to pick up their own guns. We can't stop them. And I'm not sure I would, given what's walking in the woods out there." He gestured with the hand holding the gun, which Kaya quickly motioned for him to hand over. She switched the safety and held it aimed down toward the ground at her side.

"See?" Nate said, gesturing to the gun in her hand. "*We* shouldn't have guns. And if *they* shouldn't have guns, it's better that they learn it now. Better than if they figure it out later with an accident of some kind."

The kids were standing off to the side, pretending they were out of earshot. Kaya knew they weren't. Nate must know, too. But he kept talking in that low, soothing voice that said he knew he was right and he wanted to let her know gently. "Given what's roaming in the woods, I wouldn't necessarily begrudge them wanting to carry weapons."

Kaya loved her husband more than the sun rising in the morning. But damn, when he was logical, he could argue her down into a pulp. It was easier to concede. She could tell that, while the gun was out of ammo, he was not.

"You're right," she whispered. It was the best she could do. Reluctantly, she'd handed the gun to her children.

Cage had been a natural. He'd held the firearm as though he were born to it. *How?* she wondered. *I'm a damned pacifist!* But with little instruction from his father, Cage had simply lifted the gun and fired. He, of course, had nailed the bullseye all six times he pulled the trigger.

With no words and a look that only a teenage boy could give his parents, he turned and handed the gun carefully back to her as though to say, *Well, you wanted to know.* She knew now.

Next, she handed the gun to Joule. Her daughter, in typical fashion, was far more cautious. She set her feet shoulder width apart and squared her shoulders. She lifted the gun in a straight line from the ground to the bullseye and took careful aim. Then she rapidly pulled the trigger and nailed the fuck out of the target.

Behind the kids' backs, Nate had only shrugged at her again. Cage was the more casual shot, Joule far more meticulous. But both had easily outshot both her and Nate. That made her think that, with a little training, they might be able to protect themselves.

But one of the reasons she had been so against guns was that guns were for killing. And, once you killed something, you couldn't un-kill it. Even a squirrel or a bird. Even by accident.

Becoming an instrument of death was a burden she wanted to save her children from. But she had never run across a creature before where she couldn't talk herself into some level of peace. The coyotes had lived here before the houses had come.

Some of the neighbors shot them, but Kaya thought they should have a little respect for the wildlife and just bring their cats in at night. Even the cougar she had seen a few times was here because this was the edge of its natural territory.

But these dogs? She felt no mercy. It was them or her.

Worse, it was them or *her kids*.

Holding her hand out to ask Joule for the gun back, she traded out the empty magazine for a loaded one. It was shocking how easy that became, even in just a few repetitions. While her hands moved cleanly with the motion, her stomach turned with the thought.

Cataloging where the current holes were in the target, so she could figure out if she'd made any new ones and where, she lifted the gun and aimed again. Again, she sucked at it.

Her shots hit the target, but in a few cases only because the rectangle of paper extended well beyond the colored circles. Several shots hit the hay bale directly, not even on the paper, and each one sent up a small puff of hay dust to let her know of her failure.

She shot again. And again. Her family waited while she tried, but eventually, even she gave up on herself. This wasn't going to happen.

Turning to Joule and Cage, she asked "So, do either of you think that you can shoot a living animal?"

15

Cage headed out into the woods again, his sister following along again. He hoped to find something. Again. But he didn't expect it to happen.

They'd been checking the traps every afternoon. Despite what they'd all thought was an excellent design, nothing had worked. Where to put the traps had been a full-family debate. They wanted to be able to check them daily, yet the traps needed to be far enough apart that the dogs wouldn't be able to call for help if they got stuck. Traps were no good if the dog could summon a brethren to break them free.

But having baited traps near homes was a crappy idea. Purposefully bringing one of the dogs closer to the people was a terrible strategy. So they had gone out into the cow pastures and set the traps.

This meant they'd had to talk to several of the farmers, so it had taken several days to get everything up. Luckily, the farmers had not had the same reservations about baiting the dogs into the pastures. It seemed the cows themselves were already more than tempting, and the farmers were glad to have something to distract the dogs from their livestock.

Between getting permission and jury rigging the traps, it had taken a while to get going. This was finally the third day of trapping.

The third probably failed *day of trapping*, Cage thought. He turned to his sister, "What's the over under on the traps?"

"Zero." Clearly, her hopes were no higher than his. She had the bow clutched in her hand again, the metal arrow hooked across the grasp and notched onto the string—not pulled back, but ready.

They'd spent the money and made four traps. Now it was taking a good hour and a half daily to check them. Nate had come home early yesterday and he and Cage had gone out. The first day, it had been Kaya and Joule. But Cage and Joule were on duty by themselves for the weekend. Now the twins were out hiking through the woods while their parents stayed home making up for missed work during the week.

Pretty much everyone who had a job these days was working double time. If you made tacos, you had extra tacos to make for the FEMA workers in your area and for the people who didn't have a home anymore.

Cage's parents worked in think tanks, and most of the think tanks had turned their gaze away from flying cars and shooting for Mars. Now they were looking at alternative fuels, installing solar arrays, and designing devices for flooding safety, earthquake braces for houses, compact and safe heating and cooling systems for power outages, and more.

Cage looked around the woods, trying to remember where they had put the next trap. They hadn't fully camouflaged it, but if they didn't get close, they wouldn't see it.

The two out in the farmers' pastures had been empty, but the bait was missing. There were two more traps in the woods. Cage was wondering if there would be a dog inside or if the bait would be missing here as well.

He didn't see it, but he knew they were close.

"I don't hear anything," Joule told him, her way of saying she suspected this one would be empty, too. As they came up closer, he saw that she was right and the bait was gone from this one as well.

But the trap was not closed. On closer inspection... "Damn it," he said. "Look, Joule." Kneeling down, he looked inside and he checked it out. "Look at the door."

"Fuck," Joule muttered. "It's completely bent. We're going to have to haul it back with us." She was starting to pick it up.

They'd designed the contraptions out of dog crates, using a basic wildlife trap designs where the door slid shut after the animal went inside and tugged on the bait. The family had spent time rigging one end of the door to be open and slide down once the bait was touched. But they'd maintained the basic dog crate design so they could fold it up and carry it by the handle.

"It won't even fold up," Joule moaned as she lifted one corner of the trap.

"Shit," Cage spat as he joined her, circling it to look at the damage. "We have to go look at the other one, first. I would hate to spend the effort to carry this back and then have a dog sitting in the other one and not get it checked."

Joule nodded in agreement and began stepping carefully down the trail toward the last stop.

"What do you think," he asked her a few minutes later, "are the chances that no one has killed one of these dogs yet?"

"If they have, they're not talking about it."

Cage stopped in the woods then, letting her walk a few feet ahead before she realized and swung back to look at him. "Joule, you survived the night out with them. You got away... and we don't tell people that."

"Well, we never specifically agreed to *not* tell people that." She was almost looking at him now, but her eyes still darted from side to side, checking the area around them. She'd always been vigilant, but she was much more so since they'd seen the dog in the daylight. "It was just kind of something we did."

"I know," Cage said, "but maybe other people did it, too. Maybe they killed one of the dogs and they just don't tell people... kind of like us. Maybe they're afraid of the backlash."

"It's plausible," she mused. "But it doesn't matter. If they did it, they're not talking. And if not, then how are we going to find them anyway? They aren't bringing us a carcass. We need our own."

"That's true," he said. "But I'm still having a hard time believing that one of these gun nuts hasn't gotten his AR-15 out and just mowed a dog down. I think you're probably right. Maybe they just aren't sharing."

"But," she said as she turned, "I'm not sure that bullets would stop them."

"You think they're *bulletproof?*" Cage stopped again, his brain overriding his feet.

"No, not really. I just think they're a lot more bulletproof than we are. Obviously, a single bullet would kill you or me, but it's not taking *them* down. The police put so many bullets into them. I think they might have mortally wounded some of them, but the pack still killed the officers and managed to get away."

"That's true." Cage sighed, not liking where the conversation was going. "Remember how our psych class in Curie talked about the horrible irregularities in eyewitness testimony? And they said even trained police officers only hit their target less than forty percent of the time. So my guess is, if people have been shooting at these dogs, they're probably missing more than they're hitting."

Joule nodded along as he talked, then turned and put a finger to her lips as she whispered, "We're getting close to the last cage."

In another fifteen steps, she let out the words, "Son of a bitch!"

16

J oule stopped dead in the woods. The late morning
sunlight filtered through the trees, making the path
bright. The foot trail was cleared enough to walk on
comfortably, but that wasn't where they expected to
find a dog. So they'd laid the trap about ten feet away from
where they walked.

She could see the twisted bars from here. What a mess the
trap was! "It's completely mangled," she said to her brother. Not
that he needed her commentary. "We managed to get another
dog inside the cage, and—"

"How do you know?" he interrupted.

"Because the bait is gone."

"But another animal could have eaten the bait."

"Sure, but what other animal could have taken all of it and
then fought their way out from the inside?" She sighed. "It's too
much of a mess to even be worth carrying home. Clearly, our
design sucks."

Joule turned to look at her brother, her bow and arrow still
in hand, her eyes scanning, her ears listening beyond their

conversation. As she flicked her eyes up to Cage, she could see that he agreed.

She would have rolled her eyes, but she didn't want to take them off the surrounding area. The look of that cage only irritated her. "Back to the drawing board."

It was something her parents had said since she was small, and it seemed so appropriate right now. All that money lost on the cages. All the time spent designing them and trying to trap a dog. It seemed so useless. Or worse. "All we did is *feed* them."

"That's true." Cage waved his hand at the twisted metal, indicating it was a loss. "Let's go back and get the other one."

Nodding, Joule followed him back along the path they'd just come down. Today's hike was about efficiency, not about finding things.

"The good news about feeding them is that we seem to have fed them the right things," Cage offered into the general air. The words held a little bit of snark, and Joule nodded her agreement.

They'd fed the dogs whole, raw chickens stuffed with mushrooms. Normal dogs weren't supposed to have chicken. The bones could splinter when chewed with a dog's powerful jaws and the shards could then rip up their intestinal track. A good chicken bone—splintering as the dog ate it—could kill a dog.

To be fair, it was what they were hoping for.

Mushrooms were rumored to have possible deadly effects on many dogs. So they'd bought several containers at the grocery and stuffed the chickens full, hoping that these guys didn't have a good enough sense of smell—or sense, period—to stay away.

Joule walked softly and spoke just loud enough for her brother to hear her. "All four pieces of bait were gone. So they ate them."

"Well, *something* ate them."

She was relatively certain that the offending party was one

of the dogs. A smaller animal should have been stuck in the converted dog crate. The metal was sturdy, welded, and designed to hold household pet dogs up to eighty pounds in weight. So a good shoulder thrust by a German Shepherd or a Rottweiler shouldn't have accomplished anything more than a dent. This trap had been broken out of from the inside.

What she had was logic. It would be better to have proof. "Let's look around."

Joule was thinking that the bones might have been left behind for them to find, or the dog might have rejected the mushrooms and spit them out somewhere. There might be footprints in the vicinity of the crate or some other evidence of what had eaten their bait—something she hadn't thought of but would hopefully recognize when she saw it.

While they headed back to the other crate—the one they would do the work to haul in—she tried to think of other, less obvious possibilities. "I suppose it's possible the bait attracted a different animal, like a coyote or something. Then the dogs came in and got it. So the bait didn't work, but it baited something that *then* served as bait."

That would provide reasoning for the mangled crate, too. And it would mean they *were* serving up the wrong bait. They didn't want to catch a coyote. They wanted to catch one of the dogs.

Joule thought for a moment. When had she last seen a coyote? She'd just assumed that they were pack animals and that would afford them protection from the dogs. But she didn't know.

Cage interrupted her musings. "I'm assuming that would leave blood everywhere. And wouldn't eating a coyote make them cannibalistic?"

Joule hadn't thought of that. "Would they eat wolves? They did eat a bunch of the neighborhood dogs. So yeah, that would make them cannibalistic."

She thought another moment and amended her answer. "Eating coyotes doesn't make them cannibalistic. Coyotes have been known to eat small dogs. Cats, too, but dogs are the important standard here. That's not cannibalism."

"Because coyotes aren't dogs." Cage picked up the thread of her logic. "So that takes a good measure of cannibalism out of it. You have to eat within your species."

Something about that last phrase nagged at her, but she couldn't afford to get distracted. She'd seen a dog in the daylight. She'd seen a pack of them coming straight at her. Even though it was barely midday, she needed to be prepared. Just in case.

Nodding at her brother's back, she followed him just off the trail to the previous cage. It took more effort than she would have liked to get it partially folded up. Broken and bent, it wouldn't clip down into its planned, compact carrying shape.

For a while they carried it between them, each with a hand looped through the bars and holding up one side of the mess. But as Joule quickly pointed out, "I have only one free hand right now. If something comes up on us, I'm going to drop this and that's going to cause you problems. One of us needs to have the bow and arrow ready, and that means one of us needs to carry the crate by themselves."

She figured it was pretty obvious which of them should do which part of her suggestion.

"I've got it," Cage volunteered immediately, showing he understood their skills the same as she did. It looked awkward as fuck to walk with the crate bouncing against his leg each time he took a step, but Cage made it work somehow, not slowing his pace much at all. The dogs were good motivation to get home quickly.

Joule stayed behind him, swinging her gaze and her hands wide, keeping her arrow notched, if aimed toward the ground, always ready to go.

As they emerged at the edge of the woods, their dad was pulling up the driveway, probably having run errands while they were out. Everything had to be done during the daylight now. Nothing could happen after dusk—not getting a gallon of milk, not even watching TV.

Nate climbed out of the car and looked up at the kids. He stopped from where he was rummaging in the back seat and turned to face them, clearly picking up on their glum expressions. "It didn't work... What's that?"

"This one's broken," Cage said, lifting the folded metal a little as a gesture. "There was another one, also mangled, but so beyond repair that it wasn't even worth carrying home."

Nate's lips pressed together as he made an assessing nod. "Well, I guess we have to start over."

Finally, Joule let her arms relax at her sides. She wasn't ready to throw the bow over her shoulder and put the arrow back into the quiver—that was for when she was inside, or trying to impress her mother with how safe it was. *How safe it was was always a lie*, she thought.

"We don't have to start over from the top," she told her dad. "We think the bait worked."

But they all headed inside, tired at the end of the day and with their results. As soon as he set his things down, Nate called into the space of the house, knowing Kaya was already home, even if he couldn't see her. "We need all brains at the table!"

It was an hour later that they had a plan in place.

Kaya looked around the family, and Joule felt her mother's gaze as if it were a physical touch. "If we split up into teams of two and go different directions, I think we could have the setup before nightfall tonight."

Everyone agreed.

But, Joule thought, *the timing would be tight*.

17

Kaya was exhausted, but she wasn't about to give up. She'd given the gun to Cage along with a holster she'd bought earlier this week. The idea was that he could clip it to the side of his jeans and have it at the ready without having to do something stupid, like tuck it into his waistband. The dogs were threat enough. She wasn't going to lose a child to something else.

That was why she'd put her foot down when Cage asked about a fully-automatic assault rifle. They were too easy to mis-use. The bullets went everywhere, and she could imagine firing at a dog and hitting a neighbor, or a family member.

Right now, all four of her family members were healthy. They were physically fit—able to run, jump, and climb. She'd always known she would love one of her family members through any disability, but now their health had become exponentially more important. Fitness skills were exactly the ones that had saved Joule's life. Kaya wasn't going to put either of her kids or her husband in a situation—like unsafe gun use—that would put any of that in jeopardy.

"I don't like this one." She said it to her family and to the woods in general.

Joule had her bow and arrow out and only nodded in response to her mother's statement. They seemed to be silently betting on which trap would work best. Just then, Kaya realized that she and Nate were setting out the traps while the kids held all the weapons.

She would have preferred she carry the gun and take the responsibility of killing something. But her children were far superior at defense than either she or Nate. Kaya had to come to terms with this being the correct setup. She just didn't like relying on her children this way. The dogs left them no choice.

Nate was working to pry open the old-fashioned bear trap. Kaya could feel her adrenaline kicking up, but she didn't want to say anything. The trap needed to be opened, even though it looked horrifically unsafe to do so. She didn't want the kids doing it, so it had to be her or Nate. But they were chalkboard kind of people, and it seemed too way easy to dick up something like a bear trap. Too easy to catch one of *them* rather than one of the dogs.

With the jaws open, Nate slid the small latch into place and Kaya reminded herself that—while it was easy to slip the latch out—a combination of forces was holding it in place. Friction. Tension. Opposing forces were working—the latch wanted to go up, the notch at the corresponding piece held it down—until something put weight on the flat plate in the middle.

Nate eyed his handiwork and they both stepped back for a moment.

"Bait?" he asked into the air as he pulled the coat hanger hook out of his back pocket. He'd decided when they bought the trap that there was too much chance of putting the bait on wrong. He was not going get snapped into the trap. *At least he worked hard to stay ahead of potential problems*, Kaya reminded herself. She looked to her daughter, who was carrying the chickens today.

Joule swept her gaze one last time, but neither of the adults said anything about her taking a moment she clearly needed. Then she shrugged her backpack off and unzipped it with one hand the other still holding the bow, finger across the shaft, ready to go. She pulled out a gallon bag and tossed her father raw chicken already stuffed with broken pieces of bittersweet chocolate.

"Chocolate?" He looked up at her.

"I read it online. Store bought mushrooms may not be a threat. That's dark chocolate. It has a better kill rate," she told him.

It took him a few minutes to pull the bait out, hook it onto his makeshift wire and set it ever so carefully into the trap. With an uneasy exhale, they all stepped back.

"That was the last one," Kaya announced. "Good work, Nate." She almost expected as they walked away that they would hear the trap snapping behind them. She didn't expect that a dog had been stalking them or anything so sinister, but that they were rank idiots and the trap would simply snap shut on its own because they'd done it all wrong.

She didn't hear it, and her breathing got easier with each step she took toward home.

The day was wearing on and they all needed dinner and now showers, too. In the end, though, she liked this better than the original plan. Originally, they had hoped to catch a live animal. Their intent had been to then either tranquilize or kill it.

They now owned tranquilizer darts for the rifle—one of the errands from earlier today—and more bullets for the 9mm handgun. She and Joule had gone on that errand, as Kaya had thought it might help her daughter sleep better if she had a sense that they could stop the animal, if need be.

Kaya had invested in hollow points. Joule had nodded her agreement and the clerk at the gun shop hadn't questioned a mother and teenage daughter buying bullets that had originally been designed to pierce Kevlar.

When she'd asked the kids, could they kill a live animal? Both had said *yes*. She'd tried to explain that it wasn't always the kind of thing you understood until you had done it. By then, it was too late. Neither of her children seemed to have any qualms about taking out one of the dogs, though, and Kaya had let it stand. At least it wasn't like zombie movies where the characters had to decide to shoot a parent in the head.

Of the four traps they had set out, two would kill the animal on contact. One trap was a simple snare: a net laid out on the ground, strong and sturdy enough to hold up to a fighting dog. Or at least, they thought it was. After all, they'd been wrong about the dog crates serving as a suitable cage.

The net was much stronger, it's flexibility a point in its favor. At each of the four corners a nylon rope tied it up to a pulley system in the tree above. A counterweight had been set to pull the animal up high and out of reach of any other dogs.

They'd made all these decisions thinking through a live scenario. The dogs traveled in packs; they might catch two. So they'd made the counterweight heavy enough for that scenario. The pack might try to get a member back, so they'd made the lift high enough that they shouldn't be able to jump and snare it. But it was overall a simple design. Snap the trigger and up goes the net—a live animal captured. "Just like Wile E. Coyote," Joule had commented.

Another trap had earned the nickname "the Venus flytrap." Should an animal step into it, full planks would zip down from both sides. The added weight would crush a ribcage enough to kill the animal, they hoped. This was the one Kaya almost wished wouldn't work.

"That Venus flytrap," she started off, "is going to mangle the animal it catches. Which means we might lose information."

"That's the whole point," Cage replied with force. "We're trying to get *information*."

Kaya didn't follow his reasoning. "Exactly, and crushing it will lose that."

Her son shook his head as he lead the way back through the woods, on track to get them home well before dark. "*Not* catching animals is what's losing us information."

Kaya couldn't find an argument, now that she understood his point.

"Once we get one," he continued, "we can get *some* information out of it. We can look at most, if not all, of it. Maybe we can figure out a better way to trap it or design better bait. Learn how much force is necessary to not mangle the next one, that kind of thing. Then we can use that information to catch a live one."

Behind her, Nate muttered, "Besides, the more of them we take them out in the process, the better off we'll all be."

They were almost home and the children's phones beeped simultaneously, making Kaya's head snap up at the sound. They should have had them off in the woods, but she hadn't thought of reminding them. All their phones were programmed to go silent at dusk, in case they forgot to turn them off. *Another thing to add to the list*, she thought.

The noise didn't worry Nate, as it was broad daylight. She talked herself down: Even the one dog the children had seen in the daylight had been solo, which gave the four of them much better odds, and that might have been a fluke, anyway.

She looked at the kids then, when she noticed they didn't say anything, though both had looked at their phones. The expressions on their faces made her stop cold. "What is it?"

When neither child replied right away, Kaya waited. She knew her kids. Nate stayed silent behind her, also waiting as though with no agenda. They had learned a long time ago that sometimes the children just needed a moment to process and then they would talk. Somehow, that trick had carried almost into their adulthood. She had no idea if it was a good thing or a bad thing.

But eventually Cage looked up at her. "It's Mitchell from school."

"He wasn't in class on Friday," Joule added, and Kaya felt her heart drop. It couldn't be good news. She just hoped it wasn't the worst.

Still, she waited. Probably the hardest part of being a parent for her was letting her two kids arrive where they needed to be in their own time. It was Joule who spoke up again and said, "His parents found evidence." She didn't specify what that "evidence" might be.

A few years ago, Kaya would have thought that statement meant he was cheating on tests or there was indication of drug use. Not anymore.

"He was out too late and..." Joule didn't finish.

That was all Kaya had needed to hear to know their friend Mitchell would not be coming back to school. Mitchell had been caught outside after dark.

Just like Joule.

Only Mitchell hadn't made it home.

The Mazur family trudged across the wide yard, and Kaya was beyond grateful that all four of them were still together. But she turned and looked over her shoulder. These traps had to work.

18

C age walked through the woods trying to make as little noise as he could. He wanted to stomp out his anger but knew that wasn't smart.

The gun sat on his hip, a heavy weight reminding him of what was at stake every time he walked out here. With the weapon holstered, he had both hands free. In case he had forgotten the consequences, his father now carried a machete.

Cage hadn't failed to notice that they were slightly more armed each week.

"What about Tennessee?" he asked his father. They'd continued looking for places to move. And there was still the question of where he and Joule would go to college.

He could almost hear Nate shaking his head on the path behind him. "Too many rivers. It's the same all the way down into Georgia. The land is too soft to hold back the flooding. We can't move there now, anyway," his father said, as though it might have been an option a while ago.

Cage heard one swift hack as the machete hit branches that Nate must have decided were in his way. Or maybe he was just angry and taking it out on the foliage. "Besides, can't get a house anywhere near Nashville anymore. And that's where the think tanks would be. That's where your mother and I could work."

"Why not?" Cage asked, even though he assumed he wouldn't like the answer. He didn't.

"Mud slides," were the only words that came back. His father hacked another branch or two and Cage ignored the sound.

"California?" he asked. It was a one place he and Joule had been looking at college.

"Tidal waves." Only this time Nate said it with a tone that asked *Why would Cage have even asked? Everyone knew about the tidal waves.*

They weren't full tidal waves, but they were more than big enough to wash into the middle of town and take out homes and some of the less sturdy buildings. The waves had taken out bridges and roads, turning the LA/San Diego area into a royal mess.

"I meant inland," he told his father. But all that followed was a deep sigh.

"Sinkholes, big ones. The random kind they used to show on the news about Florida. Those are now in the places where they aren't having the tidal wave problem."

Cage could hear his father's frustration leaking out in every word, and he opted for a little bit of positive. "Joule and I have decided we're going to go to school together."

"Oh, thank God." The breathed relief in the words made Cage realize the conversation he and his sister had a few days earlier had been spot on.

When he and Joule had talked, he'd told her, "I think mom and dad will breathe easier if we're together. There will still be two people for them to call if anything goes wrong, but we'll be in one place. I'll be able to vouch that you're safe and you'll be able to vouch that I am."

"I really thought we'd go different places." Joule had been digging a tiny hole in the yard with the end of her bow. Despite the afternoon sun, she'd held onto it. "We've always been together, and that's good. But I thought maybe it was time to go somewhere different... to each become our own person, separate from our parents and from each other..." But she'd trailed off.

She didn't have to say it.

And Cage didn't say it either. The night that she had spent out alone had changed everything.

So, as simply as that, they had decided to go to the same college, and to push on as though there weren't wildfires and blizzards and droughts. They still needed an education. What Cage and Joule hadn't decided yet was where to go.

Staying together was one thing. There were a handful of schools they had both gotten scholarships to. Cage figured that was due to the time they had spent in Curie, Nebraska. The town they had lived in for a handful of years had an IQ requirement and a high school so advanced that it shot students into the stratosphere. Even now, he and his sister were almost entirely enrolled in advanced classes. They'd wailed on their standardized tests and had full scholarships to most of the schools they'd applied to.

Initially, it had felt a bit excessive to him. Now, he thought it was a good thing. His parents could spend their money finding somewhere else to live, rather than paying tuition and textbook fees and such. His brain wandered, but as he and his father walked up to the last of the traps, he saw it was just like the other three. Empty.

Both of the Mazur men swore at it like sailors.

Hands on his hips, Cage turned to his father. "This isn't working any better than the last one."

His father stood over the net trap, the one that would have lifted a dog that walked across the path high into the air.

Looking up and down, Nate started talking. Cage wasn't sure if he was telling his son what was going on or talking to himself. "Either they're not walking here or the trap isn't working."

They both looked at each other. "Gotta test the trap."

They would have to reset it but it would suck if dogs had been walking through here and the trap simply hadn't worked.

"What do we got?" Nate asked, looking around.

"Neither of us!" was Cage's reply. It would take both of them to set it back and they couldn't risk one of them getting tangled and caught if it worked after all. If one of the dogs died while hanging in the trap, that was fine. It was not okay if it was either of them. Cage had no desire to get stuck and spend the night as swinging bait above a pack of hungry dogs.

"Log." Cage pointed off into the woods. "We need something heavy enough to activate the trap."

He and his father spent the next fifteen minutes rolling the massive, rotting piece of wood over and making faces at the worms that turned up underneath it. Next they got their fingers under the edges, which took a little more effort than he'd expected. It took a few minutes to work out a grip that would allow them to chuck it into the middle of the trap.

"Three, Two," he and his father swung it back and forth with each count and let the log fly. "One!"

It landed a little further than center, but it worked. With a sudden jolt, the net swung sharply upward, the log caught firmly inside. Leaves that they had used to camouflage it fluttered down around them.

Nate looked at Cage with crossed arms. "Well, it works."

"And that log wasn't as heavy as a dog." It wasn't really the answer Cage had been looking for. If it was broken, they could fix it and hope for a better answer tomorrow. But if it wasn't broken... what could they change?

They went ahead and reset it. Cage offered a shrug and an,

"I mean, it's already here. And I think it would take the four of us to move it." They needed a better location, clearly.

It took the next twenty-five minutes to haul the counterweight up, lower the trap back into place, and anchor the four corners of the net until the pulley lines could be hidden again. Getting the log out of it had been the hardest part.

Chucking the log to the side of the trail with a heave and a sigh that he wasn't as strong as he'd thought, his dad said, "Do you think they're too smart to go in?"

"I hope not." Cage's brain ran away with ideas, and his mouth followed. "I'm tempted to get out here at night. Just come out with a full arsenal—guns, smoke bombs, grenades, everything. Even night vision goggles."

Suddenly, Cage changed his mind. "Not night vision goggles." He noticed his father was about to protest coming out hunting at night with any kind of goggles that would restrict peripheral vision. That was a recipe for disaster. "No, we need a night vision *camera*. We need to know where they're going and how many and all that."

Nate tossed his head back and laughed. Not the reaction Cage had expected.

"You're absolutely right," his father said. "You want to know how I know? Because your mother ordered one last night."

19

Kaya watched the footage of her backyard displayed in grainy shades of grey and green.

Though it was interesting to see what was happening in her yard overnight, mostly it was boring work and not at all what she was supposed to be doing to earn money. But the fact of the matter was, no one was going to fire her, and she intended to do this work—the work that mattered most.

It had now been several weeks since the night Joule had spent outside. That night had changed everything for her family, but to Kaya, it felt that time was dragging. The deadline for the kids to decide what college they wanted to attend was looming closer. Though they had decided to go together—much to her relief and their father's—they still hadn't decided where.

She and Nate had also put off deciding if they would follow the kids. Normally, she would never follow her child to college, but there was no *normal* anymore. She was edging closer and closer to survival mode, as was everyone else. It had become a very real possibility that they might move close to her children's school and at least attempt to keep the family unit somewhat together.

Right now, she couldn't make that decision. She wanted Cage and Joule to decide where they wanted to go on their own. She would make her decisions later. All she could do today was learn what the dogs were doing at night.

If she could figure that out, maybe she could protect her family. At least, that's what she wanted to believe. She had ideas. An electrified fence might be a great plan, but it was a lot of work and a lot of money. If it didn't keep the dogs out of their yard at night, then it wasn't worth it. A tall fence might work, but not if they could jump or climb it. There were too many options, and the Mazurs couldn't enact any of them until they knew more of what they were up against.

She forwarded through several hours of nothing happening, but then paused as—in rapid fast forward—the screen lit up with shapes. Backtracking for a bit, she tried hard not to guess what was happening before she could really watch what was on the screen.

As it finally played in regular speed, Kaya saw a pack of coyotes had come through close to the back of the house around two a.m. She wondered: Had they always come that close and she hadn't known it, or did they just do so now? Was it a tactic? The coyotes might think they'd be safer from the dogs if they were closer to humans.

She waited with bated breath, but nothing happened to the coyotes. There was no sound with her system, so she watched in silence as mouths opened and the coyotes presumably yipped or bayed. They did seem to communicate well and eventually the mid-sized pack had given a little jog and disappeared into the woods.

With the yard empty again, Kaya fast forwarded until she saw another, smaller shape. It turned out to be two possums, one with lumps that looked like babies clinging to her back. For a moment, Kay smiled at the cute animals—but then, from nowhere, three dogs descended on the two possums and ripped them to shreds.

With a gasp she couldn't hold in, Kaya leapt back into her seat. She was grateful no one was around to see her visceral reaction. Even though the dogs couldn't get to her, even though the event was already over and they were simply on a screen, the attack was stunning and disturbing.

It was like Wild Kingdom in her own backyard—the *worst* of Wild Kingdom.

She swallowed hard, and then forced herself to rewind and watch the footage again. This time as she watched, she checked to see how close the dogs came to the house—almost as close as the coyotes. That was the scary part. She and her children were sleeping behind walls probably less than fifteen to twenty feet away from where the dogs had come.

Previously, Kaya and Nate had slept downstairs and the kids upstairs. But when the dogs had come, they'd moved their bedroom upstairs, trading out with her office in an effort to have just a few more seconds to get away, if it ever came to that. There was a tin roof over the first-story patio below their new bedroom window. She and Nate had quietly reinforced it one day while the kids were at school.

That was the plan: Get the kids out of their rooms and then bolt through the parents' bedroom and out onto the roof, if necessary.

While Kaya watched the video again, the dogs made short work of the possums. Forcing herself, she went back through it a third time. This time, she didn't pay attention to the possums at all. Only to the dogs.

The green and black shades made it hard to glean much detail, but she could see that her kids' description had been quite accurate. The twins had nailed the thick legs, barrel chest, and wide face. Even in this grainy image, the heavy jaws were as scary as Cage and Joule had suggested. That was about all she could say. The clarity wasn't great and she couldn't see color or anything else she wanted. But what she could see was disturbing enough.

One more time, the last *time,* she told herself and started it again.

This round, she watched for how the dogs attacked. Kaya noticed they surrounded the possums first and then dove all at once. She was surprised they didn't conk their thick heads, but the attack was eerily well-coordinated.

So far, she was counting the night vision camera as incredibly informative. It was well worth the time she and Joule had spent installing it. Unfortunately, all of the information had been negative. It seemed the dogs were bigger than she'd originally thought. Kaya was hoping the kids had overestimated their size but, if anything, they had underestimated it.

She'd known they worked in packs, but now she knew they worked almost as though they had a hive mind—all striking with a precision that concerned her.

When she had gone through the entire previous night, and thankfully not found any other instances of the dogs in the range of the camera, she turned back to her other research. Her *pet project,* as she was calling it.

Kaya Mazur was now the proud owner of three veterinary texts, and she was focusing her research on canine physiology. What she'd learned so far were all things that wouldn't help, but that might stop her from trying something in the first place.

Dogs carried their heads forward, as all canines did, and thus had thick necks and tended to be hard to strangle. *Check that off the list of possible counter-attack methods,* she thought.

They had massive immune systems. In fact, most veterinary surgeries were done in open air, not even in a sterile operating room. Thus, they were hard to kill by infecting them with something. Open wounds didn't carry much of a threat to canines. In fact, it seemed dogs were made for them. They licked the wound and didn't suffer much unless it was horribly deep. Even then, they sometimes survived.

She had few options left. Up until now, they had avoided considering poison, not wanting to poison the entire local animal population. Not knowing how the dogs had come about in the first place made Kaya even more wary of setting out chemicals.

Maybe these dogs had developed as a reaction to somebody trying to poison feral dogs. She didn't know. But as she flipped the pages, she learned more.

20

J oule sat behind her school desk during last period, basically doing nothing. It was their third consecutive day with no AP Chemistry teacher.

Mrs. Wintston simply had not shown up at the end of last week. In the ensuing days, the school must have called her house, tried to find her, and come up shy.

The class had been assigned to a substitute, but it was difficult to find a anyone who could not only teach Advanced Placement Chemistry, but could also come into another teacher's course and pick up exactly where the other teacher had left off. In fact, it was difficult enough that it hadn't happened.

Joule pulled a deck of cards out of her backpack and was playing solitaire to burn the time. The sub had suggested they study for their next test. Several of the more dedicated students had taken the suggestion and were nose deep in review. Others had ignored it.

Joule knew it didn't really apply to her. She understood Mrs. Winston easily, and the test material came with little effort— the way it did when the teaching style was a good match.

Despite getting almost kicked out of physics, Joule and Cage had never actually blown up the lab.

She would have pulled out her laptop and looked up information on the dogs or could have tried to do research on traps, that kind of thing. But the last name "Mazur" had not afforded her a seat at the back of the room. All it had done was place her one seat behind her brother.

That meant anyone who was sitting behind her would be able to see her screen. Anyone who got up and walked around the room would know what she was looking up, and then it would become a thing. She didn't want to tell them what she and her family were trying to do. Everyone had their own theories about the dogs, and Joule was in no hurry to share hers.

The kids who'd thought they were invincible were now mostly missing. They'd learned ... one way or another. Some of the others didn't even want to acknowledge that the dogs existed. They simply said they went to bed early and had no idea what people were complaining about. Joule didn't have either problem.

She was laying down an ace as Cage ended whatever conversation he was having and turned around to whisper to her. "I think we need new traps."

She shook her head. "Not here," she hissed, although she agreed with his assessment. It had been three days since Cage and their dad had checked the net trap and shown that it worked. It simply wasn't catching any dogs.

The twins had gone to the store for bait, and she was beginning to think the clerks had to have noticed they were buying far too many chickens—so much so that the online coupon generator was sending them discounts specifically on cheap, whole, raw chickens and boxes of very dark chocolate bars. As of yet, none of the traps had sprung closed—not with a dog caught in them—although the chickens continually went missing.

They had jimmied the latch on the bear trap in an attempt to make it much more sensitive. An online video showed them how to file the notch down, putting the whole system on a hair trigger rather than the safer, ten-pound trigger. Though they had again found it sprung closed and the chicken missing, there had been no dog inside.

They discovered no random dead dogs on their trips through the woods, despite seeing evidence that the dogs passed through there regularly. She'd hoped if the traps didn't get them, they might have choked on chicken bones or been poisoned by the chocolate. Joule was beginning to think the dogs weren't even eating the chickens, and maybe her family was just feeding the other wildlife and fattening it up for the dogs.

"When we get home, we'll talk." She put her brother off because there was far more she wanted to discuss than was acceptable in this classroom, and she went back to flipping cards, though her brain stayed focused on making plans.

For far too long, they had been failing at trapping a dog.

The sheer scope of their failure was becoming concerning. Joule was beginning to think the dogs weren't just hive minded, but actually rather intelligent. She had talked her mother into letting her watch some of the footage, even though Kaya had told her it was violent.

Joule didn't like it, but she was smart enough to know that if they were going to trap a dog, violence was going to be involved.

When she finally got bored playing cards by herself, she and her friend Sarah started up a game of Gin. The substitute didn't really seem to care that what they were doing had absolutely nothing to do with chemistry. Basically, the woman was a warm body in the seat.

Leaning toward Sarah, Joule played a card. "What number teacher is Mrs. Winston?"

Sarah didn't need further clarification, which is probably why they were friends. "Fifteen."

The Chem teacher was the fifteenth to go missing since the dogs had first appeared. Joule sat with that thought for a moment until Sarah nudged her that her turn had come again. The school was reasonably large. They could lose fifteen teachers, and it was likely none of the students would have known all fifteen of them. But it was still a big number.

"Far more students than that," Sarah added, out of the blue.

That was probably the case. They *should be* losing more students than teachers in a purely mathematical sense. *But,* she thought, *how many more?* She asked Sarah.

"More than the right ratio." Sarah played another card, though her words indicated she had been thinking along exactly the same line.

Joule began to wonder. "Is it because we're smaller? Are we just easier prey?"

Stopping her motion of throwing down cards and rapidly snaring points, Sarah looked around the room surreptitiously. Then she played another card, flipping over everything in her hand to show Joule just how soundly she had lost. Her words didn't match the game. "Honestly, as a group, we're stupider."

Despite having told Cage that she didn't want to talk about it, she and Sarah were now having the conversation. But Sarah wasn't coming home with her, and she couldn't simply put her off until later. Besides, it was Sarah who offered up that perhaps they should just hang one of their less-well-liked classmates out as bait.

"We might be able to solve this whole problem." Sarah had shrugged as she shuffled the deck again.

Joule had taken that thought home with her that afternoon. She and Cage had arrived at the house just a handful of minutes after the last bell. They took turns driving an old hybrid their parents had recently bought for them. Kaya had liked that it was heavy; Nate had liked that it didn't cost much for gas. Neither of their parents said anything about the dogs. But Joule liked that she was no longer on the bus—or as she was now referring to it: The Moveable Feast.

The family afternoon had worn on as it usually did, checking traps—and of course, finding them empty, making dinner, doing homework. Closing the curtains and clipping them tightly down the middle so no light got in or out. Then going to bed early.

Joule hadn't had a chance to tell her brother what she thought. It wasn't quite Sarah's "sacrifice a classmate" idea, not straight up. But that had gotten her thinking, and Joule smiled to herself. She did have a few fellow students she wished she could use for bait.

She had decided she would bring up her new idea in the morning over breakfast. But just as she was beginning to fall asleep, sirens went off all around the room.

21

Cage came awake to the hideous noise, initially thinking it was some kind of alert from his cell phone —but his cell phone was off. It was off for exactly this reason.

No one needed an alert on a kidnapped child in the middle of the night. Not when he wasn't even outside to help spot the relevant silver sedan, anyway. All sound would do was draw the dogs to the house.

Distant family members might have heart attacks, it was true. Someone might need the Mazur family in the middle of the night, but they would not be coming, because their phones would be *off*.

So Cage sat up, still not fully alert, and reached out beside the bed, grabbing for the phone. He held it up to his squinting eyes, only to see in the dark gloom that it was, in fact, off. He dared not press a button to check, but the sirens still wailed and it wasn't his phone.

His sister stuck her head the room with her own phone in her hands. "It's coming from outside," she told him. "I think it's a tornado warning."

The sound of his parents rustling on the other side of the hall had him looking to his sister in her night shirt and him and his shorts. "We'd better get dressed."

Nodding, Joule turned around then replied absently, "Shoes too."

Yes. If it was a tornado warning, they might need to go somewhere. Get out of the way. The knock came at his door just as he was pulling on his jeans. "I'm getting dressed, Mom."

"It's a tornado warning." When he called back that he knew, she continued to give him information he already had. He let her. "Yes, oh, good, your sister's up."

"Yes." He sat on the bed to pull on socks and shoes. "Be there in a minute!"

It was less than that. Joule was already in the hallway when he stepped out, hopping into the sneakers that she never bothered untie as their dad pulled a sweatshirt over his head.

As his head popped out the top, Nate began making announcements. He was the *de facto* head of emergency services in the Mazur family. Cage watched as his dad did a quick visual assessment of each member and apparently declared them acceptable.

"All right," Nate said. "We'll be meeting downstairs in the bathroom." He waited for a nod from each of them before continuing. "Water bottles are in the rec room, Joule. You know where they are. Grab as many as you can carry. Use one of the bags that we grocery shop with." Joule nodded but knew better than to leave until they were dismissed.

Cage was given his assignment next: Get Joule's bow and arrow and the gun.

"Kaya, you're on food. Get a bag like Joule, pack it up. I'm getting the machete and blankets. Everyone, meet downstairs as fast as you can." With that, they were dismissed.

Joule ran to the other end of the house, and for a moment Cage wondered if they were too late. He could hear the wind howling outside. But his father had decided they had time, and there was no second guessing in a command situation. He headed back to their rooms, thinking that his parents had changed quite a bit to allow them to sleep with weapons near their grasp. It was also disturbing that his father was sending him for weapons... in the case of a tornado.

But if a tornado came through—which was luckily unlikely —and if it blew out the windows, they would need protection from the dogs.

"Heading down to check it out," Nate told him in hushed tones from the hallway. He couldn't yell it to the house. Despite the tornado warning siren, they still couldn't risk the noise.

Cage was already in his room with the holster clipped to the waistband of his jeans. Spare magazines he already had loaded were tucked into his back pockets. Heading into Joule's room, he grabbed the next round of weapons. She had several bows and sets of arrows—not just the one she'd originally gotten, but also the one that he had been given. He'd passed it off to her, since archery clearly wasn't his skill.

Cage grabbed all of it. Joule had more than one quiver full of arrows. Old wooden ones and a nice batch of new metal ones. Throwing the cases over his shoulder, he headed down the stairs as fast and quietly as he could. Then Joule was coming down into the lower level right behind him.

The bathroom down here had only one high window. His mother had always commented that she enjoyed the windows and the light of the place, but with the dogs, and now the tornado, the window was no longer safe.

The house didn't have a tornado shelter. The closest they had was a closet, and it wasn't big enough for the four of them.

As the family huddled together in the bathroom—Kaya coming in last—Cage was grateful there were no younger siblings who didn't know how to run a drill like this. There were too many moving pieces, things to gather, noises not to make, light switches not to turn on.

He was grateful the blare of the sirens was outside the house. Had the alarms been going off inside, it would have attracted the dogs. Although, with the commotion outside, they must be going crazy. He found himself hoping that maybe a tornado would come through and throw the dogs into Oz or something.

Looking up, he double-checked the window covering. His dad had long ago covered the high window with a piece of wainscoting. Cut to fit the space, it blocked out all the light, and the thick curtain drawn over it made it so anyone who was caught downstairs in the middle of the night could hole up in here and hopefully not worry about activating a dog attack.

Now Cage saw that the covering was not sufficient to keep out a dog, only to block most of the noise—and it certainly would not keep out a tornado.

Turning to the activity at hand, he saw that his father had spread out one thick blanket on the floor for all of them to sit on and left several others stacked around. He then pulled out two decks of cards, though there was really not enough light to see them by.

But as he shuffled, Cage saw what he hadn't noticed before. "Oh, they're luminescent," he whispered with a smile.

They still couldn't talk at normal volume. The last thing they needed on top of a tornado—one that was clearly close enough to set off the sirens—was the dogs knowing they were in here. Still, his father had thought this out, and Cage was grateful. He saw Joule's face as she smiled in the very dim light of the cards.

Slowly, they played the game until Cage glanced at his watch. It was going on four a.m., but he wasn't tired. They'd be sleeping in tomorrow, he thought, as there would certainly be no school.

That thought had just passed through his brain when he heard the sound of a freight train barreling down on them. His parents' heads popped up, looking immediately to the kids.

"That's an actual tornado," Kaya said, trying to keep the panic out of her voice, though Cage could still hear it. Whether Joule got it from her mother or her panic was her own, she clearly had started breathing more heavily. Cage tried to slow his pounding heart rate, because it was the only thing he could do.

It was clear that something needed to be done. Now.

Nate and Kaya nodded to each other.

"Blankets," was all his father said, and Kaya immediately opened one up and chucked it into the closet in the bathroom. She let it settle into a small space tucked beside the washer and dryer. "Kids," she motioned with one finger, "up and over. Get down in the space."

"What about you?" his sister whispered back, louder now, to be heard above the raging winds.

But Kaya shook her head. "We're the parents, you get the best space. No worries, we're coming, too. We'll be bundled into another blanket."

As Cage watched, his parents climbed on top of the washer and dryer. They threw a blanket on top of the kids and pulled yet another one over themselves as the freight train sound got closer and closer.

Cage waited it out, his arm looped through his sister's. Side by side, they sat with their backs against the wall, their knees under their chins, the only way they fit. It wasn't an outside wall, so he assumed it wouldn't blow away behind them. There were no windows in the tiny laundry cubby. And even if the window burst out, the flying debris shouldn't get them.

They heard the windows shuddering around the house as the pressure outside changed rapidly. The freight train sound went by incredibly close. Cage knew when they went out of the house in the morning, they would easily be able to see the damage. He could hear it happening and considered that they would be lucky if it had not destroyed part of the house.

Without speaking, they all waited as the noise reached a crescendo and eventually began to fade away. The fact that the house had not shuddered and shook harder was the only thing that convinced Cage that a corner of the place had not been bitten off by the passing tornado.

Slowly, much slower than he would have liked, the noise got farther away.

"Stay put," his mother said. "There could always be more of them. I think we're here until morning."

All four Mazurs huddled down, staying low and out of range. Cage's legs cramped from the tight space and he might have even eventually dozed off. They hadn't heard another tornado go through.

He was just beginning to breathe easier when they heard the window shatter.

22

They all heard the breaking glass. For a moment, Kaya was able to pretend it was just the storm, just the wind coming in. So she waited with fingers and toes crossed and prayers sent up, even though she wasn't quite sure where she was sending them.

Beside her, Nate's whole body went rigid. He was listening, the same as she was. She hadn't heard anythi—

There. The scrape of nails on hardwood floor.

Shit, she thought. They had been prepared to be upstairs at night if the dogs came in. They were not prepared to be down here. There was no real way out of the lower portion of the split level house.

Out the window? Into the lawn where dogs most likely waited. Out the back door to the patio? Into a pack of dogs and chances she wasn't willing to take. They had planned to go out onto the tin patio roof, but they hadn't planned for this.

They had planned for extreme weather and they had planned for dogs, but not both in one night. The tornado was gone, but it had somehow led the dogs inside, and Kaya and Nate and the kids were merely waiting, under blankets. There wasn't even a door between them and the intruders now. The closet was just the open space protected only by the curtains they pulled in front of the washer and dryer.

She stayed perfectly still and clutched at the machete her husband had brought under the blanket with them.

The dogs seemed to have a poor sense of smell, which was lucky. If they had a decent one, they would walk right down here to them. Instead, she could hear them exploring around the main floor of the house, their nails clicking on the hardwood floor. Then they walked farther away, into the extension that had been built on before they moved there. The game room had a tile floor, and the sound the dogs made was different.

Slowly, not ready to feel the relief her body was forcing on her, Kaya let her lungs deflate. Though the noise of the dogs on the tile was louder, it was also at greater distance. Still, the small noises rang out in the bone chilling silence the tornado had left in its wake. There were no cars driving by, no animals rustling in the woods, no birds chirping in the dead of night, only the sound of the dogs prowling her house looking for food.

Kaya couldn't see the kids, and none of them could afford to have her look. She couldn't see the room. It was dark, and they were under the blanket. The kids were smart enough not to move and she was suddenly very, very grateful that she had put the children down in the corner.

Cage and Joule were almost adults. If anything happened to orphan them, they would be okay. She had done her job as a parent and set them up well to live on their own. Though it was a little early to be thinking such morbid thoughts, she wasn't able to fully push them away. In a sick way, they were comforting.

After a little while, the click of nails faded, and she was almost beginning to take a breath.

Then she heard them on the stairs.

Fuck.

There was no doubt, several of the dogs were coming down here. The curtains were pulled in front of the washer and dryer. She and Nate had done it thinking it might protect them if the window gave way and any debris went flying through the room. They would not be worth anything against the dogs. But she hoped against all hope that the dogs might just walk by. There was every possibility that they would come in and poke at them but smell nothing and leave.

If she could just stay quiet and still enough—even if the dogs came into the room or even poked around—they might just walk away. Could she get lucky enough that their sense of smell was that bad?

Kaya didn't know.

While she counted the seconds, she wondered if any of the neighbors down the street had lost their homes. She and Nate had installed plush, thickly padded carpet down here. She'd wanted to sink her feet into it when she came out of her bedroom in the morning. Now it muted the sounds of the dogs coming closer. It ended what she could hear, a thin layer of false hope she'd been clinging to.

Turning her thoughts again, she wondered if only the windows had been broken or if the house might have taken more damage. Maybe there was no roof anymore. The place had shuddered so much with the high winds, she couldn't be sure. The tornado had been so loud that it might have been right on top of them.

She waited again, counting slowly in her head. And then she heard it: nails on tile at the doorway to the bathroom.

She hadn't closed the door when she'd rushed in here. In fact, they had needed it open. If the windows had blown and the tornado had come through, having the door closed would have created pressure problems.

She wished now that she had gotten up and shut it once the tornado had gone. But she cut herself a break. That wasn't fair. It was more than possible a second or third tornado could come through, and closing the door would have been a bad idea.

Click.

Click.

Click.

She could smell the dog now, even if it couldn't smell her. It was so close it took all her willpower to keep her nostrils from flaring. Wet dog. Rotting leaves. Fetid breath.

Even if it couldn't smell her, she was stuck smelling it.

Ever so slightly, Nate's hand gripped hers more tightly, but they didn't dare move. She could only trust that her children understood the same.

Low growls let her know that there was more than one dog in here and that they were discussing something in whatever language they understood.

Fuck, she thought again. The last thing she'd wanted to learn was that they communicated more than she'd already guessed.

Then she felt it, the weight of the dog. The front paws up on the edge of the washer. Now inches away, the nose nudging at the blanket. She felt the first brush against her leg. Then her side. She held still, trying to be furniture, but it didn't work.

Maybe they could smell well enough to know that she was a person and not a thing. In a moment, a growl came and the dog jumped up onto her.

In that split second, she made her decision. The dog needed something—*someone*—and it wasn't going to be her kids. It wasn't going to be her husband, either.

"Nate, *stay.*" She hissed the words to him, even as she threw the blanket off, startling the dog standing over her. Grabbing the machete tightly, Kaya raised her hand, wielding it like an avenging angel, and she jumped away.

She wanted to ask Cage for the gun, but didn't dare risk exposing him.

With a hard jab of her elbow and a body check, she tossed the surprised dog onto its side and offered a rebel yell to her family. "I've got this. I've been studying up. Don't worry."

But the last words came as she ran up the stairs, three dogs too close behind her.

23

Kaya ran like the world was on her heels. In a way, it was. If she didn't make it out of this, she would never see her family again. She wasn't afraid of a painful death; she was afraid of not leaving anything behind.

With a deep breath she thought about it as her feet pounded through the kitchen and toward the other side of the house. Three dogs right behind her.

She would leave Joule and Cage behind, but what a legacy they would be. She would leave Nate, and that would be a tragedy. The two of them were truly better together. Kaya only hoped she had made Nate's world richer.

The soles of her feet felt as though she had been running for so long, but it had only been a few bounding steps. Considering a hard turn, she could run directly upstairs and go out onto the reinforced tin roof. If she did that, she could evade the dogs. But she didn't actually want to evade them. Leaving the dogs in the house might end with them wandering back downstairs and finding her family again. She had to end this.

So she ran, knowing the dogs were following her. With a quick turn of her head, she counted that she had all three, and could only pray there weren't more. But that had been her calculated move when she jumped. Nate was still with the kids in case more were coming.

Kaya bolted across the main body of the house to the other side, as far away as she could get without going outside. She led the dogs into the game room, where they would likely smash the electronics as they fought, but the things weren't worth as much as her family. She led the chase around the large couch and then, jumping over it, headed back around and slammed the door to the kitchen. The dogs could no longer get back into the main house without breaking down that door.

There Kaya stood her ground.

She had to kill them. Actually, she had to kill at least enough of them to make the others leave. The three circled and growled at her. She growled back as she mentally checked that she hadn't seen more. She could only hope that this was the total that were in the house.

The veterinary texts had been truly enlightening, though she'd needed references for her references. She'd watched videos online, and though she had zero practice, she had her brains and she knew what to do now. And even if she didn't really know how to do it, she at least had a plan.

When they stared her down, she did the opposite of what was expected. From what she had learned, dogs had tremendous fighting skills. They had superior jaw strength and an ability to pull with brute force, but if you *pushed* the dog, it lost some of its power.

Not wanting to lose the machete, Kaya clutched it tightly in her right hand. With her left arm out in front of her as a small shield, she wished she'd thought to wrap a blanket or towel around it first, done *something* to protect herself. But it was too late, and she held her arm out with her hand in a fist, jamming her forearm into the dog's mouth as she ran at it.

At least her bold move startled all three of the dogs. Using the machete, she then jabbed at the dog's body. The first time, she missed. She didn't get the tip of the machete in, and wound up cutting the dog's skin and making it bite down harder.

She heard her bone crack, but didn't feel it. Her adrenaline must be far too high to know what was truly going on. But her brain was working at hyper speed, so she thought through her moves. Then, using her right hand, she pulled back and took advantage of the machete's length. Rotating it ever so slightly, Kaya tried to make up for the error on her last hit.

She had to get the blade between ribs. She tried again, and finally, on the third try, she did it.

Pulling with her broken arm still tightly in the dog's mouth, she managed to control the dog's head. As long as he didn't let go, he would follow where she led. So she yanked her arm in close to her own body, and used the tip of the machete, where she'd gotten it between the ribs, and pushed.

She felt various organs give way under her touch, and she pushed anyway, sinking the blade almost to the handle. Then, with a strength she hadn't realized she possessed, she used her grip and stirred the blade inside the dog.

Yes! she thought, as she felt the dog slip for just a moment. The pain flared as the hold on her arm softened slightly. The dog let a whine out around her bruised, bloodied, broken skin, but didn't quite give up its hold. She wasn't willing to pull the arm back herself, not confident she'd get the whole thing.

Kaya was in serious trouble, but she was triumphant. *Yes,* she thought again, as she pulled the machete out and felt the hold on her arm slacken enough to get her arm back.

But just as the triumph passed through her brain, she felt the clamp of jaws on her right thigh. They attacked in unison, she remembered, and this one must have bitten and she hadn't realized it. Turning, flailing, fighting, she used the handle of the machete this time and bashed it into the dog's skull.

It had no effect. The dog was too thick-headed, and even the hard hit with the weight of the weapon was not enough to slow it down. Though it let go for a moment, she wasn't able to slip out of its reach and it bit again, pulling on her. She would have traveled with it, but she felt a second bite on her other leg.

Both dogs now, she thought, her brain again in full hyperdrive as the adrenaline flooded her again. Her victory over the first hadn't made them flee. However much need there had been to fight before was now doubled. She breathed in deep and felt nothing, she only saw and calculated and acted.

She'd learned so many things in her research, and so much that simply didn't work on dogs. She'd made notes on everything. Now, she knew what wasn't worth her time to try. So she purposefully laid down on the floor.

Though the dogs had a firm grip on her, the seemingly surrendering move was to her advantage. Kaya rolled. By doing so, she twisted the dogs. They had to let go or roll with her now. And her new position on the ground had them at a position of severe disadvantage.

She wielded the machete again, hacking at the neck of the dog that held her right leg—the only one she could reach. Kaya swung and chopped, not cutting through his neck. The muscles were far too thick for that, but she was able to make reasonably deep cuts.

She watched as an artery spurted, and then she took aim for the other side. She could feel and calculate the damage being caused on her left leg, but she ignored it.

One dog at a time.

She understood full well that humans didn't stand a chance against the *pack*—but one dog at a time she could do. She had already proven she could kill one. It lay on the floor, just out of reach, bleeding out, if not already dead.

One triumph, she thought, *now go for two*.

She hacked again at the neck, and again and again, but it didn't slow the dog much. She had read that dogs could circumvent the carotid flow if hit in the neck. Thus, if this dog was like other dogs, it might survive lacerations that would be fatal to humans.

She felt her own blood escaping her then. Not because she felt blood leaving her system or saw it pooling on the floor. She only noticed that her arm was growing week and her cuts were lacking the force she should have been putting behind it.

She maybe had one or two good cuts left in her, and she lifted the machete up under the dog and aimed for the inside of his back leg. She hit the femoral artery on the first try.

Yes, she thought, it would take a minute, but he would bleed out from there. She'd made too many cuts on him, deep enough to add up. The clock ticked, but she counted two dogs down.

All she had to do was wait him out, but then she felt the teeth sink deeper into her other leg.

The remaining dog let go of her, grabbed her again, and began dragging her across the floor. Trying again to hack with the machete, she discovered he was out of reach and she couldn't get closer. She couldn't sit up to reach at him while he was dragging her. There wasn't much she could do, but wait until she had an opportunity.

The plan was to act when he stopped dragging her for a moment. Kaya would bolt up and jab her thumb through his eye. But as he stopped and adjusted his hold on her leg, she tried it. She could no longer sit up, her muscles weren't responding to her commands and so she was dragged across the floor as the darkened room became darker than it had been, and she let her eyes fall closed.

24

Cage sat behind the washer, still curled into a little ball, his arms still looped through Joule's. She couldn't have let go if she wanted to. He was too rigid to move, too tightly wound to let go of her.

He had been counting the seconds. His father had not moved from the top of the washer, but he understood. His parents had had the conversation with the kids earlier, about "the plan." He knew his parents: There was always a plan, and they always did their best to follow it.

The deal was, one parent would go and the other would stay behind, in case a second situation arose. The idea was that the kids were not left by themselves. That had always been the goal.

But now, Cage thought they didn't have to plan like they had when he and Joule were little. The twins were almost adults, and the dogs and the mudslides and tornadoes had broken them of the idea that teenagers were immortal.

Still, his parents insisted. They would split up and always keep him and Joule covered. Right now, he hated the plan.

But there was nothing he could do. His mother had left to

fight the dogs. She had yelled that she had this, and he had begun counting. He heard her yell twice more, but they had been rebel yells, not the screams of someone being tortured. He consoled himself with that fact.

His brain flashed back to a memory from childhood. He'd been struggling with his shoes, probably six or seven years old, maybe eight. He had tied double knots and couldn't get them undone. He was panicked because he couldn't get his feet out of his shoes. Joule had found him. He remembered her small, round face, wide hazel eyes, and her deep understanding of her twin's nervous fear. She had remained calm.

"Stay here," she told him. "I'm going to get Mom. Mom can do it. You know, Mom can do anything."

He held on to that now—his sister's tiny voice saying *Mom can do anything.*

Mom can fight off the dogs.

He wasn't sure he didn't hear Joule chanting the same thing right beside him. Low and under her breath, her voice a whisper with no sound, she must be saying the same thing. So he began counting from the last yell.

He was keeping two separate counts, one from the last time he'd heard his mother and another from the last time he'd heard the dogs. The dogs had been quiet longer. He'd heard them running through the house behind her, but then mom sounded like she was on the other side of their home. He'd heard those two yells, fierce, angry bursts like he had learned while he was in karate class. It was a sharp yell, designed to startle your opponent. Though his mother had not taken karate with the rest of them, she had surely sat through enough classes, and that's what she was doing now.

He counted again, and when he reached a thousand, he sneaked his hand up and under the blanket on top. Patting around, he searched until his father's hand reached out and held him. He couldn't see and could only hope no dogs were in the vicinity to see his movement, but he couldn't smell them, and he'd not been able to fight the urge.

Nate's finger wrapped around to tap the back of his hand—a few taps, in a slow steady rhythm. Cage understood—*Be patient!*— and he wondered how hard that was for his father. As hard as it was for him. Maybe worse.

He stayed there, unmoving, gripping his father's hand until his own fingers cramped and eventually—*far, far too late*, he thought—he felt his father's hand tap at him again.

One. Two. Three. Nate was tapping out.

Cage had to let go. If his mother needed anything, his father would be the one to find out.

"Stay there," the whisper slipped through the air, and he felt more than heard his father slowly pull off the blankets, look around, and slide down to the ground.

Then Cage heard nothing, nothing but soft footsteps, nothing but a long and drawn-out silence.

Thankfully, no dogs.

Unfortunately, no sound of his mother's voice, no footsteps that he could identify as hers. And much, much later, when the footsteps came back onto the steps, he made out the sound of the ever-so-soft single tread—his father.

The dogs must be gone. His father was walking relatively freely around the house, but it still wasn't quite light out. Soon, but not yet.

He heard and felt the bathroom door close, then his father slowly climbed back up on top of the washer, and pulled the blanket over him.

Cage knew then, though he asked dad as softly as he could, "Mom?"

In reply, he heard a voice that clearly echoed of tears. "There's nothing we can do. We have to stay here until daylight."

25

J oule walked into her bedroom and peeled off the blouse she'd been wearing. She stepped out of her skirt, and yanked off the low heels she'd shoved her feet into today.

Throwing all of it into the corner, she told herself it would be folded and given away. Later. She would never want to wear it again. It would always be the clothing she'd worn to her mother's funeral.

Her father had suggested that she wear the pink sweater her mother liked so much, but Joule had refused. If she wore it today, she would never wear it again. And she wanted to wear it again and again and again. Something to keep for later, when she needed her mother close and couldn't have her.

Several people from the neighborhood had shown up for the service. A handful of her friends and her friends' parents had come, as had Cage's. Nate's friends and coworkers had turned out in large numbers and, of course, her mother's coworkers also came and said how much they'd loved her. Kaya had loved her work.

They talked about her mother in the past tense, and Joule was not ready for it.

Extended family had not made the trip. It was too hard to travel in many cases—storms raged between large cities. Gas didn't always make it to the remote locations, making driving more expensive. Planes were still the fastest, but becoming increasingly more iffy as large, sudden lightning storms kept popping up. People were afraid that if they left home, when they came back, it wouldn't be there. Joule understood.

So it was only locals at the funeral.

Joule couldn't say for sure—as she hadn't been to too many funerals—but it seemed the vibe was all *off*.

It had taken her a while to place her finger on it. The hushed voices sounded like something one would expect with a casket at the front of the room, but they'd been more like gossip than reverence. Eventually, Joule thought she'd figured it out: Her family had a body to bury, and almost nobody else did.

Her mother was actually declared *dead*, not just missing. They'd not had to find a piece of her and try to decide if the loss was survivable. It didn't matter anyway: the dogs were not survivable. It didn't matter how much or how little the officials found of a person later.

Her mother's body had been there, lying in the game room. She had obvious and fatal bites in several places. So it was clear that she had bled out—but her body was intact.

Though she was dead, Kaya had been the victor in that battle. That was what Joule chose to remember. That was all she wanted to take away from this day with its stupid clothing —not her mother's favorite—and its ridiculous handshaking, and all the parts where she and her brother and her father consoled other people about their own loss.

She changed into jeans and a long sleeve T-shirt. The weather was starting to get warmer and time was now moving on without her mother. The day was wearing. It almost felt wasted spending it at a funeral, especially when her mother had died getting them the information they wanted.

They had spent the first day cleaning up. Joule and her brother bagged the bodies of the two dogs Kaya had killed. They'd found them on the tile floor beside her. Her dad had not been able to look at them. But Joule had said, "It's okay, Dad. We've got this."

She and Cage had cleaned the bodies. There had been at least three dogs in the house, but the third must have run off. Despite following a blood trail, they hadn't been able to find it anywhere. She shrugged at Cage. "Just the two."

"Two is plenty," he'd replied as they figured out what to do with them.

Their father had taken care of the other major task: boarding up the windows for the night. Even before he'd gone to bed, he'd gotten an appointment and an order to have the windows replaced the next morning. The work crews seemed to understand the importance of getting that job done quickly.

The man installing it had said as he hung the window, "This one's really expensive, but it's a double-pane window, with argon between. The panes aren't glass. It's a nearly indestructible polymer."

Joule had thought the word "nearly" was a legal loophole, because the dogs had made "nearly" as close to definite as a product could be.

Nate had only nodded his response, not speaking unless he had to, and the men had gone about installing the new window. When they finished, they sprayed it down with something from a pressurized can and the installer returned to explain. "It's a repellent. Keeps things away."

He didn't say what things. Joule looked back and forth between the man and her father.

"Would you like me to spray all the windows?" he prompted.

Nate had nodded and the man headed off to tell the crew to do the whole house.

And that, Joule thought, was the extent of it. They should have done that before. If a *dog repellent* existed, they should have sprayed all the windows long before this. She had said as much to her father, but he shook his head.

"We hadn't heard of it before this. But don't you think we would have, if it worked?"

"You're paying for it," Joule pointed out.

"Can't afford not to, but I don't have faith in it."

They stood there in the living room, watching as the workers headed around the house, dousing each window in turn with their spray gun.

The dead dogs remained in large plastic storage tubs on ice. They'd gotten the ice from the grocery store and left it in the bags, not wanting to let their specimens get wet or float in a puddle as the ice melted. They'd already replaced it twice.

Now, Joule knocked on Cage's door. She had to get this day moving. She had to get anything moving. "Are you ready?"

"Give me a minute," he hollered back, and she wondered why she was the fast one.

Heading downstairs, she started working. There was a job to be done.

No one had touched the table since her mother had been there. They were eating directly from the refrigerator as they could. No one was hungry and they'd left everything as it sat. So now she was the one who closed her mother's laptop for possibly the last time and picked up the textbooks and the notes that were laid out around it.

But as she went to move the pieces of her mother's life, she noticed something. These weren't work texts.

"Cage!" she called, "Dad! Look!"

Her father came running. He, too, was still tying up his shoes, having obviously changed his clothes. Maybe none of them could handle wearing the things they had worn to the funeral.

"Notes." Joule smiled as she held them up. "Remember, Mom said she had a research project. She left it out for us. I guess we were all too busy with our own things to see what it was."

Nate began thumbing through the loose pages, frowning at her mother's handwriting, but it was Joule who put it together. "It's veterinary texts."

Cage already had one in his hands and Joule held another one. There were sticky notes protruding between the pages, and Cage quickly flipped from cover to cover, looking at each tagged note.

Joule thumbed through the heavy book she held. The twins looked up at each other almost simultaneously. "She was trying to figure out how to kill a dog."

Nate's voice was far too calm for the situation, but still he said, "I'd say she figured it out."

"She left them for us," Joule replied. Something struck her then. She'd been low, despondent, and afraid since the night that she'd been outside. She'd been scared, but here she was: still standing, when even her mother wasn't.

If she died, she'd only be the same as her mother. Being like mom wasn't a bad thing, so there was no longer any reason to fear it. If she went, she was going to go out like her mother did, with a machete in her hand and a win on her chart.

There wasn't time to grieve but, suddenly, Joule didn't feel the need for it.

She closed her book and grabbed the one out of Cage's hands, closing it, too. She took the notes from her father and set them all aside. "We're going to look through these later. We can read them at night if we huddle in the middle of the house—in the upstairs hallway and use small flashlights."

Both of them looked at her almost as though she were

insane, but she'd stopped caring. So what if a dog saw the lights? They couldn't anyway, not from the upstairs hall—and if they came in, she would kill them. Just like her mother had.

"Right now, while we have daylight, we have to examine those dogs." Moving everything aside, she pulled at the table-cloth and threw it into the corner before heading into the kitchen to grab trash bags. "You two go get the bodies."

26

C age looked at his sister, as though to question her. But she only looked back at him. "Go. It's going to take both of you to carry each dog. And you need to bring both of them in."

They'd been storing the bodies in the garage. No one wanted them in the house, but they'd had to be kept where the other dogs wouldn't get to them, which meant keeping them under heavy locks.

Now, Cage realized that, while he didn't have quite her level of determination, he found it was a bit infectious.

His father moved as though ignoring every feeling he had, though Cage understood where his sister was coming from. Their mother was not going to die in vain.

In fact, she already hadn't. She had given them the one thing they really needed. The thing the whole family had been working toward for two weeks, and had been unable to accomplish. Kaya had handed to them, not one, but *two* of the dogs.

The *two* part was important. He knew if they only had one, if it had any unusual features, they might assume that feature was true for all the dogs. Having two gave them an exponential increase in information. "Come on, Dad."

He headed out to the garage, not looking back, only listening for his father's footsteps following along. His father was on leave from his job and Cage wasn't sure Nate would ever go back. He didn't know what his father would do without his mother. But right now, what they were going to do was check out these dogs.

It took fifteen minutes to unlock the multiple padlocks, get a good grip on the heavy tubs, and haul both of them in.

While they had been out, Joule had set up the dining room like a well-stocked laboratory. She laid out boxes of latex gloves. Cage knew they'd been stored in his mother's office. She kept them in several sizes, because they weren't like other families and they occasionally ran physics or chemistry experiments when they could. When the twins had found a dead animal, or a baby lost from its family, their mother had encouraged them to pick it up. But always with gloves.

Under the window, Joule had opened a TV tray, covered it with a white trash bag, and set up the microscope their mother had bought them. She and Nate had always said they didn't understand much biology or chemistry, but they'd encouraged the kids to try everything. So when she'd found the laboratory-grade microscope in the thrift shop, she'd not only bought it for them, but immediately invested in glass slides and coverslips.

His eyes drifted to the center of the room. Joule had extended the table with the leaf and wrapped they whole thing in plastic. She had trays out. They would no longer be baking cookies on these; Joule was ready to possibly dissect organs. Three steak knives sat at the ready.

But Cage looked at her and at the knives. "We have dissection kits. Remember?"

Quickly, she'd nodded and run upstairs as he and his father pulled in the second of the heavy tubs. Putting in the ice had been a good move. The dogs didn't smell any worse now than they had when they'd been alive.

Joule came back, not only with two leather dissection kits that they had purchased for high school, but also the scale from her parents bathroom. She set it on the floor and motioned to Nate to not lift the lid yet.

"Weigh the whole thing," she said as Cage and Nate caught on quickly.

Holding the tub onto the scale, he watched as she tilted her head around to read and then record the weight. "Now take out the dog."

Following her instructions, they hoisted the carcass onto the table. The body almost didn't look real, it was so stiff. But Joule wasn't looking. She again looked down at the scale, calculated the difference, and said, "Approximately eighty-two pounds. Next."

The second dog, though visually a little smaller, and in a tub that seemed to have more ice in it, had still outweighed the first. It clocked in at eighty-five pounds. Joule had it all written down in a lab notebook she must have pulled from her room.

The two dogs were laid out on the table, side by side, snouts aimed away, legs pointing to the left, as the three of them stood there and looked. Nate took the spot in the middle, and Joule looked ready to record with her notebook and pen in hand.

"Alright." Cage breathed in heavily. They could do this. "Visual assessment first. What do we see?"

They did their initial walk around, the three of them counting toes, bending legs to see if they moved like regular dog legs, and tipping the heads. They measured the circumference of the tails and the waists. Joule recorded length of each dog from the tip of his nose to the base of his tail.

They measured around one head, then the other dog's, and recorded everything. Cage walked to the front of the table, and did something that felt very scary despite the fact that he knew the dogs were dead. He lifted one eyelid and shone his small flashlight at it.

For a fraction of a second, he expected it to jump up and growl, snarl, and bite. But it did no such thing.

"These eyes are light brown," he said. "And when I shine the light, they reflect back a little bit. I think that's normal for dogs. I mean, sometimes you can see their eyes in the dark. Right?"

Joule nodded. Nate shrugged, but his father finally held a hand out, asking for the flashlight. Moving to the second dog, Cage watched as he repeated the test. That made Cage notably happier.

His father had merely been going through the motions, doing what he was told to set up the funeral and letting the kids take lead. This was the first time that he had made a move on his own in days. Cage wanted to tell his father he'd be okay. But he didn't know if that was true.

The best he could do was show his father that *he* would be okay.

So he reached out to the dog's jaw and pried it open. Pulling back the lips, he scanned the space. "The gums are almost black," he told his father and sister. "The teeth are yellow... hey, look at this." He pointed into the mouth.

Joule came around his side, and looked and frowned. Nate joined them as they all stared into the mouth. Holding the jaw open so his father could shine the flashlight on it. They peered in and tried to count.

"Those are molars..."

Joule made notes as Cage counted the long and multi-ridged teeth that lined the back of the dog's mouth. The front incisors didn't appear quite as tiny as those on a regular dog.

"I don't know if these are normal." More comfortable now, he ran his latex covered finger over the teeth. "Let's check the other dog."

Cage stepped over and pulled that jaw open, too, and then leaned back to let both his father and sister check out what they were seeing.

"It looks pretty much the same as the other," his father commented with the tone he used when he was examining something. *At least he wasn't using the flat, unaffected sound of the past three days,* Cage thought.

But he turned to Joule, waving the flashlight as a cue. "Do you want to grab one of those veterinary texts, see if we can match it?"

She was moving before he finished the sentence, flipping pages and holding up a diagram.

"Look," she said. Cage read where she'd held the page up to him, then turned to show it to their father. Normal dogs had incisors, canines, and premolars—much like humans. Though the individual teeth were shaped very differently, he could see they were in roughly the same layout.

The premolars in the book were sharp and pointy, but not like the canines. They were short, and wouldn't do much damage in a bite. Once they figured out which teeth were molars and which were premolars, they frowned. "I only counted two on each side." Joule said.

"Those are premolars." Cage countered.

"No, look." She held up the book, where the description of a premolar tooth was clear. "They don't have enough cusps to be premolars. These are canines."

That gave the dogs three canines in each of the four quadrants.

The canines were the sharp teeth made for tearing into meat, and these dogs had an abundance of them. The Mazurs stepped back and looked at each other, confused.

Cage looked first to Joule and then turned to his father. But Nate only shrugged; this wasn't his forte.

Cage checked out the dog quickly, thinking what he now

needed to do. They needed to check the internal organs. They needed to take samples and look at them under the microscope later. Suddenly, this project had gotten huge.

But right now, he and Joule were comparing the teeth they saw to the teeth in the textbook. Looking at his dad, he explained. "We learned something very important in biology class," he said. "Teeth are conservative."

His father shrugged. "I guess I always thought they were liberal?"

"Ha ha, funny," Joule dead-panned. And, for the first time, despite the conversation and the dead dogs lying on the table, the tone of the room felt a little closer to normal.

But Cage was about to change that.

"No, Dad," he said. "It means, teeth don't change. All dogs have the same teeth, and that's how you know that they're the same species. Any time the teeth change, you can declare it a speciation event."

He and Joule looked at each other then up at their dad.

"These extra canines are consistent between both the dogs. They're not just a mutation. This is a whole new species."

27

J oule stood at the table with her hands on her hips as she surveyed their work.

The dogs, laid out and clearly autopsied, barely resembled dogs anymore. They had been cut into and their organs removed, weighed on the kitchen scale, and checked against the veterinary texts.

It had taken them three days to get to this point. Each night, they would pack the dogs back up into the hard plastic bins, stuffing the extra area with ice. They put ice packs on top of the bodies when they weren't working on a particular dog and packed them as best they could at all times, in hopes of slowing the decay process.

Joule looked at her father and brother now. "I'm starting to smell them. I think this is the last day." She looked back and forth and when neither of them spoke, she pushed a little harder. "What else do we need before we dispose of them?"

Cage, mimicking her stance, also surveyed the table. "What we need is to figure out how to kill them."

At the head of the table, Nate nodded.

None of them had left the house for several days. If they had been eating at a regular pace, they would have run out of food yesterday, but instead, today was the day.

"We need to get to the grocery store before dark tonight," Joule said, feeling like she was the only one who had her head on her shoulders. Her father was despondent, though understandably so. Her brother was neck deep in the dogs, learning everything he could and not paying attention to much else. Also, understandably so.

But Joule was the one making sure they were fed, and that they showered regularly.

"Here's what we know," Nate told the room at large, almost shocking her. He'd spoken so infrequently this last week. "Their physiology is slightly different from normal dogs, at least according to the text and the two specimens we have. However, compared to our other books, their physiology is generally mammalian and, within that grouping, generally canine."

Cage recited what they'd learned. "Kingdom, Animalia. Phylum, Chordata. Class, Mammalia. Order, Carnivora. Family, Canidae. Genus ... and here's where we can't classify anymore ..."

"They have to be *Canis* like dogs, wolves, and coyotes." Joule was reading the text in her hands as she talked. "They aren't Lycalopex or Vulpes, because those are foxes. But the individual species doesn't match anything here ..."

"That means we should be able to kill them in generally canine ways," Cage added.

Joule nodded, following along. Though the family had not stayed awake in the hallway with flashlights, reading—as she had suggested they do—she had.

Each night, she would sneak out of her room. She had a halogen flashlight that she dialed way down and she would read her mother's notes and textbooks. For several hours, in the otherwise dark space, she would take her own notes from her mother's, mark significant passages, or check what her mother had flagged. No one questioned her. No one asked when she said, "But this book says dogs do X," or "But wolves do Y."

Now, she looked back and forth between the two men. "My books should be here today. I ordered two more texts. One on animal behavior and another on general mammalian behavior and learning."

"Good idea," Cage said, though Joule only nodded.

She wanted to say, "Yes, it is. It was mom's." But she held her tongue, not sure if that would help or hurt. She also hadn't told them that she had answered the door for the delivery man yesterday. The package he'd placed in her hands held a book— one that her mother had ordered before she died. *Animal Minds*. Joule had begun reading it last night.

"I'm going to clean up the dogs here." She motioned to the table, to organs cut out and laid onto the cake pans. To the slides that they had made with tissue samples and blood smears and examined under the microscope. "You two should go to the grocery store. And then when you get home, we can all carry the dogs back into the garage or figure out what to do with them."

But Nate shook his head, startling her. His expression held determination she'd not seen in too long. Though she was grateful, she was also wary.

"No." He didn't protest, he just stated it like lord of the manor. "*We all* clean up. And *we all* go to the store. We don't split up. Not again."

Though his voice was quiet, the force came through loud and clear.

Joule was in no position to argue, and he was in no position for a fight. She wouldn't do that to her father. So she nodded her agreement. Besides, he may have just said the first parental thing he'd said in a week, but he did make sense.

"Is there anything we need to keep?" She looped back to her original question. The last thing she wanted to do was clean up then later wish she had something to compare and have thrown it away.

"The slides," Cage replied and promptly ran off, presumably to get a box to keep them in.

"Let's keep everything we can," Nate said and Joule shook her head.

Though she agreed in theory, it wouldn't work in reality. "It's biological, dad. It's going to rot. I can already smell it starting to turn."

Her father nodded as he seemed to think about it. A minute later, he looked up with an idea in his eyes. "Let's swing by the home store and buy ourselves a freezer."

Joule nodded, because who was she to argue? Of course, that's what they would do. It was the smart thing to do. Her father had always commented that the actual report was better than the summary. The pictures were better than the report. And setup itself was better than the pictures. So they would keep the dogs in a freezer for anything they needed to learn about them later.

With a nod, she began shoving the organs—still in ziplock baggies—back inside the hollowed-out dogs. It was the best place to keep the organs. Right organs with right dog. She felt like the creepiest kind of Dr. Frankenstein, but it didn't stop her. They had to learn as much as they could.

When everything was back in place—generally speaking— Joule positioned the bags of ice on top of the animals. They would leave them on the table while they went out.

"Groceries first? Dogs second?" she asked her dad, and he nodded.

"We need vegetables," Nate declared as Cage came down

the stairs with a small, wooden box in his hand, presumably for the slides.

It was Cage who joined the conversation he'd only heard the last line of. "What we need is a way to kill the dogs."

Joule looked up at Cage then over to her father, and said, "Actually, mom already found that."

28

C age stretched his back. It was sore from the heavy lifting they'd all been doing.

They had not made it to get a freezer the afternoon before. When they'd left the grocery store, spring clouds had been rolling in and they voted that they had just enough time to get home and get the dogs packed up. That was a necessity.

So yesterday, they'd packed the dogs on ice again. Today, they headed first to the store and picked out a freezer. Getting it delivered had cost another several hours, but it had arrived in the afternoon. Luckily, getting it delivered also included getting it hauled into the garage. Directing someone to put it in place seemed as though it should be easy, except they'd had to clear a spot for it first. That had been Cage's labor input.

Then they'd gotten it plugged in and realized it would take a good twenty-four hours for it to come down to the right temperature. Cage sighed at yet another setback, but his father just looked at what was there.

"I think both tubs will fit inside." Nate stuck his head into the freezer of a size that suggested to Cage his father had bigger plans than just these two dogs.

So he and his father had lifted each tub up and over the edge into the freezer.

As he put the lid down, and felt it click shut, he had to admit, "It is a well-sealed, insulated system."

Even though the temperature wasn't down yet, the carcasses would still fare better inside. The ice they were packed in would probably help drop the internal temperature faster. All the physics added up.

Just inside the door, Joule turned back to them asking, "Who's first in the shower?"

Cage noticed that she was no longer asking her father if he needed to shower, but simply stating that the three of them would do it. She was only asking, what order did they want to go in? Somehow, he and Joule always managed to put their father in the middle, ensuring that things happened. They were doing the same thing with food, making sure he ate.

This time, it was voted that Joule should get the first shower and as she left the room, Cage turned to his father and asked, "Was it all worth it?"

It was the first time he'd really broached the topic of his mother.

"Kaya?" Nate asked.

Cage nodded, realizing only then that his question was horrifyingly unclear and he could be glad his father hadn't answered about the freezer. But Nate didn't really see the humor. Instead, he breathed in deep.

"It was worth every second of this hell." His father spoke the words with a conviction that Cage and Joule had not heard since their mother had died. Nate continued, "I got you guys out of the deal. And I guess I need to tell Joule, too, because I realized it doesn't seem like I know that right now. But I am living for you two. That's why I'm going on."

Cage had to sigh—he needed some kind of release of air in exchange for taking in that depth of information. On the breath out, he floated his own words. "I love you, Dad."

But it was too much, or too quiet, or too something, and his father only offered a nod before he went off to take his turn at a quick shower.

When Joule returned, with her jeans and sweatshirt on, her feet bare and hair wet, Cage told her, "I asked Dad... I think he'll be okay. It's going to take some time, but he'll be okay."

"He should come to college with us," Joule replied, "I mean, move to wherever we go."

It was an easy statement to agree with. Without their mother, they were their Dad's family. Having him at a distance —alone—didn't make any sense. "We'll have to look for a place that has a think tank he can work in."

They needed Nate close, if only for their own peace of mind. Later, Cage wondered if his question had snapped his father out of something. Because, when he came out of the shower, Nate was wearing a decidedly different attitude.

His eyes searched for Cage and he called, "Your turn!"

Even that had been snappier than anything else that week, but when Cage returned, there was a whole chicken in the oven. It sat upright on an opened beer can in a tray. Whoever had made it seemed to have also added lemon and herbs. Scattered and roasting on the tray around the chicken were the vegetables that his dad had commented earlier that they needed. And the rice cooker was out and turned on, presumably making a batch of sticky white rice to go with all of it

"Did you do this?" Cage mouthed to Joule, his brows pulling together as the kitchen filled with smells of the first real food they had eaten in well over a week.

"Dad," she mouthed back, to Cage's relief.

As he looked around, he saw more changes that had occurred during the short time he'd been out of the room. The table had been peeled of its plastic and scrubbed down. The microscope was put away and the room generally returned to rights.

As they sat around the dinner table that night, he thought maybe he had his Dad back. Nate looked at the two kids sitting on the other side across from him as he finished up a full plate of food. From the light in his eyes, Cage knew something was coming.

"I have ideas, but I want to know what you think is next."

With a quick glance to his sister, seeing she was on the same page, Cage asked, "Are we going back to school?"

"Do you want to?"

"No, but we need to graduate. So I'm guessing we have to."

Nate nodded, but it looked more like he was trying to figure out how to get them out of it.

Cage had something else to add. "We need to take down the traps. They're not working. The least we can do is reclaim the material. We certainly don't want a trap to catch something *now* because it's not worth checking them regularly."

Nate looked to Joule and as she agreed, his father nodded his consent as well. Then he turned to Joule, "What do *you* think we need to do next?"

"I think we all need to read Mom's notes. I've been up at night reading. Did you know that?"

Cage did, but his father seemed surprised by it.

Joule checked their expressions and that seemed to be enough. She went on, "I'm through most of her notes and I've been going through the textbooks as much as I can. But I'm just one person, and there are several full-course texts. We all need to be researching for the next couple of days before we make the next move... so we can make the right one."

Nate again nodded in agreement and Cage realized that— somewhere in the past couple of years—he and Joule had graduated from being "just kids" to being at least partially equal family members. Their father could, and certainly would, outvote them if he wanted to. He'd claim fatherhood as the ultimate be-all/end-all and demand his way be enacted. Immediately. Cage had seen it happen. But it hadn't happened in a while.

As his parents had explained to Cage and Joule years ago, while Nate and Kaya were paying the bills, they had the option to declare themselves overlords. Cage fully understood. He thoroughly enjoyed not making a house payment, or dealing with utilities bills, and yet still getting to live in a home with heat, light, and clean running water.

Until the dogs had truly invaded the neighborhood, he'd enjoyed playing video games during his down hours. He'd binge-watched his favorite TV show on his laptop and did the piddly job of keeping up with his homework. So he tried not to complain when his father pulled rank. But right now, he was trying hard to think of the last time Nate had done such a thing, and he couldn't remember it.

Here at the table, his father was consulting him and his sister as equals and accepting their suggestions. But then Nate spoke up with his own plan for what to do next. "I want to look into some kind of armor. I want to find it and get it ordered ASAP."

"Armor against what?" Cage asked, thinking bullets, or maybe the full medieval suits of mail and metal that his friends had worn in Curie when they had cosplayed knights and swordsmen.

"Probably chain mail," his father said far too casually. It made Cage suspicious, but he stayed silent.

"Lightweight, but impervious to dog bites, something like that." Nate's enthusiasm was concerning.

"Why would you need that?" Joule asked, caution creeping

into her tone. She clearly had her suspicions, but she was going to make her father say it out loud.

Then Cage lost every good feeling he'd had about his father coming back around because Nate said, "I want to go out and fight them."

29

Joule was exhausted. Somehow, they'd been outside, in the dark, for three hours, with no sighting of any dogs.

Truthfully, she thought she'd maybe seen one go by in the distance, keeping to the shadows. She'd heard rustling noises in the woods, and even in nearby bushes. But in neither case could she say that it was, specifically, one of the dogs.

She was exhausted because she'd been walking in the dark, tense and hyper-alert, for three hours, holding her bow, with an arrow notched and ready, the whole time. She'd done all this while wearing approximately sixteen pounds of high-quality chain mail. The armor was necessary but growing heavier by the minute.

Her father had ordered it online. He'd surprised them one day by suddenly measuring each of them—shoulder to shoulder, shoulder to hip, hip to floor, and so on. Next, he'd made them measure him.

Delivery of his very precise orders had taken longer than he'd wanted. He'd hoped to find armor he could get in two to three days. But custom orders weren't that simple, and it had taken much longer for the chain mail to arrive at the house. So Joule and Cage had gone back to school. The weather had warmed up a bit too, which now only worked against the chain mail.

Joule was hot as fuck, sweating beneath the lightweight shirt she'd worn. It was long-sleeved, because no one wanted chain mail rubbing on their bare skin. And it wasn't thick, but it was slippery—again, to keep the mail from causing her skin any problems—and that made it hot.

Because the wait for the mail had taken so long, Nate had turned to other ideas. He'd sat at the dining table designing traps, reading the texts as though he were getting another degree in mammalian and canine biology and behavior. He had not gone back to work.

When Joule questioned his ability to pay for the house and more, he'd answered her almost ambiguously. "I don't worry about it." He'd shrugged her off without even looking up from a design she couldn't distinguish from the one he'd done yesterday.

"But I worry," she replied, calmly and cautiously.

"You're going to college soon."

"Yes, but I thought we would still have this house. I realized later that that may not be the case—that you and mom might prefer to move closer to us. Honestly, Cage and I were hoping that you would." She paused for a moment, but still couldn't tell if her father was listening. "But that means we should be able to sell this house, which means you have to keep up with the payments."

It was a conversation she'd never expected to have with her father. Then again, she'd never expected to lose her mother. She'd not been given the opportunity to be a grieving child. But, as Cage pointed out, her parents had been treating them mostly like adults for some time. Now, she was having to step up fully and act like it.

"Dad, you need to make the payments on the house. Are you still getting paid from work?"

"Yes, I have four more weeks of leave," he told her, still without looking up. Finally, a straightforward answer to her questions. She'd been afraid he would put her in a position in which she needed to call his job and see what was going on. That would not go over well.

After a few more questions—very pointed and specific—he caught on. Looking up at her, Nate said, "Your mother left a good-sized life insurance policy. I cashed it a week ago, and it was more than enough to pay off the house. Also, it was designed to let me live at home with you two kids until you graduated."

It would only be a few more months before they graduated, then three more before they left for college, Joules thought.

Nate shook his head. Apparently, her line of reasoning had shown on her face.

"No, honey." His words were gentle and he finally seemed to see how worried she was. "We set up this policy when you were four. There's enough money for me to stay home with you for fourteen more years... We never changed it. It will cover your college without worries, and I can stay home. I can go where you go, without having to worry about finding a job for a long time. We are okay."

He'd stood up, putting his hands on her shoulders to comfort her, and at last, she nodded.

But then he said something that shocked her. "It really wouldn't matter if we didn't pay off the house anyway. Who's going to come here and reclaim it? Not the bank. People are losing houses—physically—left and right. They aren't going to pay their loans. The banks are going to collapse any day now."

For a moment, Joule stared at him. None of that was right. Yes, people were leaving their homes. And yes, the housing market was crap and the banks were suffering. But they were not on the verge of Apocalypse Now—*were they?*

She stared at her father, hard. Even so, she figured just telling him he was wrong was a bad idea. "Dad, that's not a plan. Pay the house. When the bank stops asking, you can stop paying. But until then, *pay for the house.*"

She'd walked away then, ending the conversation because she simply couldn't deal with any more of it.

And then, the next day, the chain mail had arrived and her father had asked them to try it out. They'd worn it for two full evenings before going outside with it. They'd all known it would be heavy and that they needed to get used to it.

That had been an understatement.

Cage turned to her at one point and said, "It's heavy enough that I noticed it's taking more effort to breathe."

For a moment, Joule flashed back. "Just like what they did to Marat and Johanna." She remembered old friends of theirs from Curie, Nebraska. Their murders were a big part of the reason their family had left that state.

Now the remaining three Mazurs stood out in the street, chain mail on and weapons at the ready, waiting on dogs that might not show.

Joule was almost relieved when she heard the growl behind her. With a deep breath and bark of her own, she hollered, "*Now!*" and turned to face the three dogs coming toward her.

Aiming her bow, she took stock. Still at enough distance to use it, she pulled back on the string, and waited.

30

J oule let her second arrow fly. The first was already sticking out of the dog's chest, having lodged between his ribs. Yet the injury was not slowing him down.

Even as the second arrow flew, she was reaching for one more, aiming and hitting a second of the three dogs before she made her move.

Nate and her dad were on either side of her—giving her just enough room to work the bow and arrow—but the dogs were now closer than her range. Also, no one was watching their backs, with the three of them lined up to face the dogs. Either the dogs couldn't count, or they could and they thought the match was still in their favor.

Joule didn't like it. She'd almost yelled to her dad to watch their backs as the dogs tended to circle. If there were three dogs in front of them, there might be four—or five or ten—more coming around the other side.

Her father had wanted to fight the dogs, and this was his chance.

Clearly, she and Cage had reluctantly agreed. Though neither of wanted this, they'd known Nate needed to do it. He mentioned going out by himself, and the twins wound up arguing their way into a plan neither of them wanted any part of.

"No one goes alone," they'd told him, throwing his own words back. "The family sticks together." So here they were, suddenly in the middle of a dogfight Nate had sought out.

Now, dropping her aim with the bow toward the ground, she turned swiftly, another arrow notched as she raised it facing the other side. Using sweeping motions, she searched for dogs circling, but didn't see them.

Behind her, she heard the fight. They wore small army helmets, buckles under their chins, and she knew they must look like ridiculous warriors in their loose and heavy chain mail and tiny helmets. Wasn't this too close to what those bands of soldier wannabes had tried to do? Hadn't they all gone missing?

She was bumped into from behind and recognized it immediately as her father. Straightening her legs, she offered him support, and he bounced off, heading back into the fray. At least it sounded like they were winning the fight. That was what her father wanted. She and Cage just wanted to survive with all their limbs intact.

Nate had originally considered carrying a broadsword, but after testing the one he'd bought he found the weight of it—along with the heft of the chain mail—gave it all the same problems the Crusaders had originally encountered. It was far too heavy and unwieldy. Quick movements were nearly impossible, and he'd set it aside in favor of her mother's machete. He added a dagger he liked the heft and balance of.

That choice of weaponry meant he was only doing close fighting with the dogs—hand to hand, as it were. Not like her with her arrows and the ability to wound at a distance. That was why she'd brought the bow and why she'd turned around to protect their backs now. She still saw no other dogs approaching and thought that was out of their usual pattern.

Cage had chosen a short sword and a long dagger for himself, while Joule had two stilettos, one sheathed at each side, in addition to her bow. As far as she was concerned, she could not be armed enough.

The three stood back to back in the middle of the street, though only Cage and her father were fighting right now. Sweeping her gaze again, Joule spotted another dog approaching from her direction. She was opening her mouth to let her father and brother know, when she saw the second one coming in close on the first's heels.

"Two!" she hollered out. "Ten o'clock."

"Got it!" Cage called back over his shoulder.

Nate didn't respond, except for the grunts of his hits coming through to Joule. At least they were comforting sounds that he seemed to be winning whatever skirmish he was in. Joule wasn't hearing screams or yelps or swearing that he'd been hit.

Joule let an arrow fly, hitting the first dog and—just like the last time—angering it more than wounding it. It darted toward her, as though now set on a faster speed. There was only enough time to put one arrow in this dog. Aiming another, she turned to face the second.

Then she had a choice to make.

Pull the stilettos or stay with the bow?

Though her focus was on the dog she was shooting at, she saw movement on her left. "Eleven o'clock," she said. By her account, if no more had joined Cage and her dad on the other side, then they were at seven. Three of them against seven dogs.

Turning, she put one more arrow into the dog on her left, leaving one dog without any wounds yet. He would be the one to be wary of. But he held back, watching the fight, watching the other three in her sight stalk toward the little trio, barely giving her time to think.

It was the best she could do with the ones on her right. They were getting too close, and slung her bow over her shoulder with her right hand even as she pulled her stiletto out with the left. In one smooth move, she unsheathed it and jabbed it forward, sweeping her now free right arm up in a practice arc. Her forearm clashed with an embedded arrow as the first dog came for her.

Brilliant. It made her smile as she realized the dog was controlled.

The arrow had embedded into its sternum, and now, the metal rod forced the dog to turn to the right with her motion. It didn't even require much strength from her. She was using the arrow against the dog's motion, and the dog had no chance. That was a small reward for excellent aim and hitting the dogs, even if it had just made them angry at first.

The stiletto in her hand was long and sharp, and she had studied her mother's notes. With a jab, and knowing she had to be quick, she aimed now to the dog's side. She didn't have to kill the dog, she simply had to render it unable to fight. Incapacitated was fine.

Shoving the stiletto in between his ribs as her mother had instructed, Joule now *stirred*. After a moment of feeling the insides give beneath the sharp edge, she pulled the stiletto back, sliding it between organs she had shredded, removing it with blood dripping.

With her right arm, she continued to push the dog out of her way. And she heard a sick thud as it fell over onto its side. *One down.*

It was a heady feeling, but one she couldn't dwell on for long. Unfortunately, the dog's friends didn't seem to care that their friend was injured and they kept coming. "Caaaaage!" she called out, lengthening his name. If her brother and father had three dogs to fight and she had four, then she needed reinforcements. Though—as she looked at the one bleeding out on the street—she only had three now.

A quick glance around told her no other dogs had joined the fray.

Cage, already at her back on her right, pushed at her side a bit. Then the whole little party of three rotated as a unit, leaving her father facing the original dogs and Cage, with Joule, facing the newcomers.

"Got this one," her brother said, and she breathed a little sigh of relief.

The second dog got close and Cage swiped his sword into the air, hoping to stop it. He'd aimed for the neck, knowing that it likely wouldn't kill. Her mother had made those cuts on the dogs in the house and had still had to get underneath and cut a different artery before they died.

They had discussed this already—what their best defenses and offenses were, what Kaya had found in her books and when she fought, what information she'd left behind for them. So Joule knew Cage's cuts right now were intended to wound and that was it.

But a wounded dog was more controllable, and Joule also anticipated what he would do next. He used the sword against the cuts in the neck, the pain probably making the dog faster to comply, to move out of the way of where the sword pressed. It kept the mouth, and those teeth, away from him and let him get the dagger underneath the dog and go for a femoral artery.

But Joule couldn't watch her brother's moves. She was already dealing with the dog coming at her now, full on.

She pulled her second stiletto from its sheath, the bow still up and over her shoulder, across her chest. She'd practiced fighting with the bow in place, with one stiletto and, like this, with two. She'd practiced while having Cage bump her unexpectedly, and she'd practiced with everything except actual dogs coming at her.

But when she faced this one, she was ready with two weapons in her hands. So far, she hadn't been bitten, hadn't put the mail to the test. If she was lucky, she could keep it that way.

Joule was prepared—if she lost her stilettos, she had more sharp, pointy things on her back than she had hands. She had tried using the arrows as weapons in and of themselves, but they didn't offer a good grip. They didn't let her grasp and shove and pull back without her hand sliding along the shaft, but they were backup, if she needed it.

Joule was ready to cut and stab and smack the creature coming at her, because it was ready to tear her limb from limb. Since cutting the carotid arteries wouldn't make him bleed out the way a human would, Joule bent her knees and leaned forward to put her weight into heftier cuts.

Turning her shoulders sideways, she aimed to make herself a smaller target. The hardest part was waiting for the animal to get close. The stilettos were not a long-range weapon, and her arms were not the longest either.

Three.

Two.

She held herself calm, waiting for the right moment as the dog came closer and closer. One.

As he lifted up to come at her face, she jabbed the stilettos into each side of his neck, letting them cross somewhere in between their entry points. It was not an easy flick of her wrists. This was much harder work than that.

The veterinary texts had shown them—and her experience was agreeing—that the dogs had incredibly thick, muscular necks. Human necks were weak and spindly in comparison. Thus, on the dogs, slicing was harder. But she put her shoulders into it and wrenched the blades back and forth scissoring beyond where she'd pierced him. Then she watched as the dog —just like the frog in her bio lab—piece by piece, stopped moving. The mouth whimpered once, and then blood gurgled toward her.

Using her foot, Joule shoved him back. It worked and the dog, no longer fighting her, went flying further away then. She was stronger than she'd thought.

But as she pulled the foot back, she saw and felt as a pair of jaws clamped around her ankle.

31

Cage, noting the two dogs in front of him were dead, and knowing that one behind him was as well, now rotated to his left again. He was trying to face the still living dog or dogs.

Joule still had a live dog she was fighting off. The growls were unmistakable—it was still healthy enough to put up a good effort. As he came around, his mouth fell open at the sight of the creature clamped on his sister's ankle. He also saw his father coming from the other side.

Nate's eyes were full of light and anger. And something else, maybe glee. He seemed to be enjoying the killing. All week, he'd enjoyed getting ready for the fight.

Cage had seen it as a task he could not get out of. In fact, he would have much preferred to stay home in the dark—the far safer place to be—but his father insisted on coming out, insisted that knowing they could fight and how to do so efficiently was a necessary part of their forward movement. Now, here was Joule, the dog clamped around her ankle. The jaws were firmly on the mail, though whether it was working, he couldn't tell. She shoved with her foot, but the dog didn't come loose.

"Are you okay?" Cage asked, getting in her face and enunciating each word. His father hadn't asked; he was just assessing how to get at the dog.

"Yes," she answered calmly, eyes still on the dog as she shoved at it again.

But it was Nate who, after a moment of contemplation, put an arm across Joule's chest as though to hold her back. Cage grabbed her then, lifting her off the ground, giving her an advantage so that her leg was at the same height as the dog's mouth. The dog was trying to use his strength to pull on her, and though Cage wanted to fight, his sister's foot was more important.

With no warning, Nate leaned over the dog. Using the machete, he laid a harsh cut into the middle of its back. Despite his apparent effort, the cut was not deep, but it must have been enough. Maybe the processes on the vertebrae had led the knife through the V down between the bones, severing the spinal cord, Cage thought. Because, as he watched, the back half of the dog went limp.

Joule shook her foot again, but the jaws did not want to let go.

"Careful," Nate said, once again holding his arm out the way Cage remembered his father doing if they had to stop suddenly while he was in the front seat of the car. It probably worked just about as well here. Maybe it was only intended to be a gesture; Nate certainly hadn't spared a look at his daughter.

Still, Joule leaned back, Cage's arm clamped around her as he lifted her. In his other hand, the sword was ready to fight. Her hands still clenched the stilettos, but it was hard to reach down by her ankle with any force.

The dog should have let go. Logic said there were far more

blades than the dog could withstand. But for all Cage was willing to credit them with intelligence and cunning, this dog wasn't figuring out that it was time to let go and run.

It was Nate again who chopped at the dog. Without warning, he brought the machete down in another hard arc. He was clearly trying not to get too close to the head. But the swing had made Cage nervous, *incredibly nervous,* for a split second as it swung down too close to Joule's foot.

However, this time, the dog let go.

The three Mazurs staggered back as Cage saw the last of the dogs fall. A quick spin revealed that no more were coming, and that his father would have missed it if they were. He was too busy lording over the last dog as it twitched on the ground in front of him. Cage looked away, finishing his turn to the sight of his sister putting weight on the ankle and testing it.

"Does it work? Are you okay?" he asked. Even as the words came out of his mouth, he realized it probably wasn't anything she could answer yet. Certainly not until tomorrow, not until the ankle did or didn't swell up.

"I think it's good." She shook it, the chain mail rattling ever so slightly with the movement.

Nate had wanted something silent. The pants they had on were made of chain mail stripes alternating with carbon fiber cloth. The carbon fiber didn't protect against punctures as well as the mail, but it could not be torn outright and lessened the weight of the pants by half. The maker had believed there was enough chain mail in strategic locations that a bite would not go through.

He'd made these on the other side of the country and mailed them. He'd done it while asking questions about needs, but not exactly what it was for. Perhaps he was getting many strange orders these days.

Cage thought the mail did well, protecting against bites, but he'd withhold judgment until he got a good look at Joule's ankle. He wanted to see how it protected against the pressure of the bite or the rubbing of the mail against the skin as the dog held on and shook his head. His sister had become their unintentional test case.

Joule put weight on the ankle again, lifting it and stepping down gingerly while Cage and Nate looked around, watching for more dogs, any late entries into their fight.

None appeared.

The only dogs he could see were the seven dead, now in a circle around them, at varying distances from where he stood. But all were too close for Cage's comfort.

It was Joule who asked, "What do we do now?"

Cage looked to his father for that answer. He saw that Nate had not heard his sister, but was still looking at the dogs with a triumphant grin and a gleam in his eye. That bothered Cage more than the fact that they had been out at night—and more than the issue that they had fought off *seven dogs* without backup.

That his father saw this as a victory was the worst thing he'd seen tonight. A quick glance between him and his sister told Cage they were on the same page. Their next job would be to hold Nate back from thinking this was anything they should repeat.

Joule asked again, this time louder, "What do we *do*?"

"Do you think anyone saw us?" Nate asked in reply, too casually looking up at the windows on the houses down the street. Almost half the places were abandoned, but that meant more than half still had people in them. People who might have looked out. But Joule shook her head.

"I doubt it." Her gaze bounced between them. "We heard the noises in the night before and I would *never* have cracked the curtains to look. Not as long as it's dark." She looked up at the sky. "I don't think anyone was watching. The problem is we can't leave dead dogs in a circle in the middle of the street. *That* will draw suspicion. And the last thing you want is to advertise that we just did this." Her voice grew angrier as she spoke, and Cage felt the weight of her words in his chest.

She was right. What they had done was monumentally stupid. It was possible they had done something no one else had done. Or, possibly, it was something crews all over the area were doing as they spoke. But none of that mattered. The last thing they wanted was to get a reputation as a vigilante crew.

Cage hoped their job was done here. *We fought them. We proved we can do it. And now we go back to other methods.* But he didn't say that. Nate wouldn't hear it and Cage couldn't afford to miscalculate, or they would wind up out here every night.

Looking to his father, he said, "We have to dispose of the bodies. We have to at least get them out of the street. It will be bad enough, because several are bleeding heavily, and we're going to leave streaks. Hopefully, it will look enough like what we've seen before that no one will think twice."

His father still stood looking at the dogs, not acknowledging that his children were speaking. Dagger and machete in hand, he turned in a circle, surveying all that he had done.

"Dad! We have to at least drag the bodies off the street," Cage said with more force this time.

Nate only nodded absently, and it was Cage who leaned over to grab the first dog. The skin was a little loose, though not as loose as he would have expected. Again, he reminded himself, they needed a new name: These weren't *dogs*. They were something different.

He began to drag the bleeding body off the road toward a little copse of trees, where he hoped no one would look. It was hard work, pulling in that bent over position, the weight of the animal in his hands and the weight of the chain mail making him even more tired. The work was much slower than he wanted.

As they reached together for the last carcass, Cage offered a half smile to his sister. Joule was walking fine, he was glad to note.

But Nate came up to them as she strode back from shoving a dead dog into the overgrown front landscaping of a nearby abandoned house. He reached down, strength and energy renewed with their unwarranted victory. "I've got this."

Both kids nodded at him, not knowing what else to do.

Cage leaned toward Joule and though he knew his father couldn't hear him, he whispered the words anyway. "Sun's coming up. We have to get home."

32

By the time Joule woke, the day was almost gone. The three of them had dragged their exhausted butts inside just as the sun had peeked above the trees, just as they'd finally been relatively certain the dogs would not walk in behind them. The creatures should be heading wherever they went during the day—something the Mazurs still hadn't been able to figure out.

Joule had been dragging, and she could see that Cage had, too. But Nate walked on disturbingly light feet. When they'd gotten inside the house, they still hadn't spoken, just taken turns running through the shower, pulling on pajamas, and climbing under their covers.

This is a shitty setup, Joule thought as she lay down. They should not be sleeping during the day. That should be saved for the night, when there wasn't much else they could do. Given the way the house was built, there wasn't a safe space to read or have any light at night except in the hallway—and it wasn't set up for anything like that.

An older house, theirs was designed to let in the light. Most of the interior was accessible by curtains. That meant, once it got dark, they couldn't be in the game room; they couldn't be in the living room or have a light on in their bedrooms. Even the kitchen and the downstairs had too many windows to keep them safe.

She'd thought more than once about covering them completely. Joule wasn't a fan of artificial light, but having a place she could go and something she could do at night was looking more and more appealing. The problem of having to go downstairs to get there was something she only now considered as she truly entertained the thought and noticed the previously unforeseen problems.

Being downstairs meant any light leaking out was on a level the dogs could directly access by coming through the windows. It meant that, if the dogs did come through the windows, she would have to run through the main house to get upstairs. Not safe. *Bad ideas all around,* she thought as she fell asleep.

So far, the hallway and the dimmed halogen flashlight still seemed to be her best bet. But sleeping during the day was a waste of usable time.

She woke, refreshed but starving, and found Cage must have had similar ideas. His head was in the refrigerator and his hand was reaching in and out, piling items on the counter.

"Are you making dinner?" she asked, noting just how late she'd slept. From the looks of him, he hadn't been up much longer than she had.

He mumbled something about being the only one who was going to do it. Joule turned then to look at the table, at her father, who sat there scribbling on paper, piles of other pages around him.

Looking back to her brother, she watched as Cage took a moment to pull his head out of the fridge, look at her, and shrug his shoulders. But it wasn't a casual shrug or dismissive shrug. It was a worried one—a heavily worried one—and the shrug only meant that he had no idea what to do about it.

Letting Cage plan the meal, she walked over and looked at what her father was drawing. There was no need to ask, once she saw the sketches. Nate glanced up with a grin on his face that she didn't like at all.

"It will work better if we redesign the pants so that we have slightly more mail. Or, alternately, more, thinner stripes. With thinner pieces of mail versus carbon fiber, we can keep the weight low, but also keep the dogs inability to bite through very high." He spoke quickly, a cadence that would have been indicative of drug use of some kind if she didn't know what her family had just been through—and what her father had just lost.

It had been several weeks now, and it was time. A quick glance to Cage, eyebrows up, and a quick nod back from her brother, and it was decided between them.

Reaching around the table, Joule picked up the sketches her father had been making for the new armor. She gathered them, stacking them neatly as though to respect them more than she did. Then she set them in front of her father and said, "No. No, Dad, we can't do this. We're not going out again."

Nate looked up at her, confused by her declaration. "It's almost dark. We can go out again tonight."

"No," she replied again, her voice firm. "We're not going out again tonight. We just woke up. It's going to be hard enough for Cage and me to get our butts to school tomorrow morning, given that we just woke up now."

Her father's eyes darted around the room and ended up looking at the floor, even as he shook his head at her. "I don't think you need to go to school anymore."

Joule froze. If there was one thing her parents had always supported it was their children's education. Nate and Kaya were both highly educated, both holding their own doctorates. Her mother had two advanced degrees. Her grandparents were immigrants on both sides, and they had come here to escape hard situations but also for opportunity and education for their children. That sentiment was something her parents had both carried on from their own parents, and she and Cage had always known they could be anything they wanted—but they'd be educated.

Her father's words now were mind-blowing, and she saw that Cage had paused in his activity and was turning to lean against the fridge, watching from a slight distance.

"No," Joule said again, wishing she had something to bang on the table to make her point and holding herself back from letting that show in her voice. "Cage and I *have to* go back to school. We're going to finish. We're very, very close to graduation. We have honors, even with the missed days. We're going to graduate with four-point-oh GPAs, Dad. So we're going to school tomorrow. *None of us* are going out tonight."

She felt the need to add the last part because she was afraid if she said that she and Cage weren't going tonight, Nate might take it upon himself. There was time for the argument now, and she was ready. Cage came up beside her, his arms still crossed. Feeling the frown on her face, Joule fought to relax and used her elbow to subtly nudge her brother. Seeming to get her point, his arms uncrossed and the combative stance shook out a little bit.

"Dad, we can't go out tonight. Joule and I have to go to school. We have to graduate."

They both backed it up with nodding.

"Friday night, then," their father countered.

A quick glance passed between the twins, and Joule picked up the argument again. "No, Dad, we went out once. But now we need to study it. They did not attack the way we expected."

Nate frowned. "What do you mean? They attacked, we killed. We have a method now and we can take them out."

Joule fought the sigh that wanted to rise in her chest. There was nothing about her father's statement that was okay.

"Dad," Cage jumped in, his voice soft. Joule could tell he was trying to be gentle, though he didn't quite make it. "You could go out and kill seven dogs every single night for years. But we don't even know how they breed. Probably faster than you can take them out. So we can't just go out with machetes and arrows. We need to figure out a mass method to remove or subdue them."

Joule hopped in when her brother lost steam. "We need to use last night's information to figure that out. Because what they did last night wasn't the way we've seen them attack before. And we need to know why."

Nate looked between the two kids, and as he nodded at their argument, something seemed to change in him. Then he said, "Exactly. Things have changed. And we have to change with it."

But it was Joule who shook her head. "No, Dad, things have changed. Things changed dramatically, painfully, quickly, and without our permission. Several times—all the way up until losing mom." Her voice had a hitch, she could hear it, but she couldn't stop talking.

"And those kinds of changes, when they come at us... they throw us off our game. Dad, we are off—*way off*—and now is not the time to make any big decisions. All these changes, they will change us and we will change to accommodate them. But we need to do it later, when we're—" she almost said "sane" but held the word back. "—when we are prepared. We thought about it." She motioned between her and Cage.

"So tonight—at least tonight—we need to stay home. Cage and I will go to school tomorrow, and tomorrow night we'll talk about it more."

Nate seemed to absorb what she said, and she saw her father's expression slowly changing, forming from a frown to a nod. *He'd agreed,* and she could only hope she'd actually gotten through to him.

But there was something about his expression she didn't believe.

33

Cage walked in the door after school the next day to find his father standing at the counter pouring himself what looked like a second or third or maybe tenth cup of coffee.

"Did you sleep?" he asked, wary of the answer.

His dad nodded as he lifted the mug to his mouth. The nod and the gesture were neither concerning nor reassuring.

Cage and Joule had been late to school this morning—not that anyone cared. No one was marking tardies anymore, especially when the morning light had been slow to come. It wasn't as if truant officers were going around looking for all the missing kids. There were more kids missing than anything else, it seemed. But Cage had met a lot of those kids and it didn't surprise him that they'd gotten themselves in trouble.

Those kids weren't like him and Joule. The twins had stayed up most of the night with their dad, reading textbooks and making notes. They continued to search through the notes their mother had made. The three of them lined the hallway, butts pushed into the corners, small flashlights in their hands.

But whatever they found, they had to just take notes and

wait. The rule was always *no talking*. They could pass notes, and sometimes did, if the question was small. But it was a crappy way to communicate, especially on the level they needed when talking about the dogs. They couldn't use their phones to text, either. The phones had to be *off*; any alert coming in could be enough noise and possibly signal the dogs outside.

Cage and his sister had crawled into bed just before the morning hours, and at least he'd managed to find some sleep before carting his ass off to school. Now, he looked at his father and wondered if Nate had slept at all.

Not surprisingly, he saw his sister grab food from the fridge. Cage followed her lead. Food seemed like a good idea, both because he needed it and it tempered a conversation. So the three of them sat around the end of the table as though it were preordained.

"Let's talk." Cage used his best negotiating tone as he put his hands flat on the table. The food in front of him was calling, but his father was more important. "They didn't attack the way we expected. The dogs moved almost one by one."

Joule put her hand up. "They're not dogs. We know this and we need to stop calling them that. We need to make a plan, and that starts with distinguishing these animals from dogs. These animals need to experience an Extinction Level Event or an equivalent amount of hunting. *Dogs* don't." She paused and then whispered, "I like dogs."

Cage smiled. Joule had tried to convince their parents to get a dog, any dog. It had never happened. *Good thing now, or it would have been the first of us to go*, he thought.

She didn't look up until their father asked, "So what do we call this new species? If we're the ones who found them, then we get to name them."

"No." Joule was firm. "I don't want to go public with this. And do you really want those creatures to be called *Mazurs*? Do you want their scientific name to be *Canis Mazuri*?"

It hit Cage that, if that happened, the creature would bear the same name as his mother—the woman they had killed. He shook his head in agreement with his sister.

"We don't put our own name on this." Joule reiterated it in case Nate wasn't fully catching on. "They need a name that everyone will recognize on hearing it. A name that's different from *dog*, *wolf*, or *coyote*. Those are protected species."

Cage was impressed with her determination. And he offered up "Drolves."

He was met with crickets. "Dogotes?"

Joule closed her eyes, shaking her head at him, letting him know she was disappointed in his efforts. "The terms *wolves*, *dogs*, and *coyotes* are distinct words. Coyotes aren't Coyodogs. These creatures get a distinct name."

"Assholes?" Cage suggested, and at least that made his sister and his father laugh.

"Wendigo? Trolls!" Nate offered up a few more suggestions, both as ridiculous as what Cage had said.

"Those are already *things*. And people know what wendigo are. That's not this. Also, giving them mythical names gives them power. So, *no*." She paused then offered her own. "I think we should call them Pack Hunters. I think if we say that, then people will know what we're talking about just from hearing that term."

"Night hunters," Cage offered.

"That works. Somebody else can come up with their scientific name later. I just don't want *our* name on it."

Cage nodded in full agreement, and Nate seemed to go along. Cage threw out the next question. "Okay, so now that they're night hunters, how do we kill them?"

"Blade between the ribs," Nate answered. "It's pretty clear."

"Absolutely." Cage agreed, because it would make his father happy. Both teens were handling their father with kid gloves these days. It didn't feel good. He understood his father was grieving the loss of his wife. He was left alone with two children and a world falling apart at both the macro and micro level. But it didn't make Cage feel any better about having to hold it all together.

"The math doesn't add up," Cage told his dad, echoing Joule's words from the day before. "We could kill night hunters on a daily basis, but we don't know how fast they breed. And that won't get them gone anywhere near fast enough."

"List," Joule announced, standing up and heading into the kitchen. It took a moment for Cage to process but, when she came back, she had written down *Where do they sleep?* And *What poisons them?*

Cage added to what was clearly a list of things they needed to learn—soon. "Why they attacked differently last night?"

Joule added his question, speaking as she wrote, and then said, "What are they eating?"

Cage feared the answer was *people.*

"Mass methods for what we did last night," Joule said, her hand flying as she recorded their questions.

That one was the first item that made Nate perk up, and that scared Cage. His father was enjoying the fight too much. Nate looked between the two of them. "You're right. We can train people. Because three of us can't go out and do this. But maybe more of us can…"

Cage and Joule looked at each other and Cage felt his blood run cold.

34

Cage flipped the eggs in the pan as he heard the footsteps tromping down the stairs, startling him. Clearly, it was his father.

This was not the Saturday morning he had expected.

"Faraday!" Nate snapped as he turned the corner.

Shit, Cage thought, he was getting *real-named*. "Yes, Dad?"

"It's Saturday." His father supplied the obvious. "We have no traps. We haven't killed any dogs since Tuesday night—"

"Night hunters," Cage said, slipping in the new term they had come up with.

"Regardless, we haven't killed any since Tuesday night." Nate looked at the coffee pot and his expression turned sour when he saw it was empty. He started moving around to fill it, but it didn't stop his little evidentiary tirade. "If they're breeding the way you seem to think they are, then we've let them get way ahead. Every one we take out now stops a future exponential chain of birth. Just like spaying and neutering!"

Jesus, Cage thought, his father was likening going out in chain mail at night to the local spay and neuter program that had been necessary before all the cats had disappeared.

It was then Cage noticed his father held his laptop under his arm. He also spotted the dark circles under his father's eyes. He was growing more convinced that Nate wasn't sleeping enough, if at all. He blurted out something he probably shouldn't have. "Dad, have you seen a therapist?"

Nate waved his hand as though to brush Cage off. It matched the dismissive expression on his face, but then he seemed to catch on to just how worried his son was. He stopped messing with the coffee maker and turned to look directly at Cage. With clear eyes, he said, "I'm *okay*. This whole thing is crazy. And everything we've been through is crazier. But *I'm okay*."

His father emphasized each of the last words, and Cage could only take him at what he said. But the reassurance did make him feel better.

"Look at this," his dad said, motioning to the laptop. "No, wait. Get your sister first."

Nodding, Cage turned off the heat under the eggs. "Check the oven," he told his father. "There's bacon." Then he ran upstairs to get his sister, only to find she was already awake, lying in bed, and—shocking no one—reading.

Cage didn't recognize the book. "What's that one?"

"New veterinary text I ordered. I'll tell you later."

"Come on downstairs. There's something Dad wants to show us on the computer."

When they headed back down, it was to discover their father setting out plates of food at each place at the table. A glass of orange juice was ready by each meal. The only thing abnormal was that there were three seats instead of four. The laptop sat in between and was already queued up as his father emerged from the kitchen with napkins and forks in his hand.

"Sit down," Nate motioned as he handed out the goods, "and we'll hit the button."

Cage was three bites in as the video got rolling. It was an

older gentleman in a wheelchair rolling around his house in the dark. Up and down ramps he went, and then out the front door on a bumpy path to the street.

"Can't move my legs," the man said to the camera, almost jovially. "Been in this chair for five years. I'm probably the weakest of any of us. My family's been doin' a good job protecting me from those dogs that come out at night."

Reaching out quickly, Cage slapped at the button, stopping the video. "*Where is he?*"

It took a moment and Joule tapping several buttons as she looked for the initial upload information. "Other side of Little Rock," she eventually said.

"Holy shit!" Cage looked around the table, but the other two were calmer than him. "They've gotten *that far.*"

"Sounds like he's talking about the same night hunters we have here." Joule looked at him with an expression he could read but his father probably could not. The two of them had talked about the range of the animals, but neither had thought the population had spread that wide.

In fact, it seemed initially that the night hunters were local. But here he was, seeing a report from a farther place than he'd expected. Cage had gotten caught up in his own neighborhood, in the happenings in his own backyard, and he had not thought to look further. That had been a miss, but it completely reinforced the idea that going out hunting every night wasn't going to make a dent in this creature's population.

His father motioned them to start the video again. And as they watched, the old man tooled around his house and talked about his disabilities to the point where Cage wondered where this was going.

But just as he had that thought, the video cut to an amateur edit into a dark scene. This time, the old man was rolling down the street in the dead of night. The streetlights were just bright enough to illuminate his journey.

It appeared he was using a phone, recording himself on some kind of a selfie stick. No one was with him.

"Is this a snuff film?" Joule asked, already appalled. "Is he committing suicide? He has been talking about the night hunters."

"Just watch," their father said, motioning with his fork as though he wasn't showing his kids an old man about to get ripped limb from limb. Nate's attitude was the only thing that made Cage think it might be okay to watch, and he kept his eyes on the screen.

The old man narrated, rambling about empty houses he passed—just like their own neighborhood—people gone missing, no more house pets, and more.

One thing Cage caught was the old man's timeline of events. Even though he hadn't said it that way, he mentioned the night hunters coming into the neighborhood in more recent terms than Cage remembered it happening here. *No*, he thought, *more recent than he* knew *it had happened here.* His mother had started taking notes when the abundance of missing pet signs had grown eerie. Cage didn't remember specifically, but he could look up exact dates.

This man talked about it being a few months that they'd been closing the windows, and Cage cataloged that maybe his own neighborhood was the epicenter.

But then the man said something that pulled Cage's thoughts back to the video.

"They don't come after me. They come up close. They growl. They lick me, but they walk away. Don't know if it's the chair or what but look..." and he scanned the phone around, giving a wider view behind him.

Cage gulped down a gasp and he heard Joule do the same right in time with him as he saw five dogs stalking the wheelchair. They were within several feet of the old man, their lips curled, and as the phone narrowed in on one, the old man did an admirable job of tracking the dog's face.

It came within inches of the hand sitting idle at the wheelchair control.

The old man held still as the dog sniffed around, licked him once, grunted, and trotted away.

35

J oule was Sisyphus.

It had been three days now that she kept pushing the boulder up the hill, telling her father that going out and fighting by hand at night was not the answer. And each day, he turned up again suggesting the same damn thing. It was a constant battle to rein her father in. She ignored the fact that she cried herself to sleep each night, the loss of her mother at times more than she could bear. But she got up each morning and tried to save the parent she had left.

"Dad, just because that man went out and the dogs didn't attack him, doesn't mean we can do the same thing."

Her father countered quickly, clearly ready for her argument. "If we knew what he had, we *could*. The night hunters wouldn't attack us, and we'd be safe. It would be even better than the chain mail."

Joule sighed. "We can't attack them if they won't get close, Dad. If we figure it out and we get whatever he has, they'll just leave before we can fight." She didn't even address that the first step hadn't been made—they *didn't* have what that man had, and they knew it because the night hunters *had* attacked them.

"You have bows and arrows," her father countered deftly. "You can get them as they turn away."

And then what? she thought. *Nate and Cage would run them down, hacking the night hunters with machetes?*

No.

"We can't do it, Dad. We don't even know what *it* is. And I don't feel like going out and waiting to see if the dogs attack us is a suitable experimental method."

Joule had loved growing up in a family that argued and required that she support her own arguments with evidence. Her parents had trained her to make a case logically. She'd seen other people argue, and it was often just a fight. They would hit below the belt. They name-called. But her mother had been a fierce advocate of a fair fight.

Right now, her mother would have told her there was a lesson in this—that Joule was using a piece of evidence to tell her father he couldn't go out and he had turned around and used the exact same piece of evidence to say why she was wrong and he was right.

The sharp, piercing feeling of loss hit her again. She could have been one of the night hunters going limp as the machete hit her square in the back.

She missed her mother desperately. Truth be told, she missed her father, too.

This Nate was not the man she had grown up with. Her Nate Mazur was kind and reasonable to a fault. Her father—as he'd been—was actually slower to act than her mother was. Now, he was gung ho and pumped full of revenge. Nothing she or her brother ever did seemed to rein him back in for more than a day.

It was an ongoing fight to keep her father in the house at night—and to keep the sword and the machete out of his hand.

She and Cage had sat up in the hallway for a few hours in the middle of the night while Nate slept. They studied and talked and, without saying so specifically, they made decisions without their father involved.

She'd developed a pattern, and so had her brother: fall asleep, get in a few good hours, and then wake up in the middle of the night. Inevitably, some noise would jostle her from sleep, so she would tap on Cage's door, or he would tap on hers. Very quietly, they would meet in the hallway with a book or a stack of notes and paper and pen and the small flashlights. When they were set up, they would get to work. A few hours later, they would return to bed, able to get up in time to get ready for school.

She had no idea if their father knew what they were doing. They'd done it again last night, though they'd gotten a little more lax about being perfectly quiet. She leaned over and whispered in her brother's ear, "We should get Dad."

But Cage shook his head, and she saw in his eyes that he didn't like it, but it was how he felt that had to be. He'd replied, "Dad needs sleep," his voice as soft as her own words had been.

She'd felt the tears well. "It's hard enough doing things without Mom, but doing them without Dad ... well, he's right here!" She pointed at his closed bedroom door. "This is hard, too."

Cage shook his head again, talking as though he were the voice of reason. "But what if we tell him and he uses this—" he lifted their notes as a gesture, "as a reason to go out? You know that's what he wants to do. Every day he lets us talk him out of it, but—"

"Shhhhhh," she shushed him as his voice rose, but she nodded. It had been said. It wasn't possible to go on believing that their father just randomly wasn't in these late night sessions, or that they "just forgot" to tell him some of the discussions they had. They were actively holding back information from their own father.

Joule realized then there wasn't much they could do. Just

wait. They had to hope that Nate worked through his loss and came back around to being himself. She hoped it wasn't much longer.

It was Thursday afternoon now, twenty-four hours to the weekend, twenty-four hours until their father tried again to turn them into a pack of merry hunters. They had decided their only recourse was to give their father something else to focus on.

"Poison," Joule offered now, dangling the word like bait and praying it worked. "Let's figure out what they eat and use that to figure out how to get rid of them *en masse*."

Cage nodded along with her, as though he, too, thought it might be enough of a distraction to keep Nate from wanting to go out at night.

"Dad," she started again when her father didn't speak in response to her first attempt. She fought to keep the tone in her voice light. "Cage and I were chatting on the way home from school." That part wasn't true. They'd been talking about it for several days, but she kept going, "and we were thinking we need to run some experiments this weekend. Figure out what the night hunters eat. Then we can make our next move."

Her father nodded this time, and they sat down for a few minutes, planning out what they needed to know, what their best experimental setup would be, and what they might need to buy that afternoon to get ready.

Once it was mostly set, they hit a concerning point.

"I don't know any other way to do it," her father had protested.

Sadly, Joule didn't have a response either. She looked to Cage, but he shrugged slightly when their father wasn't looking.

Shit, she thought. There was no other way.

It was Nate who looked back and forth between them, still going. "If we're going to do it, we must observe it. We've got the camera, and we need to know that it worked. We need to know the night hunters are eating what we set out—otherwise, we only learn what gets eaten. That's not necessarily what *they* eat. If we're going to know the night hunters actually ate what we put out, we have to watch it happen. And that means we have to bait them right into the front yard."

36

C age struggled to keep his eyes open for the first few hours. He was used to sleeping at night.

Aside from the one night out with his father and Joule, fighting the night hunters, they had been sleeping—at least in part—during the dark. Sometimes, they would review footage from the night camera and see all kinds of things walking through the yard. He now knew the night hunters came right up to the house more nights than he cared to think about

Their experimental setup, he thought, was wonderful, but no one was showing up. At least, not the creatures he wanted to see. Though it was reassuring to see that many nocturnal animals were still around.

He and his father and sister had begun getting prepped the night before. They'd bought all kinds of food—chicken, steak, hamburger, pork, vegetables (just in case), and more. Even hot dogs were on the menu.

This first night was a merely a "What will they eat? And what won't they?" kind of test. But Nate had protested before they even started.

"It's all laid out in the front yard and we've got this beautiful window. We need to find a way to watch!"

"We're not opening the window!" Joule had jumped in before he even finished the sentence.

"Of course not," Nate replied, trying to sound reasonable.

"We've got the camera," Cage supplied quickly, as though trying to fill cracks in his father's reasoning.

But Nate waved him off. "That's not enough. It's delayed. We can't watch until after the fact and we need to see it live."

Cage didn't agree that they had to. He and Joule had decided a while ago that what they *had to do* was stay alive. The decision had begun a long debate about how to do make it happen.

The idea of a periscope had been thrown around and tossed out.

Joule protested quickly. "The dogs—night hunters—will see the movement and come right through the window."

"What if we put it on a window they can't see? Or can't see well? Like on the second floor?" Nate fired back.

"It's still movement. It will still attract them to the house. Are we willing to risk that?" Cage had jumped in, not wanting his sister to bear the full brunt of the fight and not wanting his father to think his son agreed. But he regretted the words as soon as they were out of his mouth. He should have said, *No, we aren't willing to risk that.*

Nate came at it again, worse this time. "We can get binoculars and lay up on the roof. We'll stay still."

Cage put a hand out, clasping his sister's wrist, silently pulling her back from the brink as he watched her get ready to explode. He replied in the calmest voice he could find. "Dad, we can't lay on the roof. They'll see us. It's even worse than the periscope. I can't imagine we could stay still—"

"Of course not!" Nate had shrugged, as though the need to not draw attention from the night hunters was no longer of any consequence. That scared Cage to his bones. "But they can't get us on the roof."

Cage heard his sister take in a forced sigh, but he spoke so she didn't have to. "Let's just say you're right. Let's say they can't get us on the roof. They see us up there, though, because there's no way we can stay still enough. Then they barge into the house and wreck all our windows trying to figure out a way to get up to us! We're not going to be safe tomorrow night if we do that."

That at least got Nate nodding and thinking, but it didn't shut down his need to watch the action live. In the end, they had bought several small cameras and set them up to create a live feed to the laptops.

In the dark, they sat in the hallway, side by side. They'd fed one camera to each laptop, and the three of them each watched a screen there in the dark. There was little enough activity that Cage was beginning to wonder if this was normal. Then again, what was normal anymore?

After all, they had carefully left various piles of raw meat inside wooden square frames they had built for just this purpose—to maintain a feeding space and to be able to record what was done within it. They needed to see who ate what, how much, what was consumed there in the space, and what might be picked up and carried off. If any food was dragged, then what distance away? The squares were a simple but excellent method to let them have a clear point of measurement.

But if the night hunters weren't here, wouldn't he have seen tons of other animals coming out? There was a feast in their front yard. Cage watched for another hour as a few birds swooped in and picked at some of the meats. Not surprisingly, they left the vegetables and hot dogs alone.

It was long enough that he was starting to nod off, when Joule whispered harshly, "Look!"

Finally, something! He didn't see it in his view but noticed her motion to her own screen. Her camera was aimed to the far right of the yard.

Nate, sitting in between them, watched the camera feed to the middle of the yard. Joule took the right. The three of them had lined up so the laptops made a makeshift panorama of their experiment.

"Raccoons," his sister whispered with a smile. "I guess raccoons like hot dogs."

Cage grinned, too. Though, as he understood it, raccoons liked everything. He was leaning across his father, watching as Joule tilted her screen toward him, only to hear her say, "Shit, shit, shit. Look!"

She was pointing toward his own screen now, where he was no longer looking. That was a failure of their scientific method. For some reason—maybe he was tired, or bored, or brain dead —he turned his head expecting to see more raccoons or maybe something cute eating hamburger or such.

But that wasn't it. They all watched as a pair of night hunters moved into the yard from Cage's side of the screen.

Suddenly, he was more than alert.

37

With his back straight now, Cage pushed at his laptop, lining it up with his father's and his sister's, so they could watch the night hunters as they moved through the camera's field of vision.

Slowly, the large canines stalked into the yard.

Somehow, the raccoons remained unaware, feasting on the hot dogs as though there were no threat closing in on them.

It was plausible, Cage thought, *that they might not know the hunters were there*. Cage had been impressed by how much their experiment smelled when they'd first set it out. It could be that the smell of the food overwhelmed any olfactory sense the raccoons might have had that the large night hunters were approaching.

Cage felt his heart beating hard. He had a bad feeling about what was going to happen next, but he tried to think like a scientist. Even as he reminded himself to stay focused and logical, it was Joule who leaned over and pointed at the hunters.

"Look how they're staying low to the ground. Moving slowly and steadily. They're getting as far as they can without any sharp movements. They really are stalking."

And they were doing it as a unit, Cage thought as he nodded in reply to Joule. But his sister was whispering again.

"They haven't made enough noise to get the raccoons' attention."

She was right. He'd thought about the smell, and the fact that the hunters' movements were smooth enough to not draw attention. But he hadn't accounted for the fact that their video had no sound.

These were raccoons that were still alive, despite evidence of the hunters being in the area for over a year now. So they wouldn't be oblivious to the threat. They truly didn't know the canines were there...

It didn't bode well for the raccoons. Sucking in a breath, Cage braced himself.

He felt his features pull together and his head turn to the side because he didn't want to watch. Raccoons were cute. He had a general fondness for most wildlife—except the night hunters.

The three Mazurs sat silently now, watching, not speaking. Even Nate didn't comment, just adjusted his laptop so all three of them could watch as the night hunters passed from the view of one camera to another and came into focus on his screen.

It was a tense minute or two, but Cage knew it might have just felt drawn out by his own reaction. By the time the raccoons realized what was near them, it was too late.

They tried. They jumped. They ran.

"They didn't—" Joule said sharply, cutting herself off as apparently she noticed the same thing Cage did.

He'd noted that though the raccoons ran, the night hunters did not take that opportunity to bolt after them. They simply continued stalking at a pace that would have let their prey escape.

It was less than a split second—hence Joule cutting herself off as she saw it—that they all saw the reason why the hunters didn't pounce. The raccoons ran straight into three others coming from the other direction.

This time Joule whispered, "They were corralled!"

Cage sat back, trying to absorb what he'd just seen. There was no doubt that it had been a coordinated attack. That was an advanced tactic. He'd originally thought of the hunters as mindless beasts, smelling food and going after it with vicious dedication.

Instead, it looked as though almost everything about his original presumption had been wrong.

"They're very smart," he said, his voice as low as he could keep it. "Smarter than we even gave them credit for the other night." He didn't say *the night we went out and fought them.*

Though Nate didn't speak, Joule nodded from the other side of her father and picked up the conversation. "That was a lot of raw meat out there. It's not warm, and it doesn't fight. It's free food—but the hunters went right by all of it. I thought that would be a feast, but they only wanted the raccoons."

"Do you think they're like snakes?" he asked. "They only want food if it's live?"

In the dim glow from the laptop screens, he saw his sister's eyebrows rise, as though she were considering that thought for the first time.

The action on the screen distracted them. He'd not been able to watch as the hunters slowly caged in the raccoons into a smaller and smaller space. He squeezed his eyes shut, grateful that there was no audio, because it appeared the raccoons had squealed. Mercifully, their death was quick.

Within moments, all the screens were clear. The raccoons were gone—only a few scraps left behind, which Cage tried not to look at. Luckily, it was dark outside and the cameras didn't offer light. They just caught what was there in the greens and grays of night vision, so he was able to ignore the detritus of the fight.

What he'd not been prepared for was how fast the hunters disappeared, too. They split up and were all out of range before he could even think about what they might have done. Pointing his finger back and forth, he motioned to his sister to look. "They've gone off in different directions..."

"Are they resetting?" she asked, cautiously. But Cage didn't know.

The screens remained clear of wildlife for some time. Another hour or more later, just as he was about to nod off, an owl came in. A typical bird of prey, it swooped down to pick at the meat and was gone almost before he realized what had happened. But no night hunter showed up to make a play for the bird.

Several bird strikes later, Cage figured the hunters must have concluded that birds weren't worth their time. Whether that was because of all the feathers, or the speed needed to catch one, or what, he didn't know.

It was when another possum came through that they watched the flanking of the hunters' two-pronged attack work again, netting them another small animal.

The threat of dawn was evident in the slightly changing light when the third set of mammals—another band of raccoons—came through. Cage watched with a heavy heart and bated breath as the little animals used hand-like paws to pick through what was left of the vegetables and grab at some chicken. Again, the steel trap stalking strategy of the hunters caught the entire batch.

Cage looked at Joule, wanting to do anything to distract from what he was seeing, anything to take away the feeling that he'd baited the raccoons to their death. "Do we need chickens with feathers? Butcher items? Legs of cows?"

Joule was nodding. "We need to dangle them on string or something and make them look alive. They need to move."

For the first time in hours, Nate spoke up, and he said something that stunned Cage, something that he never would have expected his father to say. Not Nate the pacifist, Nate the gentle father, Nate the man who had no emotional reactions now at all.

He calmly looked at his two children and said, "This is easy. What we need is live bait."

Cage felt his stomach turn as he shook his head.

38

J oule woke up groggy. The three of them had gone to bed in the wee hours of dawn and slept until late morning.

But then her alarm had gone off and she'd dragged herself awake. They had things to do. It had taken a while for the twins to convince their father not to try to trap live bait. Neither of them had been able to stomach the idea of setting out a live animal for the sole purpose of letting the hunters rip it apart.

"Those night hunters are going to kill those animals anyway!" Nate had argued. At least his logic remained intact, but his sense of morals seemed to have swayed a bit in the recent weeks. "We're not doing anything to them, just making their deaths useful."

"I know, Dad. We're trying to stop the night hunters so they don't rip up any more people, but we also need to protect those animals. We need our local wildlife! The hunters are already changing the ecology. And I can't be the one to put a live animal into a certain-death situation."

She watched him for a reaction, but was only shrugged off with the statement, "Then I'll do it."

"No! None of us will do it! We need to find something they'll eat that we can buy at the store, Dad." She could feel her blood pressure rising with her anger and a fear that seemed misplaced. Her father wasn't going to hurt *her,* but the cold feeling of lurking danger at his comments cut deep. Cage was off somewhere on the other side of the house, and she wished to hell she had some backup right now. She knew her brother wouldn't agree with sacrificing a live animal, either.

It was becoming exhausting, repeatedly pulling their father back off the ledge. He seemed convinced he needed to jump. It was a constant battle to find anything to distract him from this idea that he could simply go out at night and battle these creatures by hand. He seemed to believe he would be the victor. Somehow, their night out in chain mail—however petrifying— had only convinced him he was right. It had convinced the twins it wasn't worth carrying the extra weight.

"Come in here," Cage called from the living area, and Joule and her father headed down the steps to see what he had. She hoped it was distracting enough.

Ironically, it literally was.

"Look." Cage sat in front of a wildly waving machine, as though the thing wasn't going bonkers in front of him. "I'm curious if, instead of using a solid cut of meat, which is really heavy, and making it move, we can use this instead." He pointed to the thing Joule still hadn't figured out.

"So I'm thinking if we tack little bits of meat all over—" he moved his hands around his contraption, "—it will be light- weight enough to keep moving, because at this cut-down size, the air should be pretty forceful. But the extra weight of the meat will slow it down a bit. It won't be so erratic as it is right now, and maybe it will look more like something alive."

Joule looked again and finally figured out what it was. Cage had modified their father's Halloween inflatable. After cutting down the fabric in the normally wildly waving ghost, he'd taped it back together until it was only a small piece that now jumped in the generated wind.

Cage turned it side to side, demonstrating his new bait. As he did, Joule felt some of the air escaping out the top hit her in the face. She held up a hand to block it.

"See?" he said with a smile, blasting her again. "I think it's strong enough that we could put little pieces of meat on it, and hopefully it moves enough that it will attract the hunters."

"It's worth a try." Anything was worth a try. Anything that didn't involve combat. "I think we might only get one use out of it, though."

Cage nodded. Nate stood by, still not speaking. And that bothered Joule as much as anything, but she tried to work around it.

"I hope," Cage continued as though he needed to fill the space—and Joule appreciated the effort, even if their dad didn't —"that they'll tear at the fabric and not get to the mechanism on the bottom." He held up the huge swath of fabric leftover from the original ghost, which had been about ten feet tall.

Well, she thought, *they wouldn't be putting that out for Halloween again.* But with the hunters on the prowl, Halloween yard ornaments were a thing of the past. She sucked in a breath as she remembered. "Two years ago, someone vandalized all the Halloween decorations down the street..."

She watched as her brother caught on, but her father was too busy frowning at the setup, as though it still required his analysis.

"Maybe it was the night hunters?" Cage asked. "Out even earlier than we thought?"

"Maybe." But there was nothing more she could do with that idea except tuck it away for later. She turned her attention back to the contraption her brother still hadn't turned off. "I say we do it. It's as good a plan as any."

And it was excellent bait to keep her father away from rushing into the fray.

"Alright," Cage said, thinking out loud. "Maybe... chicken skin, meat strips, things like that. Definitely raw."

"Go for it." Joule watched her brother head into the kitchen and set out the chicken. It would be warm by the time they put it in the yard, more like live meat—as much as it could be. At least she was not setting out a live animal. She was not going full "Jurassic Park goat" tonight.

And hopefully, never.

While Cage got to work, cutting thin strips of meat and hooking them to the fabric with toothpicks, Joule watched. She almost protested the toothpicks, but then thought, *who cares if they all get toothpicks stuck in their throats?*

Joule broached another idea she had. Nate was standing by still listening, and she wanted his attention for this. So she carefully turned and caught her father's gaze for once, then motioned to Cage and opened her new topic. "Do you remember the vet who used to come to our animal biology class?"

"Dr. Brett," Cage said, showing he did remember the man. The vet would come into class once every few months, bringing an animal to show off or use for a demonstration. The students would learn training, diagnostics, musculature, and more. They often discussed what kind of veterinary care was required if it was a pet or a farm animal.

"Well, what if we contacted him?" Joule asked. "He gave us his card."

Cage shook his head pretty quickly. "He left town."

The vet had stopped coming to class about six months ago and Mrs. Beaman hadn't been able to find anyone to replace him. "I know. I think all the vets moved away. They were pretty much driven out of business when no one had any cats or dogs left."

"Is anyone even left locally?" Cage asked her, still pinning meat chunks to his fabric moving-bait setup. Their dad stayed strangely silent.

Joule shook her head. "Probably not. Shockingly, there are only two left. One doesn't even have an office you can go into. They're fully mobile, because they go to farm to farm. The big animals are the only ones left. And the other vet has a very small practice now, and they only treat exotics—birds, sugar gliders, things like that. Pets that never leave the house are the only ones still around."

"So there's no one to really call," Cage said.

"True. There's no one local who can come and help evaluate things. But Dr. Brett gave us his card. I'm hoping the phone number on the card will have a message or tell us how to contact him. I say we call him and find out." She waited a beat before pushing her agenda a little more. "He probably won't know specifics about them, because they're not dogs. But he does know animal physiology, and we can tell him what we figured out. Maybe he can help."

Her brother nodded, a smile forming on his face. His eyes showed that he was clearly thinking through her idea. Joule felt hopeful about Cage's setup for the meat, so they didn't have to put out a live animal. And she was starting to feel hopeful about the idea to call the vet. When he'd been in class, Dr. Brett had been genuine and welcoming to the kids, telling them to use his first name and call him Dr. Brett. Joule hoped he'd be the same now.

But then she turned to look at her father, and found he was walking out of the room having not said a word.

39

J oule headed downstairs, her hand in her hair, her feet thumping down the steps. She didn't quite have the fully-awake coordination to make her descent gracefully.

Cage sat at the table, cutting fabric for his wind contraption. Beside him sat the old chewed up one—what was left of it anyway—along with scissors, packing tape, safety pins and other fabric. It looked as though he was trying to build the whole thing out of a different color. Maybe the bright white of the original ghost hadn't been their best bet.

"How long have you been up?" she asked.

"About fifteen minutes," he replied. "Just had the urge to get working."

The night before, the machine had done its job. The smell of the meat and the movement of the wind in the fabric had brought the hunters right to it. It might not have looked like a live animal, but it was good enough.

As the three of them had sat watching in the hallway, the night hunters had attacked the little moving bait. However, as the Mazurs quickly discovered, it only worked once. The hunters had torn into it, shredding the makeshift critter. They ate meat pieces and fabric scraps alike, before seeming to declare it had nothing left to offer and trotting off toward the east.

Despite the fact that they had torn the fabric and meat off of it and left the machinery beautifully intact, there was no way to go out and reset it at night. So they'd left the cameras on, gone to bed, and waited until daylight.

"Is Dad still asleep?" Joule asked as she slid into the chair beside her brother, watching as he worked.

"I think so." Cage didn't look up at her, but stayed focused on lining up his fabric. He had some design in mind, making it narrower at the top this time. "I haven't seen him."

She sighed as the thought settled in. It was good that her father was finally getting some sleep. It took a moment to let the swirl of feelings in her chest settle down before she said it out loud.

"I think he hasn't been sleeping well."

Though he didn't say anything in response, her brother seemed to agree. Maybe there just wasn't anything to be done for it other than to say it and know that they all understood.

Turning, she looked up the stairs toward the bedrooms, hoping that her father's door remained closed. Leaning in close to her brother, she asked more softly this time, "Do you think he'll ever be okay again?"

Joule watched as her brother's shoulders deflated with the thought she'd given him. This time, he set down the work and his eyes darted toward the ceiling. "I think so." He paused. "I *hope* so. I just don't think he was ever prepared to go on without Mom."

"I don't think any of us was prepared for that," Joule said. For a moment, she resented that she and her brother—the kids —were having to pick up the slack in the family. In that same moment, she felt horrid because they *were* the kids.

Her father had lost the person that he'd *chosen* to spend the rest of his life with, and he'd been thrust into a big, bold, scary *rest of his life* without the best person he could have possibly had by his side. He'd made a choice, and then had it ripped away from him in one of the worst ways possible.

Joule had grown up expecting to outlive her parents. Not at this age, certainly, but she'd always known one day, she would lose her mother. "Do you think he'll ever get married again?"

She watched as her brother's head snapped back at her question.

"Jesus, Joule. It's been less than a month!"

Her brother was being obtuse, and she hoped her sigh conveyed that adequately. "I'm not talking about *tomorrow*. I'm actually talking about how good he and Mom were together."

With a small nod of acknowledgment, Cage turned back to his task and spoke downward toward the table, as though the words didn't merit looking at her directly. "I'm guessing he'll never find anyone who fits him the way she did. And the same would have been true if it was the reverse."

At least her brother did seem to understand that her line of thinking wasn't that of trying to marry their dad off. Certainly she didn't think "a wife" would solve whatever problems he was having. Right now, adding anything more to the mix might collapse the delicate balance their family was barely maintaining.

"How long do you think until he gets his head out of his ass?" Joule asked boldly this time, taking the conversation somewhere she hadn't dared before.

"Give him time," Cage replied as he taped together two pieces of fabric and held it up to inspect his work. "I mean, he lost his wife."

That time, it was Joule who snapped. "I lost my mother! I never had a life without her, and neither did you. He did have a life without her. They made an agreement with each other when we were little if they ever had to choose, they would choose us over each other. And that's exactly what she did! He did have a life before mom. I'm not saying his loss isn't huge, but so is mine! So is *yours!*"

"Fair." The word was barely whispered into the air, and it seemed to signal the end, or at least as much conversation as they could handle on this topic at once. Maybe ever.

"Are we going to school tomorrow?" The topic change felt necessary and was welcome. She felt her blood pressure drop.

"I don't know." Her brother still didn't look up. "Do we need to?"

"I'm supposed to have a Chem exam," she said, the words tumbling out as though they were of little consequence. But it was true. "You know, we all take our exams when we show up. So, maybe we don't need to go. I can make it up. But I called Dr. Brett's number and it lists the new office number—which, of course, isn't open on Sundays. I didn't want to leave a message, so I thought I'd call tomorrow when they're in."

When she paused and nothing changed in Cage's movement or acknowledgment of her words, she pushed on. "I'd rather call from home, in case he's busy and has to call us back. And I'd rather not wait until the end of the school day."

Another pause in the conversation and she waited while Cage seemed to think about it. *It always goes like this these days,* she thought, *even if one of them was ill.* They stayed home or went to school together. Maybe it was just an offshoot of their father saying *we don't split up.* So if she wanted to stay home, Cage would stay with her.

As Joule had that thought, a second one crashed in close on its heels. "What does Dad do when we're at school?"

"He builds things. He designed some of the traps."

"He did," Joule said, "but that was just a day or two here or there. What does he do during the rest of the time?"

Her brother's hand stopped moving but there was no

answer coming. Instead, Cage changed the subject. "Actually, I think our next question is, *What do we do next?*"

"Well, depending on what the vet says, I don't know." She shifted in her seat, her stomach rumbling for something. There wouldn't be eggs and bacon today. "But my thought was that we put a little tracking device in that meat." She pointed to the fabric her brother was designing as a delivery system. "Maybe we can do more with that than just study how they attack and when. Maybe they don't chew well. Maybe they'll swallow a small tracker.

"Then, maybe, we can figure out where they go."

40

Cage watched silently as Joule spoke into the phone. She'd put the call on speakerphone and now reintroduced herself to the veterinarian. She'd mentioned he was on speaker phone and that Cage and her dad were there with her, following their mother's instructions on phone etiquette to the letter.

Dr. Brett was very kind, acting as though he remembered the two of them from class and that he was glad they'd decided to call with questions. He acted as though this kind of out-of-the-blue call was exactly why he'd handed out the cards.

He didn't offer any explanation for why he had left town. Maybe there was just an implicit agreement that it didn't need to be said. He was, however, very open to questions. "Sure, what do you want to know?"

"We saw a video of an older man, out at night in a wheelchair. He was trailed by several... of these *dogs*..." Cage heard the pause as his sister wasn't quite ready to use their new term yet. She went on to explain how the night hunters had licked him and left.

"Honestly, it sounds like he has a disease of some kind. I

wouldn't be able to tell without looking at him. And I'm no human MD. But dogs can certainly detect—and will often turn their noses up—at cancers, diabetes, things like that."

There was a pause, but he seemed to be thinking, and the Mazurs waited Dr. Brett out. "I haven't known those things to actually make a dog *turn away* in the past, but it could. I know for a fact many medicines can be detected as a smell on the skin. Even things as simple as garlic. That's an example of something we humans can smell well after it's consumed and digested, and we don't have noses anywhere near as sensitive as a dog's."

Caged look to his sister and Joule nodded, indicating he go ahead. "Hi, Dr. Brett, this is Faraday," he introduced himself. "We have something really odd to discuss with you, and we'd like to know that you can keep it between us..."

Though Joule nodded along, supporting what Cage was saying, Nate simply stood there with his arms crossed, listening and making no commentary on the conversation.

This morning, Nate had gotten up at the usual time, though the kids had told him they weren't going to go to school. He'd puttered around the house, but given Joule's question the day before, Cage watched more carefully now. As he did, he came to the realization that his father hadn't really done anything. He hadn't even spent time making food or eating anything. In fact, Nate had been up for several hours and had nothing to show for the time.

Cage took a deep breath and pulled his thoughts from his father to the vet on the phone. He had no idea how his information would be received, but he felt the only thing to do was dive in. "My sister and my father and I got one of the dogs."

There was a pause on the other end of the line. "One of the dogs?"

"The ones who come out at night," Cage clarified carefully, knowing there was no common language for the new creature.

"You *caught* one?" the vet asked, his tone bordering on incredulous.

"Well, not so much." Cage felt himself wanting to skirt around the words, but there was no good way to do it. "It was dead." He felt the lump in his throat as the thoughts tumbled through his brain. It was dead because his mother had killed it. His mother was dead because it had killed her.

"What about this dead dog?" the vet asked cautiously. "Go on."

"Have you seen one?" Cage asked, suddenly realizing it was better to lead by getting information first rather than just throwing it out there without being able to even see the man's reaction.

"No," the vet replied, but quickly amended his answer. "Not actually, aside from a few instances from a distance. I saw some on the street one night, but I didn't look for long. I saw that they move in packs. But..."

He paused and there was a change in the tone of that single word that made Cage frown. When he looked to his sister, he saw that she, too, had pulled back from the phone for a bit. It took only a beat or two for the vet to continue talking.

"My son was in college. Undergrad."

Cage didn't miss the use of the past tense.

"He was home for break and he was visiting his girlfriend, who lived two streets over from us. One night, he left her place at seven and he never made it home... It took three months before I found—"

Again there was a long pause and a change in tone that held Cage back from filling in the silence. "I found a piece of his shirt."

They all knew what that meant: The vet's son was one of the missing.

"Is that why you moved?" Joule asked, her words soft and comforting.

"Oh, yeah. The business was going downhill. All the cats and dogs were reported missing. Standard domestic pets were our bread and butter, and no one was bringing any in anymore. Our bulletin board couldn't hold all of the missing notices. There were no more notices of litters of kittens or found dogs needing adoption.

"When my son first went missing, well, we stayed put. You know, we wanted to be there in case he came back. But after what I found... there was no reason to stay anymore."

"I understand," Joule said, and then somehow she found the strength to say what Cage hadn't been able to. "The dog that we got had broken into our home, and our mother took a machete and she fought it. She killed it, but it fatally wounded her. And we decided that, as good scientists, we needed to figure out what was going on. We needed to see if we could tell what was different about these... dogs."

Cage could almost hear the held breath on the other end of the phone. Clearly the vet had not decided to go as far as they had. Despite probably having dissected many animals in veterinary school, Cage could tell he hadn't dissected one of these, or he would already know what they did.

"What did you do?" the vet asked.

"An autopsy... well, a necropsy," Joule replied.

"What did you learn?" Dr. Brett asked again, his tone curious but cautious.

"It has three canines in each position, not just one," Cage began. He felt that he could contribute to the conversation now that it wasn't about exactly how they had come to be in possession of a dead night hunter.

He could almost hear the smile on the vet's voice. "Actually, those are premolars."

"No," Joule replied quickly and cleanly. "These don't match the size or shape or cusp number requirements for premolars. We got a veterinary textbook that our mother had—"

"Was your mother a vet?"

"No," Joule said, once again, seeming far more emotionally stable than Cage felt when talking about their mother. "She was a scientist. And she was very interested in the dogs. So she ordered veterinary texts."

"Okay, so go on... you had a veterinarian text," Dr. Brett prodded. "And you looked at the teeth."

"Yes," Cage replied, knowing the nod he wanted to add wasn't sufficient over the phone. "And my sister is right. The dog has incisors like normal. And molars—just like normal. Normal places, normal numbers, but it had two fewer premolars and three canines in each position."

"That's an unusual mutation." Cage heard the vet's tone changing even throughout the sentence, as though he were thinking through how a mutation like that might occur.

"Well, it's not an individual mutation," Joule said. "Because, actually, three dogs got into our house and my mother killed two of them. The third got away, but we examined both the ones we have. And they both have the same mutation."

"We have video of them in the yard, and I'll bet we can blow up the pictures." Even as Cage said it, the idea was lighting up in his thoughts, coming out of his mouth as fast as his realizations hit.

They should be looking at the images they had. They'd saved all the video from the past nights—his father made sure they had the storage for it. But he jumped back into the conversation and repeated what he had learned in bio class. "Our teacher for the animal biology class—the one you visited—told us that teeth are conservative. That any change in dentition is a speciation event."

The vet didn't say anything suggesting they were right. Nate still hadn't said a word or lent his scientific weight to the conversation, and Cage was willing to bet that Dr. Brett Christian—as nice as he was—wasn't willing to just tell them they'd discovered a new species.

The vet asked cautiously, "Do you have any pictures? Anything you can send me?" Then he sucked in a breath and his tone changed rapidly. "I promise you, this will be *your* discovery. I won't take that away from you."

Cage almost jumped in to say, *We don't want it. We don't want our name on it at all.*

But the vet kept talking. "If you can send me pictures, maybe I can verify something until we can get our hands on one."

Cage looked to his sister, not needing words to ask his question. She seemed to think about it, but only for a moment. When she nodded back at him, he said, "We can go one better than that. We still have the bodies, if you want to see them."

41

J oule surveyed the table. It was Thursday, and she and Cage were home from school again today.

It had taken three days for the vet to find time off of his job so that he could come back into town and see the night hunter corpses they'd saved. He was no longer popping over from several miles away; he now lived in a different town, and the drive was several hours. That told Joule how interested he was in seeing the animals they had.

The Mazurs had set to work, once again wrapping the entire tabletop in kitchen style poly film and then covering it again with a layer of black plastic. This time, they had invested in a real tarp, not split-at-the-seams black trash bags, and they'd taped the corners, wrapping them under the edges of the table to keep it from moving. Joule was aiming to impress.

She was surprised to find she was nervous. This was a real veterinarian coming to survey her work. She would be showing a trained professional how they had the hunters' organs in plastic baggies labeled with black marker and stuffed back inside the cavity of its body. She was about to hand over the lab notebooks they had kept where they'd weighed everything, measured the creatures, and ultimately decided that they had a new species.

What if the vet said they were wrong?

Her hands wrung absentmindedly while Dr. Brett stood at the table doing a cursory visual check of the animals, labeled bags, and her notebook. Cage reached out and touched her arm, making her realize what she was doing so she could stop it.

"This looks good at first glance. Can I put on some gloves and check things myself?" The vet's voice was kind. He was treating them as though these were *their* specimens and *their* science.

They'd opened the door when he arrived and readily let the man into their home. But then again, Cage and Joule had met him several times at class. He wasn't a stranger.

And now, he was standing at their table, awkward as he hunched over at the height that was not appropriate for lab work. He didn't comment and continued checking out the animals that they had taken out of the freezer on Monday to start thawing. Both were now a little wet, plenty pliable, and more than a bit smelly. If Joule were squeamish, she'd be making faces right now, but none of them did.

Dr. Brett's finger ran down the page of lab notes Joule had recorded as he picked up each labeled organ in its bag.

Though she tried to fight the surge of adrenaline fueled by fear, she couldn't keep it fully at bay. She was afraid of being a bad student. What if she'd labeled something wrong? Mixed up the organs? What if that wasn't a kidney but a... she didn't even know, but she was afraid she'd screwed up.

Dr. Brett he looked up at Nate and said, "You guys did a really good job with this."

But Nate didn't answer. He was standing back, still with his arms crossed. He only pointed to the kids.

It suddenly occurred to Joule that her father had been in almost that same position for three straight days. While she and her brother had discussed buying a tracking device and what that might entail, Nate had barely spoken but finally agreed. The whole time, he'd stood several feet away with his arms crossed.

He'd done the same while they cooked dinner each night and while they set out the mechanical bait. Sometimes, he'd reached in and helped, but Joule realized now that he was staying out of most everything and just watching.

It must be some new stage of grief. She wondered again when he would come out the other side of it. *If* he would come out the other side of it.

A friend of hers, who'd lost her boyfriend to suicide the year before, had once quietly said, "Grief changes people." Joule could hear that in her head now as she tried not to watch her father too closely. Then she wondered how her own grief had changed her.

Sometimes Nate had changed his position... sometimes. Each night, they'd set up their little wind-blowing bait machine and watched their videos. The first two nights, they'd quietly, but excitedly, whispered in the hallway as the hunters came by and tore it to shreds.

Her father sat down for meals, at least, and he sat down in the hallway with them at night. But Joule found she was struggling to remember any other times when her father wasn't in his current position.

She glanced up at her brother, hoping to nudge him to ask. Cage caught on, finding a voice she couldn't, and asking the vet. "Do you think it is a new species?"

Dr. Brett snapped his gloves off efficiently, clearly someone who did this multiple times every day. "I think you're right and it is."

"So what do we do now?" Joule asked. Finally, letting

herself breathe and join the conversation. "Do we name it? Or what?"

"Well..." The vet looked back and forth between the two kids, having seemed to have figured out that Nate Mazur wasn't a real part of this conversation. "I think you need to find someone higher up the food chain than me. Someone at a university, someone who maybe studies canines specifically. I would look for a researcher who has a PhD in this and works in biodiversity. They can help with the naming and getting the species declared in all the documentation."

Though the vet smiled at his announcement, Joule was more than a little disappointed now. She nodded politely, thinking that didn't sound like anything she and Cage were in for.

"It'll look good on your college applications." The vet smiled. "Finding a new species—that's pretty big."

Joule had nodded absently again. Their college applications didn't need anything. They had decided on Stanford now. The only question was whether they could get their dad to come along to California with them.

"Can we show you the video of the old man in the wheel-chair?" she asked, just as Dr. Brett looked like he was starting to pack up.

He agreed and Joule set up a tablet quickly so they could watch together. She tried to hang back and not crowd the screen. She tried to watch the vet as he watched the old man wheel himself down the street and the dogs rejected him.

"I don't know what caused that." Dr. Brett leaned back with a frown. "For all they can smell, dogs often like people with diseases—diabetics are hypothesized to be a little sweet. People with Cystic Fibrosis are salty. But I don't know of anything that would make them *turn away* like that."

"Actually," Joule began tentatively, and watched as Cage looked toward her—probably thinking the same thing she was

—"We don't think these night hunters have a very good sense of smell."

"Is that what you're calling them?" the vet asked for the first time, though it wasn't the first time she'd used the term "night hunters" in front of him.

"We decided we didn't want our name on it. And we wanted a term that most people would understand or at least recognize what we were talking about if we didn't fully explain."

Dr. Brett's smile suggested that he understood. "You're right, though, the night hunters *aren't* dogs, and they might not have a dog's senses." His eyes glazed a bit as he seemed to recall other information. "Now, wolves have an excellent sense of smell. Coyotes are maybe just less so than wolves. Dogs tend to be more variable."

"What do you mean?" Cage asked.

"Well, some dog breeds were chosen and designed to have a great sense of smell, others are worse. Short-nosed dogs—" he pointed his finger at the hunters on the table, "—tended to fare the worst in the studies I've seen."

"Would you call these short-nosed?" Joule was leaning over now, looking at the faces she was getting very familiar with.

"Compared to the width of their head... yes. And maybe that's why they turned their nose up at the old man." He paused again, then looked to the kids, a question on his face. "Why is it that you think they have a poor sense of smell?"

Joule and Cage talked over each other then, explaining how the hunters seemed to recognize their prey by sight, rather than honing in on it.

"I've never seen them put their noses to the ground and sniff along like they're following anything," Joule commented. "And wouldn't they know we were in the house? A dog would know you were in the house."

"They don't come to the house, unless you make noise. And then they come through the doors and windows because they're so aggressive," her brother added. "Once they know you're there, they don't quit. But they don't seem to realize anyone or anything is inside until there's noise or light."

The vet's whole stance changed as though he was remembering something horrid. The nod he gave was tight and sharp as he agreed with them. "Assuming they don't have a good sense of smell..." he started, then jolted up. "Wait."

Reaching into the box of gloves Joule had set out, he snapped on another set and motioned for Joule and Cage to do the same.

"We have more to do. If this is a new species—and I'm confident that you're right—then we need to figure out everything we can from this physiology."

He pointed to the night hunter on the table. And then, with renewed purpose he began a more thorough examination, pointing to the kids, having them take specific measurements and look things up. "Let's see what we can learn from the features."

42

C age had been happy to play assistant as the vet had run his preliminary inspection.

Dr. Brett found no anomalies in the internal organs, but had commented, "Most canines have virtually indistinguishable internal organs. If you just handed me the organs, even still inside the animal, I wouldn't be able to tell the difference between a wolf or coyote or dog."

He then set the organs aside and started by examining the night hunters' feet. Pointing to certain features, he seemed glad that the twins were taking copious notes, though he didn't ask for a copy. "Their paws are wider than normal. And they're relatively flat. Look at the nails."

The vet held up the foot for them to see. "There's something about these nails ... I've seen this shape before. They're certainly strong."

He'd grabbed the tip of one nail and used it to move the toe back and forth. "The shape resembles... *something else*. I'll have to look it up and email or call when I figure it out."

He'd checked out the foot even more thoroughly. "The pad

of the foot isn't as rough as a dog's. I'd say it's still tough, but it may be softer."

"Is that to help keep them quiet as they stalk prey?" Joule asked. Cage appreciated that she'd just said "prey" and not "us."

"Possibly." Dr. Brett smiled, but went on to point out discrepancies in the size and shape of the face. Placing his gloved hands on either side of the head, he felt around the orbitals of the eyes and then moved his fingers along the back of the jaw.

He pointed out things that Cage and Joule had never noticed. Then he directed them to take photographs. "Take pictures of everything. You can smell them already. You did an excellent job of preserving them, but they won't last forever. Not if we keep thawing them."

Cage appreciated the use of the word "we." It felt good to have a professional by their side.

Dr. Brett ran his hand slowly along the dog's body. "The fur seems a little different. It's on both specimens, so I'd say it's likely not an anomaly. Both of them have what I would call a kind of wiry, but softer, fur."

"What do you mean?" Joule had asked, ever curious, while Cage took his turn at the notebook and jotted down what the doctor had said.

"The fur itself—the hair shaft—feels thicker than regular dog fur. At least to me. It's hard to tell with the gloves on, but I'm not really anxious to touch a dead animal with my bare hand. Still, it feels almost as though it's softer on the outside of the hair shaft. May I take some of it with me, so I can go home and look at it under my microscope?"

Cage enjoyed the man's surprised reaction when he offered, "We have a microscope and slides here. I think it's probably a high enough quality piece—it's the same as the ones at the school."

Dr. Brett raised his eyebrows and then looked impressed

when Cage brought the setup down to the table. "Not many people have a high-end microscope in their home."

"We're nerds." Joule shrugged it off. She offered to take the notebook from Cage for a turn.

The vet had set up the slide and looked at several samples of hair from both hunters before saying, "Yeah, this is a bit different from normal dog fur."

He'd lined up the optics and let them each have a look as he guided them through what they were seeing. "I don't have regular dog fur to compare to. But I can at the office, if I take this with me. It would be another piece of evidence that this is a new species."

Cage was nodding as he caught sight of the clock on the wall. Feeling himself go tense, he told the doctor, "You need to leave. You have a couple hours of driving, right? You'll need to go now if you're going to make it home before dark."

They'd been caught up the renewed examination of the hunters. It seemed Dr. Brett had come here thinking he would tell them that they didn't have a new species. But now that it was clear they did, he was diving in and squeezing out every bit of information he and his two new assistants could gather.

The veterinarian glanced toward his wrist, his eyes suddenly going wide. "Shit. Yes. Sorry."

As the man apologized, Cage waved him away. He and Joule had far worse language in their back pockets than anything this man had said today. "We'll clean all this up."

"Can I take pictures of the night hunters?" The vet was snapping his gloves off and reaching for his phone. Cage didn't comment, but he noticed the man had started using their terminology.

The whole time they'd examined the hunters, Nate had stood a few feet back, just watching the goings on. Cage couldn't remember if his father had even said a word.

He and Joule turned to the task of putting the organs back

into the dogs. They hadn't taken many of the organs out of the bags, only a couple for the doctor to look at. So that, at least, was easy to clean up.

Dr. Brett thanked them for the opportunity and said he'd stay in touch, but he was gone almost as fast as it had taken to look out the window and see the sun was already lower in the sky. Cage understood and hoped he made it home on time.

The twins put the hunters back together, lifted them into bags, and stripped the table. Nate helped haul the bodies to the garage freezer, but then left before Cage even closed the lid.

Cage noticed—though he didn't say so to his father—that they had not put any more creatures into the freezer, despite the large size of the unit. Clearly, Nate had bought it expecting to fill it up. That hadn't happened.

After dinner at the cleaned-down dinner table, in the room that smelled heavily of air freshener, they had voted not to put up the bait that night. Nate hadn't voted, maybe realizing it was already two against one and there was no point.

"We need sleep," Joule said, as though needing to defend the choice. "I need to show up for school tomorrow. I'm assuming you do too, Cage."

"I have the same World History test you do." It was a required class, and neither of them could afford to fail the course.

He next broached the subject of college. "Are you coming with us next year, Dad? It's less than six months away."

"We want you to be near us, if you can do it," Joule added between bites, her tone a little over-eager, a little too worried. "Or we could all stay here."

"There's not a good school for you here." His dad had finally said something, but he didn't look up. He continued eating his dinner as though he hadn't spoken at all. He stabbed at his meat with the fork, seemingly angry at everything now, even food. "I like that you picked Stanford, and I think you definitely need to go."

"We want you to come, too," Joule prodded.

Nate nodded absently, but Cage could tell that it wasn't an agreement. It was merely an acceptance of what he and his sister had said. He'd seen that before from both of his parents. And that had been all Nate was willing to give. Dinner had gone on with him and Joule talking, but keeping the conversation simple.

Cage had fallen into bed that night, exhausted from staying up watching the video of the hunters going after his mechanical bait each night. They'd learned a lot.

But the previous night, the hunters had not come.

It was another good reason to sleep the night through. Joule had suggested it that morning, as they'd finished a night with no hunters in view of the cameras and the bait still intact, waving its little fabric arms in the manufactured wind.

Though his brain had run rampant even after he'd laid down, Cage had fallen asleep quickly. The alarm was going off before it felt as though he had even slept at all.

Rolling out of bed, he almost hit the floor before his reflexes kicked in. He'd brushed his teeth, gotten dressed, and was sitting at the table eating a bowl of cereal when Joule came down the stairs. Fully dressed, she had her schoolbag slung over her shoulder, but the expression on her face worried him.

She'd speculated, "Do you think they figured it out that our bait man is not real? Or that there's not enough meat on it to make it worth coming anymore?"

He wondered, but before he could think about it, she looked at him and asked, "Where's Dad?"

43

J oule was exhausted. They'd not gone to school and had missed an English exam. Though the twins had been gung ho about showing up for their tests—on time—before, she'd lost some of that luster and was now thinking she would test when she could.

At least the teachers just seemed glad when students showed back up to take the test. But now she and Cage had been out all day looking for their father.

As soon as she'd walked down the steps, she'd asked where her father was. Cage didn't know... and that had changed everything this morning.

They'd immediately searched the whole house, top to bottom, and found no sign of their father. They'd next checked the driveway and saw all three cars were still there. So they searched the house again, figuring surely they had just missed their dad the first time around.

When that didn't work, Cage insisted Joule eat something.

Grabbing a granola bar, she headed out the door behind her brother. They scoured the entire property. There were a good handful of acres that they owned, and Joule walked through the woods where they had seen the night hunter during the day before. She was now not only afraid that they wouldn't find her father, but that she wasn't alert enough. What if one of the night hunters was out during the day and she didn't see it until it was too late?

She turned to Cage then. "Do you think dad would have come out here into the woods?"

Cage shook his head as he held a branch out of the way for her, his eyes scanning as far in to the brush as he could. "I don't know. I don't think so. But I'd hate if he was out here walking around and we were at home worried."

She shrugged. "We already missed the test. The day is shot. I just want to find Dad." She realized as soon as it was out of her mouth that it was a dumb thing to say. Of course, Cage wanted exactly the same thing.

Nate had not turned up in the woods or behind the barn or in any of the corners of their property. They hadn't seen him—or anyone—in the distance and they turned around, eyes still open, hope still on hold. Joule arrived back at the house, a little bit sweaty, a little bit irritable, and a lot afraid.

She opened the door and immediately yelled into the empty space of the game room, hoping it would reverberate through the house. "Dad. Dad!"

Cage had let her be the one to holler out, but he followed behind. Rather than sticking with her as she ran through the house yelling, he'd stayed and opened every door, checked every closet and every bathroom.

Finding nothing in the far reaches of the house, but hearing Cage opening doors behind her, Joule turned back. She crossed paths with him in the living room as he was peering behind the couch.

"Do you really think Dad's hiding back there?"

Cage looked up, not appreciating her sense of humor. "No, I think he might have had a heart attack or a stroke and fallen over. I think it's possible all we're going to see is a foot. So I'm looking everywhere."

Joule, duly chastised, suddenly began thinking of other options. "I'm going to go check the cars." She'd run outside then, wondering if her father had fallen over in the backseat and they simply hadn't been able to see him. Each new idea brought a surge of hope—even that he might have had a heart attack and was lying somewhere, waiting to be found.

Unfortunately, Nate Mazur wasn't in or under any of the cars.

She'd come back inside to find Cage standing in the living room, his hands on his hips as he turned a circle, as though he might see his father if he just rotated one more time.

"What's next?" she posed, then answered her own question. "The neighborhood. We have to go around the neighborhood."

Cage, apparently having given up on finding their father in the house, motioned for her to lead the way. Then, as she was heading out the door, he remembered to stuff her pockets with cracker packs and more granola bars.

He'd handed her a soda, popping the tab on it as he did and saying, "Sugar and fizz. It will help." Then he darted back inside to get his own.

They were down the street, soda and food in hand, as quick as they could be. She ate by rote, knowing she had to stay fueled, because if they found her father they might have to leap into action—save him, carry him, do some number of hours of rescue. So she ate and drank quickly, but tried to keep her eyes alert.

Joule pulled out her phone and was dialing her father's number, wondering why she hadn't thought of that before, but the panic Nate Mazur had inspired by going missing was making her think in odd circles.

"Good idea," Cage said almost absently, his eyes scanning

the houses they passed as though his father might peek out a window.

They walked the length of the street and back up. Almost no one was out. The neighbors who had jobs had gone to work. In the distance around the corner, one mother pushed her child in a stroller, but she barely even waved to the two teenagers now almost running up and down the street. They passed quickly through the little neighborhood intersection, checking in every direction before turning around and heading back home.

Joule warred with herself as she tried to keep her thoughts steady and her breathing even. Each time a thought crept in that her father had gone truly missing, she tamped it down. Nate Mazur was too smart for that. Nate Mazur knew how to stay alive. Nate Mazur wouldn't leave his kids like this. Nate Mazur...

She dialed the phone again for something to do. Again it rang until it went to voicemail, but she'd already left a message. She'd already sent texts. And she'd already waited and gotten nothing back.

Reaching the end of the long driveway, Cage turned to her and said, "What we need to do now is be smart. We've been panicked, but we need to toughen up and we need to figure this out. So we're going to go back into the house and we're going to figure out what we missed the first time."

Joule shook her head and shrugged at him, showing just how confused she was at his comments. "We didn't do anything wrong. We haven't been dumb. I don't understand."

Cage looked at her. "We did what we should have, but we're done with it. We were looking for Dad. I'm hoping he is in that house right now," he said, his pace eating up the driveway and getting him closer to the door.

"We're going into the game room, and if we're lucky, he'll be sitting there watching TV wondering where we are. But if he's not, we need to play it smart now. We can't find Dad, so we need to find information. We need to figure out if his phone is gone or if it's in the house. We need to figure out if he left us a note that maybe—I don't know—fell off of the table or behind the fridge. We need to figure out if anything is missing besides him."

Joule caught on. It was time to play detective, and she could do that. She could keep her head in the game and figure out where her father was. Her brother was right; Investigating was far better than panicking.

Cage bolted through open the door, hope obviously still leading him. This time, he was the one yelling for their father as he barreled through the house, no longer checking in closets or behind couches. That had all been tried. He called out again, though there was no answer.

"Dial his phone," Cage commanded and Joule did it, but they didn't hear it ring.

"It's either not in the house or it's not on." She wondered why and how they had not put tracking devices on their phones. She told her brother exactly that and he agreed, but suggested they do it later.

They spent thirty minutes searching the house again, but not for a person this time. They found no note, either missed or misplaced, and no cell phone left behind. But they did figure out that the machete was gone, and so was the short sword her father favored.

Joule stood in front of her parents' closet and held the door open, pointing to the clothing that hung there. Two sets of chain mail hung next to each other—but only two. "Cage, his chain mail is missing. And look, look at these clothes in the bottom of the closet. I never saw him wear these."

Nate favored khakis and lightweight, light-colored pants. He liked button-down shirts. In a heap in the closet were heavy black pants; black, long-sleeved, tight-knit shirts; and the occasional dark, knit hat.

That was when it hit Joule.

"He's been going out," she said to Cage, but as she turned, her brother was closer than she expected, his face drawing into a tight knot of anger as he looked at the missing pieces.

"Where do you think he is?" she asked, but Cage only shook his head in a tight way that said he didn't want to talk about it.

"We need to go back out. At least this gives us a better idea of where to start." She pressed the issue, but Cage shook his head again and pointed out the window.

"We have to close up, Joule. It's getting dark."

44

T he first night that Nate was missing, Cage lay in his
bed wide awake and stunned.

Though he heard the soft sounds of crying
coming from his sister's room, and he understood them, he
wasn't as far along in the process as she was. He'd not yet
admitted to himself what had really happened.

So the next day, he'd gotten them both up and ready and
they'd gone out searching again. They'd done the same things
—walking in the woods, checking down the streets, calling
their father's cell phone, with basically the same results.

This time, they checked where they could in the backyards
of neighbors, went farther down each street, hopped the fences
at the back of their property, and combed through the open
fields. They still found no trace of their father.

It was Joule who turned to him as he dragged a long stick
through a pond and hoped he didn't snag on anything. She
said, "We don't have a way to track dad's phone, but the cell
phone company does!"

She had a signal and so immediately called in. She was told
that *yes*, a reasonable triangulation of the phone itself could be

made if it was still on. If not, they could locate the last known point where the phone was active.

Cage listened in as the man's voice came over the line. "I understand that you're looking for a person, and it's important that you understand we can't locate the person, only the phone."

Cage rolled his eyes as Joule replied sweetly, "Of course. But that would be excellent if you could run that for us." Joule was keeping herself together in a way that Cage was unable to. Maybe it was because she'd cried herself to sleep the night before.

But when she asked the operator for a time frame, she was told there was nothing they could offer. Their request would be placed in a queue and performed in the order received. "The number of requests we've been getting have been soaring over the past year. We have more coming in every day. I'm sorry."

They would have to get in line. Cage realized then that it didn't matter to the phone company that their father was missing. Every request in that line was for a missing person.

His sister politely answered all the questions to make the inquiry official and said, "Thank you," as she tried to hide the deep disappointment from her voice. But Cage heard it. Or maybe that was his own disappointment.

That night, he'd fallen into bed, exhausted both emotionally and physically. Cage thought that would help him fall asleep immediately, but instead, he found that it was him who curled up into the fetal position as silent tears rolled down his face, dampening his pillow. He tried to imagine what had possibly gone so wrong.

He wanted to run into the other room, shake his sister awake, and ask her, "Why did Dad not stay? Was it just because he couldn't live without Mom? Did he really think he would win against the dogs? Or was it a suicide mission?"

Cage did none of that. There were no sounds coming from

Joule's room tonight, and he wasn't willing to wake her up if she was finally getting some rest. He prayed that his father would turn back up—and the strange way Nate had been acting recently, it seemed as if he might.

But Nate didn't come back Sunday, either. They hadn't gone out looking. There was nowhere else to look. The phone company wasn't going to call, not in twenty-four hours. So they'd made breakfast, talked casually, watched TV, and hadn't left the house.

"Are you ready for the World History exam tomorrow?" Joule had asked him over lunch of mac and cheese served on trays in front of the TV.

"Are we going back tomorrow?"

Joule paused as though thinking, though it was clear she'd already thought this through. Maybe she was just letting him catch up. "I think we have to go. It's plausible that Dad will turn up in a day or two. If he does, we'll all be glad we put in the effort to graduate. And if he doesn't, well, it will be even more important that we put in the effort to graduate."

Cage felt the hand reach into his chest, grab him, and squeeze hard. It was the first time either of them had spoken the idea out loud: *If Dad doesn't return.*

"Do you have it all figured out?" he asked his sister.

The look on her face—the way she suddenly stopped eating and stared into space—said clearly that *no, she didn't.* But it was equally as clear that she had been thinking about some of it.

"I'm sure I've missed plenty. And it will pop up and bite us in the ass. I'm just trying to stay ahead of the tidal wave of crap that keeps coming."

That was something Cage understood. But Joule was way ahead of him, and he struggled to catch up to her as she started in again.

"Like, right now, I just realized that I told Dad he had to pay for the house. And now, I don't think that we do."

"What do you mean?"

"Well, as dad pointed out, no one is going to come and repossess a house like this."

"*Like this*? It's a great house," her brother protested immediately.

"No, it's not. It's our home. And structure-wise, it's fantastic. As far as I know, Mom and Dad did a good job keeping up with the routine maintenance. This house would sell for a lot, except that death roams the streets at night—as evidenced by the fact that there were four of us just a month and a half ago, and now there are two, Cage."

She'd sucker punched him again. He knew she didn't mean to hit him hard. She was the only family he had left, so he wasn't going to say anything, even though he was having trouble breathing.

Besides, she was right. He was the one dutifully ignoring the fact that his father had not come home for three days. And he couldn't think of anyone else who had reappeared miraculously after that kind of time span.

"So we don't pay the house," he asked. "Then what happens?"

"The bank comes after it."

"That will ruin our credit."

"No, it won't." Joule smiled at that one. "Though it will ruin Mom and Dad's credit. You and I aren't invested. We aren't listed on the title or the loans. We can let any credit card bills go, any car payments—no, wait, they might try to repossess those." She paused and thought for a moment. "A car can be repossessed easily during the daylight hours and it can be transported for sale. So we need to make any payments on the cars. I don't know if there are any to be made."

Cage was struggling to keep up, but he tried. "So we need to pay the cars and the insurance on them."

Joule added, "We need to gain access to the bank accounts.

And we need to graduate so we can get to get our butts to Stanford in the fall."

Cage sank back into the couch, his food forgotten as Joule's words squirmed uncomfortably inside of him. They had three weeks until the end of school for the senior class. Then another week until their graduation ceremony. It occurred to him then that no one would be there for them. No parents. No grandparents. No one would come here to visit, and even if there wasn't something wrong in Rowena Heights and the city at large, travel wasn't as safe as it used to be. But Joule seemed to have it all mapped out.

"Do we leave as soon as we graduate?"

She shook her head. "Dad and I started the paperwork. Stanford's all set for both of us. Free ride and all," she smiled, "but we don't have dorm rooms until the week before classes. So we should stay until then."

"What if Dad comes back?" He hated that he had asked *what if?*

Joule stared at him. "If Dad comes back, all this is moot. All this goes out the window and we start from scratch. I would love nothing more than that, but it's been three days, Cage. Have you ever seen anyone come back after three days?" Her voice was rising as she went, but she was a steamroller and Cage was jumping out of the way. "And we *know* he went out to fight them."

"But he was protected by that mail and hopefully the machete and sword. We've been *out there*," he protested. "We fought them, and we *lived*."

"Yes, Cage." Joule's tone was at odds with her words. "*We* did. Not him *alone*. Unless he's out marauding with some band of happy hunters, the chances that he survived are *slim*." She emphasized the last word.

"We—all three of us together—barely made it through seven dogs. That all came at us at once. For a single fighter, I don't think any number of hunters higher than two or maybe three is survivable. The odds are shitty. Which is exactly why we didn't want to go out again. We didn't like our odds at *three to seven*. And dad decided to take one against however-many-showed-up."

She was so logical and he was so hurt. He couldn't stop the words that came out of his mouth. "You're so cold, Joule, calculating all this out. Dad might come back!"

She jumped up, nearly flipping the tray in front of her. "*I'm* cold? Mom saved us. Mom sacrificed herself so the hunters would be distracted and the rest of us could live. Dad went *crazy*. I don't think he meant to hurt us. But he did. That's what *cold* is. He made his own decision without us, for no reason I can see, and now the rest of it doesn't matter." She stopped suddenly, and he watched her through slightly blurry eyes as she sucked in a breath before continuing.

"Cage, my cold calculation is going to be what keeps you and me alive, because we're all that's left of this family! And if we don't survive, no one does."

45

Thursday, as Cage pulled the car up the driveway after school, Joule immediately spotted the package on the front porch.

They'd been to school every day this week—a record. Joule couldn't help but think that maybe it was because her father was gone and not in spite of it. She hated to think it, but the world was less work without having to talk Nate out of his crazy ideas each day.

Getting to the end of the school year now seemed achievable. For the twins, it was barely two weeks away, because the seniors finished early as all their grades had to be in and calculated well before graduation. The way things were going, Joule couldn't imagine any of their teachers stopping them from getting their diplomas.

The school had numbers to make, after all, and she and her brother had full-ride scholarships to Stanford. Any bean counter at the administration would see the Mazurs counted in the plus column—or they would—and failing to graduate them would only be the school officials shooting themselves in the foot.

Regardless of graduating, getting up every morning, going to class, and seeing her friends was comforting in its routine.

Now, she made her brother stop the car and let her out where she could run toward the front porch and pick up the package. Far bigger than it needed to be, it was almost light-weight enough to feel empty.

Cage came through the house and unlocked the front door, pulling it open for her. "What is it?"

"The trackers," she said with a happy smile. She and Cage had a plan, a full plan—and that felt good, too. It sucked being on their own, but having things laid out felt better than anything had in a long while.

They would stay here and use their father's bank card to take out cash, as much as they could each day. They were slowly setting it aside into their own accounts for their future.

They had agreed that, if their father showed up before it was time to leave for college, they would happily reevaluate everything. But for now, the plan was to stay in Rowena Heights, graduate high school, and take care of the night hunters.

The first two were easy. Joule figured not moving was the easiest—it meant doing nothing. Graduation was something she'd almost actively have to spoil, and neither of them would do that.

The night hunters were the real problem.

"Taking care of them" meant either creating a scenario where humans were no longer night hunter prey or making the new species extinct.

The trackers were her first step toward that goal. Before she could successfully wipe them out, she had to know where they lived, what they ate, and how they reproduced.

The tech had been her idea originally, and she knew there were a lot of flaws in the plan. She and her brother had been raised to double check everything—to do a walk-through test before moving forward, to catch flaws before they happened.

So she wasn't surprised when Cage asked, "What if they chew them up?"

"Then we've wasted our money," she replied. "But we will have learned something, even if it wasn't what we meant to learn."

Money was something they had, and time was something they didn't. Joule wasn't capable of sitting back and rocking her way through her grief. She fully understood her father's desire for revenge on the creatures, but she had no need to personally hack each one to death. Her revenge would be cold.

Cage tossed her the next question. "How do we get them to eat the trackers? They won't even eat the moving bait anymore."

It seemed the night hunters were smarter than they'd given them credit for. The creatures had figured out the air machine was not providing real food and they'd quickly abandoned it.

Joule and Cage had continued to run the cameras through the night, and Joule watched the footage in the afternoons. Only yesterday had she confessed to Cage that she hoped to see her father walk across the yard one night. But it hadn't happened.

Her head knew Nate was gone. Her heart hadn't been forced to believe it yet, and she'd chosen not to fully embrace the idea. So she watched the video from each night, foolishly hoping her father—clad in his mail and swinging his machete—would wander into the image.

Cage had looked at her when she confessed that. "I always find it interesting that when I wanted to hold on to hope, you were convinced it was gone. And now when I finally believe that he couldn't possibly have just been *missing* for all this time, and still come back, you're the one who's looking for him on the night cameras."

Joule could only shrug. Cage was right. Grief was like that.

And without any solid evidence that their father was truly gone, it was hard to hold on and equally hard to let go.

Despite all his questions about the box and the trackers, her brother had fetched the scissors and now handed them to her, handles first. She excitedly cut open the box, aware of all the ways this experiment could go wrong, but desperately wanting to try anyway.

When she finally unpeeled one from the bubble wrap and pried it from the plastic packaging, she held it up. It was about the size of a large capsule.

"I could swallow it," she commented.

"Hopefully, they don't crush it."

With a breath in, she analyzed what she held. It was perfect —if she could get it inside one of the hunters at night, and then find it again during the day. "So. How do we get one to eat it?"

Her brother had no answer, so she dove in and started tossing ideas out. They were possibly crap, but as her dad had liked to say, "Crap often led to gold." So she told Cage, "I think we can use what we learned and get the hunters to eat a piece of meat if we make it move. Probably only once, though. It seems, once they realize what we've done and that it isn't alive, they won't eat the bait again."

"Well, we might get a second feeding, but likely not a third," he corrected, obviously thinking back to the air machine.

"We need to make it move a different way. That method is used and they figured it out."

"What about a full side of meat. Something big, from the butcher. Maybe even with bones in it?"

"You think we should just slice it open and push the tracker down in?" she asked.

Once he agreed, she popped her next question. "Do we want to put in one or two?"

After a little thought, Cage concluded, "I think we have to

only do one. I mean, how good is the signal if he eats it? Are we going to be able to find it? How close do we have to get to read a signal out of that thing once it's inside a hunter's body? All those problems make me think we shouldn't burn two of them if we don't know the answers first."

He was right. So she opened her mouth as though she were going to swallow it. "Want to find out?"

Her brother's hand flashed out and slapped the device out of her hand.

"Hey, douchewaffle! I was kidding."

"Hard to tell," he replied, as he bent over to pick up the tracker from where it had bounced along the floor.

The good news was that she'd invested in sturdy devices. There was no telling what the night hunters might do to them. Surely a tracker wouldn't survive a good chomping of their jaws, but it did need to be able to survive being thrown around, picked up, and gobbled down.

"I really thought you were going to swallow it and then we'd have to... *reclaim* it."

"That's shit-tastic." She'd felt her face pulling into disgust as she thought about what her brother was suggesting to find the tracker once one of them had swallowed it. But the face she made must have amused him, because he laughed whole-heartedly.

It felt good to hear her brother laugh. It had been a long time, too long. Even though she was getting used to their new reality, so was he, and she tried to remember that.

"Let's test it—but not like that!" She pulled her hand back at his startled expression. "You hide it on the other side of the house and see if I can find it. Let's see how far away we can pick up a signal."

He was following along. "If that works, then maybe we get that side of meat. We can stick it inside and see how much that masks the signal." He was thinking his way through, the way they'd been taught, when he tilted his head. "We're not going to get this set up live tonight, are we?"

"No," she replied. "Maybe tomorrow at the earliest. Too much testing first." Though they'd been laughing, she didn't hesitate to alter the mood. "We have to be very careful. We can't afford to go up against the hunters without knowing how we stay safe first."

They spent the next several hours testing the tracker as best they could inside the house. They hid it and found it. They tried masking it with a variety of materials and yet, gleefully, they still picked up the signal.

Joule had hidden it in the back of the closet inside her father's fireproof safe. Cage still found it, though the box clearly dampened the signal.

"At least it works," she said. "Hopefully, if it's in the stomach of a night hunter, it'll still broadcast better than being in a safe."

She looked outside, wanting to do further testing, but realizing that—even though it was still relatively bright—the day was waning. Having been caught outside once before, she found she was still wary of the late afternoon.

"Let's make dinner!" She aimed for casual, hoping the light tone would mask her own uneasiness. Or maybe it was PTSD. Hard to tell. She was still striving for *normal* whenever possible.

Luckily, her brother didn't hear the tone riding softly under her request, or maybe he did and he was catering to her. They cooked together, making broiled chicken breasts and serving them with broccoli and baked potatoes.

And again, Joule noticed but didn't comment—dinner was another thing that was going a little easier now that so much of her day wasn't filled with talking her father down.

She missed him horribly, and she would gladly have continued talking him down. But she remembered her mother had once told her for every downside, there was an upside. And that sometimes you'll lose, and you'll lose big, and it will hurt and it will suck—but there will always be some little upside. And maybe you could enjoy that.

So Joule had made a pact with herself to enjoy an evening of TV and a nice dinner, even if her family was desperately smaller today.

She was doing a good job of it when the house phone rang.

Turning, Cage looked to her, but he was closer than she was. With a shrug, she asked, "Can you grab it?"

But she was speaking just as he did it. He almost had it to his ear when he froze.

When he looked up at her, his eyes were bleak. "It's the cell phone company."

C age wrote down the coordinates of the last known location of his father's cell phone.

"Yes," he said abruptly, also agreeing to receive a text of the same information.

"The next thing we have," the woman said, not kindly, but not unkindly, either, "is the last time the phone was used. It was six days ago at four-thirty-seven p.m."

As was now usual in any kind of business dealings, he and Joule often put the phones on speaker so they could both stay up to speed on their conversations. They were the only ones left, and they were team.

Joule's eyes were wide, and he saw his sister was calculating back. A small nod told him that the time listed was in fact the last night that they had gone to bed and seen their father.

The news was as bad as they thought.

"It hasn't been used at all since then?" he asked.

"It hasn't pinged a satellite, so if it's been on," the voice on the phone told him, "it hasn't been able to connect."

In the end, there was nothing else he could ask. So he thanked the woman and got a number to reach her in case he

had any other questions. But he didn't think he would. Of all
the things he wanted to know, none of them were things the
information on his father's phone would likely answer.

Hanging up, he looked to Joule, their dinner forgotten. It
took a few moments to find a device to plug the given coordinates into, but in a moment, they saw what they hadn't really
expected.

"It looks like we're standing on top of it."

"Not quite," Joule said, her head leaning in close to the
small screen. "It should be that way." She pointed up the stairs.
"It's probably in his room, and we just didn't find it."

Cage couldn't disagree. Though they'd gone through his
father's room before, they hadn't been looking for the phone.
They'd just assumed Nate had either taken it with him, or it
wasn't important. He didn't know why they hadn't found it
though.

His sister gave a reason. "We always turn off the phones at
night. No beeping. No ringing. No alerts. So if dad was heading
out, the phone would just have been a nuisance. Another thing
to carry that he couldn't use."

Cage felt his lips pull together. He didn't like the sour taste
in his mouth. "It wasn't useless. If he'd gotten stuck, he could
have called or texted us."

But Joule was already shaking her head at him, as though to
say, *you know better.* "If he was stuck, he wouldn't have had time
to turn the phone on, let alone for it to find a cell tower and get
a message out. And it would have been too noisy."

"Texting is quiet." He didn't have to wait long for her to
shoot that idea down, too.

"It's light. So no. The phone would have just been an extra
weight to carry in the end."

Cage quit trying to justify why his father should have
carried the phone he hadn't. And that was the end of the story.

Perhaps the phone would have led them to him *if* he'd had

it on him. But even so—if it had happened that way—that would mean that he and his sister would find his father. Cage wasn't sure that was what he really wanted.

If his father was alive, then, certainly. But, given what he suspected happened, he didn't want to follow a signal to his father's last known place. He didn't want to face what he would find there, nor the evidence that his father was truly gone. Right now, he held a thread of hope, even though his thoughts were rolling firmly toward belief.

Maybe he didn't want to find whatever was left of Nate Mazur.

"Let's check his room." Joule was already marching up the stairs. That was the most logical place, even though they'd looked before. This time, they checked everywhere—drawers, pockets of coats, under the edge of the bed—and still found nothing.

"Do you think he took it with him?" Joule asked.

"You just argued that he didn't!" Cage huffed his reply.

"I know." Her voice was low and soft, as though she understood she was being contradictory. But it didn't stop her. "The coordinates they gave us are for the last place the phone pinged. It just occurred to me that we're maybe looking for a phone that isn't here."

"It was last here. That's what she said."

"Well, it was last *on* in this location," Joule clarified. "Since we can't find it, I'm now thinking it's possible that he used it here, turned it off, and left with it. Maybe he did think he'd be out and could call us from where he wound up."

Cage groaned again in disbelief. They'd spent all this time looking for a phone that probably wasn't even here. She was right.

They stood on opposite sides of their parents' bed, unused now for going on a week, and looked at each other. Without needing words, Cage asked her, *Then what do we do now?*

His sister's gift—or one of them, she had many—was cold practicality in the face of a crisis. Not being able to find the phone hardly qualified as that, but when Cage analyzed it, he felt as though his whole life had been one big crisis for a month and a half now. So he looked to Joule, who didn't disappoint.

"There's laundry in dad's closet. I have a growing pile myself. So let's do laundry. If he comes back, he'll be glad for clean clothes." She paused a moment. "And so will I."

Cage didn't know if she also purposefully gave them a menial task that was time intensive. She might have done it just to keep them focused on something normal, something they could accomplish. So he agreed.

She grabbed his father's laundry basket and headed into her room to get her own. Cage was still standing in the same spot when he heard her feet on the steps to downstairs. With a jolt, he looked around the room.

The bed. *If his father came back...* he'd appreciate a clean bed. If he didn't, then leaving the bed dirty was pointless and unsanitary.

See? Cage told himself. *He could be practical, too.*

He tugged off the pillowcases and pulled back the sheet. As he did, the phone fell out from where Nate must have tucked it under a pillow.

C age set down his own basket of laundry next to where his sister was beginning to paw through her clothes and put blue things into the washer.

She was turning her attention to his father's laundry as he said, "Look, I found it." And held up the phone.

Her eyes widened as she sat back, suddenly still. "Where was it?"

"It fell out with the sheets." He was still holding it up as though it was going to reveal a secret of the universe. It wasn't going to do that, though—the battery was completely dead. He'd already tried three times to turn it on. "I was pulling back the covers and it hit the ground, so maybe it was under his pillow."

"That's good that you found it."

"I'm going to go upstairs and plug it in," he offered. "Once we get this load started, maybe it will have enough juice to power on."

Ten minutes later, with the washer chugging from downstairs in a show of domesticity, they hit the power button on the phone and watched as it lit up.

Quickly they pushed buttons, calling up their father's most recent interactions. They combed through text messages, but there wasn't much there that was new information.

Cage felt his breath hitch when they stumbled on a few back-and-forths between Nate and their mom that he hadn't deleted. Of course he hadn't deleted them. They might have been his last recorded conversation with his wife.

As Cage read it, he realized his parents were exactly as they appeared. They texted each other with the same love and snarky comments that they passed around in person. They had been the model for his own future thoughts of a family, but having watched as his father devolved after his mother died, he was no longer so sure.

Joule, however, was grabbing the phone, reading quickly and clicking buttons almost before he was ready for the next screen.

"Look," she said. "He was using one of the other messenger options and sending himself notes on the dogs. Holy Fucknuts."

Despite the swear words, the sound was reverent. She'd turned the phone closer to her own face to read, but now rotated it back toward Cage. He looked and read as fast as he could, before she could yank it away again.

Stunned, Cage tried to filter the words—they almost seemed to not make any sense to him. "Dad was going out almost *every night.*"

He'd thought the words would come out of his mouth as a solid sentence, but they had pushed by weakly, almost as a whisper. He couldn't believe what he was reading.

Joule only nodded in reply, seemingly unable to find her own words. But she scrolled through more of the notes and read the messages out loud.

"The pack was seven. I killed three, wounded two, and ran

from the others." With a pause and a quick scroll to the next entry, his sister added her own breathed out, "*Jesus*."

"I hid from the pack. Eight total. Too big. All eight of them bigger than what I've been seeing."

Cage interrupted. "He saw bigger hunters than what we normally saw?"

With a shake of her head that said she didn't know, Joule looked back down and finished reading that entry. "Saw two lone dogs, dispatched both via machete."

As Cage read the odd little missives for himself, he occasionally looked up at his sister to see that her face was pulling back in horror, though whether it was horror at what their father had done or at his casual note-taking system, Cage didn't know. He only knew what he was feeling himself and expected his expression mirrored hers.

"I'm trying to count how many he killed in total," Joule said at the same time as Cage commented, "I was looking at how many nights he'd gone out."

His sister looked up at him, her eyes wide and clear, but the spark behind them missing. "These first notes are long before I even suspected he wanted to go out and fight."

Cage nodded. He, too, had expected it started after he and Joule refused to go back out—well after the night the three of them fought together. But apparently, Nate had been out by himself long before that.

"Look." He pointed to one of the small entries. "He called them *dogs* in all the ones before, but then calls them *night hunters* after this one."

"The date matches," she agreed with a sigh that said she was more disturbed by the find than pleased or even relieved.

What bothered Cage was that his father had pushed *them* to agree they all had to stick together. Cage and Joule had gone out the one night in part because they felt dragged into the fight by that exact promise. Though Cage hadn't quite believed his father bought into it, he had desperately wanted to believe his father would hold to the vow.

But the promise itself had been made on a lie. Nate had already been going out, and slaughtering whatever dogs he could, long before he'd taken Cage and Joule out.

"Holy shitballs." His sister's calm swear brought his attention back to the phone.

Her swears were not uncommon, but her artistry with them was. She whispered the phrase again. "Holy shitballs."

"What?"

"Cage, he was going out before he even had the chain mail."

She scrolled a couple of times, moving the words faster than Cage could follow, not knowing what she was looking for. She summed it up as she moved up and down through the entries. "He mostly used the machete. He really only walked up and down the street—"

"Do you think anyone saw him?" Cage interrupted.

"God. I hope not."

They were still thumbing through the records in the phone much later when the washer dinged, reminding them that they'd left their dinner to sit out and they had tasks to do. And that, despite the notes their father had taken, his phone didn't seem to be much help in finding him.

Joule handed the phone to Cage with a shrug and a sigh, indicating she was done with it. She waved her hands and her tone wavered, too. "There's nothing in here we can use to find them." She sounded almost angry. "He didn't have any techniques we can use that are safe."

Cage started to open his mouth to say his father had survived plenty doing things this way, but Joule shook her finger at him before he even got the words out.

"It's not safe! He *died* doing this."

Again, it was a punch to Cage that she was willing to say it out loud, even though he knew it and believed it in his heart.

His jaw clenched with the pain of the words that now both his parents were gone, and he turned his head to the side in an effort to fight the sudden smack of tears that threatened to come.

And then his heart stopped.

"We fucked up." He whispered the words as he looked out the window.

It was way too dark outside already.

"Joule, turn it *off*. We have to close up. Now!"

He tried not to yell. He desperately didn't want to make noise—in case there were night hunters out at the edge of the yard, already stalking in the shadows.

Without breathing he stepped slowly and cautiously toward the window to close the curtains.

"Don't," she whispered harshly. "Don't touch them. I think I see movement... We can't afford to close the curtains." Her tone pleaded with him to agree. "It's already too late. I'm just hoping there's enough daylight left that we can turn off the lights without getting noticed."

Slowly, she dropped to the floor then, and crawled. He caught on that she was hoping to stay under the level of the windows, and he followed.

"You get the lights. I'll lock the doors," he said as quietly as he could above the pounding of his heart.

Piece by piece, they secured what they could of the house and came back on their bellies to the middle floor.

"Now what?" he asked.

"Hallway." She pointed one finger toward the upstairs, and added, "Attic."

When they got into the hall and out of the view of any of the windows, they pulled down the makeshift staircase Kaya had installed for exactly this kind of incident. The ladder-like stairs slid down smoothly, despite the roughness of the wood-work, and they climbed up.

There was no way to see from the outside into the hallway, so at least this movement was free. Cage breathed a little easier as Joule grabbed the stairs and pulled them up behind her. They slid back into their folded position and she crawled awkwardly around the opening, reaching down into the hallway and grabbing the long string. Joule pulled the cord up with them and secured the door.

That was protocol. They had to pull up the knob and string, because what if the hunters jumped up and grabbed it? This was safer.

Looking at his sister, he allowed himself to let out the breath he'd been holding. They would be okay in the attic overnight. At least he wanted to believe that. He told himself that his mother had saved her children once again, and she would be proud. He hoped she could see that they would be okay.

But even as that thought passed through his head, Cage heard the sound of breaking glass and nails on hardwood.

48

J oule was convinced she was going to have a heart attack.

Her heart was beating erratically. She knew the exact out-of-cadence rhythm because, unlike a normal day, she felt every heavy hit of pressure in every portion of her body, particularly in her head. Her brain might explode as well as her chest.

Her breathing was labored, too—probably PTSD from the last time she'd spent the night in an attic, listening to the night hunters roam through the house below.

The click of their nails on the hardwood floor was even more disturbing this time. She hadn't realized it before, but sitting here all night, she had nothing but time to think.

Thinking, at least was quiet.

The houses in the neighborhood were all built around the same time, probably by the same manufacturer. Which was why the click of the nails on her own floor sounded exactly like they had the night she had spent terrified and convinced she was going to die and her family wouldn't know what had happened to her.

Now, only her brother remained to miss her. And if she went, he likely would, too.

Her hand reached out and clutched his, a physical reminder that this time was different. She tried to console herself with the numbers. She had done this once before, and she had survived. She was more knowledgeable now. The first time, she'd ducked into an attic on a whim. This time, it was a plan, and they had followed it to a tee. They would be okay.

Unfortunately, she followed the numbers right back into a serious round of hyperventilation and heart-thumping fear.

The first time, the hunters had stalked her and then eventually let her get away. She'd waited them out, and in the morning, she'd come home. She was smarter now, but so were they...

They would have learned, too, and they might have figured out how to get into an attic.

She couldn't tell what Cage was thinking, only that he held her hand tightly. He wasn't speaking, but she could still hear, loud and clear, that he wasn't immune to these kinds of thoughts.

Did he grip her hand as hard as she gripped his back? She didn't know, and she couldn't ask.

It was constant work to keep her breathing as silent as possible. It was exhausting, with only short moments without sounds when she could relax just a little.

She heard two of them.

Then three. Coming up the stairs.

She and Cage sat, still with hands clutched, waiting as the creatures walked the hallway directly below them.

Joule heard them as they passed from wood to carpet, going into the bedrooms. They didn't smell well, so she didn't know what they would do in there. Did they sniff at her things? Nudge them and roll them around?

She thought of the jeans she'd left on the floor. The shirt she had peeled and left out a few nights ago that she should have picked up and put in her hamper. Now, she would throw it all out and never wear it again.

Though she listened as carefully as possible, Joule couldn't tell. Did they climb up on her bed, walk across, curl up?

From the sounds of steps, one of the hunters stayed in the hall. Then another came back into the narrow space. She could hear them right below her.

Her fingers clenched involuntarily. Her breathing shallowed out and sped up.

She talked herself through, counting to six for breaths in and never quite making it. She tried counting to six to breathe out, too, and barely made it to four.

Eventually, the night hunters seemed to have left. She hadn't heard anything in a while. She must have missed them leaving down the steps and out the front. Maybe she'd dozed. Joule didn't know.

But, ever so slowly, her breathing returned to normal.

Then she heard it. Just below her.

Another tap—a tail, perhaps hitting a wall—and she froze.

They knew she and Cage were up here.

The night hunters hadn't left. They were sitting there in the hallway, waiting them out.

49

J oule breathed in and out as slowly as she could, forcing herself to painfully hold each breath to five seconds. She wanted to talk to her brother, but even that was dangerous. Waving her hands or shifting, even just an accidental bump, would be a reminder that they were up here.

The night hunters always left before morning. Or they had. But did they have to?

Was it the sunlight that drove them off? Because it sure seemed to be the dark that brought them out.

What happened if she and her brother opened the attic door and the hunters were still there?

It had been pitch black in the attic throughout the night. She'd only known she was with her brother because she was holding his hand. In fact, she'd had an incredibly creepy thought that maybe he was gone and only his hand was left with her holding it.

Had she fallen asleep and dreamed that? It was hard to believe that she could have possibly slept through the tension that haunted her all night. But she didn't know.

She listened through the stillness, cataloging each creak of a branch outside the attic. Each pop as the houses settled. Each thump of a tail on the wall. Each touch of a softly padded foot on the floor she walked barefoot most mornings.

A series of soft thumps made her believe she was hearing them leave. It sounded like paws on steps, heading downward. Then through the living room.

Cage grabbed her hand and gave a couple of quick squeezes indicating that he heard something happening, too.

Another sound followed the first. Maybe only two of them had left, and now she heard another walking along the hall and down the stairs.

Was there a fourth waiting? Had she counted correctly?

If she'd been wrong at any point in her estimates, then she and Cage could open the door and find a killer waiting for them.

Her next question was: Had they simply gone all the way into the lowest floor of the house? If they decided to stay down there, that was trouble, too. Then the twins would need to find a way out of the attic without going through the house, a task that would be difficult at best.

Contacting someone on a cell phone would be their best bet, but neither of them had one on them. They'd made the mistake of coming up here without anything on them. No chain mail—which was too time-consuming to make happen even if they'd thought of it. But they'd come with no communication, and no protection, and maybe worst of all, no weapons.

Eventually, they would have to open the attic door and pray the house was empty.

Slowly, light seeped into the attic. It was just enough for her eyes to adjust, to see that her brother still sat across from her, his hands in hers, both of them cross-legged. Joule desperately wanted to move. Her legs were dead asleep. If she had to jump up and run, she wasn't sure she would be able do it.

But she hadn't dared. Flexing her legs might have meant killing them both.

Seeing her brother's outline indicated that there was light outside enough to get into the attic. It meant daylight had arrived. But did it mean the hunters were gone?

She lifted her watch to check the time.

The attic had been more tightly built than she'd thought. It was already well into the daylight hours. She looked to Cage and mouthed, "Can we move?"

He nodded, and slowly they began moving one leg each. Soundlessly, carefully, she lifted one leg and flexed it in the air. When that didn't bring any sounds from below her, she leaned one hand behind her and slowly put her weight on it, not knowing if the attic would creak below her. Or whether she would suddenly hear the hunters jumping up, growling, hissing, and calling for her death.

She had a sudden vision of the creatures being angry and aggressive enough to climb onto the bed and jump upward until they came through the thin subflooring here. But she heard nothing.

It must have been an hour later that they were stretched out toes flexing, moving relatively freely.

Joule quietly asked, "Should we head downstairs?"

Cage frowned at her slightly and pointed to his ear.

She shook her head back at him, not understanding. But his hand came out flat, suddenly stopping her. Freezing, Joule waited, listening for whatever she could hear. At first, she heard nothing.

But then she heard the noise.

Something near the door.

Her head snapped back.

What was at the door? Had the night hunters not left?

But next she heard footsteps, the clear sounds of heavy— human—feet bursting through the house.

Reaching out for Cage—she could see clearly now and she wasn't waving her hand blindly, as she had the night before—she grabbed her brother and held his hand firmly in hers again as they listened.

Whoever it was was reasonably big.

Whoever it was was running through their house slamming doors open or closed, she couldn't tell.

As she looked to her brother, Cage shrugged frantically. She had no idea who it could be.

It occurred to her then that the front window was obviously smashed in. Clearly, the hunters had come into the house overnight and done their best to find a meal. If they left, they'd left an unsecured property.

Joule wondered why it hadn't happened before, or why she hadn't heard of it before.

But she turned to Cage and whispered, "Looters."

50

C age stared at his sister in the dim light of the attic. It was growing brighter every moment, and normally that would have made him happy, but the feet pounding through the house below scared the crap out of him.

He thought he was ready for night hunters, though he really wasn't. He and his sister had darted up here with only the thought of getting away. The attic entry had been prepped and ready, but they hadn't thought beyond getting out of reach.

If someone could have come and safely scoped the house out for them before they came down, that would have been a huge help. But it wasn't an option. Now they'd survived the night only to face an unexpected threat from humans during the day.

Cage didn't even breathe in.

But then he heard it.

"Joule! Cage!"

The voice called out their names, making Cage frown as his sister froze, at the obvious recognition.

"Nate?" it asked loudly into the echoing silence.

Cage could only try to piece together the hint of recognition he had. But friend or foe? He couldn't tell.

It occurred to him then, the biggest loss from both their parents being gone: If something happened to both him and Joule, who would look for them?

The voice yelled out again, "Mazur family! Is anyone home?"

Clearly, it was someone who knew them. As Cage tried again to place the voice he knew he'd heard before, Joule leaned over and whispered, "Only one set of feet."

He thought about calling out, "Who is it?" but even as he thought that, the feet pounded down the hallway to the other end of the house.

"It's me! It's Dr. Brett Christian! Are you home? Are you okay? Make noise, any noise, if you can!"

His lungs expanding suddenly, Cage felt his head snap toward his sister and they both sprang into action. He pounded on the plywood flooring beneath him. "We're up here! We're in the attic. Is the house clear?"

But even as he said it, Joule was reaching for the handle to the attic entrance and she was pulling on the door, releasing the mechanism to let the stairs down. She did it carefully, so the stairs didn't drop on the vet's head and damage the one person who had come for them.

"What? Where?" the doctor's voice called back, and the sound of his feet changed direction, aiming back toward them. The short, barked words were still frantic in their tone.

"We're okay," Cage hollered back. "We're in the attic. We're coming down."

Joule ran down first, her feet pounding down the steps, and though the attic ladder stairs weren't designed for it, Cage started down before she'd even hopped off.

Dr. Brett appeared at the base of the short staircase, his eyes wide, his expression still alarmed. Looking up at them, he sucked in a deep breath and then suddenly fell forward, his hands braced on his knees as he sucked in labored gulps. He looked as though he had run a marathon and finally hit the finish line.

"Did the hunters get in last night?" He followed that with a now almost-out-of-place "Thank God, you're both okay." But then he looked around. Up the attic stairs, as though waiting for more. "Where's your dad? Is he—?"

The expressions on their faces must have answered.

"Oh no." Just when he had started to stand up straight again, the vet's shoulders collapsed inward with the perceived loss.

It was Joule who shook her head when Cage couldn't find the words. She answered clearly. "It was a week ago."

Cage thought it through then. They should not be telling an adult that they no longer had any known parents. In front of him, he saw Joule suddenly stiffen as though she, too, had suddenly realized the problem, but moments too late.

"He'll come back!" she blurted out, but the sad expression in Dr. Brett's eyes was clear even from over her shoulder. Cage knew the doctor wasn't buying it.

The question was: Did he buy that Joule believed it?

Stepping forward, Cage put a hand on his sister's shoulder, and decided to go for honesty. He hoped that would keep this from becoming yet another shit show. "Our father isn't coming back. He disappeared a week ago. He'd been going out at night to hunt the hunters. Apparently, he'd been doing reasonably well for a one-man crew. But eventually, he didn't win one."

Cage watched as the man's eyes seemed to acknowledge their loss and notice that Cage and his sister had been working through it for a while already. What Cage was concerned about now was what the veterinarian was going to do about it.

Rather than waiting and letting the man get some ideas of what should happen, Cage decided to head it off. "We're just a few months from eighteen—" more like seven, but he didn't say that. "We're graduating with honors in two weeks, and we're going to Stanford. We've got this. Please don't throw a wrench into it."

He watched as the vet stood upright, looking between the two kids and seeming to make some kind of decision. "I understand."

Attempting to put them into foster care would be crazy. Even just getting the courts to declare them emancipated would take so much time and effort, it probably couldn't even happen before they reached legal age. It would just be a mess and might ruin the last of their schooling.

"Would it be okay if I check in on you?" the doctor asked, and Cage nodded. He felt relieved, both that the man wasn't going to make trouble for them and that it was good to have someone checking in on them. It hadn't occurred to him until just that moment that it might be good to network a little.

The vet was the first person they'd told that their father was gone. They hadn't even called their grandparents and let them know what had happened to their son. Not yet, anyway.

Joule nodded. "I'm sorry I lied," she offered quietly. "We know he's not coming back."

That, at least, made the veterinarian smile just a little. Dr. Brett seemed to appreciate that she was trying to protect herself, but also that she could acknowledge that she'd done it.

He gave a small, tight nod in return, but then everything in his stance changed. He waved his hand at the living area. "They got in last night," he said. "It looks like they got everything."

For the first time, Cage looked around the house. Dinner had been knocked from the TV trays, one of which was broken now. Splinters of wood stuck out like broken bones.

The macaroni and cheese had been licked up, the plates clean, one broken into several pieces. The large window into the living room was shattered, with glass shards and bits of blood everywhere—both inside and out on the front porch.

The floor would need to be swept. The dinner table looked like it had been run into and rammed across the floor. It was definitely out of place, and the deep scratches in the wood indicated the movement had not occurred gently.

Joule was leaned over now, her head down low, worrying Cage that she was struggling to catch her breath, or that she was crying, but she was doing neither. Instead, it turned out she was examining the floor.

"Look." She pointed. "They scratched it with their nails."

With a wry voice, Cage looked between the other two, and said, "Well, this is really going to devalue the house."

Luckily, both of them laughed.

It was Joule who then looked up at the Doctor. "What are you doing here?"

"I sometimes come back into town. There's a vet who still works here. She takes care of the exotics—the ferrets, birds, turtles—the ones who remain inside. And sometimes I come by and offer a hand with surgeries or such." He paused. "I was going to go in this morning but woke up to my lower floor flooded... *again*. I told her I'd make it in if I could. I came out to see if you had any more data. But, if you'd like, I'll stay and help clean up."

Joule nodded. As Cage watched, he noted his sister's movement was a little bit restrained. *What was she thinking?*

But then she asked, "So you *just* came by to check?"

Cage caught it. When Dr. Brett had last seen them, they'd had a father. There was no need to see if they were doing okay. For a moment, his thoughts tripped, wondering what the doctor knew that he didn't.

But Dr. Brett looked between them, standing straight, ignoring the glass on the floor around his feet, the tipped chairs, the general disarray of the house that would have to be cleaned up before dark.

"Well," he said, "I only have Joule's phone number, or maybe it's the house number. I don't know. I don't have email for either of you. And I got some information I would have sent. But, since I was halfway here, I thought I'd bring it to show you."

That was the first time Cage noticed the folder in his hand.

51

J oule looked over the printed pages of notes that Dr. Brett pulled out of the first manila envelope.

"You printed them out?" she asked.

"I didn't have an email address for either of you. It seemed easiest to print it." He waved the now-empty envelope, "I thought I could leave it in the door or on the porch if I didn't see you."

She nodded. He was running old-school style. She could deal with that.

Holding the pages, she read down the lines. A lot of the information sounded familiar. Looking at Cage, who was reading a different page, she asked, "Do you want to go grab Mom's notes?"

With a nod, her brother darted down the hall. She wondered what he would find, and whether the hunters had destroyed their mother's things as well. They hadn't checked everything before sitting down at the table, amid the broken glass on the floor and the window letting in the outside air and a few bugs.

The three of them tipped the chairs upright and pulled the

tablecloth back into place. It looked like one of the hunters had tugged at the tablecloth their mom had always put out. The things that had been on the table were skewed at best. Much of it had fallen onto the floor—her backpack, the plaid shirt she liked, and scattered school books that were now so damaged they would have to be paid for.

"My mom found this out," Joule pointed to a spot in the list about circulation in dogs bypassing the carotid arteries in some cases. "It was in her reading. That's why she went for the femoral arteries."

"Good call," Dr. Brett said calmly, as though they weren't talking about the night her mother was killed. "If you go back another couple pages, I listed some things I think might work. One option is rat poison."

"We thought of that. It will kill them, right?"

"Probably. It works on most mammals. But if we're right, and these guys are a new species, they could be one that's immune."

"That would be an odd coincidence, wouldn't it?"

For a moment, the doctor thought, and then he shook his head. "I don't know. It depends on what evolutionary pressure created them."

"Is it normal for something like this to develop so fast?"

The vet nodded. "People think evolution is a slow roll, but it's really a series of snap revolutions. So things change that aren't expected."

That made sense. "But the poison will still most likely work, right?" When she got a nod, Joule continued. "What we don't know is how to get them to eat it. And I don't know how to keep all the other creatures from eating it—which is our main concern with just laying out poison."

She sighed. "Our other wildlife populations have already been decimated by the hunters."

There was something about the look on Dr. Brett's face that

said he was impressed with either her vocabulary or conservancy concerns. But this was merely the way she'd been raised—on a five-and-a-half acre lot with herons and snakes, both of which her parents had given equal reverence. They had foxes and ground-hogs and mice and voles. Once, an otter had swum up their creek.

"The bird populations seem to be mostly okay," she told him. "We still see owls and peacocks and crane in mostly the amounts we'd seen them before the night hunters came. But we did get pelicans earlier this season, which is really weird. They shouldn't migrate through here."

He'd once again raised his hands, palm up, as if to say, *What are you going to do?* His words said, "Climate change has messed everything up." As if that were enough.

She could only agree. "So what can we use that will only get to the night hunters?"

"That's a hard sell," he replied, thinking again. "Most of these things will affect most mammalian animals. So we can't let it into the ecology, either before the hunters get it or after."

"After?"

"Anything that consumes them after they're dead."

That was a new thought for her. She hadn't ever found a dead hunter in the wild, and hadn't followed up to check on the ones they'd killed with their dad. Were the bodies still there? Or—as Dr. Brett had suggested—had something come along and eaten them?

Looking for something a little less system-wide harmful, she asked about the poison.

"It's Warfarin. The ingredient in the human medication Warfarin. In low doses, it's a blood thinner. It's not the fastest, but eventually a decent-size dose will kill them. They'll bleed out easier, which also means anyone who encounters them has a better chance against them in a fight."

She thought again, always looking for holes in the game

plan before she called it. "If we gave the Warfarin to the raccoons, would it then get into the hunters—" Before she even finished the sentence, she was holding up her hands, warding off the idea she'd just thrown out. "I would *never* do that. I can't stomach the idea of using a live animal as bait to get another animal. But I'm trying to think about how it would pass from animal to animal. How do we get it into the hunter's system? They seem to only eat other live animals."

"I don't know. For reference, I think if you dosed a raccoon for it's size, even if the hunter ate the whole raccoon, the dose wouldn't be big enough to also kill the hunter. So you'd kill the raccoon trying to get enough into your actual target. Vice versa, I'm hoping if it kills a hunter, then a vulture or something that ate it wouldn't get enough to kill them. It would make them more vulnerable, but would eventually pass out of their system. The upside is that dogs, at least, *like* the taste of this medication. That's part of why I picked it. If you can deliver it, they should eat it."

"Nice!" Joule said and almost smiled. Then she looked up the stairs and listened for a moment, hoping Cage wasn't having too much trouble finding their mother's papers.

But the vet was talking again. "I still haven't figured out what the older gentleman in the video had that made the animals turn away. I did reach out and contact him. But most of his answers don't make sense—not as something that would cause that kind of reaction. At least, not if we're looking at the hunters as canines or standard domestic dogs. But I listed what he said on one of the pages." He pointed to the manila envelope Joule was still holding.

She was about to ask what the man had said when Cage finally came back downstairs, notes in hand.

"Were they okay?" she asked, noticing as she did that her heart had kicked up. Nothing in his hand was neat.

"It's a mess," he sighed. "They knocked dad's computer off his desk. I think it's dead."

"Mom's?" She was almost on her feet, but there was nothing she could do but look. That didn't change anything.

"It's okay."

Joule and Cage had already checked on their own. Hers had slid from her backpack when it had fallen from the table, but it seemed alright. Cage's was untouched. *Well, we have three out of four*, she thought. She probably couldn't ask for more than that.

Joule looked at Dr. Brett again—this time, with fight in her eyes. "We have to figure out how to kill them in groups. How to take out *all* of them. I'm not doing this zombie TV show shit where we kill them one at a time, and we're still fighting the same stupid way seven years later."

Despite the seriousness of her expression, Dr. Brett had laughed at that. "You're right," he agreed. "We need something serious."

"We have to get their numbers down low enough where they're no longer a threat to humans," Cage added. "At the very least, we need to achieve a technical extinction."

"Well, these are my lists of things to try." The doctor pointed to the pages in Joule's hands.

"The Warfarin sounds the best. We just have to deliver it carefully," Joule said, bringing her brother up to speed on what they'd been discussing.

It was Cage who asked the most pertinent question then, one Joule hadn't thought of. "How do we get Warfarin?"

Her head had turned to her brother, but it was Dr. Brett who said, "You can just buy rat poison, but some kinds are better than others. I'll get you what I think will work best. Although I have to admit, your safety with the delivery system concerns me."

"Well, it concerns us, too," Cage replied with a smile. "Which is why we're working on exactly how to do it with us not in the equation." His expression turned more serious. "We want the same things my father wanted, but we want to survive it. We've got college to get to in the fall. And we're all that's left."

Joule listened more to the tone of her brother's words than the words themselves. She'd heard it before, but the tone was becoming stronger each time he said it. And that made her feel stronger.

"We leave in just under four months for school," she told Dr. Brett. "That's how long we have to get this done."

The doctor nodded at her. "That makes sense. But... be aware, it's spring now. There may be juveniles out there that you haven't seen yet. And they'll probably start coming out in the summer months."

"Well, shit," she said. It was another thing she'd not even thought of.

"Maybe this will make you feel better." He handed over a second envelope.

Joule opened it, scanning the pages and showing it to Cage before she asked her question. "There's an application to declare a new species of animal in here?"

It looked as though she simply filled in her information on the form and *voila*, Species declared! But that didn't make any sense.

Again, the doctor smiled. "It's not that easy. This actually goes to a coalition of university biodiversity professors. They range from five different fields and seven different universities. The problem is that everybody and his brother thinks he's the one who found some new species. My guess is they got tired of fielding useless information, so they created an application. If you fill it out and give them enough information, and if they agree, this will get you an answer on whether or not they think it's worth sending someone out to test your new animal."

"Interesting," Joule mused, and then asked, "Are you going to sign it?"

"Me? No." The vet shook his head. "Not unless I have to cosign it because you're underage. This is yours."

"Well, I don't want the hunters called *Mazurs*."

"I'm pretty sure," he said, "that the team will let you keep your name off the animal if you want. Lots of people find new snakes, but they don't want snakes named after them."

Joule almost huffed. She'd be thrilled to have a snake named after her—but not these guys. "We don't have a lot of the things they want."

She was looking at a list that included skin samples, blood samples, habitat information and more. "Maybe we can get it as we catch some more. Our samples are old. After we thaw them again, they won't be good samples. The freezing is going to break the cell membranes."

The doctor smiled again, as though he were surprised she'd paid attention in her biology classes. "Well, we'll send it and see what happens."

He stood up, pushing his hands downward on the table top as though making a declaration. "We have a lot of cleaning up to do." He pointed around the house. "We've got to get those windows boarded up before tonight, or you can't stay here."

She would have argued, but she couldn't. He was right.

Then, he turned and pointed toward the jagged glass of the window. "But the good news in all of this is that we have blood samples."

52

C age helped his sister close the attic door and crawled into his makeshift bed.

It was a sleeping bag with a comforter laid out over it. Both were on top of a twin-sized, inflatable mattress.

On the other side of the attic door, his sister was climbing into a similar setup. He'd brought up one pillow. She'd brought up three.

He'd brought up a sheet and a comforter. She brought a softer comforter, a smaller fleece blanket, and a pair of socks thicker than his finger. He wasn't sure how she wasn't going to boil in all that.

Cage had assured Dr. Brett before he left that they were going to sleep in the attic. He'd also had to explain that the hunters had not come into the house for no reason. It had been their own stupidity and lack of attention that had alerted the canines they were inside. It was a mistake they wouldn't make again, and one they would be ready for if they did.

In addition to pillows and inflatable mattresses, Cage had brought with him a store of weapons this time. Joule's stilettos lay on the ground on either side of her. She'd considered stuffing them under her pillow, and it seemed like a great idea until they remembered the mattress was inflatable.

Cage had his short sword and his dagger and the gun. Everything in close reach, just in case.

The beds were on either side of the attic door. Their thinking was, if something managed to come up that way, it would have to choose to take on one or the other of them. Whoever wasn't getting attacked could defend.

It was tough to admit that strategies like these were things he'd not thought about a year ago, when he crawled into bed and was most concerned with whether or not he could join an online game and still get enough sleep to wake up for school in the morning. Now he was worried about communication and long-term survival.

They'd brought up cell phones and mag lights, snacks and more. Not that they would use any of those overnight, but if they ended up trapped, they might be key to getting out or to surviving long enough until they could.

The attic was stuffier up here than he remembered. Of course, the previous night, nothing had been about comfort, only survival. They hadn't discussed whether they would remain sleeping up here for the duration—until they left for school. He knew it was only going to get hotter as the weather changed.

Cage had suggested they bring a fan up with them, but Joule quickly shut the idea down. "Noise. Can't do it."

She was right. Even the low hum of a fan might be enough to alert the predators.

Dr. Brett had stayed to help Cage haul the multi-density fiberboard from the garage. As the two of them had picked out several pieces and carried them back toward the house, he'd said, "You've got a nice setup here with the wood ready."

They'd propped up the boards close to the window and Cage had shown the vet where they kept the tools. "My dad got ready. He knew the hunters could come and take the windows out at any time. He'd seen it happen to the neighbors. He figured it was better to invest and be ready to close up shop quick than to have to deal with something like a motel and an exposed home."

"Smart man," was all Dr. Brett had said, as he set about anchoring the piece in so that hopefully the dogs could not get through it. They discussed the best method for a little while, thinking about how to board the gaping hole up with the strongest results.

"I think we should do it more like for hurricanes," the vet had offered. "Put the board on the outside, because the hunters are going to try to push in. If you tack up the board from the inside, they'll push from the outside and need only bust out the nails. If you put it on the outside, they'll have to actually get through the board itself. Good thing your dad bought the good stuff."

They stood outside as the day warmed up, hammering and attaching the boards as best they could. Neither was a carpenter, Cage thought, and it showed. But it was a good enough job. Though a few of the neighbors walked by and waved, none of them seemed to find their project weird.

Joule had stayed inside, cleaning up, gathering splinters from broken wood, determining what could be kept and what needed to be tossed, and basically putting the place back to rights. They'd watch her haul trash bag after trash bag out to the bins.

"It's really good to have an extra set of hands on this," Cage began, "but I'm curious. You could have been at work today. Why are you helping us?"

The vet didn't look at him, and the answer wasn't what Cage had expected. Not that he was sure what to expect. But it hadn't been this.

"My son was only a few years older than you," he said.

"When he was your age, he worked in the office with me a lot of the time. He really was very good with the animals. He knew more than maybe an average vet tech by the time he'd hit that age. He had plans to go to vet school. I thought I was going to pass the business on to him... and then he didn't come home one night."

There was a pause and a breath. Then the vet put it in simple terms. "Though you guys clearly have this under as much control as any of us, you're not actually adults. Not yet. You're kids with no parents and I'm a parent without my son. It works." There was another deep pause and Cage let it ride.

"If it had been the other way around, and I was gone... If your dad was helping my son clean up after something like this, I would have been eternally grateful."

Cage could only nod. It was a sad situation. But, as he thought about it, maybe it didn't have to be. The vet was right. They didn't have any parents left. And though they felt okay on their own, like they could handle it, it was nice to have a backup set of hands, an adult, and some advice. The vet was helping them figure out what drugs they could use to poison the night hunters. He was going to get them a supply. He was boarding up the window of a home he didn't live in.

Cage had been sure to thank the man as the two of them worked the late morning away in the growing heat.

At the end of the job, they'd collected blood from the window shards and wrapped it up for Dr. Brett to take with him. They'd filled out the paperwork and promised that they would get a skin sample as soon as they could.

But the priority was killing the hunters, and the blood sample they already had would probably suffice for DNA.

Dr. Brett had gotten copies of some of the pictures they had as well: the triplicate canines, the back feet, and most of the things he'd found that were different from other, known canine species.

Once again, the vet had had to leave in time to get home before his own house grew dark. Cage wondered if he was also going to try some of the tricks they had talked about, like getting a tracker and using meat as bait. Maybe he'd try following the packs of night hunters around his own home or find out where they were sleeping.

He was finding them enough rat poison for their needs and had promised to bring them a supply the next time he came, in a few days.

Cage and Joule had agreed that the tracker needed to be the first priority. If they tried both at once, they risked ruining the information from the tracking device. If they got a tracker into a hunter, but also poisoned that same hunter in the process, then he might not make it back wherever home was. That would ruin their information.

One experiment before the next, Cage reminded himself.

They could do what their father had done and angrily hack at the night hunters, killing them one at a time, but it wasn't going to solve the problem. So they had to work smart.

"Good night," Joule said in the dim light of the attic as the late afternoon faded into night. It was far too early to go to bed, but there would be no more sitting up in the hallway, watching the night cameras on the laptops. They couldn't risk it. So Cage turned over, snuggling under his covers, and attempting to fall asleep.

He had a lot to think about. He had three more exams before the end of school, and he figured he could just show up on those days. He had to eradicate an entire colony of killers. He had to keep his name off a species of canines that Dr. Brett had already sent in the information for. And he had to survive the night.

But when he woke up in the morning, he checked the cameras and saw something.

53

Cage was scrolling through the feed from the night vision cameras. With both screens rolling at double time, his eyes were darting back and forth. He slowed down when he thought he caught activity, but he ended up watching the occasional deer, a handful of foxes. Several times, a pack of night hunters roamed the streets in front of the house. Since they did nothing but walk down the street or across the yard in search of something, Cage scrolled on.

Things that happened in the front yard were relatively clear. What happened down the street was too far away to know exactly what was going on. He'd stopped and watched a deer three times just to be sure that's what it was.

When the night hunters had taken out the front window the other night, they had knocked out one of the cameras. It had survived, but he would need to remount it today. He and Joule would put it up aimed to catch activity in the backyard again. They had decided repositioning it would limit their span in the front, but catching what happened in the back would yield so much more than they lost.

He looked up at his sister. She was leaning over his

shoulder now, watching the screen roll by in front of them. "Tomorrow we have to go take that Geography test."

She only nodded in response, but pointed to the screen "Cage, is that a person? Go back, go back!"

The staccato of her voice jolted him to attention and focused his blurring eyes. It took three tries to catch the image, as the man—or woman, it was hard to tell—was further down the street. Whoever it was seemed tall and lumbered a bit.

"Is it Dad?" Joule whispered, but Cage couldn't tell. He looked more closely. Rewound. Tried to find anything he could definitely say was a yes or a no.

"Watch the walk," she whispered again. No longer hovering over him, leaning in and actively fidgeting in his personal space, she'd gone stock still.

"That's not the way Dad moves," Cage countered. Nothing said it was his father.

She looked at him with worry mixed with hope. She'd never been the optimistic one before, but now she said, "Maybe he moves differently after being out for several weeks. Maybe it's the chain mail?"

"Do you really think that?"

"Of course not," she replied, leaning back now. The sheen of hope vanished and was replaced with her usual practicality.

In general, the practicality was great—Joule was a straight shooter, always ready to dive in, but wanting to do it the best way possible. But this time, it was just an erasure of hope. "I can't imagine how Dad could have possibly survived this long. Or why he wouldn't have come to see us if he did. But on the off chance that that's our father, we have to figure it out."

In the end, the person hadn't come close enough to the house for them to tell.

Cage had headed outside and re-aimed one of the cameras. He refocused the lens to get better shots down the street. But what Cage suspected was that one of the other neighbors had gotten pissed off enough or crazy enough to take up the call. He hoped he and Joule could get an answer in the next night or two.

They headed to the butcher's next, collecting several large sides of beef rib, one leg, and additional smaller chunks of meat and bone. While Cage was holding his breath and trying to think of a good answer for two teenagers buying a reasonable chunk of a cow, the butcher didn't ask any questions.

Cage had no idea if that was normal—if people just occasionally picked up huge hunks of meat for their own backyard barbecues—or if maybe the last six months had brought such weird orders in that the butchers had quit commenting.

After getting most of the meat wedged into the fridge as best they could, they used Nate's phone. It was a treasure trove of information that—despite getting knocked off his dresser when the night hunters had come through the house—had survived the fall.

As Joule worked to string up the meat on a system that would make it move, Cage logged into his father's banking system.

"Moving large amounts of money will get us flagged," he said as he pressed the appropriate buttons for a transfer, "but Dad's account has access to mom's accounts and mine and yours. So I'm going to move some about every third day or so. Not in a regular system, not in the same amounts. I don't want to trigger anything. So you won't be getting the same amount I do with each transfer."

She'd paused and raised her eyebrows at him, as though he might be cheating her out of the money they were siphoning from their parents' accounts.

"You can log in, too. Check my math. I'll make sure they wind up even. But we've got to have access to the money. Sooner or later, they would shut him down for inactivity. Better we have it before then."

"What if someone finds out we did it after he was gone?" Joule looked up at him again. Her hands were on the hunk of meat in front of her, with pop-up germ-killing wipes sitting next to her.

Cage had wanted to shrug. "But that's just it: he's not dead. It doesn't become a problem until they can prove that he died and *when*. Well, even then, maybe not." He was thinking it through. "Dad did give us permission to access these accounts. We have his password. So we're not actually doing anything illegal. Maybe just a little sketchy."

He looked at his sister, sitting at the table. It was once again covered in plastic as she baited a tracker to catch a killer species. Colorado had avalanches. DC was having problems with bees. Florida was slowly disappearing under the sea level —exactly as predicted. His father's bank accounts were really no one's first concern these days. "Honestly, the way things are going, I don't think anyone is going to come after us. Kind of like the house."

He looked up. They had not yet even received their first message of an overdue payment. But he was waiting. "Should we pay the house? I'm thinking if we can take out the hunters, the place will be valuable again."

"I don't know," his sister replied. "I mean, there's particle board over the big front window. The hardwood has scratches all over it now. Even if we take out all the night hunters, I don't know that the housing market is ever going to recover—or at least not in our lifetimes."

"Well, if it comes to it—if we change our minds and we're still here—we have enough to back pay the mortgage."

"True point," she said, and she went back to looking at the hook and the meat system she'd designed.

"Are you trying to catch it like a fish?" Cage asked.

"No, that's the problem. I don't want to *catch* it. I just want to feed it. I think I need to cut off the point of the hook and push the wire back around so that no night hunters can get caught on it." She looked at the piece, balanced up on one end on the table, and turned her head this way and that as she analyzed it. "I think," she said, pointing, "I need to put a small slit here and push the tracker in right to the middle of the muscle."

They still had no idea if the night hunters would even fall for it. But it was worth trying.

Once she had it done and strung up, they'd had to go outside and build the contraption to make it dance. With a pulley and nylon cord, they strung the meat to a motor that wound and unwound a small amount at various random times. Cage programmed it so the motor would never go longer than four seconds without moving. Though the meat would only move only up and down, he hoped the randomness would be enough to get a hunter to bite into it.

Joule pointed upward into the tree, but away from the pulley. "We can put up a second pulley over here. The single motor could still then move it back and forth. But as it would hang at the bottom of a V of cord, which would give it a little more lifelike motion."

"True," Cage had said, considering her upgraded option, but he was already wiping sweat from his forehead and in need of a shower.

There were now more and more things to do during daylight. And though the summer days were getting longer, which was helpful, he and his sister had lost their ability to stay up and read at night or do anything after dark. So he compromised. "Tomorrow. If this doesn't work, we'll do it your way tomorrow."

His phone pinged then, giving him the break he wanted as he pulled it out.

"Dr. Christian," he said, absently telling his sister what he saw. Then he held up the message. Though she was a few feet away, she had excellent eyesight and could probably read it fine.

The email contained pictures of the application as though Dr. Brett just wanted to be sure that they knew that he had sent the form in with their information and wasn't exchanging it for his own. The second picture showed where he'd created several slides from the blood. He'd used supplies from his own office and covered the mailing, which Cage thought was very generous of him.

The email also included a date when the doctor would come by again, next time bringing the Warfarin in his preferred brands of rat poison. It would take a few days, since he often only found one kind at a store, and he didn't want to trigger any questions if anyone he knew found him buying that much poison.

Cage replied to the email, agreeing to the ideas.

Dr. Brett must have been online and watching his email come in, because just as Cage had turned away, his phone dinged again. He pulled it out again and called up the return email, once again turning and holding it up to Joule.

"I was thinking through the things we saw during the necropsy," Dr. Brett had written. "Those feet. Remember I told you I recognized something familiar about them? Well, I found something interesting. Look at the pictures—"

Several pictures of mammalian feet showed on the screen. Cage was looking at foot pads from a variety of species, even though he couldn't have named them by their feet alone. Dr. Brett had circled the pads in several of the images. In a few others, he'd marked around the scoop-shaped nails.

Cage held up the phone, showing the pictures to his sister. "That's a really interesting option."

54

J oule stood in the woods, feet planted, arrow notched into the bow, string pulled back ever so slightly. As ready as she could be, she scanned her eyes first left then right.

Though it hadn't happened the last time she'd been out, or even the time before that, having seen one night hunter walking during the daytime was enough to keep her vigilant. It had been in this section of the woods, too. She was not going to get caught unaware again.

She was also concerned this time because they were making noise.

Cage stood behind her, swinging the radio receiver one way and then another. It was a very simple system—the closer the signal, the higher the frequency. But this meant it was difficult to know which direction to go—a dangerous game of warmer/colder. It involved a lot of Cage waving the receiver at arm's length, trying to pick up the differences in signal.

Because they'd turned the volume up to hear the distinction in the frequencies, Joule was even more nervous. She pulled back on the bow string just a little harder, even though she hadn't seen anything.

The butcher-meat bait had been successful on their first try, and Joule had been incredibly pleased. The night camera had shown that the meat raising and lowering on the pulley system —even as slightly as it did—had been enough to attract the attention of the hunters.

The only thing that had gone wrong was that the eight-hundred-pound test rope of nylon had not held up to the canines. They'd frayed it, then snapped it and pulled the meat down, torn into it and left the broken cord and bone behind.

Between the detritus of their work in the morning and the camera, Joule had enough evidence to be convinced the tracker had been consumed.

The second camera—now aimed down the street—had shown their street fighter had come out again. He appeared to be carrying a broadsword, which Joule found more than a bit inefficient. He'd come a little closer to their camera this time. It was enough to identify the person as male, but though Joule didn't think it was her father, she didn't yet have enough information to completely rule that out. She had to admit, the broadsword was the best evidence against it being her father. He would never have thought such an unwieldy weapon was in his best interest.

"Shh! Stop!" Joule hissed.

It felt like it took milliseconds too long for Cage to turn off the receiver, for her to perk her ears and reach for the sound that she thought she had heard. They stayed like that for a while, quiet and only listening, ready to act. But whether it was thirty seconds or three minutes, she didn't know.

When they didn't hear anything, she relaxed her shoulders a little bit. "I'm sorry. I thought I heard something."

Cage looked at her, his frown almost chastising. "Don't be sorry. We have a tracker. We're getting close. We have scholarships to Stanford. We're going, and *this* is how: we're going to be overly cautious. We'll stop and listen a hundred times and be glad if we don't hear anything. We're not going to make the same mistakes..."

He trailed off. He didn't add "as Dad did." But she understood.

"Thank you," was all she said. In her head, she heard her mother's voice, reminding her that her brother would be her best friend, if the fighting kids could get their crap together. No one would ever understand her the way her brother would. Not only had they grown up together—same house, same experiences, same parents—but they had the advantage of being twins, the same age, neither being the older or the younger child.

Though Joule was two minutes older, her mother had broken her of the habit of lording it over her brother a long time ago. That had been wise, as Cage had ended up a good four inches taller than her.

With a breath, she nodded to him. "Now you can turn the receiver back on."

She lifted the bow and they walked about five feet in the direction they agreed the sound was indicating. They had a few more hours of sunlight to operate. They'd gone to school, taken their Geography test, and she was confident she'd done well. When her brother texted her at lunch, it seemed like a good idea to just disappear.

They never would have gotten away with this kind of truancy, even last year. Last year, they'd missed just as much school, but that had been days the school declared off—not skips. The school board had used up every single snow day, but they'd had heat days and cold days, and flood days and high wind days.

Still, the students had all missed those days together. This year, they were missing randomly, but no one complained. So

Joule and Cage had snuck out to the parking lot at lunch and come home. They had bigger fish to fry. And only four days of class left.

They walked another fifteen slow feet, her muscles tense, her body tight. This was her workout these days. When they were kids, she and Cage had taken karate classes, and both she and her brother each held a second-degree black belt in mixed martial arts. They had used some of that when fighting the hunters with their dad.

But after that second black belt, they'd both left the program. Though their parents had encouraged them to keep exercising, neither of the kids had felt any burning need to get to the gym. Right now, Joule's tension was burning calories. She could feel it.

While she had the bow and arrow in hand, she was ready to roundhouse kick a hunter, if that was the better option. She would happily make use of the hard heel on her shoe—a shoe she'd chosen for just that purpose—and kick one of these night hunters upside the head.

Three more turns, fifteen more minutes of getting deeper into the woods, of going the wrong way, realizing the frequency was dropping, and turning back, and Cage finally held the receiver up. "This is close. Very close."

"I know," Joule was whispering, despite the fact that her brother wasn't. "Where are they?"

"Who knows? There's only one tracking device. And there's not more than one hunter hiding right here... is there?" He was turning again, looking up in the trees, down at the ground. None of it made sense. Despite the clear signal from the meter, there were no night hunters.

Joule felt the same confusion. "I just assumed they would sleep in packs and during the day, because they're up at night. It makes sense they would sleep now. We know they hunt in packs." She too stared at the forest around her. "Are we looking right at them and not seeing?"

That had been her concern all along, that the brindle-like coloring on the creatures would blend right into the forest floor. That she could stub her toe on a sleeping evil before she even knew she was on top of it.

She and Cage walked the full circle, and the indicator was very clear that they had gone all the way around the tracking device. It was functioning perfectly and it was right here.

But there was no night hunter here.

Not a pack, not even a single one curled up on the forest floor.

Cage's words were long, drawn out, and questioning. "Do you think it's just the tracker that's here?"

"I don't know." She was looking around as though she might just spot the tiny thing. "They ate it. We saw it on the video. Do you think he didn't really swallow it and spit it out over here? Or barfed it up?" She was wracking her brain for scenarios that made it possible for the tracker to move from the meat in the yard to here, but without a canine attached.

"That's a long way to carry it," Cage put in. "Do you think he crapped it out?"

Joule shook her head. "That's the very first tracker. We only put it out less than twelve hours ago. I mean, they are a different species, but I don't know any mammalian system— except maybe a newborn puppy—that could poop something out that fast."

Cage was reaching down to the forest floor as though to scatter the leaves and see if he could spot a tracker the size of a pill. Joule was shaking her head at him, her hands still occupied with the bow as she spoke over her shoulder. "You're going to put your hand in poop."

"I'm being careful," he protested.

But he was cut off by the growl from behind them.

55

J oule swung around sharply. She had the bow string pulled tight, ready to let the arrow fly. Sure enough, she was staring into the eyes of a night hunter, the broad daylight making its almost black irises glossy.

It growled at her and her brother again.

This one was larger than any she'd seen before. She thought for a moment of her father's notes saying that he'd seen some of these bigger ones. Was this species getting larger? Could it happen this fast? She didn't know. Dr. Brett had said evolution was revolution.

But this wasn't the time to figure it out.

Throwing her shoulders into it, she pulled the bow tight as she could.

"Now," her brother whispered.

She couldn't afford to look around and see if others were coming or wait and analyze this one's actions. She let go of the bowstring.

With a thunk, the arrow buried itself deep into the canine's neck, aiming back toward the chest.

It squealed and tried to toss its head back. But she must have hit some important muscles, because—though it tried to move its head—it couldn't. The front legs came up into the air, almost like a horse pawing at the sky. However, the vocal cords remained intact and it let out a hideous sound somewhere between a howl and a scream.

Joule yanked another arrow from the quiver on her back, notched it, pulled back, and swung wide. Cage faced down the now-injured hunter with the receiver in one hand and his dagger in the other. At least now he faced a disabled animal.

She was going to watch his back. It was hard to turn away, but this was the plan. Despite the fact that her father hadn't followed what he'd said, he'd been right.

Stick together.

She and Cage had added two more rules.

Stay in formation.

Don't let them get behind you.

Working with that plan, she scanned the area in front of her, her eyes alternately focusing and glazing with the hope that she could catch movement. Hoping she could spot things that were too well hidden to see with her normal vision.

This was her big concern. If she was standing in the middle of the street and a pack of night hunters came toward her, she couldn't miss them. But here in the dappled light of the woods, the creatures could hide right in front of her.

This one had come up behind them, and they wouldn't have known it was there if it hadn't growled. If it had jumped first, one of them might have gone down. She almost hyperventilated with the thought, but then reminded herself that it hadn't happened that way, and they would use this mistake to prepare better for next time.

She both heard and felt her brother working behind her. He grunted as he jabbed the hunter harshly with the dagger. In turn, it squealed and she heard the sound of flesh being struck.

With her scan completed, she rotated back quickly to check on her brother, to be sure he was holding up okay. From behind, she watched his shoulders as he put in the effort to pull the dagger out of the hunter and then to jam it in again.

This time, the night hunter fell over.

Cage breathed an audible sigh of relief that the job was done.

Joule turned another full circle before she looked again—at her brother and at the creature lying on its side, its rib cage moving rapidly as it waited to breathe its last. Cage, too, was looking around. They could not afford to rest. They could not afford to be surprised again.

She wondered if her brother would stab the hunter again, put it out of its misery, but he didn't seem to have it in him. The creature wasn't long for this world.

"We need to get out of here," she told him. "Before more find us."

"Yes, but this is our new one. This is our fresh skin sample. We need to take him home."

"He's still breathing."

"Not for long," Cage replied, right on the heels of her words, and he was right.

"We don't have any way to get him home." *He doesn't even have a stupid collar like a real dog,* she thought, *so we could drag him.* But she didn't say it. Even if there was something so silly as a collar on a wild animal, she wasn't going to put her hand that close to the mouth—not while it was still alive. It had taken her a while to get used to getting close to the gaping jaws of the ones on the table, and they were well and dead.

"We also need video," she said, pulling out her phone and starting a film of the night hunter. Lying on its side, breathing heavily and harshly, her arrow still sticking out of its sternum, it blinked one eye rapidly. The gaping holes in its side predicted a quick death. Cage had done his work.

Keeping at a suitable distance, in case the dog jumped up and snapped at her, Joule walked a full circle around it. If she could have, she would have flipped it over and gotten video of the other side. But it wasn't dead yet.

"We need to go home and rig up a way to get it back," Cage said, and she mistakenly caught her brother's voice on film. She clicked it off.

"We can get a tarp. Roll him onto it. Hopefully, he'll be dead by then, and we'll drag it back."

She'd thought about a wagon, but dismissed it because of the rough path. She'd thought about tying the animal's legs to a sturdy branch, the way the old deer hunters did. Then she and Cage could lift it across their shoulders and heft it home.

But the deer hunters weren't being hunted by the deer. She and Cage needed their hands free.

They did not discuss the option of leaving one of them to guard it while the other went home for the tarp.

They stuck together.

They stayed in formation.

And they never let anything get behind their backs.

She wasn't used to being so callous about life. But even while she was recording, she'd almost made several comments that the creature wasn't dead yet, and that they would just wait. With a look over her shoulder, they left it there to bleed out and breathe its last while they trudged home.

By the time they grabbed a tarp and a spare, they'd decided a shovel would be a good idea—to help roll him onto it. So they didn't have to touch him. Adding to that thought, she shoved extra lab gloves in her pockets for both of them. Twice more, they went back for just one more thing.

She wasn't looking forward to the march back into the woods. She was tired and she wanted to sit down. She wanted to make savory food and eat dinner watching a TV show before it got dark. But they had a fresh sample and they had a huge freezer and there was work to do.

However, when they arrived back at the spot in the woods, they could not find the hunter.

Joule turned a circle, looking all around her. It had been a brindle dog, but it should not have been camouflaged. "He's not here... Did he get up and walk away?"

"He couldn't have," Cage replied, his eyes still scanning the ground.

"Are we in the wrong place?" It was the only other logical solution.

"Maybe," her brother said, the word hanging before he seemed to realize that he still had the frequency reader in his pocket. Turning on the receiver, he held it out and immediately picked up the signal. The noise indicated they were clearly right on top of the tracker. There was only one tracker out, only one activated, and it was *here*.

This was the same place.

"Look," she said, "there's blood."

It had bled plenty when Cage had stabbed it. This time, Cage asked, "*Could* it have gotten up and walked away?"

It seemed the only reasonable answer, since the dog had been lying in this spot, bleeding heavily, and now he had vanished.

But Joule knelt down to check the ground. "Watch my back."

No, he hadn't gotten up and walked away. He had been dragged.

She pointed the marks out to Cage and, without her saying anything, he seemed to catch on. They'd lost their find.

But as they headed back to the house, Joule wondered what could possibly be big enough to drag away a big night hunter. An even bigger one?

Only a bear, she decided, and there were no bears here. At

least, not that she knew of. The only remaining scenario was that at least a second—if not a third, and maybe even a fourth —night hunter had come out and dragged the first one away.

Which meant the creatures were definitely out during the day.

56

Cage hopped up the front steps to check out the package that had been pushed between the storm door and the heavily locked front door.

He walked past the front window, still boarded with the solid particle board he and the veterinarian had put up. He would need to get that replaced, and soon. The task was another thing on a to-do list bigger than he'd ever intended to own.

He and Joule had just come back from school, having stayed for the whole day. There were only one and a half days left, and he and his sister had decided to attend. It was possibly their last chance to spend time with some of their friends.

Without being able to stay out after dark, and with the work that the two of them were trying to accomplish during the daylight, they hadn't gotten to see much of anyone recently. Cage supposed it would make leaving easier in the fall. In fact, many of their friend groups had already fallen away. It was hard when a clique lost a member—especially when that member disappeared, with the suspicion of having been eaten by wild animals—so even the school social hierarchy had been suffering.

Joule had parked the car and walked around to see what he had gotten. "Who is it from? And what is it?"

"Dr. Brett," he replied, picking up the box that rattled when he shook it. "It wasn't mailed. Looks like it must be the rat poison. He must have come by and we were at school."

"Good thing he boxed it," his sister mused. At least it doesn't look like poison left on the doorstep."

Cage hadn't thought about that, but it made sense. Dr. Brett had left them a supply of the Warfarin in a large enough quantity that—if it had been of the human variety—it would have required a prescription and an explanation.

He pushed his key in and unlocked the door. The house was blessedly cool and he took a deep breath. The heat had kicked up this week, and sleeping in the attic was getting rough.

He set the box on the table and it rattled oddly again. He had to wonder just how much was in there. "Do you think he included dosage for eighty-pound canines?"

"If not, we'll email him." Joule was dumping her own things onto the table.

"If we don't get a quick reply," Cage countered, "then we can't start poisoning them tonight. We don't want to waste it. So we can't start until we know what the proper dose is."

"We could maybe find the dose in the textbooks. I'll bet the drug—Warfarin—is in there. But we can't start poisoning them tonight anyway."

Joule was pulling items out of her backpack and piling them in the middle of the kitchen table, things she had packed up from her locker and was bringing home for the final time. She held up a locker shelf and frowned at it as though it held no more purpose in her world.

The table was usually heaped with their things, and periodically cleared to run experiments. They'd been eating dinner in front of the TV and leaving the kitchen table for all things school- and night hunter-related.

But there were fewer than two more days of school.

"What do you mean we can't start poisoning them tonight?" Cage's own bag was much lighter today, after handing in four library books.

Joule was standing at the table looking at him like he was nuts. She pulled out her laptop and laid it down and then picked it up again and looked around. "I don't want to put this where it might get damaged if one of the night hunters gets in. But I don't think I need to carry it to school anymore. Maybe I will, just to have something other than my phone..."

But she switched topics rapidly and without warning. "We can't poison them. It doesn't work immediately. They're not going to fall dead in our front yard so we can come out and clean up the bodies. We need to know where they go first, so we can follow them and be sure that they're dead... Otherwise, we're just wasting our drugs and we get to wait for months on end to see if we've made an effective dent in the population."

Cage had another thought then, and it shifted the conversation. Their topic zigzagged in a way that no one else would have been able to follow. "We should ask Dr. Brett if we need to pay him back for all this. It might have been expensive."

He grabbed a pair of scissors and cut the box open. He figured the dose was probably listed on the box, but for rats. That small amount wouldn't do anything more than help the night hunters with blood pressure problems. They weren't trying to medicate their canines; they were trying to kill them.

Boxes of rat poison fell out. One of them had a note taped to it. "Dogs and other mammals like the taste, so you shouldn't have to worry about getting them to eat it." He did comment about keeping it away from other wildlife and how much he recommended they distribute into the bait.

As Joule lined the boxes up on the table, turning all the

labels one direction, Cage asked, "Then what do we do? Do we put the next piece of meat out with a tracker in it and try again?"

"I think we have to. We have to find where they go, so we can be sure they're gone. We also need to get these—" she picked up one of the boxes, "off the table and somewhere safe. If the hunters get in and knock everything over again, they might eat it, but we'll lose all the information."

He understood. She wanted to control how it went down.

Normally, he'd say it didn't matter, but control would let them duplicate what worked... until all the night hunters were gone.

They cleaned up the boxes and put them in a low cabinet behind the pots and pans. If anyone came by—if anyone even cared what they were doing—hopefully they wouldn't even see the poison. And the hunters couldn't smell well enough to root it out.

Doing his regular check, Cage pulled up the camera footage from the night before. This time, the man down the street was out again, though he didn't come as close. Cage could tell it was the same person over and over. He just couldn't tell if it was or wasn't his father.

He was losing any last thread of hope that the mysterious prowler might be Nate Mazur. Even if that body had once belonged to his dad, the man wasn't coming near his own home. That indicated a severe head injury, or madness. If that was Nate, it probably wasn't the man he'd known anymore.

Cage truly thought it was someone totally different. He and his family couldn't be the only ones to think about fighting back. He knew for a fact they weren't the only ones to lose a family member.

"We need to clear the table," his sister announced as she looked over his shoulder. She saw the footage and commented,

"I'm becoming more and more afraid to watch him. One night he will go up against the dogs and lose."

Cage moved the things from the table and pulled out the tarp they were now keeping handy. Joule chose one of the other huge pieces of meat, this one a section of ribs, from the freezer. Hauling it to the newly prepped workstation, she worked on stringing it up.

She began to jab it with another huge fishhook, but sighed. "Last time, they broke the cord. Maybe I shouldn't put the hook in. Maybe I should just drill a hole in the meat and loop the cord through. Can we do that?"

Cage joined her as they tried to rework the initial system. What had been a thirty-minute project became an hour and a half. But they got the meat strung up on the pulleys, which luckily had not broken, and ready to go for the evening. If the neighbors saw them hanging huge pieces of beef or pork from the tree in their front yard, they didn't say anything.

The two of them ate dinner and headed upstairs into the attic—where the air was now almost unbelievably hot.

Turning to his sister, Cage said, "We've got to figure out how to sleep in the house again."

She whispered back, "I think we can sleep in your room. You have two beds in there, and you have access to the bathroom. That means we can barricade your door and the bathroom door and have a room to move through. It means if they get in, we have another door we can barricade if we have to." Clearly, she'd been thinking about this. "Also, you have windows."

He'd been thinking about windows, too. "Let's rig the windows with some kind of method to get *up* to the roof rather than down to the ground."

"Maybe." She rolled over, hands behind her head as though she were looking at the stars and not at old attic beams.

Camping, he thought. Lying outside and looking up at the stars. Gone forever—unless they could kill the hunters.

Joule interrupted his thoughts. "Maybe we should just put attic access in your room, you know, as a backup."

"We'd also need something from the bathroom, in case they breach and get into the bedroom and then we're stuck in the bath..." he was thinking out loud. So many options, so many precautions necessary, just to sleep in his own bed.

But they'd watched their mother, he thought. They'd watched her install the attic access in the hall. "I think we can do it."

His sister was right. This house was never going to sell again. Still, he'd not seen a notice from the bank.

He had one and a half days of school left. How many days until they found where the tracker had gone?

They had to get one to work. Joule was right about that, too. They couldn't poison the dogs until they could follow them.

It took him a long time to fall asleep that night. His brain was churning with questions about dosage, about whether or not the large piece of meat on a pulley system would still work as bait, or whether the night hunters would figure it out...

As he fell asleep, he heard a series of growls and deep barks. He heard them close to the house. The night hunters were always close.

57

J oule surveyed the yard in the afternoon light, hands on her hips, a frown pulling her brows together at the mess.

They'd managed to sleep through their alarm that morning, probably due to the heat of the attic. The two of them had thrown off their covers in a rush to get ready, and a few minutes later, squealed out of the driveway heading for school late.

They'd considered skipping, but it was the last full day and now not even a full day for them. Yearbooks were coming in. So Joule had gotten hers signed by everybody who was left to offer a word of encouragement for the future or fun memories of the past.

It hadn't been quite the joyous day she'd been looking forward to, and she reconsidered skipping tomorrow. There was plenty to do here, and she thought maybe it was better not to say goodbye.

Now, they had to make a decision. They needed to find a barricade for the bedroom, clean up after the night hunters took the bait, and track the device that appeared to have been eaten. There wasn't enough daylight left for all of it. So they were going to spend another night in the attic.

The yard clean up had been more than she'd bargained for. The hunters must have played with the food. She admitted to herself that the mess was a bitch, but she didn't really care. She cared that the hunters ate the tracker and that their meter could track it. This gave her a second chance.

They could fortify the room tomorrow. Or even the next day. They had gotten their yearbooks signed today. So at least that was done.

But now the yearbook was in her backpack, sitting on the kitchen table, full of the multicolored scrawls and signatures. Her classmates' handwriting was crappy, while hers and Cage's were neat and precise. Their mother had read up on handwriting and development, then handwriting and memory, and she and her brother were homeschooled in penmanship. So far, Joule had only found the skill useful when signing yearbooks.

But she quickly pushed those thoughts aside as she surveyed the yard. Her brother stood beside her, looking at the once-again broken nylon cord. Cage leaned over into the grass and produced a glove from his back pocket, snapping on the blue nitrile like a pro before picking something up. He held it up for her. "Piece of rib."

Joule looked at the slightly curved bone with tiny bits of beef still hanging on it and agreed. She joined him, searching around for others.

"Well, I'm glad we took the hook out of it, or one of them would have eaten it," Joule said.

"I'm not really sure that's such a problem," he countered, speaking downward to the grass where he plucked up something else. "We're trying to kill them. Even though we're trying to kill them in large numbers, getting the occasional one as a side gig doesn't seem so bad to me."

"It's not that." She was still looking around while she talked.

"If we hook it, it might very well wind up hanging here. What if the rope didn't break? If it was caught like a fish, what would happen? It wouldn't die. It would almost definitely thrash and lash out. We'd probably have to shoot it, and the neighbors haven't asked any questions, but shooting one hanging from a hook in our front yard might very well raise some eyebrows. Or even worse, the other hunters might stay with it, and we'd wake up to a yard where we couldn't even get to the car."

From the look her brother gave her, he hadn't thought all those options through. She knew she did not want to catch hunters like fish. Not until she knew what to do with one.

"Okay, no hooks." He turned and surveyed the other damage. "It looks like they ate it all the way up the cord this time."

There were no snapped pieces, only a frayed end that looked like it had slid out of the pulley. It now lay like a snake across the yard, the bright color like a warning. Luckily, it hadn't seemed to draw any attention to the motor twenty feet away that was still running. While everything was hooked up, the motor had pulled the meat up and down.

Joule analyzed the whole scene. "Only a few bones left. It looks like they took the bait." She paused, "That means we go out and track again."

"Clean up first," her brother said, turning and heading over to the cord. Coiling that around his arm, he next picked up the machine and set it inside the front door. There was every possibility they'd put it out again tonight. But if not, they weren't leaving anything valuable out to get trampled, chewed, or dragged away.

Joule was not looking forward to going out after the tracker. The last time that hunter had appeared behind them, seemingly out of nowhere. And when they'd gone back to get it, the body was gone. The creatures seemed to be hauling away their dead. At least, *something* was.

Honestly, Joule didn't think she wanted to find out what that something might be. Even if it was just a standard issue Black Bear, that was more than she could handle. Hell, she was growing more certain that the night hunters themselves were more than she could handle.

"We need a backpack," Cage said

"I've got my quiver. No more room on my back," she replied. "Why?"

"Tarp, spare tarp, folding shovel," he went on, and she realized he was right. They wanted to be ready to haul an animal back if they found one. They didn't want to lose it like last time, and making a trip back home for supplies was clearly the way to do that.

Nodding to her brother, she started to gather their supplies. It took a little while. Each time they thought they were finished, they realized they had missed something.

"Water bottle." Her brother filled one up. "To drink and in case somebody gets cut."

They added the folding shovel, tarps, gloves, and more. Cage had a full backpack by the time they were ready. He was also carrying the loaded gun.

No one said it, but if they found a hunter this time, they would have to kill it. A mercy shot to the head or something similar. There would be no leaving it to die.

Even as she crossed over the small creek and into the woods, Joule could feel her lungs getting tighter. This was where she had encountered the night hunters during the day. She didn't like it.

She didn't feel safe. She hadn't felt safe the first time, but this time it wasn't just a hunch but evidence-based knowledge. She kept her stilettos in sheaths along the sides of her legs, one ready for each hand.

But she didn't hold them now. The bow was once again in

her hands, the string pulled tight. She figured she could measure her own tension right along with the string.

Cage was using the tracker once again, holding it out at arm's length and swinging it wide to pick up the signal changes. "We're headed the same way," he said. Eventually, they wound up at the same place.

Joule took a sweeping glance around, wanting to look at her brother and read his face, but no longer trusting even that moment. She kept her eyes on the brush and the trees in the distance.

"Are we following the first tracker by mistake?" she asked, still not looking over her shoulder.

"It's possible," but he held the receiver up toward her. "It sounds louder, doesn't it?"

"But you have the volume up."

"I have it at the same level we set it at yesterday. I wanted to be able to hear it and distinguish the frequencies. But we don't want to be so loud as to wake something."

Made sense, she thought, then added, "It does sound louder."

"Which means, plausibly, *both* trackers are here."

She swung around to look at him, then snapped her eyes back into the trees scanning for movement, for threat. She shouldn't have looked at her brother. She asked her question to the space around her. "Do you think one of the hunters ate *both* of the trackers?"

"It's plausible," he said again. "It's also possible that they move in a pack, and the pack is territorial. Like, this is *our* pack. We haven't made any effort to identify individual animals, but we could go back into the night vision cameras and check see if we're getting the same number each night. See if we're getting the same ones that show up repeatedly."

Joule nodded and it all made sense, but it didn't help right now.

"So if two of the animals from the same pack ate the two trackers, they would wind up in the same place... which means..." she paused, sweeping the arrow again, pulling back just a little tighter on the string, "that they're *sleeping* in the same place."

"Or barfing them up in the same place," her brother added, obviously irritated at the thought that their trackers had not lead them to the dogs.

For a moment, they were quiet. Only the staticky squeal of the frequency meter kept time to their thoughts. Nothing moved, and she swept the point of the arrow back and forth, ready to aim and let fly.

What would bring both the trackers right here—right to a spot where there weren't any night hunters?

They weren't here. She was looking. She was testing. She was even nudging the leaves, but the dogs weren't in them.

And then she figured it out.

She realized how the trackers were, in fact, *right here*, and how the one night hunter had popped up behind them so quietly the last time.

With jerky movements, expecting an attack at any second, she swept the arrow up and down, side to side, and watched for ambush. When she saw nothing, Joule turned to her brother. In her softest but harshest voice, she said, *"Run!"*

58

J oule's feet pounded through the leaves and sticks that littered the trail. Beneath her feet, a twig cracked, but she was gone before the sound hit her ears. She was going as fast as she could.

She would have held her brother's hand, but they both needed their hands free in case one of the night hunters popped up behind them. Or in front of them. And she now believed the canines could do that—just pop up.

Cage had pushed her to the front. She didn't understand the move, but she just had to assume he had a reason, and there wasn't time to argue.

As her feet pounded the trail, making far too much noise, she swept the tip of her arrow toward the brush, then the trees, and back again. Though she was ready to shoot if she saw one, she wasn't sure they would fight if a hunter found them. Could she outrun it? She didn't know, but she was moving like she would try.

Joule was going so fast that everything blurred around her, she couldn't focus on anything. She was afraid that the initial tweak of movement in her peripheral vision—the one that would trigger her to look—would not register at this speed. A hunter could be on her before she even knew it was there.

But she decided that stopping wasn't worth the risk, and her feet pounded on, the earth slapping upward at her with each step. Her lungs felt as though they were going to burst, but she had no options.

Cage occasionally looked back over his shoulder, checking the trail behind them. She knew because, every handful of steps, she looked over her shoulder for him. She could not afford to lose her brother, and she was glad he was watching their backs.

Perhaps he'd put himself in the back because he had the short dagger and the sword. He would be the first to attack at close range, by their plans. Snapping her head back for another quick glance, she saw he had the gun in his hand now, not just waiting at his hip anymore. She ran onward.

The place where the tracker pinged was deep into the woods, well beyond the edge of their own property. There was a good distance to cover to get back. Too far.

Her lungs soughed, and she hoped that she would make it all the way. When she got close, she spotted the creek and her hope soared. During the day hours, they'd only seen the hunters in the woods.

If they could just get across the creek, she told herself. She held her breath.

Ten more steps. Five. Two. When she hit the edge, she leapt the water in one jump, landing hard on her left ankle. She'd hit a rock she hadn't seen and her ankle twisted beneath her.

Turning her shoulder into the fall, she rolled, the hard metal of her quiver smacking against her back and adding insult to injury. Joule kept moving, rolling up onto hands and knees. Cage bounded just a few feet beyond her before stopping, leaning over, and breathing as though he'd just finished a marathon.

When she added in the adrenaline and the fear, they had run the equivalent of a marathon. But Joule climbed to her feet, grabbed at her brother and said through her scattered breath, "Keep going. Keep going... Inside!"

They ran together to the front door. They hadn't been locking it, not until dark. There seemed to be no need. They'd reconsidered once they thought there were looters, but of course, it had only turned out to be Dr. Brett. And they'd decided once more against locking themselves out.

She was glad now that it was open. Despite the deep twinge in her ankle every time she stepped down on it, Joule bounded up the front steps, yanked at the storm door, and threw herself into the house with enough force to smash the door wide. The knob surely had left an impression in the drywall.

She made it three feet further before she stopped and rolled onto her ass. Dropping the bow and arrow, she pulled the quiver off over her head and watched as Cage followed her through the doorway. Turning around, he slammed the door shut and threw all three bolts as fast as he could.

Safe at last, she sucked in the deepest breath she could.

At least he'd understood when she told him to run. At least he listened and didn't demand an explanation first, even though he didn't understand why they were running. He hadn't questioned when they were already in their yard and she tapped his arm. Farther. Faster.

Her lungs were still heaving too rapidly to talk and she held up a finger to say, *just a moment.* It appeared her brother had not figured out what she had. But she still couldn't talk. Finally, her adrenaline began fading, almost as though it was leaching out through her skin wherever she contacted the floor and draining into the wood.

She spoke before she had the air for it, thinking she was further along in recovery than she was. "Their feet," she said, breathing the words with no voice behind them.

"Their feet?" Cage asked, his own words coming on an unsteady cadence. "What do you mean?"

She tried again, her lungs huffing once more, but this was important. "Dr. Brett told us he recognized their feet and the nails. They're *digging* feet. They were there," she huffed it out. "We found them."

When Cage still looked at her like she wasn't making sense, she added, "They dig. They burrow. They're sleeping in a pack, probably with both the trackers. Probably not in the same dog." Jesus, she wasn't making any sense. "One second."

She leaned back onto her hands and tried to open her lungs. She tried to steady her breathing and slow her heart, and she started again. "I mean, statistically it's unlikely—"

Shit. Her breath had run out and she stopped, and she sucked in another lungful of air. It hit her then, that she was no longer breathing heavily from the run. Now it was out of fear. She tried again, but Cage was already nodding along.

"Probably we have a local pack, like you said. One set of dogs that most likely lives with an alpha and a beta leader. They have a territory that they claim and defend and feed from."

"You think we are seeing the same dogs each night."

She nodded. "I do now."

All she had energy for was sitting on the floor, her feet flat, her arm propped on her knee. Thinking better of that position, she tipped her left leg then, taking the weight off the ankle, hoping it wasn't any more damaged than just a little twist that would feel better by tonight.

"So you think probably two different hunters ate the trackers, and they wound up sleeping in the same batch in the forest," Cage filled in.

"In a burrow. That's how the hunter appeared so quietly behind us. He didn't walk up to us. He just came out of his burrow."

"Underground." Cage was nodding along with her.

"I think if we had moved the leaves, we might have seen the entrance," she said, her oxygen safe now, her voice coming back, her words resuming their normal force, even if the fear of what she was discussing still remained behind them. "But we might have woken them."

Cage's expression told her he understood. That he knew why she'd demanded they run.

"I think," she said, "that we were standing right on top of them."

age watched the house as he drove up the driveway. The whole day felt odd. Last day of school. The problems with the hunters. That they weren't ready and wouldn't be. They were still sleeping in the attic, and he hoped he didn't suffocate up there.

At the porch, he pulled the door open and held it while his sister walked into the game room ahead of him. She was still limping just a little bit. She was trying to claim it wasn't that bad. He was trying to believe her.

They'd attended the last half day of school, which had gone pretty much as he'd thought. Aside from seeing his friends, he'd hugged a handful of teachers goodbye, he'd thanked them for recommendation letters and such, and not much else. The day had no academic purpose, so he was surprised that it hit him as hard as it did.

Maybe that was why their house—their *home*—felt like brick and wood and high-end siding. Maybe that was a good feeling to have, since they'd be leaving it behind.

Joule flopped down onto the couch, her now-empty backpack still in her hand. "That's it. No more high school functions ever."

Though Cage didn't flop, he sank down next to her. "Actually, I think we have to attend graduation."

They had decided to skip the ceremony, as both of them had wondered, *what was the point?*

It wasn't like either of them was valedictorian or anything. Their old school in Curie, Nebraska had been *hard*. He'd gotten a B+ in statistics. Joule had gotten several A- grades in various history classes. Those classes should have been curved when they transferred in here, but this school hadn't done it. So while they ranked well, and bumped up their GPAs with advanced placement classes, neither of them was valedictorian.

Clearly, he was just a little bitter about that, and so was his sister. But they'd decided it was a good thing, as neither had to give a speech. Now, she turned and looked at him as if to ask him what in the blazing hell he was talking about.

"I think we have to get that sheet of paper, and I'm not positive that we can get it at any other time."

"Why?" she asked, still not having moved from her Jell-O-like position. "The sheet of paper doesn't mean much. It's the school records that—" she cut herself off as she caught on. "—that will burn down when the school burns to the ground or the hunters rip all the administration apart, and no one's willing to come back into the school to get it. Crap."

Cage nodded at her. "Assumedly, there's some kind of backup system—another high school or some national database—but I don't want to be the one tracking that down later. We do have to prove to Stanford that we graduated. If their administration calls here and no one answers, I want that paper in my hand."

Joule offered him a wry press of her lips that—while she didn't speak—made it clear she agreed it had to be done.

"Let's have lunch," he told her, not quite ready to do everything that was still necessary today. They still had to get the room barricaded, and it wasn't going to happen today. But he had to admit he had a powerful urge to sleep *in* the air conditioning rather than three feet above it.

Ultimately, he thought it was a good thing that they had gone to school. The extra time had changed their plans about how to fortify the room. Their initial designs had conjured up an image of chairs shoved under doorknobs or hurricane window boarding. At one time, they had discussed covering the doors permanently and putting a ladder to the window. They would lift it up and close the window to get in ... and not be able to get from the house to the bedroom, or vice versa.

What they had wound up with instead was a medieval barrier system. They'd bought steel strips and contrived a device to bend them. They'd bought solid two-by-eight pieces of wood and cut them down on their father's saw into four-foot strips.

Joule had pointed to the name *Mazur* written in permanent marker on the side of the saw. "What are we going to do with all of their stuff?" she'd asked. But Cage had no answer and no drive to answer it. He just wanted to sleep in his room.

So now, four thick boards sat ready by each door. They slid through the steel holders almost the way a bathroom door closure did and much the way the movies always portrayed medieval fortresses as blocking the door. They had sunk heavy wood screws into the studs, and then tested them, though they were no hunters.

The two-by-eights themselves should be hard enough to get through. But there was the anchor into the walls, and the doors themselves. At least they were real wood. *Old houses*, he thought.

If the night hunters were going to get in, they would have to break through all of it. Unfortunately, while Cage believed in the system, it didn't matter what he *believed*. It mattered how determined the hunters were. It did help that Joule believed in it as well.

"Time me," she said five hours later, hot and sweaty from sinking anchors into the walls and lifting wood bars. Steel strips held the two-by-eights to the left of the door, ready to slide into place once the door closed.

He was exhausted, but Joule seemed ready to go. Pulling his phone out, Cage called up the stopwatch and said, "Go!"

Joule moved quickly. At least she was tall, reaching up to slide the top one across. But before she had the second crossbar in place, he said, "Stop."

"I didn't get anywhere near finished." She turned around with her hands on her hips. "Well, how long did that take?"

"Barely two seconds. Less than that, I think," he told her as he looked at the clock. "That's good."

"But why stop me?"

"If we're timing for speed, we're timing for a panic situation." She nodded, as though that were obvious. Hopefully it wouldn't come to this. Ever. They both wanted every evening to happen that they simply slid the crossbars into place, put themselves to bed, and slept in a safe place at night. But they were running the drill in case that failed.

He continued, "If the night hunters are on the other side of the door, you shouldn't slide the top one first. It's the one they're least likely to hit at."

Catching on, she examined the setup for a moment. There were four bars across each door—one just below the doorknob and another between there and the floor. In fact, for a hunter to get between them would be incredibly difficult. Another one slid across just above the doorknob, clearing it by maybe six inches, and at the top, another one split the remaining space at the top of the door.

They'd designed it this way specifically because the night hunters were most likely to come in low.

"Ready?" Joule asked. "Let's do this again, and for the sake of accuracy and overestimation..." She stepped back. "I'm going to start from the middle of the room. Tell me when to go."

He looked around the room, at the stopwatch, hit the button and said, "Go."

This time, his sister ran so fast to the door she practically slammed into it. She slid the bolt below the doorknob first, making practical maneuvers this time. Next, she worked the one above it. Then the bottom, and last the top one.

"Ten seconds," he hollered, but she was already around the corner to the private entrance he had to the hallway bathroom. She was sliding around the corner and bouncing off the sink, before she hit the door like there was already a hunter on the other side.

She pushed her shoulder against the top as, once again, she slid the piece across under the doorknob. Though still the most important bar, this one had had to be jury rigged. The bathroom was not wide enough to slide the whole piece across. So she slipped in into notches they'd designed and he watched as she considered what to do next. They hadn't pre-planned this.

These had locks, since they dropped in from the top. Joule didn't lock them and instead slid in the other three. Cage hollered to her, "Eighteen seconds!" but she waved him off as she set the linchpins in at last.

She stepped back then, breathing heavily.

"Total twenty-two seconds." He grinned.

She nodded as she spoke. "Possibly survivable for one of us, if they don't figure out to try the other door first. But it's a good time if there are two of us."

"I saw what you did at the bathroom door." He smiled as though that was enough. It wasn't. They still had to get the attic access.

Though he wanted to believe the hunters wouldn't have a

way into the room, Cage refused to sleep in the room until he had a way out of it, too.

They were well-barricaded in. It made him smile until he heard the knocking at the front door.

Joule turned to look at him as though to say she had no idea who it was.

His first thought was that it was Dr. Brett, but his wasn't the voice that called out.

"Hello?" Sweet and gentle, female and older, it called out again as the person knocked.

Cage and Joule practically clawed at the barriers. Getting out fast was not something he'd anticipated a need for. But it was obvious they were home and while Dr. Brett seemed to have no problem leaving the Department of Child Services out of the equation, Cage knew nothing of the kind about anyone else.

"Hello, is anyone home? I'm your neighbor from down the street."

60

J oule opened the front door, bursting through as the woman walked down the front sidewalk and hung a right hand turn onto the driveway.

"Hello," she called out to the woman's back.

The woman turned around before Joule could say anything else, a frown marring her face. Her white hair was pulled back harshly into a headband and her sweater had some kind of design that Joule couldn't make out but she was pretty sure she didn't want to.

Joule was trying to hide the fact that she was breathing heavily from running down the stairs. So she stood, just barely onto the front porch, and waved as she fake-smiled.

Act normal, she reminded herself.

"No one answered the door." The woman's tone was flat. As though not answering a door was criminal.

On the one hand, she was stating the obvious. *On the other hand*, Joule thought, *Actually, I did answer the door and I'm standing right here.* She felt her lips press together, but tried to maintain the smile. "What can I help you with?"

Somehow, the woman's expression soured just a bit more.

Maybe she'd wanted to walk away with nothing so she could bitch about it later. Joule wasn't going to let her. Counting in her head, she waited as patiently as she could.

The woman motioned with one hand, flipping it toward the space in the front yard. "I just wanted ask your parents about what was here in the front yard."

Shit, Joule thought as she felt her brother step up behind her. She wondered if he might be better able to maintain a happy face than she was, but the answer was *probably not*.

"Oh," Joule replied, as cheerfully as she could muster, "You can see we cleaned it up." She wasn't going to say what it was.

"But it was out all day." Her tone sharpened to a fine edge.

Joule replied, still internally talking herself down from a good verbal bitchslap, "We had to go to school this morning. It was the last day. It won't happen again."

This time, the woman's eyes narrowed, and she began walking back up the sidewalk toward them. Joule didn't like it.

"Well," she started in with a tone that said she was about to say, *I don't mean to be rude,* but then she was going to be. "I've seen it several times but didn't say anything."

Joule knew that smile wasn't hitting her eyes. "It shouldn't be a worry in the future."

That was probably a lie, but she wanted the woman to go away.

"May I speak to one of your parents?"

"My father is at work right now. He had to stay late tonight." A lie, for sure.

The woman's eyes narrowed. "Well, I would love to speak with him when he's home."

"Absolutely. Which house are you in? And what's your name? I'll send him down later. It might be after ten, though."

It was hard to fight the cackle that rose up in her. This woman was a blazing idiot if she thought anyone was wandering out after ten. Surely, she wouldn't open the door then, even if Nate Mazur did knock. But if she called Joule on the issue, then Joule would force her to admit that what happened on the Mazur's front lawn was none of her fucking business. Joule's smile tightened.

"I'm the green one, three doors down on the right," the woman pointed.

Interesting. No name given. And Joule thought that the woman whose grass often remained un-mowed was not in any position to be bitching about other people's yards. In fact, Joule had thought... "Oh, I thought maybe that house had been abandoned, too."

She normally would have had a snappier comeback. Would have said that *no*, no one was going to give out any answers about their yard. It's not your place to judge. But she didn't have a parent to back her up and she had a handful more months before she turned eighteen. She tried the smile again.

If this old hussy called Child Protective Services, Joule and Cage could just disappear. But if they went missing, it would be that much harder to turn up at Stanford in the fall.

In her head, she thought of several different replies about *that mess in the yard.*

That mess was to kill the things that are going to kill you, old lady. Whoever this woman was, she didn't look like she could run very fast, and she didn't look like she would handle a sword or even a good, hand-size hammer very well.

When no one said anything because Joule was biting her tongue, the old woman said, "Well, if it happens again, I'm going to have to file a complaint."

"To whom?" Cage asked from behind Joule on the porch. He seemed to have finally jumped into the conversation. Maybe he'd been standing back there as the muscle and just giving dirty looks. Joule didn't know.

At the same time, Joule opened her mouth. "Listen, if you'd like to file a complaint, I don't know who you would even file it with. There's not a homeowner's association here, and the police don't care. Half the people in the neighborhood have gone missing. And if you're going to file a complaint, you need to mow your own lawn first, and then you need to get a pressure washer to clean your house and fix the windows!" Joule finally snapped her mouth shut. She'd had enough.

It was a dumb move. The woman could conceivably make trouble for them. They didn't have parents anymore, and they could be thrown into foster care.

But high school was done now, and she would graduate and go to Stanford. And hopefully, this woman would shut up. Joule decided then that, since she'd started a fight, she needed to finish it. All pretense of the smile dropped. *Fuck this shit.* "Be sure to let us know who you file that complaint with, so we can file one on your house. Wouldn't want to be un-neighborly."

It was Cage who took over the conversation then with far better tact than she had. "Look," he said, "the yard may have a few messes here in the future and that's just the way it's going to be. No one's yard has been beautiful, not in this neighborhood. Not this last year. You'll have to file one on everybody."

"We'll make sure they all know who started it," Joule added. This time her smile was genuine, even though Cage elbowed her slightly in the back. She held the grin even though her brother was right and she should shut up.

Before the woman could say anything else, he pointed to the sky. "It's turning into dusk and beginning to get dark. Would you like me to walk you home?"

No! Joule screamed inside her head. *Don't! Don't get caught out late.* Reaching out, she grabbed at her brother's wrist, luckily, behind her back so the woman didn't see. Also luckily, the woman didn't seem to like them very much and she said, "I'm sure I'll be fine."

Joule wasn't so certain. She'd been caught outside when the dark came on quickly. So they stood on this front step and watched the woman walk all the way until she made it to her door. Even though Joule wouldn't miss her. But even as the front door on the dingy green house swung shut, Joule looked up. It was dark enough to feel uncomfortable.

"You shouldn't have said that," Cage chided as they slipped back inside. He threw all the bolts while Joule closed the curtains, clipping them shut. They turned off the lights and headed upstairs and Joule pulled down the attic entry, still lamenting that there was no way to close off the hallway so that they could just use this entrance and sleep in their own beds again.

Tomorrow, she told herself. There were no classes, they could put in the attic door, and they could figure out how to spread the rat poison.

She was pulling the door up behind her—once again, bringing the cord up with them, so that no one and nothing below them could open it. But, even as she did it, she heard the howls and the barks outside.

Quietly, they climbed into their beds. No light. No noise.

But then she whispered to her brother.

"We did it. We didn't mean to, but we've been baiting them right into our front yard."

Hopefully, she hadn't baited them right into the house.

61

Cage lowered the attic door. Though he wanted to watch his steps as he descended into the middle of the hallway, he was mostly paying attention to breathing in. Fresh, air-conditioned air. Cool oxygen flowing into his lungs.

A weight lifted from his shoulders, and in that moment, he was determined to get to sleep in a bed that night. The temperatures had been climbing, and it sucked to have the air conditioning on but not getting to him.

Joule looked at him with a smile and her own deep breath in.

"It can't wait another night," she said, turning her head and looking at the medieval barriers they had installed on the door. "We're going to suffocate in our sleep up there if it gets any hotter. And I'm not willing to die over something so stupid."

They spent the morning installing the rest of the attic door. They had everything ready, so the work went pretty quickly. When he went up and down the steps to check it, he felt his lungs constricting at the hot air in the attic.

"Should we leave everything up there?"

Joule thought for a moment. "Yes to the beds, so they'll be ready if we need them. We should have backup weapons up there... and Mom's cell phone, in case we forget or can't get to our own."

Though his lungs balked each time he climbed up into the reservoir of heat and humidity, he did it anyway. Before eleven, it was all done, and he wouldn't have to sleep up there again unless something went wrong. He hoped that was never.

The afternoon was reserved for poison. They had to figure out how to distribute it. Dr. Brett had given them dosing information and they'd watched several online videos, educating themselves about how other people had set it out and what designs they used to be sure the poison only got to the intended creatures.

"Well," Joule had told him. "At least the hunters are top of the chain. That means we don't have to worry about owls eating our poisoned carcasses. But we do need to worry about the vultures and the scavengers..."

"I don't know that we can. We can only hope they don't eat enough from any one source to get too sick. And that they learn to stay away." He hadn't heard of scavenger problems with poisons in the past, just up the food chain. He made a note to ask Dr. Brett. So they'd sat at the table, sketching and talking as they worked through their design options.

"We have big hunks of meat," his sister pointed out. "I don't think we need as big of a hunk as we used to hide the trackers. We don't have to bait them to the yard, and we want the rat poison all mixed in. So I think we need smaller pieces."

"That means we get to butcher up one of those sides ourselves." He wasn't sure if he was looking forward to that or not. There was a certain glee in imagining his work taking out a human predator though.

"I also don't think we should use the last of the trackers. We know where the hunters are now—at least one pack of them. I'm hoping we'll find the next pack once these guys are dead."

"So we go out," Cage reiterated, "and we take the meat and the rat poison and we put it all near their burrow."

"That's what I'm thinking," his sister said. "Dr. Brett says that they love the taste. I'm concerned about the other animals eating it. I'm still trying to figure out how to make it so a squirrel or a raccoon can't eat it."

It took a few minutes for the solution to come through. "Maybe we hang something from a tree."

This time, though, Cage knew they'd be hanging the bait right near where the tracker had signaled them—. They would no longer be in their own front yard. Hopefully, they would nail an ideal location on the first try, and the night hunters would come out of their burrow, see the meat, and eat it first. That would deliver maximum dosage and the least likely case of something else getting to it.

"If we hang it from the tree, squirrels can climb down to get to it." He sighed. It had seemed like such a good idea, but it was hard to keep the other animals out. He wasn't sure what he would decide if they couldn't come up with a design that would only target the night hunters.

"Can we put one of those cones on the chain? Like an umbrella, or a dog's neck cone. Then the squirrel can't get around it."

He sketched a cone into their idea. They decided on chain, so the hunters couldn't chew their way through rope and spill the poison on the ground—thus ruining all the design plans.

"We have to make it work. Poisoning the smaller animals won't deliver enough poison and the results will take so long. I don't even know how we would measure if it worked."

Being raised by two scientists had created the need to always measure results. They'd been taught this from a young age. They had charts that their parents had marked with good and bad behaviors and rewards when the numbers improved. The twins hadn't known it at the time, but their parents had been training them to create measurable parameters and track their data.

Cage looked at the online pictures of the squirrel cones and agreed this was the trick. Placing an order of ten—more than they needed, and because they were cheap enough it wasn't worth a trip to get more—on hold at the local hardware store, he looked back at the design.

Do lots of iterations, try again, and brainstorm until you've got it right—another thing Kaya and Nate Mazur had taught their children. Even if they were both gone, they'd left a lot of legacy for the twins to carry.

They scoured the designs, searching for flaws, problems with setups, and the need to deliver the poison only to the hunters.

Cage thought it through. The rat poison came in blocks and pellets. Dr. Brett had given them several of his most preferred options. Later, they would purchase their own, once they'd seen what worked best with the hunters.

"So do we make a trough like a bird feeder? With slots? I'd thought about that, because if we put it in a mesh bag... well, *one,* we're going to lose the bag. The hunters will chew it and the poison will fall out and get onto the ground." With a gloved hand, he held up one of the pellets.

"I'd thought that, too, but more like a hay feeder for cows. But it doesn't matter at all if the cows or horses get hay on the ground. Even scattered bird seed isn't a big deal, but this is." She paused. "Maybe a hanging trough? Made of wood. High sides. If it's not on the ground, smaller animals can't scale it."

They sketched it out and liked the design. It was going to have to do. The day was wearing on, and they had to pick something if they were going to have it out by tonight.

They grabbed a fast food lunch on their run to pick up the

squirrel-stopper cones. And in a short while after that, they'd gone into the barn and pulled out their father's tools. They set up saw horses and the tabletop that Nate would spread across them to make a work station under the carport. Cutting plywood, they then nailed and screwed it together until they had a two-by-four-foot feeding trough with eight-inch-high sides that they hoped would keep the food inside, even if the hunters pushed it around.

"I hate the thought of rat poison spilling onto the ground," Joule lamented as they built.

Though Cage agreed, he had to play the devil's advocate. "I do too, but it needs to move and a few dead squirrels is better than if we let the hunters live." He wouldn't choose it, but he wanted to give Joule the option. "Do you want to wait? Go back to the drawing board and maybe try to find a better design?"

To his relief, she shook her head. "We need to be sure the hunters stay in the same place. Honestly, I think there's every possibility we go out this evening to hang this and they've moved. We may have already missed them. It's been a few days."

Cage had not considered that the hunters might periodically change their location. But the twins had been fixing the bedroom and installing yet another easy attic access, and the hunters might have been making just as good of use of the time. Especially if they'd come out and smelled that humans had been around their home more than once.

He only hoped they couldn't smell well enough to know.

Luckily, the day had gotten off to an early start. It had not been hard to construct the trough. They had chain. Though their father was a physicist and a mild mannered pacifist, he'd maintained an excellent workshop in the barn.

Nate Mazur's handiwork was obvious around their yard. Several years earlier, they'd gone to a bird show and taken home instructions. Nate had helped them build houses for a specific breed of owl. When it hadn't worked, their father had helped them catch field mice and tuck them into the boxes as bait. They now had owls in the little houses.

Later, after a conservation discussion in school, the three of them had gone about the very specific and detailed task of building bat houses. Two of those now existed in the yard as well. So Nate Mazur was still here, in his own way.

When they were done, they piled everything into the trough and used suitcase straps to sling it over their shoulders. It was hot, sweaty work hauling everything to the site. In fact, Joule didn't have her bow and arrows with her—it was simply too much to carry.

They couldn't move the parts in batches—a rogue hunter might destroy or carry off anything they left. So it was a basic-training-like hump out to the site. Then it took longer than Cage had expected to rig up the trough. He pushed it and watched it swing, angry that the design wasn't more stable.

"I'm not ready to put food into this. They'll spill it every-where." Joule echoed his thoughts.

It took them fifteen minutes of standing there, looking up into the trees, checking the forest floor around them, and waiting for a night hunter to pop up behind them, before they could figure it out.

Cage eventually pointed up into a tree. "Over there. If we stretch these chains tighter and increase the distance from where they anchor in the trees, it won't swing as much."

"If we do it at angles, it will still move, but not tip!" she said, nodding along. "Do we have enough chain for an anchor?"

Luckily, they just barely did

They restrung half of it, still hot work, but worth it. Then—while Joule stood guard—Cage opened the plastic baggies and dumped the poison laced meat into the trough. With a quick look around, he whispered, "Let's get the fuck out of here!"

They were halfway home when they saw the hunter cross

the path at a distance in front of them. Something hanging from its mouth was a dull gray and made a clinking noise.

Cage froze, saying back, weapons now out and in hand. Joule froze beside him. Now, having left the bulk of the weight back near the site where they believed the night hunters had burrowed in for the day, they were much lighter and their hands were free to fight if it came to that.

But the hunter walked on by, the clinking gray piece draped from its jaws, and masked any sounds that might have warned it of their presence.

The sky was starting to turn dark when they got home. They cleaned up, grabbed food, and hurriedly barricaded the doors, eating a quick dinner in the bedroom for once. Cage was grateful to fall into a bed, but his boneless relief lasted only for a moment because Joule turned to him and said, "That hunter? I think what it had in its mouth was chain mail."

62

J oule sat in one of the large chairs in the living room facing the front bay window. She and Cage had replaced the ugly particle board with yet another sturdy window. Once again, she could see the front yard, the driveway, and the long street in front of them.

The street looked almost normal in the summer light. Though the bait had been cleaned up, she could still see where the ladder hung against the trunk. The nylon cord wound around so that they could unhook it, then string it up again for future use. She could see that some of the houses down the street were falling further and further into disrepair. But on the surface, it all looked okay.

The days now felt weird and anchorless. It wasn't even like summer, because they wouldn't go back to the same school in August. This fall, everything would change.

She and Cage had attended graduation the day before. The numbers were much smaller than last year. They'd always gone to the ceremony; they'd always known someone in the senior class. But this year, when it was their turn, their parents weren't there. Grandparents were no longer traveling. It was just the two of them sitting with what was left of their senior class. When it was time, Faraday and then Joule had walked across the stage to a smattering of applause.

And, of course, there were no longer any parties all night long afterwards. Graduation was now held at two in the afternoon and everyone was home before dark. The twins had come home, made dinner, watched TV, and taken pictures of the diplomas, which they then saved to an email. They'd immediately put the documents into their father's fireproof closet safe, no longer able to leave them on the table to admire. Because what if the night hunters broke in?

She'd been eating scrambled eggs and toast with the plate on her lap, looking out the window and admiring the sunshine. Down the street, four kids ran in the front yard. Joule tried to stay positive. She tried to keep the thoughts out, but even looking at the pretty day before her, they pushed in.

The chain mail in the night hunter's mouth still bothered her. She hadn't been close enough to see if it had stripes of mail interlaced with carbon fiber material. If it did, then she would know it had belonged to her father. But even if it wasn't that clear, it could still have been Nate's. It could have come from the shirt or some other piece. And the problem was, who else would even be out in chain mail?

Cage had slept in this morning, almost as though they had gone out and partied after graduation last night. She almost felt like she had the house to herself. Like it was the weekend and her parents had just run out for an errand or a breakfast by themselves. Joule turned on the TV and caught the tail end of a TV show.

She checked her recorded shows and found a queue full of baseball games her father had input. Though not a sports guy, Nate had met a Major League player during a travel assignment and the two had become friends. Nate was now following the Atlanta Braves.

Frowning at her thoughts, Joule turned on the game. She watched it in fast forward, as the game started in daylight but continued into the dark. The floodlights came on, and the players and the fans continued to cheer. People came, stayed into the night, and walked out of the stadiums in the dark.

The Braves were in Philadelphia this week. The night hunters had not gotten that far.

Had they originated in this area? she wondered.

They were spreading out. She knew that much. But clearly, people in other areas were not worried about getting torn limb from limb if they were out past dark. They had their own problems, she knew—mudslides, tornadoes, blizzards, and more—but not this. It gave her pause.

Maybe she and Cage could, in fact, eliminate the night hunters. All new species started in an ecosystem that supported them. Maybe the twins could eradicate this one.

She had her own moral qualms about that. It wasn't her place to play God. But on the other hand, she was a species too, and she wanted to be dominant. And that was the way of species: when two fought for an ecosystem, one species won and the other one went extinct.

Flipping channels, she wound up watching a show that offered bite-sized information about new scientific discoveries when Cage finally woke up.

"I made eggs," she said. "You can heat them back up and make yourself some toast if you want."

He came into the game room a few minutes later and sat on the couch next to her. Three pieces of toast and a precarious pile of poached eggs graced the plate he balanced on his lap.

They didn't talk about their dad or the chain mail, but her thoughts ran circles around the idea. Clearly, the chain mail wasn't enough, but she felt she had all the evidence she should need.

Nate hadn't come back the next morning to pretend to be

there for them, which meant he must not have survived that first night. The alternative only created crazy options. Why just stop lying to them one day? He could have had a psychogenic fugue but—despite Joule's willingness to claim one when she forgot her homework—she knew such mental breakdowns were actually incredibly rare.

The chain mail piece told her the hunters had had the garment long enough to chew it into manageable chunks. It was only more solid evidence that their father was never coming home.

The other thing it meant was that the chain mail was not good enough protection: Nate had died wearing it. She and Cage would not make the same mistake.

It was fifteen minutes later, on the science show, that she saw it. "Cage Look, look at that! That's what we need."

"What do you mean? How does that help us?"

"It's not that we need to survive the night hunters if they attack us. That's the wrong problem to solve. It's that we need them to *not attack us at all*. We know they don't have a good sense of smell. They hear and they see. And if we have *that*, they can't see us."

63

C age opened the mail he'd brought in from the box. He and Joule had let it pile up a little this week. Luckily, most of it was crap, but he pulled one piece aside, thinking it looked important.

Sure enough, in said in bold red letters that the mortgage was overdue. He wondered now if maybe the company had been emailing his father and he and Joule simply hadn't seen a paper notice because it didn't yet exist.

Whatever the reason, it was here now. He calculated it out. The paper was giving them thirty days to pay up or else the lien holder might begin procedures. He held onto the "had the right to begin" as some wishy-washy language.

He'd been told that the lender always wanted you to pay. Eviction and foreclosures were very expensive for them. He was counting on it.

He figured out the legal ninety days before the mortgage company could kick them out. Plus the thirty days to fail to pay up before that ninety days started and he arrived at one-hundred and twenty days. That would be the first day anyone would be able to legally show up on the doorstep and kick them out. By then, he and Joule would be long gone.

It was a gamble, certainly. What if his father came back? What if his father had simply lost some of his chain mail that a night hunter then carried around? Cage knew how ridiculous that sounded, but at some point, Nate Mazur *could* come home.

Looking at the letter, he tried again calculate the odds. They were too long to be worth paying the mortgage now. He would show it to Joule, get a second opinion, and almost definitely not pay.

As he double-checked the date, he realized he had no idea what day of the week it was, only that it had been seven days since the nasty neighbor had threatened them. She'd not returned and they'd seen no kind of action—no notices, no messages, nothing from anyone, let alone any authority. He didn't consider them entirely out of the woods on that yet, but he figured Joule's threat of retaliation probably played better than he'd given them credit for at the time.

A thump at the front door had his head snapping up, and he turned to see the delivery man walking away, waving at him through the large front window. Even now, Cage was calculating the cost of the window and how many more times they might have to replace it. It didn't seem like something they could just ignore.

Sunlight was hard to come by, and he appreciated it.

He headed out the front door, feeling the heat on his skin and lingering a moment before he picked up the box. They had ordered six.

His brain was working the numbers and he couldn't make it stop. The odds on this, the cost of that, the likelihood of having to fix something else a second or even third time.

They had ordered extra squirrel cones. They ordered extra food and stuffed it into the freezer. They bought extra wood when they went to the home store. They *didn't* pay the mortgage—so that was extra money they kept. But it was past time to start budgeting.

They had to have enough to get through at least four years of Stanford. What if one of them decided to stay an extra year? Or both of them did? What if Nate Mazur came home? It was their father's money they were spending left and right.

Like Nate, Cage was much more of a duck than either Joule or Kaya. Things rolled off of his back easily, and Cage was certain that if his father came home and found the money was missing, his only concern would be that his children had lived well and ate frequently while he was gone. But the looming college years concerned Cage now.

He'd managed to get most of the money distributed from Nate's accounts to his own and Joule's various accounts over the past month. Hopefully, he hadn't moved enough at any one time to raise flags. Perhaps he should leave a little bit of it in the original account. Perhaps not. If Nate Mazur turned up dead, it would then become a huge pain in the ass to get his hands on the rest of it. Maybe he should leave a little bit, Cage thought, but a little bit less than they'd been planning.

Another conversation for Joule.

She came down the stairs then, bare feet soft on the wood, hand in her curly hair. "What was that?"

"Delivery."

Her sleepy eyes flew wide. "Is it the carbon?" She'd been waiting for the substance the science TV show had told her about.

He nodded, but he waved the mortgage papers in front of her. For a few minutes, they sat down and discussed how they wanted to budget the money they had. Luckily it was a huge chunk: their parents' savings, what was in their checking accounts, and the life insurance Nate had collected when their mother died.

Yet it would be easy enough to burn through it now if they

didn't think ahead. They had to plan. What could they spend each month? How much for themselves and food and gas and bills and general life and how much on the fight? Would they pull back if they felt they were close to killing the night hunters, but were running out their budget? How much more were they willing to spend to be able to achieve that?

Joule ended the discussion by holding up one of the plastic containers. It was the kind you might get a very large amount of spice or salt in. Plastic screw on lid, heavy to the touch. "I don't think we can budget for this kind of thing." She shook the black powder inside. "We don't know how much of this we'll need. Maybe it won't work and we'll have wasted the purchase of five of the six jars. Or maybe we'll need so much that this—" she motioned to the other plastic containers still sitting in the box, "—will barely cover an outing. We can't plan for what we can't plan for."

"Well, we should at least keep track and see how much we are spending." They put together a primary list of what they'd spent on the fight against the hunters. There was meat, wood, chain, pulleys, and more.

"At least Dr. Brett bought us the rat poison. But if we run out, we'll be buying more."

"And all this was not including what Dad spent." Cage waved his hand across the list written in his small, relatively neat print. Turning his attention back to the black powder, he said, "My hope is we'll spend less and less as we go out. That we'll get the hang of it."

Nodding, Joule agreed, but added, "We have to try it. We don't know that it will work. We'll figure it out. But we can't budget for it, not until we know more."

Still, Joule was Joule, and she wasn't willing to wait. Though she might not be able to figure out how much she would spend on it, she could run her initial tests. Unscrewing the lid, she dipped in a finger and they both watched as it turned inky black with the powder.

It snuck into her fingerprints and into the grooves of her knuckles. She rubbed it a little more, between her thumb and forefinger, leaving charcoal-like smears as she went.

"Get a light," she told him and continued to look at her finger. She smudged it onto paper, producing a mark not unlike a pencil. Though she continued to rub her fingers together, the stuff didn't rub off. It only rubbed in.

"Be careful," he told her. "What if it's toxic?"

"It's just carbon." She finally looked up at him, and saw his serious expression.

"You remember in Bio Two? Back in Curie? We were studying cyanide. Dr. Pohng told us, 'Carbon is the basis of all life, but it's also the basis of some of the things most deadly to life.'"

Joule was still looking at her blackened fingertip. "Good. Carbon made them. We'll use carbon to help kill them."

He wasn't going to change her mind, so he pulled out his cell phone, shook it to activate the flashlight and they watched together as her finger absorbed the light into almost nothing.

64

"How do I look?" Joule asked, grinning at her brother. At best, she looked like a banshee and she knew it. But that was the point.

This was their first full test run with the carbon black powder on them.

The powder had been developed in recent years, and was known as the darkest substance on earth. While black things—like her t-shirt—absorbed a wider spectrum than other colors, the carbon black took in all light that touched it and conceivably bounced none of it back. If a person took a picture of something covered in black carbon, it would look as though there was a hole in the picture. And that was Joule's plan.

They'd coated themselves in it—their clothing, their hair, their exposed skin, and more. They'd done it on several occasions, to get the hang of it. Joule had even visualized her way through the process when she first thought of it, and had already ordered black contact lenses, because the whites of their eyes showed. Their teeth were another problem and, ironically, it was a tooth whitener that best turned their teeth dark as it was charcoal based. If they left it in their mouth, their teeth were mostly covered. Now she grinned at her brother, a ghoulish look at best.

Today their run was in the late afternoon—a chance to check the feeding trough they'd filled with meat and poison. They had to see if it was still standing, to see if the night hunters had eaten anything or everything in it, and to see if it needed repairs or more bait.

Their plan was to go out in the last of the good afternoon light, and return just after darkness fell. There was no good way to test whether the carbon powder worked other than to put it up against the hunters and the dark.

They carried backpacks, carefully filled with extra hunks of meat to add to the trough if it needed it. They'd set up the table and hacked and then cut slices into the hunks in which to stuff more rat poison. She couldn't give them enough, she thought.

Joule remembered when the whole Mazur family had eaten dinner around this table. As she swung the cleaver, grief hit her. Would it always be this way? Would she always feel the sharp sting of the loss of her mother? Would her father always feel like a slow draining of her ability to hold out, tempered by spikes of aberrant hope?

She swung hard at the meat, taking out her anger. Both her parents! Both lost to these night hunters. Fuck them. Fuck the fact that they looked a lot like dogs and she loved dogs. She would stab these hunters in their evil hearts.

Her anger dissipated suddenly, and she wondered what she would do when the hunters were gone. When her hate no longer had such a clean focal point. Maybe she could just get back to the business of being Joule.

"Yes?" Cage held up the hunk of meat he hacked at. Calling it a "steak" was far too generous. "I think it's big enough to cut a pocket into and fill it."

She nodded, still unable to speak and wondering if her brother saw it. Eventually she found her voice.

"Chicken?" she asked her brother and he shrugged in reply, as if to ask, "Why not?"

Joule figured if the two of them ate a whole chicken every other week until they left town, there were still three left for the hunters. The variety might serve them well. She pulled one from the freezer and didn't even thaw it, just stuffed it full of the rat poison and bad wishes.

She was concerned about what they might find. It was possible they'd get there and find the meat untouched except by flies. It was equally possible they'd find the trough bitten through and trashed.

They fully expected dusk to fall while they were out. They intended it. They had to test the carbon black powder. It was still scary as all hell, but Joule knew they had to try. Ultimately, if they were going to go out like this and face down the hunters, it would either work or it wouldn't.

Because they had so frequently seen the night hunters out during the day—one at a time—this seemed the best way to test the plan. Hopefully, they would be able to see how it worked on one hunter before they had to try it on a whole pack surrounding them. It wasn't lost on her that the last time she'd faced a pack, they'd been three people and not just two.

As they headed across the backyard—backpacks on, powder everywhere—she could still see her brother. His black, long-sleeve shirt was lightweight, but they'd rubbed everything in the carbon powder because even the dark T shirt reflected some light. They'd bought black pants, too. Now she realized the temperature was getting far too high for a good head-to-toe covering.

After they'd put the crap in their hair several times, they'd opted for thin knit caps. Her hair had been an issue, as there was so much of it. And the black dulled the gold that tended toward brass to a flat, ashy color. The hats were better, but like everything else, they had to be rubbed in the powder.

The powder went on relatively easily, but getting it off was a different story.

She was afraid someone would come to the door and she would have black in the grooves of her teeth and the lines around her eyes. She and her brother both looked older—and until close inspection, actually old and wrinkly—as carbon powder had settled into their skin wherever wrinkles formed when they made a facial expression.

It had been funny, until she walked out the door and the danger became real. She couldn't carry her bow. Blackening it had been too difficult, but they had put shoe polish on to the blades they carried. It was only so good. Eventually, if they had to be used, the color would be wiped clean as they fought. But leaving shoe polish in a cut on a night hunter was the least of her worries.

Their backpacks, also black, were rubbed in the powder as well. Nothing could afford to be missed. They'd poured it into paint trays and watched as the powder filtered up into the air. They dipped in clothes and supplies. Joule had watched, fascinated, as her fingers disappeared into the darkness. Then a mis-timed move would send a puff up into the air again. She didn't want to think about the fact that she was going to get a new breed of black lung disease. But, with the night hunters, it was kill or be killed.

She intended to be the killer. And if she and Cage didn't kill them now—if *someone* didn't—the predators' territory would expand until the entire US, and the entirety of North America and maybe even eventually South America, would be huddling inside their houses at dusk every day.

However fast the hunters had originally emerged was how fast they could evolve again. Could they become day hunters? The twins were determined to never find out.

As they slipped out the back door, they shed flakes of black powder into the plush carpet. Their parents had the carpet installed a number of years ago, and no one was allowed to walk on it with dirt of any kind. But now there were gouges in the hardwood. The window at the front of the house didn't match the others, because Cage and Joule had replaced it with the toughest, but cheapest, option, fully expecting it to get destroyed again. Half the kitchen chairs were missing, having been splintered beyond repair. So Joule didn't worry about black in the carpet. Maybe there would never be a "next family" living here to care.

She was halfway across the backyard when she said to her brother, "Whoa, do you feel it?"

His eyes wide with the sensation, he nodded and picked up his pace. The sunlight of the late afternoon and the heat of the emerging summer was absorbed by the carbon black powder. She was quickly overheating.

Of course she was. She should have thought ahead. The powder didn't reflect any light, and therefore it had to absorb it all. Light and heat went together, and now both stayed right there on her skin. She felt her temperature climbing and wondered if she could burn her skin to blisters walking around covered in this stuff.

Picking up their pace, they rushed to get out of the light. In a moment, she was in the woods and already starting to cool down. That was the reason for the test—they had to discover any unpredicted side effects that might interfere.

Weaving her way down the path, she stayed out of the light patches. They reached the trough without further incident, only her breathing kicking up each time she heard a noise.

"Look," she said, but she didn't point and she didn't raise her voice to any level beyond that necessary to reach her brother's ears. The trough was virtually empty. A few pellets of rat poison remained inside, pushed into the corners and possibly unreachable. But that was all.

"Do you want to go first?" she asked, referring to the meat they had brought in the backpacks.

"Sure." Cage looked around before reaching backward into the pack.

Standing to one side, Joule aimed her stilettos outward and watched the trees for movement. She felt safer just standing still where she could watch more carefully, but she felt less safe now that she knew she was at a feeding site. All part of the plan, though. She was as ready as she could be.

Joule had expected Cage to pull out the double-bagged packages of poison-stuffed steaks. Instead, he pulled out the receiver and turned it on low. The static and zip of a high frequency had him catching her eyes and nodding. The tracking devices were still here, or they were here again.

Most likely, they were still underground.

Joule had hoped that feeding the dogs at their burrow would keep them in the woods. If they'd fed them enough, it had maybe kept the neighborhood safe for a night. Maybe she wouldn't wind up killing the hunters but feeding them in such a way that kept them at bay. Still, the rat poison didn't really create a zoo situation.

With the receiver now turned off and put away, Cage quickly unloaded the meat he'd carried and stepped back. It was something they'd discussed—leave it quickly and get out. There was no reason for them to be confused with food.

As soon as Cage had his backpack back on and blades out, he motioned to her. Her blackened stilettos had not been used. No night hunters had been seen or heard while he worked and Joule turned to her brother, impressed at how well he blended into the shadows as the daylight dimmed. This was exactly what they had intended to happen.

She had dropped three of her zippered bags of meat into the trough and was opening the fourth when she heard the sound behind her.

65

J oule spun around at the sound. She'd dropped the bag of meat open, but unemptied, directly into the trough, plastic and all.

There had been no warning growl, only the snap of a twig. But it had been enough to turn her head and pull her blades, enough to make Cage step sideways.

This night hunter was bigger and darker than the ones she'd seen before. And he was moving toward the trough.

With deliberate movements, Joule stepped slowly out of the way. She pulled her stiletto and was ready to fight if necessary. But as she watched the scene unfold, she saw Cage pull the gun and grip it tightly.

The hunter came closer to the trough. When he was at the edge of the hanging dinner bowl, he stepped up and stuck his face down in, grabbing one of the steaks and trotting off with it.

As fast as he appeared, he was gone.

Well, she thought, *so far it was working.*

Only the hunter wasn't dead.

So the question was: Had they killed the entire first pack, and this was a new one coming into the territory? That was something they had discussed. Or it could be the other possibility: that the poison simply hadn't worked yet on the first ones who had eaten it. Perhaps he had returned for more. Perhaps the second dose would kill him. Perhaps it just needed time.

The rat poison, in the doses they had delivered, should have worked within twenty-four hours. They had waited forty-eight to come out and check. The problem was, it worked on rats, dogs, owls, gophers, and all sorts of known mammals. But did it work on night hunters?

No one knew. Joule could only watch and test. She didn't even know if this hunter had come out of one of the burrows or if he'd been walking through the woods in daylight.

She continued stepping softly backward until her foot to hit a twig. Tensing, she waited it out, praying no hunters were around to hear it.

One-alligator... two-alligator... three—alligators were much safer creatures than the hunters, she thought. *Four-alligator... five.* She turned her head and spotted another hunter between the trees.

He stopped, looked over his shoulder, and looked at her.

Shit, she thought. Maybe it didn't want her. *There's such nice meat here for you...* she thought the phrase through until she remembered they seemed to prefer their food to move.

Joule stopped breathing.

The hunter headed up to the trough, still swinging slightly from the last hunter's actions, picked out a steak and bit into it. His sharp teeth must have cut right through the meat, because she watched as pellets dripped from his jowls. That was poison he wouldn't be eating. *Fuck.*

He, too, turned and trotted off. Maybe because he didn't need to kill her. He already had a steak in his mouth.

Behind her, she could feel her brother beginning a slow turn, checking the area she couldn't watch because she was keeping an eye on this one.

"Joule." He whispered it almost too softly to catch.

Slowly, she took her eyes from the retreating hunter and turned to see another had appeared. They couldn't stay still or they'd wind up surrounded. With a measured breath out, she stepped backward. Once. Twice. A third time, until she softly bumped into her brother.

Back to back, shoulder blades touching, they stepped slowly off the path. She could only hope this new arrival would also go for the trough rather than for the people. It wasn't dark enough yet to know if the carbon powder truly worked. She could still see her brother, a dark form in the dimming gray of dusk.

His black eyes were creepy and, despite the contact lenses, the moisture seemed to be reflecting just a little light.

Slowly, they watched as the third canine also went toward the trough. They backed away as a unit until they were down the trail. It was always a gamble: to turn and face forward and move at a good pace, but not know what was behind you. Or walk out slowly, one or the other of you walking backwards, most likely stepping on something you couldn't see, making a noise and alerting a hunter.

The night was already getting dark around her and Joule decided to trust the carbon. They needed to get out faster. Her heart was pounding and she knew, while the canines didn't smell well, they could *hear*. She wondered if, with those big ears and sensitive hearing, they could hear the blood gushing through her veins, the pressure rising with her fear.

Were the hunters' eyes good enough to see the twins, despite the carbon powder absorbing the light that hit them? All of the light in the woods was reflected light. There were no sources here.

All she and Cage had to do was have enough powder on them to absorb enough light so that the hunters didn't spot them. Not even that they couldn't, but enough for an advantage. Joule moved forward faster now, hustling for home. Occasionally, she turned and looked over her shoulder, and she noted that Cage did the same.

They were well beyond the view of the trough now. Over the heaviness of her own breathing, she heard nothing and saw nothing. But all she wanted was to get inside.

She couldn't tap her brother on the shoulder; she had blades in her hand. She was ready if the need arose, but she wanted the need to not arise. The best fight was the fight avoided.

So she whispered, forward into the night, "*Run*. Let's get out of here."

For a moment she hoped that her brother heard her and that nothing else had.

There was still a small section of woods to clear before they made it to their backyard, before they made it to the open sprint to their back door. But, as Cage picked up his pace, having obviously heard her, a cloud passed in front of the sinking sun.

The night went dark, and her brother disappeared into the blackness in front of her.

66

C age ran forward at a gentle speed, his long legs eating ground.

He wasn't supposed to be running out of fear, but he found his heart pounding anyway. They'd already seen three hunters individually. Not packs, so that was good. But he'd lost his faith that they could get out of the woods without having a standoff.

It was another moment of running before he realized he didn't hear Joule behind him. He turned suddenly, almost tripping. But as he regained his balance, he looked and saw nothing. Empty path behind him shone in the dim light from the moon, but there was no Joule.

A gut-wrenching jolt of fear made him want to scream. He stopped dead, trying to decide what to do next. Cage wanted to yell out her name—find her as fast as possible—but that was possibly the worst thing he could do.

Stay calm, he told himself. *Think.* He headed backward on the trail, going deeper into the woods, instead of out of it. This was the last place he wanted to go, except that the actual last place he wanted to go was anywhere alone. Joule was the last of his family, so he was heading backward.

He'd made it all of three feet before he thumped directly into something hard.

His head hurt. His elbow smashed into something that triggered his funny bone. It was all he could do to not swear. And he was pretty sure he'd been jabbed and now had a cut in his thigh. But he'd never been so happy to recognize the grunted "Ooof!" of the person he had hit.

His arms came out, aiming not to stab her with the blades he carried, too, and he tried to steady them both. "You good?"

"Yes. Go, go!" She said it with an urgency that told him she wasn't the problem here. And he turned and ran on, listening for her this time as she surely blended into the woods again.

It took another few minutes before they emerged from the tree line, jumping over the creek. Luckily, no one twisted an ankle this time. But his right leg hurt where he'd been jabbed, and he could feel the wetness down his leg where the blood was seeping into his pants. This wasn't good.

"Why did you come back? Why were you running the wrong way?" Joule whispered harshly, her feet still moving.

"I couldn't see you."

He heard a faint chuckle. "Yes. That's the way it was supposed to be."

She was right, but Cage understood that meant they had more work to do. They couldn't be running into each other in the dark. They had to be invisible to the night hunters, but clear to each other. They couldn't afford to mistakenly stab each other... again.

As he entered the yard, he looked both toward the back and the front of the house, trying to figure out which door to use. His leg was threatening to buckle under him and, for the first time, Joule seemed to see it. Though with her light-eating form, it was hard to tell what her expression was.

It had made more sense when they were coming out to use the back door. Two pitch black creatures emerging in broad daylight would have brought stares and maybe questions from the neighbors. But now, it didn't matter so much. Except, suddenly it did. Joule's hand reached across the front of him, holding him back.

"In the front yard."

He saw them then. Three night hunters wandered the area underneath the big tree. One looked up, as though expecting meat to be waiting. Cage realized—as Joule had said—they had trained the hunters to come here to feed. The information had been invaluable, but the results, not so good.

Joule didn't say anything, just pushed him a little and steered them toward the back door, but it was too late. They'd been spotted or maybe heard. At least the night hunters didn't seem to *see* them, but they had certainly heard something and were coming to investigate.

"Slow? Or fast?" she whispered.

If he wanted to spare his leg, the answer was *slow*, but he whispered, "Fast."

He heard a clink before he realized what it was his sister had done. Putting both stilettos into one hand, probably not her smartest move, she reached for him. He felt it before he saw it, their carbon powder working against them now. In that same moment as he realized what the sound was, he felt her hand clasp around his wrist. Then he felt the tug. She pulled him along, probably realizing he was hurt worse than they'd initially thought.

Did the hunters smell blood? They didn't smell humans, it seemed, but he hadn't been a bleeding human before. As he and Joule took off across the backyard, aiming the short distance to the door at the back patio, the hunters took off, too. As though the jolt of movement triggered the canines to come running, the hunters aimed directly for them.

The hunters were fast. Heads lowered, they lengthened their strides and ate up ground. They were built for the run; he and Joule weren't. It seemed the fifteen feet to the door took all of fifteen minutes to cross.

Everything happened in slow motion. Cage was watching the canines bounding across the yard, their mouths open. The moonlight glinted off of all those canines, ready to shred him further. He was not ready to be shredded.

They hit the patio, the jolt of the cement beneath his feet reverberating up his leg. Ducking around the table and chairs was a nuisance—the patio furniture was a good idea when there had been evening barbecues, but now those items were just obstacles for the humans. Probably not for the hunters.

Joule grabbed him and threw him into the door, where he slammed with a little "Oof" of his own.

"Open it," she demanded as she spun to face away from him. While he got the door, she was going to defend his back.

Once again, they hadn't locked the house. Besides, they'd not known of a night hunter actually opening a door, only breaking them down. So he turned the knob, slid inside, and reached out to grab the back of his sister's shirt.

She yelled a war cry and stabbed at the dog in front of her even as Cage pulled her backwards.

"Fuck!" she yelled, and they tumbled inside into a heap with the door still gaping in front of him like an invitation to the hunters. Leaping up, the pain shooting through his leg, Cage pushed the door closed. He saw the hunter then, the one Joule had stabbed, on its side and gushing blood. But there wasn't time to look, and he threw the bolt, holding the door against the weight that smacked hard up against it.

Leaning in, he hollered to her. "Get a chair! We've got to brace this shit."

Why hadn't they added braces in the first place? It seemed

obvious now. The front window was a failure point. And so were these back French patio doors. Who'd thought that was a good idea to make doors that opened inward?

Now he was leaning heavily on his left leg, acting as the brace until she came back. As Joule darted upstairs, he pushed back against every hit and waited for one of the small panes of glass to explode inward, a snout pushing through. He'd seen the hunter she slashed. Whatever she'd hit, it was vital and he was bleeding out. Joule herself looked like a survivor of a massacre, black powder running along her clothes mixed with animal blood. Surely none of the gore was her own.

They had intended to come home quietly. Lock the door. Turn off the lights and climb into bed. That was not happening now. The house would not be secured. It would be broken into yet again. These hunters were mad. They knew the twins were inside, and the two remaining ones were determined.

Joule was thumping down the stairs, the chair behind her. Though their mother would have had a fit at the way she was banging it into the walls, no one was around to get upset now and the house would survive a few more nicks here and there.

Cage grabbed the chair from her and jammed it under the pair of doorknobs, pushing against it several times to brace it tightly.

Standing back, he watched it hold against the next hit, but he wasn't sure how many it was good for. "The attic!" he cried.

She nodded and together they raced up the stairs, but as they reached the top landing and heard the crack of glass from downstairs, Joule ducked into the bathroom and then into his mother's office.

"What are you doing?" he hissed as he pulled down the attic stairs. The heat had never felt so welcome. But they had only moments before the hunters were inside and skidding around the corner. He wanted the door pulled up and the two of them *gone* before that happened. If the hunters saw them, there was no telling what they might do.

"Just go," Joule told him and pushed him up the stairs.

67

"**P**ull, pull, pull!" Joule quietly hissed the command at her brother.

Her hands were full as she cleared the top step into the attic and she prayed he understood. But Cage had already been standing with the rope in his hand, and was hauling the extended staircase up behind her even as her foot left the ladder.

She would have turned and helped because the door wasn't lightweight, but she couldn't. Holding the heavy contraption with one hand—his leg still bleeding—Cage reached down and pulled up the dangling cord. He locked the staircase in the closed position, without a means for anyone—or anything—below to reach up and pull it down.

Crossing her legs, Joule quietly sat onto the floor, her heart thumping from their run. No dogs had followed her up the hallway, and for that she was grateful. But now the two of them had to sit, unmoving, and wait.

She wanted to ask Cage how his leg was, if he was bleeding freely. Was it enough to make a puddle and drip through the ceiling? She would think he would have to bleed a good amount before that happened, but the truth was, she didn't really know.

She was covered in carbon black powder and the night hunter blood was slowly drying on her. In their plan, they would have come home and taken a shower. Although that had been a stupid idea, she thought now.

No matter how they had come home—quietly, victorious, or running as they had—there would be no showers until morning. No noise, no light. No alerting the hunters they were in the house.

Of course, they'd led the small pack right back to their door. That was another missing piece of the plan that would have to be rectified. Maybe it was a good thing that they weren't in the bedroom shedding black powder crystals all over the almost-white carpeting. Carbon Black rubbed into the rug would prove impossible to remove.

Joule breathed in through her nose and out through her mouth. The over-warm air of the attic heated her lungs from the inside, feeling as though it expanded them. She wished she had a fan. She wished she had even a dim light and that she knew sign language or something better than Morse code to communicate with her brother. She wanted to know, *Was he putting pressure on the wound?* She needed to clean and treat it.

The pounding of her heart finally subsided and she listened for noises beneath her. Though she'd heard the glass break, it was possible the chair had held and the hunters hadn't come into the house. Or maybe they'd decided it was in their own best interest to drag their dead friend away, for surely he was dead.

She'd cut the hunter—badly—and he'd leapt at her while she did it. But, by the time he was close, he'd had no muscle tone left. Her slice had been wide and deep. The Warfarin, the medicine in the rat poison, was a blood thinner. Hopefully, it would make the hunters bleed out internally or from small wounds. If that hunter had eaten some of the poison they'd set out, he was likely on his last legs.

Joule's slice had filleted him wide open. There would have been no possibility of any alternate circulation. He'd bled all over her. She shuddered as she remembered it, uncontrollable shivers wracking her spine. So she didn't think of it.

Cage had a cut that needed her immediate attention. She began moving as slowly and quietly as possible, praying she didn't squeak any of the rough floorboards beneath her. She and Cage had done what they'd planned and sat themselves on opposite sides of the attic entry door. She would have loved to have climbed into bed, but surely it would have made some kind of noise. And she was not getting into that bed covered in blood and carbon powder—not unless she was burning the whole thing in the backyard tomorrow.

"Don't move," he told her. But it was too late. She reached across the space.

"Water bottle. Soap." She ignored him, and said each item as she pressed it into his hand by feel. She'd been prepared to be nearly invisible in the woods... but not here. "Clean it out."

She could see an outline of his form, and a few spots here and there where the carbon powder had rubbed off or had not lived up to its hype. But it was hardly like *seeing* her brother—more like psychically intuiting the presence of a ghost.

From what she could gather from the dim visuals, he reached behind himself and pulled the pillow off his bed, quietly tucking it under his leg. She heard the top of the water bottle. The slow, faint scrape of plastic and a slight, unavoidable chug as he poured told her he was following her instructions. The pillow would absorb the excess water and it wouldn't make a puddle or drip through the ceiling, thus alerting any hunters below to look up.

Joule could almost hear his teeth clenching and wondered

if he had made a real noise or if she'd just grown so in tune with the only other human she now had regular contact with.

"How deep?" she whispered. She wanted so badly to apologize. They'd run into each other, unable to see, but it was her stiletto that had pierced him. She was the one who'd not aimed her weapon correctly, and she'd hurt the only family she had left. Joule had not been worried about the shoe polish going into one of the hunters with a deep cut. It had never occurred to her it would go into her brother.

"Half an inch," he whispered back, the words so soft they were only a hint of movement in the dark, thick air. "Hurts like a bitch, but it isn't bad."

If she started apologizing, she would cry. She would get noisy and sob in great gulping noises for all her losses. For the fact that her blade had gone into her brother, that her mother had been killed, and that her father was missing seemingly of his own accord. Her only consolation was that her blade had gone into her brother *first* and that she had not contaminated his wound with night hunter blood.

She heard faint shuffling sound from him and tried to make out his movements in the dark. She watched his outline as he went through the motions of cleaning the wound a second time. Grabbing her fleece blanket off of the bed, she offered it up to him to stop the bleeding he'd surely restarted with his ministrations. Their clothing was dirty, and his pillow was too now, but her favorite fleece was not. It was an adequate sacrifice for the mistakes she made. She held it across to him, whispering, "Dry it."

When she'd given him a few minutes to get the blood to stop, she handed across the one thing that she thought to grab at the last minute. She was grateful she'd remembered where it was in her mother's craft supplies.

Pushing the tiny tube into his hand, she said, "Be careful. It's superglue."

68

C age stood in the shower, letting the water slide over him, impressed at the way the super glue held his leg together. The cut was much smaller than he'd originally thought it was. *Good.*

It appeared the tip of the blade had just poked him, maybe half an inch deep. It did exactly what a stiletto was designed to do, slide in easily. Luckily, Joule had pulled back before it went in even further, but it still hurt like a motherfucker.

The hunters had not made it inside the house. For that, he was supremely grateful. Less cleanup, no need to sleep in the attic again. The big canines had broken several of the tiny panes of glass in the window but had not been able to push the door open.

It seemed they'd given up. Cage began wondering if that was because of the Warfarin in their systems. Joule had mentioned that this morning, and he could only agree. The hunters weren't quite acting up to snuff. Some had wobbled when walking, and even the bigger, steadier ones had not been quite as ready to attack—as though they knew something was wrong inside them.

They hadn't even dragged the body of their slain pack mate away.

Once he and Joule were clean, they would go pick it up. His intent was to throw it into the freezer and forget about it for a while. He couldn't deal with another autopsy right now. Maybe Dr. Brett would want this one...

Cage thought through the matters at hand. He would need to bandage his leg. He wasn't sure it needed it, but he didn't want the super glue to pull open, either.

A moment later, he emerged from the shower and into the steamy bathroom. That part at least felt normal, and he could entertain a fantasy that it was still last year and the neighbor's dog still barked too early on Saturday mornings and his parents would be downstairs when he went.

But it wasn't a year ago. He hadn't lingered in the hot shower, but had cleaned up quickly because of the wound. Joule would be standing just outside, still covered in carbon black powder *and blood*.

Wrapping himself in his favorite fluffy towel, he pulled the door open. He intended to say, "It's your turn." But one look at his still-filthy sister and what came out of his mouth was, "You look like Stephen King's *Carrie*."

One corner of her lip pulled up. "I look like Carrie met Cujo."

He laughed for the first time in a while, and he couldn't decide if it felt good or weird.

"I called Dr. Brett," she said, breaking the moment of light mood. "I asked him about the super glue and about the shoe polish."

She drew out the last couple words, indicating how bad she felt about it. But Cage was shaking his head. "Don't worry. That could have gone either way. And if I had nicked you with the dagger or the short sword... well, it would have been much worse."

Her nod said she agreed, but her expression wasn't quite there yet. "He said not to worry about it but to watch it. Since we super glued it together—which was a good thing—it's not wise to open it back up. He gave me instructions, but he also said he'll come by later with antibiotics for you."

Cage motioned for her to head into the shower she so desperately needed. They'd both taken out the black-wash contact lenses, but she still looked like something from a horror movie. The door clicked shut behind her and Cage turned his attention to bandaging the glued wound. Hopefully, with the antibiotics, it would be okay. Surely the vet wouldn't give them to him unless they were safe, but he wasn't up for explaining a stiletto puncture at a walk-in clinic.

When she was clean, and looked like his sister again, Joule apologized once more and made him breakfast. They watched cartoons as though they were ten again.

"You're inside until that heals." She motioned toward his leg between bites of pancakes and sausage. "Which means both of us are."

They made mac and cheese for lunch and wound up feeding the vet when he stopped by. Cage thought it might be in part to show the doctor they could take care of themselves—puncture wound notwithstanding.

"This is good mac and cheese. Better than mine." Dr. Brett ate everything Cage had hoped to have as leftovers. But it was a small price for a medical visit and a bottle of the right antibiotics.

"You did a good field medic dressing. Totally acceptable and excellent under the circumstances," the vet told him before leaving him with the amoxicillin, instructions on dosage, and a reminder to not worry.

They packed up the dead hunter and loaded it into the back of Dr. Brett's truck and waved good-bye. As they entered the game room, Joule spotted the blinking light on the answering machine. They'd maintained the home line to have 9-1-1 access but had permanently turned it to silent more than a year ago. Occasionally, messages came through that were actually something of value. Though Joule was hitting her way through most of the charity calls and spam by jabbing the delete button, one message stopped her.

"Cage." She turned to him, suddenly quiet. He stepped up to listen as his grandmother's voice came over the digital recording. She was simply checking in wanting to know how they were doing.

He looked to his sister then. The fluffy, light-hearted afternoon dissolved around them. He'd managed to ignore the wound in his leg and the black streaks that remained around his sister's ears and had somehow wound up on her toes. He took the first dose of amoxicillin without thinking about how he needed it because he'd been running from a pack of wild canines that would readily rip him limb from limb and had probably done exactly that to his father.

But his grandmother's voice, calling to ask about the kids, was too much. She was clearly leaving the message for their father.

"I'm glad we didn't pick up." Joule's voice was low and Cage didn't say anything in return.

If Grandma Mazur had talked to them, she would have wanted to know about her son. And there was nothing to tell. There was no point in letting the woman grieve his loss when they weren't fully positive yet that he was lost.

Joule jabbed the button once more, quelling the blinking light and erasing the message—as though, if it wasn't there, they wouldn't have to deal with telling their grandparents.

The twins split up then, going to two different sides of the house. Cage spent the rest of the daylight playing online video games with whoever showed up. Joule took her tablet into the living room and draped herself sideways in one of the big, comfy chairs and drew. He wasn't sure how long it had been since she'd added to her portfolio, but he didn't ask. They stayed on separate ends of the house until dinner time.

Telling himself that the carrots he'd eaten as an afternoon snack sufficed as a solid dose of vegetables, he decided to order a pizza. While they waited, they boarded up the small, broken windows in the door downstairs, although they kept the chair shoved under the knobs.

That night, they slept safe and clean in the bedroom. On real beds. With air conditioning.

Cage slept in hard the next day, waking to find Joule already having gotten up and eaten. Her guilt was gone or she was hiding it—he'd had to make his own breakfast—and he stayed quiet and numb most of the day. But over dinner, Joule asked how he was doing and Cage had to say *much better*.

He'd been taking the antibiotics. His leg didn't hurt at all, really. There were no signs of infection—and he knew what to look for, thanks to the vet—and he was keeping it bandaged.

"It's time to go back out, isn't it?" he asked.

69

J oule's backpack was heavy. Though she didn't complain, it was hard to keep her footsteps light, to keep from snapping twigs and crunching everything she stepped on when she was lugging a backpack worthy of an army recruit.

She figured she'd qualify for some kind of creepy Army Rangers or zombie Navy SEAL status by the time this was through. But now she thought of their situation as something they would get through.

The alternative was that they didn't completely destroy the hunters. Joule could foresee a day when man-eating canines were all over North America if the job wasn't finished now. Humans had always played God with the environment. It's why the hunters were here now. Man had fucked up. She and her brother were going to remedy that, or probably die trying.

In the heavy backpack, she carried meat. Once again it was sliced and stuffed with pellets of rat poison. She'd shoved in as much as she could. This time, though, they tied the steaks shut with cotton twine, not caring if the hunters ate it or not, as long as it kept the poison inside. The fewer creatures that got poisoned, besides the night hunters, the better.

This time, she and Cage each also carried a folding shovel. They did not carry the tools to fix the trough. When they had returned to check on it last time, the trough had been intact. Though a few of the corners were chewed here and there, it had done its job and stayed in mostly one shape.

Tonight, their job was to refill it and watch.

With the hunters' poor sense of smell, she and her brother were counting on double-bagged meats. It wouldn't do to be detected as the carriers of a moveable feast.

At the trough, Joule visually swept the area with her bow pulled tight. Though she'd carried it loosely until here, this was where the fuckers kept popping up. She would not be taken unaware again.

But no hunters appeared, and after several minutes of standing guard, they opened the packs. Dumping the meat into the trough as quickly as they could, they sealed the plastic quickly into a clean bag to mask the smell and shoved it into Cage's backpack. They had been too-well trained to not litter, and she wasn't sure if the poison would linger on the plastic and hurt another creature. With the packs zipped and weapons in hand again, they made themselves as scarce as possible.

In tight whispers, Joule motioned to her brother. One of their trees with the built in ladder was nearby. They hadn't used the ladders, not even once. But that was because they hadn't let themselves get caught without a weapon or a fast path home again.

"Let's go up!" She pointed and watched as her brother caught on.

She sent Cage up first and followed behind him. He didn't waver and his leg seemed to be healing, but she wasn't ready to take a chance—not more than they already had by coming out tonight. But if the hunters required more poison, re-dosing them as soon as possible would kill them faster and dramatically lower the chances of some of them becoming immune to it.

As he sat in the crook of a branch above her head, Cage slowly raised the ladder rungs behind her. It hadn't been planned this way. They hadn't discussed the location of the ladder when they'd decided where to put the trough, only that the trough should be near where the trackers had pinpointed the hunters.

This tree had been chosen because it was roughly the center of the woods, in case someone needed an escape. The location wasn't perfect. In fact, it left their view of the trough hidden behind a great trunk in between them and where the night hunter burrow was. But sitting in the tree was better than crouching on the ground, and better than waiting for a hunter to come up behind them.

For several hours, they sat quietly as nothing happened. They couldn't eat, or talk, or even move in case it drew attention to them, and her mind wandered. Had they missed the hunters? Maybe the burrow had cleared out earlier and they were out hunting. The canines would return before morning. But Joule was glad she and Cage were up high—if the hunters were out, the whole pack would come up from the opposite direction of the one they were watching.

What if they were already dead? If the poison worked as well as Dr. Brett said it did, that might be the case. That would mean all the hunters in the pack had eaten an adequate amount to die from internal bleeding. But it was a possibility. She was still glad to sit in the tree and not see anything.

If one of the animals looked up, they'd likely only see the twins as little blobs. In their black clothes and freshly applied carbon black powder, they were dark as pitch. Still she was trying not to fall asleep, but also not to move. Joule waited.

When she saw the first hunter, her eyes almost flew wide. It came straight out of the ground, pushing up leaves, snout and front paws emerging first, almost as though the earth had birthed a hell beast.

Turning to her brother, she pointed, and then wondered if Cage could even see her. But he nodded. Perhaps the carbon black was good, but wearing it all over themselves was not quite as good as fully erasing themselves from the night.

They knew now where the hunters' burrow was, which was exactly what she'd hoped to learn. Mentally marking the location, she watched as the hunter sluggishly headed toward the trough. The pile of meat had sat untouched all this time and she wondered, were they all on their last legs? This one wasn't moving well.

Maybe he was just tired. Or maybe he was dying. She could only hope.

Another hunter emerged from another location. It surprised her. She'd expected the pack to share one sleeping place, though the points were close. Again, she was leaning to her brother when, this time, Cage slowly pointed for her to follow. A third one had appeared from behind a tree. But she couldn't be sure from exactly where. She had to calculate at least two burrows.

The second had moved behind a clump of trees and she lost sight of him. Was there a third? Did they sleep individually? She didn't know, but that was why they'd brought shovels.

They sat in the tree the remainder of the night. The difficulty lay in staying awake while nothing happened. Only the three hunters had appeared early. They'd eaten some of the meat and then woozily headed back underground.

It was wild watching them. Possibly she could have seen more in the light and it would have made more sense. But in the dark, it appeared as though the first one just pushed his nose into the leaves and sticks covering the ground and bored his way down into the earth—a hellbeast for sure.

When the sun had risen and was at last solidly shining into the woods, she and Cage turned to each other and decided it was time to head down. Slowly, she lowered the ladder, Cage once again going first. She still saw no issues with his leg, no limp or anything, and she felt better.

Without speaking, they headed together to the location where they had seen the first dog go underground. They were going to dig him up. And if it was possible, they would kill it. If there was an entire pack there, they would kill them all.

Those were the better options. There was also the possibility it was a tunnel to another place, a warren system further back that was hard to reach. She had no idea if they worked like gophers, tunneling whole systems underground, or like rabbits, which dug a shallow hole and hid almost in plain sight. They might be like ants, with an entire underground colony. She didn't know.

Moving the leaves aside, they found the opening the dog had gone into and used their shovels to pry the whole wider and wider. One of them would dig for a few minutes and then they'd trade places. Whichever of them wasn't the digger was watching the surrounding landscape for pop-ups. Though she hoped that the all the hunters were disabled, it wasn't anything they could count on.

At last, she heard Cage behind her. "Joule, look."

Turning, she saw that her brother, who had done extra work on this last dig, had uncovered an entire hunter. "Looks like the one we saw last night."

Though she waited for the creature to spring, he didn't move. His open eyes were glassy, his mouth ajar, and he made no move to attack them or even get up. She watched his ribs, noting that he didn't breathe.

Good.

Her eyes were drawn to the dirt Cage was turning over, and she did a quick check of her surroundings before looking down again. This time her brother revealed another hunter curled up next to the first. This one didn't budge, as the burrow was slowly peeled the way around her.

Joule had no idea why she thought this one was female. In her brain the first was a *him* and this was a *her*. Cage continued the heavy work of peeling dirt away.

"Do you want me to do it?" she asked, snapping out her shovel.

He stepped back, turning and scanning the area while Joule now dug in. The tool was lightweight and lacked a good force for digging and lifting, but she slowly uncovered four night hunters. The only one alive was the one she'd dubbed a female. It panted in slow, shallow breaths and looked up toward them, but its eyes never focused.

"Cage." Joule tapped his arm, drawing his attention. Though the brindle fur was pretty, and though she very much resembled a family pet at first glance, Joule could see the differences. The head was too wide, the jaw thick and scary. The fur was slick for burrowing and thick for dampening light reflection at night. She saw the added reflective gleam in the eyes— an evil look, if ever there was one.

This was no pet. It was a killer.

"Do you want to do it?"

Turning, he looked at her. "If we do this, it's the last thing we do. We'll have to leave right away. We can't check the other burrow, since this will make too much noise."

But Joule nodded. *Three down, one to go.*

This one didn't have the energy to move. "We can leave her, let her die on her own."

"What if she recovers?"

The words brought a flash of memory and Joule could see the hunter walking by in the woods, not seeing them. It had been slightly smaller, brindle like this one, and a swath of chain mail had hung from its mouth.

Looking at her brother then, Joule said, "Do it."

With a nod, he pulled the gun from its holster and put the creature out of her misery.

The retort rang through her ears, even though she'd covered them with her hands. Shaking her head to loosen the reverberation from her skull, Joule looked around, checking for anything the loud noise might have alerted. But she saw nothing.

Quickly, they headed back toward the house, shovels still in hand. She'd slung the bow over her shoulder again, and was holding one stiletto. The shovel had a sharp enough edge that she counted it as a second weapon at the ready.

They were maybe halfway back when she heard the tiny yip behind them.

Startled, Joule spun around. They'd been looking! Nothing had been behind them on the trail. Whatever this was, it had come up fast.

Whipping around, she spotted it.

Sitting in the path where they had just walked sat a puppy.

70

Cage stared at the pup, blinking as the tiny thing stared back at him, its little head tilted side to side.

It had wide puppy eyes and huge paws. The fur bordered on fuzzy and Cage bordered on wanting to take it home and feed it milkbones. It was almost adorable.

"Are you shitting me?" Joule said into the general open air of the woods, her voice no longer quiet, her tone angry.

He understood. It wasn't about him; it was about the baby on the path. No one wanted to deal with a *puppy*. But Dr. Brett had warned them this was the breeding season.

The little guy looked about eight weeks old. But what did Cage know about night hunter development? In fact, what did *anybody* know about night hunter development? This one could be anywhere from several weeks to several months along.

Cage still hadn't said anything. He felt Joule tap at his wrist with the back of her hand. She still hadn't taken her eyes off the creature, and it alternated looking between the two of them. The carbon powder was only partly effective in the daylight.

"Do you think it's a regular puppy?" Joule whispered, as though the thing might be offended by the term.

His eyes flicked sideways to her, then to the tiny, fuzzy creature sitting in the middle of the path facing them. "You mean like a *dog* puppy," he clarified. "As in *not* a night hunter."

"Right."

Here he heard the wishful tone that ran under the hard steel in her voice. Though she was trying to keep her words harsh, the *want* peeked out. She wanted to pick up the puppy. She wanted to pet it.

Both of them loved pets. Over the years, their parents had indulged them with aquarium frogs, then newts, and in the middle of elementary school, they'd gotten kittens—a pair of little fuzzy things.

The twins had played with the kittens for hours, even though Joule was slightly allergic. Cage also tried several times to smuggle the kitten to school, tucked inside his puffy coat. His mother had always caught him.

And once, when he and Joule had learned about static and sticking balloons to the walls, their mother had come in and found them rubbing the kittens against the couch cushions. It seemed the kittens could hold a charge this way, too, becoming staticky and fluffy. The problem came when the twins then tried to use the charge to stick the kittens to the walls. Needless to say, it hadn't worked, and had led to a second discussion about static electricity and the usually greater force of gravity.

Those kittens had become fluffy, snuggly cats who had died of old age about two years ago. Cage was glad that he didn't have to wonder if the hunters had gotten Samson and Delilah, too.

Both the twins loved animals. So a puppy was not a stretch.

"When was the last time you saw an actual pet dog?" he asked her.

"You're right," she replied, because the answer was well over a year ago.

"It's also the woods," he told her. His point being—and

Joule had gotten it—that no pet dog, and certainly no puppy, could have survived this area. This was night hunter territory. They would protect their own, but other species didn't stand a chance.

"You're right," Joule replied again.

A silence settled between them then, and they stared at the tiny creature for a minute, trying to decide what to do, until it offered a whine.

"Fuck," she bit out the word. "He's hungry."

Cage understood her irritation. He felt it himself. Baby animals had a way of reaching into your hard-wiring and making you want to take care of them. Joule had no special love for human babies, but animal babies did her in. Clearly, this one was no exception.

"He'll be a killer," he added. "They grow up. It's inevitable. They killed our mother and... our father, you know." It was so hard saying it out loud, but the chain mail had been hard to refute.

There was no way Nate was still alive without his mail. And there was no way Nate was still alive without coming home and checking on his kids. If there was one thing Cage knew, it was that Nate and Kaya Mazur hadn't loved anything in this world more than their kids—except maybe each other.

"Can you shoot it?" Joule's voice broke into his thoughts, and then she immediately clarified her point. "Quick and painless. It's the most humane option."

"God, *no!*" He couldn't stop the words or the revulsion that came out of his mouth. Shooting the night hunter in its den had been hard enough. That one was full grown and mostly dead. That one looked like the one he'd seen carrying the chain mail. And it had *still* hurt to pull the trigger.

He'd only been able to do it when he pictured his mother's slain form lying on the game room floor. He could not shoot a puppy—no matter what it would someday become.

"It's daylight," she offered. But as he watched, she slipped her backpack off her shoulders and pulled out her cell phone. They waited, watching the tiny creature while she powered it up and dialed. "Hello, this is Joule Mazur. I'd like to speak to Dr. Brett—Dr. Christian." She corrected herself. Cage guessed he only went by his first name with the high school students.

It was a few minutes and a good handful of "uh-huh"s later that she hung up. "If we bag it, it will smother." She referred to the trashbags that they carried rolled up in the bottom of their backpacks. "We can conk it on the head and knock it out. But if we carry it with us, we will have taken one of their babies. Dr. Brett made it clear that taking their baby is a good way to make them very angry at us. They'll almost definitely follow it and fight for it. So that's probably the worst thing we could do. If we feed it, we are training it to interact with humans."

Well, shit, he thought, *this was going nowhere good*.

It seemed the only reasonable thing left was to shoot it— and yet he couldn't do it. "Can we feed it poison?" he asked.

That way he would know it wouldn't grow up to be a killer, because it wouldn't grow up to be anything. But he wouldn't have to pull the trigger.

Joule played out his offered scenario. "That requires picking it up, carrying it back into the woods—which we just, finally, are getting out of—" she gestured toward home, "and feeding it the meat. Which we strategically placed at the entry to the hunters' burrow. So if any are still alive, they'll be there."

Yup. That was a crappy plan, too.

He nodded at the little hunter, but spoke to his sister. "Let's not do that."

"We have to leave it." She sighed. "I can't just bash it with the shovel. I don't have that in me." She didn't ask him to do it either, and for that he was grateful.

They turned and walked away. The small thing followed them for some time. But as they crossed the creek into the back yard and the bright light of day, Cage was glad to see it was no longer behind them.

As they opened the side door into the game room, Joule turned to her brother, sadness in her voice and a wish for a proper pet lacing through underneath. "It's going to starve to death, you know."

71

C age traipsed the woods again. They'd been doing this every night this week.

Joule said they looked like zombies in their black clothing and carbon black powder. But he felt like a vampire, sleeping all day, out in the woods all night, hunting things, even though hunting was not in his general nature.

He was grateful that the last three nights they'd seen no night hunters. Though they had brought meat stuffed with rat poison, they'd ended up taking it back home with them. They'd not needed to refill the trough.

They'd stood to the side of the still-full basket, Joule bringing the back of her wrist to her nose as if to block the smell. It would have left black marks all over her face, if she hadn't already been covered in the powder.

"It's starting to smell," she said from behind her wrist, which was surely doing nothing for the odor. "Do we need to clean it up? Are the scavengers going to come for it?"

He hadn't thought about it, but vultures might come down and pick at it once it reached a certain level of ripeness. They would ingest the poison if they ate from this pile of meat. "I guess so. Does it look like it's been touched since last night?"

She shook her head, and then made a full three-sixty degree turn, as she checked the woods.

Shit, he thought. *They'd gotten lax.* They'd seen no night hunters for three whole nights. They dug another hole, pulling up the second burrow. They found all the hunters within that dugout were already dead, including six pups.

He'd bagged three of them. Separately, of course. He'd carried two, and Joule had carried one. They'd met with Dr. Brett and handed off the puppy corpses. That was incredibly disturbing, he'd thought, but he had a scientific mind. The creatures were already gone. He couldn't bring them back. Letting them be studied for science made all the rest of this more worthwhile.

Even Joule, who often was logical to a fault, muttered as she stuffed the bag down into her backpack. "Oh yeah, this isn't morbid as fuck."

He'd laughed and then remembered to check his surroundings.

Tonight, they weren't carrying corpses. Tonight, they left the rest where they'd found them. Tonight, they opened up bags and shoved the meat down into it. Trash bags didn't zip shut, so they'd double- and triple-bagged it, tying the tops off tightly.

"I think we have to take it to the dump," Joule told him. "I mean, if we put it in the trashcans at the side of the house, we're just baiting everything to there. Raccoons, vultures, all the scavengers—and whatever eats it will die. It has to go."

Once inside, they set the bagged meat on the tile floor. He could smell it, even with the job they'd done trying to mask it. Surely, the night hunters could, too. Maybe they only ate their meat fresh, and that was why this was untouched. Maybe they had figured out it was poisoned, and they were staying away.

But then, why weren't they out? The night cameras had not revealed the pack roaming in the dark any more.

The man in the street with the broadsword still patrolled, but for the past few nights, he'd had nothing to fight. He wandered aimlessly now, broadsword double-clenched in his fists, taking practice swings. Mostly, he seemed to watch, but the last nights had been blessedly boring.

The twins took turns showering the black powder away. They dressed like teenagers in jeans and t-shirts and threw the decaying meat into the trunk of the car. Cage pulled out a can of air freshener and sprayed the trunk within an inch of its life once they'd dropped off their stinky cargo.

They stopped for fast food and sodas on the way home.

That night, as Joule pulled the curtains shut, she turned to him and asked, "Are we done?"

But when he watched the videos from the night cameras the next morning, he saw the man out in the street again. He'd was taking a route that was becoming his normal patrol, walking up and down the street, always swinging the hefty sword. There had been no night hunters, no fights. The street was quiet, and Cage wondered—would his neighbors start getting dogs and cats again?

But somewhere around four in the morning—according to the timestamp on the video—the man walking patrol was attacked from behind. A pack of nine or ten night hunters managed to sneak up on him. From his reaction, or lack thereof, he hadn't heard them at all. They didn't surround him the way the pack had the night Nate and the twins had gone out.

Instead, they'd crept up as a unit, all from the same direction, all jumping in concert. In seconds, they leapt on him and took him down. In minutes, they had carried off the pieces.

Cage sat stunned and forced himself to watch the video a second time, just to be sure he'd actually seen it. Finishing, he paused before running it again. He was startled to find his sister had appeared over his shoulder and was watching it, too.

"Uh-oh," she said softly, but the sound was a hurricane of feeling. She mixed regret, sadness, guilt, fear, and more into those two syllables. "I think this is our fault. Because that's not our pack. We took out *our* night hunters. We did what we meant to do, but instead we made things so much worse."

72

J oule couldn't help but stare at the video. She spoke into the air, though the words were directed at Cage. "I thought we were done. I thought we had it figured out."

"I did, too." Cage slowly closed the screen on his laptop and turned and looked at her. "What do we do now?"

"I don't even know." She shrugged her shoulders, shook her head, and felt her eyes glaze over. "I thought we did something good, but what we really did was cleared the way for a worse pack to come in."

"Is there a *worse pack*?" Cage asked, now getting philosophical. "The ones we had ate several of our neighbors."

He had a valid point. "But they didn't eat the guy with the broad sword. He managed to hold them off. It appeared he took a few of the hunters out." She thought it through. The guy with the broadsword was now dead, too. She'd seen it on the video, no denying it. "But these guys got him. So I guess yeah, they are worse."

Her brother stared into the middle distance as he thought. He was making plans; she could tell. She hadn't quite gotten there yet, still just dealing with being stunned by what she'd seen.

After a few minutes in which neither of them said anything, Joule announced, "I'm tired. I think I'm going to go to bed."

It was broad daylight, still morning, her hair still drying after her merely passable attempt to wash the carbon powder out of it. Despite the hat, her hair still had a dulled look, and so did Cage's. She was tired and thought about her brother insisting they had become vampires. She missed the sunshine. The summer days were gorgeous, but she was sleeping through them.

And now they had a new pack of hunters to find—one that was far more deadly.

"I won't be far behind you," Cage said, but his focus was back on the laptop. He opened the screen again and began hitting keys. Though she was curious, she was more exhausted and Joule headed upstairs.

She'd gotten used to falling asleep with the daylight streaming in around her. And she fell quickly, deeply asleep. But it wasn't comfortable.

Joule dreamed of running in the back door. Of the night hunter leaping at her. In her dream, she stabbed repeatedly with her stiletto. Though in real life, it had been only once—in her memory and in the evidence when they let Dr. Brett carry the dead hunter away.

But in her dream, she slashed, and stabbed, and cut, but her assailant didn't fall.

The hunter didn't back off. It didn't bleed out or have its muscles go slack. As with dreams, the scenes faded, one into another. She hacked and fought and blinked, and she was suddenly somewhere totally different, but her dream brain accepted it. It wasn't jarring, but a bit like changing the channel.

This time, she stood alone on the path in the woods.

Looking down, she found herself staring at a puppy. In a moment, it was joined by another puppy, and another. Then another. The scene would have made a wonderful internet meme, or a gif, except for the fact that these weren't puppies. Joule knew what these were.

Looking up, she spotted Cage sitting on the rooftop of their house. Though the form was merely an outline of her brother, all covered in carbon black powder, she still recognized him. Sitting at the top of the roofline was odd. They'd never done that and never discussed doing it, at least not as far as she remembered. But Dream-Joule accepted that he was there.

He held the bow and arrow that he had originally gotten for Christmas the year his parents had decided to weaponize their teenagers. Kaya and Nate Mazur had probably thought of the bows and arrows as a cool physics lesson. Cage and Joule had thought of them as the ultimate—and much more dangerous—Nerf gun. Though Cage had eventually grown bored with his toy, Joule had not. She'd practiced. So while she was the better shot and she knew it, he was now aiming at *her*.

"No!" she yelled, "No!" as her brother pulled back on the bow string and let fly.

Twisting awake, she threw off the covers as she gasped for breath in the bright sun of the bedroom.

Groggily, Cage sat upright in the other bed. He tossed aside his own covers as easily as she had twisted into hers. "Are you all right?"

"No?" She shook her head. She was awake. Her brother wasn't sitting on the rooftop trying to pick her off with her own chosen weapon. She explained the dream briefly, and then added, "That sucks. That sucks monkey balls."

"Well," he said, "if you can swear creatively, you're probably not that traumatized."

Joule had to admit he wasn't wrong. The dream had been

no more traumatizing than her real life had been recently. "What time is it?"

"A little after four. Want to get up?"

She nodded; she certainly didn't want to go back to sleep. It didn't seem to be doing her any good. She'd been asleep for far longer than the dreams had taken time to occur. But in her memory, she passed out cold, she went through hell, and then woke back up. She felt as though she'd gotten maybe an hour of rest at most, but the whole day had passed.

His feet now swung down, bare toes digging into the carpet.

Cage looked at her, the expression pulling his brows together telling her he hadn't yet come to terms with the new—deadlier—pack. "What do we do now?"

They couldn't go out and hunt the pack the way they had before. At least, she didn't think so. The new pack? Well, they didn't even know where it was.

Images flashed through her mind of the dreams she'd just wrenched herself from. As hideous as they had been, maybe they were good for something.

"I think I have an idea."

73

J oule was once again covered in the black carbon powder and blending into the night. She sat on the biggest branch of the study tree in the front yard. If the branch broke, she was fucked.

But there was only one Y where the trunk split. Because that was the sturdiest position, she'd given that spot to Cage. Her brother was slightly heavier than she was, so she had taken the branch.

He was safer. She was more comfortable.

She didn't really worry about the branch breaking, because if they didn't take care of the problem of the night hunters, they were both going to die.

The two of them had spent the morning climbing the tree, hacksaws in hand. They had crawled out along the strong-looking branches then, and cleared out the dead twigs and smaller branches that would interfere with their shots.

They let the detritus fall to the ground below. Though the intention had been to clear it, they realized the ground cover would make it more difficult for the night hunters to sneak up underneath them. It might even slow them down if Cage and

Joule were spotted up in the tree. So the twins left the kindling where it fell.

Because this was the tree where they had built the first ladder, they had relatively easy up-and-down access. The work had been in cutting and checking, cutting and checking.

Now, they sat here, blending into the night. They had hauled the ladder up behind them and waited. The trough no longer hung in the forest. That night hunter den had been empty for a few days now. There had been no activity; she and Cage had checked.

They'd done the heavy, sweaty work of hauling it out and re-setting it in the center of the cul de sac. The trough now sat on a central stilt—much the way many dinner tables were made—in hopes that smaller animals would not be able to climb underneath, around and up over the side to where this contaminated meat sat.

So far, she'd seen no smaller animals even attempt it. Still, Joule kept her eyes on the contents. Two of the pieces of meat held the remaining two tracking devices, and Joule had already placed an order for more.

They'd spent more of their money on cheap, leftover pieces of steak that the butcher had been willing to sell them at a discount. She was keeping a closer eye on the budget, certain that while her parents wouldn't disapprove, this was not how they'd intended their life insurance money and retirement savings to be spent.

She and Cage hadn't worried about making the bait dance this time, hoping that the food itself would be enough attraction for the new pack. As she sat up here and waited, though, she wondered if that hadn't been a mistake. Still, they had a plan for that, too. If the hunters didn't come tonight, they would rig the table up with the pulleys and make it move.

She was beginning to think that was going to be necessary,

as they hit three, then four, then five hours in and she'd seen nothing.

She wanted to ask Cage what he thought. Clearly, this worse pack had moved into this newly emptied territory. But if they had expanded their own territory—maybe doubled it, for example—they might spend one night in one area and one night and another. They might not have even come close enough to know there was a feast for them here.

As she followed those thoughts, Joule didn't like where they went. The new pack would give birth to more pups if they could defend the larger territory. The pack size would grow with their land size. Given the way this pack fought, that was the last thing Joule wanted.

Her bow sat loosely across her lap. She did have an arrow notched on to the string, and more waited patiently in the quiver she wore across her back. Cage had the gun ready as well as a small crossbow he'd purchased online with overnight shipping and practiced with yesterday in the large backyard.

At four a.m., when her muscles ached and she began to worry that nothing would happen tonight, she saw the shadows appear at the end of the street.

Reaching out, she tapped her brother. He offered only a small, sharp nod in return as they had agreed not to speak and not to move unless it was absolutely necessary. However, some small motions were required. If her legs fell asleep and she fell out of the tree, that was far worse than drawing attention to the tree—a place they at least believed the night hunters couldn't reach.

But what if these new ones could climb trees?

Her heart clenched as the pack of close to ten hunters headed quietly up the street. She'd watched the videos enough now that she recognized the leader with his large, pointy ears, broad shoulders, and thick face. She knew how he attacked and she knew that the others would follow without hesitation, leaping almost as a single, multi-ton unit.

Slowing her breathing—in through her nose and gently out through her mouth—Joule watched as night hunters came up the street toward the trough that now waited in the center of the cul de sac.

She'd been ready to shoot an arrow nearby and scare off a squirrel, raccoon, or possum. But maybe, in putting the trough out in the wide open, those animals were too afraid to even try to snatch any food.

Before, when the hunters had come to the bait, they'd darted between the bushes that lined the front garden. They'd snuck in between the tall grasses at the base of the fence at the edge of the yard. They'd rushed from one hiding spot to another, to the tree, and then to the meat—short bursts of activity that left them in the open but ended quickly with them hidden. This time, that would not be an option. And maybe that was keeping the smaller creatures safe. She could only hope.

Joule watched as the lead hunter trotted up to the trough and took a sniff. The others all hung back, waiting for him to make a decision. She crossed her fingers and prayed to several Gods that it worked.

The social interaction between the creatures was fascinating to watch. Most people never got to see a live wolf pack in action. Maybe on video, or on a wildlife show, but not up close. Even then, one could watch the sharks hunt and root for the sharks. One could watch the wolves or the lions take down far bigger prey by acting as a pack, and a person could easily admire the coordinated effort it all took. Right now, though, Joule couldn't admire any of the pack's maneuvers.

She'd never been the rabbit, the buffalo, or the whale the sharks went after. Not before now.

Joule almost broke their code of silence and hollered out,

Yes! when the lead dog leaned in and picked up a steak. It was a signal to those around him. The others moved, circling the trough and leaning their heads in. Piece by piece, they began to pick up the meat wrapped in cotton twine and stuffed with rat poison—and two lucky winners would get a tracker, too.

She watched as they ate, their very presence keeping away the smaller animals. Hopefully, they would eat everything in the trough. She and Cage had slightly understocked it, trying to be sure the hunters swallowed every last tracker, if possible.

Slowly, the creatures examined each piece, picking it up, chewing on it, and picking it up again. Occasionally, they fought over a morsel. But they had gobbled up most of the rat poison that had fallen to the street when one steak was torn in half from a tussle. Joule made a mental note to clean up the spill as soon as the sun came up—and the light was creeping up ever so slightly down at the end of the street.

All around her, the daylight was tiptoeing in, and she was beginning to wonder why the night hunters hadn't already left.

There was too much sun. The meat was gone. But they lingered, licking at the corners of the trough and sniffing at the edges of her yard. Had she and Cage made a heinous miscalculation? Or did this pack hunt in daylight, too?

Just then, three doors down on the dingy green house, the front door opened. A face she recognized—though she hadn't gotten the name—stood in the open space, cocked a shotgun, and lifted it to her shoulder.

74

Cage watched in horror as the night hunters turned as a group. Their attention was not focused on him or his sister, nor on the food in the trough. They also hadn't focused on leaving because it was daylight. No, they had heard the woman come out her front door.

In his head, Cage referred to her as Bad Neighbor Lady. He was not a fan, but this was not going to be a fitting end.

As the pack turned, trotting toward her, they kicked up their speed, just the way Cage's heart rate did. Turning to Joule, who was already scrambling, he said only, "Down down down!" and pulled the cord on the ladder.

They had modified it, making it faster. *Thank God.* It now zipped open, the final step lingering just eighteen inches off the ground. He rushed halfway down before letting go and jumping into the jumble of cut branches from their earlier work. One of them jammed into his calf, but he ignored it, hoping it was just a scrape and not a case of tetanus.

As he hit, his feet began running down the street, chasing the pack, but it took him only half a second to realize that was one of the dumbest things he could do. He had to wait for his sister. If they didn't have each other's backs, then they were all in danger. Only as a unit did they stand a chance. Even the broadsword man, had not survived because he hunted alone.

Joule almost ran into the back of him as he turned and looked for her. Together, they raced down the street. Cage felt the weight of the gun in his right hand; he was gripping it tighter than he intended, but he didn't know how to relax his hold. With his left hand, he reached along his thigh for the dagger that he'd sheathed there.

He felt like a wild and crazy Indiana Jones, strapped up with weapons and wishing he had a superior skill with a whip. He needed more weapons that worked at a distance. Close fighting with these creatures was too dangerous.

Bad Neighbor Lady yelled something, but the sound was indistinguishable as an English word. It came out somewhere between a growl and a war cry. But it wasn't enough warning for Cage or the hunters.

She fired off the shotgun.

As Cage jerked back with the retort, he noticed the front hunters in the pack shimmied backward a bit with the blast, too. Only, he hoped their movement was from injury, not startle.

Good for her, he thought.

Despite the jerk in his momentum, he kept running. The second blast was what drew him up short, as she was now firing and yelling indiscriminately. If he and Joule got into the fray, Bad Neighbor Lady might be the one who took them out. He was not going to die—not by some idiot's shotgun.

Joule took only a moment to grab his hand and tug him to the side of the house. It made sense; circling around would get them out of the direct line of the blast. So he sidestepped and followed his sister. The move would mean the hunters could see them, but it would also mean that they could fight head on and not be also fighting Bad Neighbor Lady and her shot pellets.

Despite getting into the field of vision of probably several hunters in the pack, none of them came after him or Joule. They aimed instead as a single unit, still focused only on Bad Neighbor Lady.

When they leapt at her, Cage fired his gun three times in rapid succession. He aimed in front of the Bad Neighbor Lady and prayed he didn't hit her. But if he didn't fire the gun, the hunters would definitely get her. There were more of them than her shotgun could hold at bay, and they didn't seem to care that she was trying to kill them.

He watched in almost slow motion as his shots—or hers— made two of them flinch. One dropped, motionless, onto the overgrown yard in front of her, another twitching his shoulder uncontrollably and shimmy-stepping sideways, as though his body no longer worked. He was no longer part of the fray.

The Neighbor Lady stared the hunters in the eyes, almost ignoring his and Joule's approach. Her gray hair, previously up in a puffy headband, now hung straight down around her face. She was clearly in her pajamas and in a rage as she stood at the top of three small steps on her cement front porch.

In the moment that she took to reload and cock the gun, Cage fired two more times, and Joule put several arrows into the hunters on this side of the pack. Still, the canines paid almost no attention to their injuries. The leader, though hit with shotgun blast several times, kept lunging toward the neighbor woman. Each time she fired, he pulled back briefly but then kept coming. Cage believed he had put a bullet into the leader as well, but it didn't seem to be stopping him entirely.

He almost shook his head then. It was daylight, and he could clearly see what was going on. The sun was well and truly up. There was light coming down the street.

The hunters growled, but at last they didn't leap.

For a few moments, they circled the yard in front of the neighbor, all their attention still on her. Then the ones who were still walking gathered and changed direction. Cage almost let out a breath of relief, but he wasn't ready to declare it over yet.

The hunters seemed to make a decision to take the two wounded with them. One, they dragged. The other, they nudged to his feet. Slowly, the remaining five headed off and left three lying dead in the neighbor lady's yard as they headed down the street toward the rising sun.

Cage stayed ready in case they changed their mind at any moment. He watched carefully, the gun still aimed. Behind him, he felt Joule's shoulder blades touch his own as she watched his back for anything coming from the other direction.

Bad Neighbor Lady didn't impress him, but Joule was always on her A-game.

When the hunters finally disappeared from sight, the three humans all stood and waited for another moment before lowering their guns. That was when Cage looked around and realized a few of the people who remained living on the street had opened their doors, too. They were looking at the leftovers from the fight.

It was the neighbor lady who made the first move. Stomping down the steps, she glared at Joule and Cage and demanded, "What in the hell do you think you're doing?"

75

C age felt his head jerk back, and he couldn't stop the snap response that came out of his mouth. "*Me?* You're the idiot who came out on your front doorstep and challenged them."

"You're the one who decided to feed them," she replied, stepping closer, as though she were a threat. He was taller, but she outweighed him and he was beginning to wonder if she had any formal training he had to worry about. He didn't want to make the mistake of thinking she was all bluster.

"That's why I came and complained about your yard! You can't feed them, you moron!"

It was Joule who turned around now and faced the woman. Somehow, she managed to keep her tone even and replied quickly, an attempt to defuse the rising heat of the situation. "We did feed them. We fed them electronic trackers and rat poison."

Cage watched as the woman's whole body moved back slightly, as though the news had physically pushed her. He watched her face as she realized perhaps they were all on the same side.

Something caught his attention to his left. Though he didn't take his eyes off Bad Neighbor Lady, in his peripheral vision he saw a neighbor man. The large man was in his own pajama pants, a thick, fuzzy robe wound tightly around his belly. He held the robe shut, a curious look on his face as he approached the old woman and the two kids covered in black powder.

The Bad Neighbor Lady had moved back, her gun aimed to the ground now, her anger having dissipated with Joule's information. So Cage turned and looked over his shoulder. He saw a woman, who was probably the new man's wife, standing timidly in the doorway, her hand on the knob, as though she was going to duck inside and bolt it if anything threatened.

Cage was opening his mouth again when the neighbor man moved purposefully forward as yet another woman came from another house in between his and the Bad Neighbor Lady's.

It was the man who spoke. "My name is Steve. What is your name?"

His tone and cadence was even and forceful, brooking no argument. He controlled the conversation now, something for which Cage was momentarily grateful. But he would have to wait and see how this went.

"My name is Cage. This is my twin sister, Joule." He didn't spell anything, and he didn't explain. He answered only what he had been asked.

Steve then turned to the woman, who was now standing in the grass in front of her porch, shotgun hanging loosely from one hand. She looked much less threatening now. "What is your name?"

"Susan," she replied.

Steve's face was wide and kind. Brown eyes and dark brown skin warm in the aftermath of a fight. He at last turned to the new woman who'd just entered the group. Without being asked, she volunteered. "My name is Kayla Reeves-Lopez. My wife, Ivy, and I live in the blue house."

She didn't point at the house, though Cage could clearly see it. She stood with her hands at her side, carefully watching the other members of the little group.

Cage watched and took notes. Each person in the circle seemed to have an attitude about the night hunters. Kayla Reeves-Lopez had volunteered her whole name and her wife's and stood with her hands on her side. No weapons. Was she aware how dangerous the hunters were?

It was Steve who turned back to Cage and Joule. "I've seen the things you had in your yard. Can you explain?"

At least, for that, Cage was grateful. The question was neutral, not accusatory like Susan's. He nodded. "My sister and I have been poisoning and baiting the night hunters."

"Night hunters?" Kayla asked, stepping closer to the circle now.

"That's what we call them."

"They're dogs?" Kayla asked again.

"No, actually." Joule stepped in and looked around the group. Cage could see her glancing at him, silently asking for permission to tell what they knew. He offered a short nod.

"They are canines, but they're not dogs. They're different from wolves and coyotes, as far as we know. We sent some samples off for genetic testing—for proof—but we're confident it will come back as a new species."

He watched as all three neighbors' eyes went wide. Another person joined them from the left. Smiling all the way to her eyes—which were almost violet in color—she said, "My name is Ivy Reeves-Lopez. And you're telling us this isn't just angry dogs but actually a new species?"

Joule nodded. The Mazur twins might be the youngest in the crowd, but they were the most heavily armed, and they were still covered in carbon black. In Cage's mind, they were the only ones who really knew what they were doing.

"That aside, you're baiting them and tracking them."

Both the twins nodded again.

This was going to go down. Cage didn't know how it was going to end. But he was getting questioned. He was seventeen-and-a-half years old, living on his own with no parents, and trying to explain to the neighbors what he and his sister had done.

It hadn't occurred to them that this was what would get them caught. He answered questions and tried not to hold his breath.

He knew the way this conversation played out would change everything.

76

J oule gave the neighbors only the barest of information of what she and Cage had figured out about the night hunters. Though she mentioned the veterinarian for reference, she did not mention Dr. Brett Christian's name.

She told them about the trackers and the fact that the night hunters slept in burrows during the day. She told them about the fur and their jaws and the ability to appear quietly behind a person in the daytime, seemingly out of nowhere, because of their giant, padded feet.

She told them that she and Cage had killed the old pack, but held back that it was their fault that this new, harsher pack had moved in. If they put those pieces together for themselves, then they could have it, but she wasn't going to hang her guilty feelings on the front fence for everyone.

Susan was the one who looked at them with pride. Steve looked at them as though they were mad. Kayla and Ivy had begun to get a little gleam in their eyes. And it was Ivy who asked, "How can we help?"

Joule almost felt her heart stop. It had never occurred to her that the neighbors would *help*. Her mouth opened like a fish, but no words came out. Before she could even shut it, Susan said, "If we're killing them, I want in. Those assholes murdered my son."

It was Cage who found his voice first. "Was he the one out at night with the broadsword?"

Susan nodded and Joule noticed that the woman had tears running down her face. The loss was fresh, and she wasn't handling it well. Probably why she'd come out with her shotgun in the first place.

Susan made a lot more sense now. Her son was going out fighting the hunters at night, and she'd thought Cage and Joule were feeding them like pets. At least everyone was getting straightened out now.

"What's on you?" Kayla asked, and Joule was able to answer, explaining about the carbon black powder.

"It absorbs light, making us almost disappear in the darkness at night. These animals don't have a good sense of smell, but they see and hear well." Luckily, the question had been about something she understood. The neighbors were throwing her for a loop and she was struggling to get her brain wrapped around it.

Joule had no idea how it had really happened, but she suddenly found herself on a *team* of more than just herself and Cage. These were people she didn't know. People she didn't trust. But people that she now had to.

"So," Steve said, bringing the conversation back around. *He must be in management*, was all Joule could think. "You fed them rat poison and a tracker today?" He pointed down the street in the direction the pack had left.

She nodded.

"Then what do we do next?"

"We sleep." She said it knowing it wasn't the answer any of them expected. "Well," she picked at her shirt, "We shower first, then sleep... and this afternoon—when we have several hours of daylight—we try to find them."

Cage stepped in then. "We know they went that direction." He pointed down the street, the same direction Steve had. "But after that, we don't know."

"How do you track them?" Kayla asked, her cadence a little clipped. Joule explained the device they had that read frequencies.

"What frequencies?" Kayla asked.

Joule shrugged. "I don't know." She hadn't thought about it. She'd ordered the tracking devices and the frequency meter. It had worked; she hadn't had time to examine it further.

"It's probably radio frequency," a neighbor said. He was looking into the distance, blue-grey eyes lost in thought.

"The problem is, we have to get close enough to pick up the signal," Joule explained.

Though everyone else was paying attention, Kayla was not.

"So we wander around for a little while," Joule continued. "It may take us a few days to figure out where they're sleeping."

Kayla shook her head. "No. We can find them right away with a wider-range device."

Ivy looked to her partner. "Can you do it?"

Kayla nodded, as though it were just that simple.

Joule looked to Cage, wondering if she could be right, and found he was looking at her with an expression that probably mirrored her own.

"When should we meet back here?" Ivy asked.

"We were going to head out at about one," Joule said, realizing their trip had been hijacked by well-meaning neighbors. But that didn't mean it was the wrong thing to do.

"I'll bring a meter to find the frequency," Kayla said, still not really looking at them. "I'll be able to dial the frequencies, so if we can figure which one it's broadcasting on, I can find it."

Interesting. This Kayla sounded confident. It was Ivy who

looked at the twins as though she had figured out that Steve might be controlling the conversation, but the young twins should be controlling the hunt. "She can do it."

"We should drive." Kayla pushed into the conversation again. "Cover more territory. If I make three signal receivers, can we split into three groups? Ivy and me. You two." She pointed to Cage and Joule. "And you two." This time she pointed to Steve and Susan—the most unlikely couple.

But they turned to each other, shrugged, and agreed.

"One o'clock. Right here. I'll hand out the receivers."

It was Susan, then, who changed the conversation. She looked to Cage and Joule. While it wasn't an apology, she said, "I thought you were feeding them like people used to feed the deer, or like pets."

"No, ma'am," Joule replied, figuring etiquette was the better part of valor here.

Susan offered no response to that, as though she'd said her piece and any apology or need to acknowledge her error was done.

It was Steve who said then, "When we find them, what do we do?"

Though Joule opened her mouth to reply, it was Susan who said, "We kill the fuckers."

77

C age drove around the neighborhood, taking the turns hand over hand, while Joule sat beside him. She'd put the windows down and held the new receiver made by the neighbor Kayla in her lap.

So far, it hadn't made any noises.

It was well after two in the afternoon and the group was late getting started, though Cage thought it was for a good reason.

Kayla had handed out her souped-up receivers—apparently having spent her morning retrofitting some old hand-held radios she had.

But she insisted on testing them first, which Cage and Joule thought was wise. There were no remaining loose trackers to toss into the yard and go find. The only one with a known location was at the burrow of the pack they had killed. So the entire group headed into the woods, Joule with her bow and arrow leading the way. Cage held the back with his dagger in hand. No one questioned that there were kids at either end of the line ready to fight, except maybe Cage.

Kayla, walking forward with the new receivers, quickly

A.J. SCUDIERE

picked up the signal and demonstrated for everyone what noise they made and how they relayed not only near/far information —like the old receiver—but also direction. She tested all three and got a positive signal. Kayla's new tech had gone off almost at the edge of their yard, indicating she had devised a way to detect the tracker with a much, much better range than the twins had before.

Thus, they hadn't even needed to go all the way into the woods for the test, so at least it had been a short trip. It beat the hell out of the way Cage and Joule had wandered, trying to figure out which direction the signal was strongest in. Maybe the neighbors *would* be a help, Cage thought. He was trying to stay optimistic.

After they'd emerged from the woods, they'd split into their three designated groups and were now out driving through their mapped-out territories. Ivy had made the maps, handed them out, and then asked for suggestions and allowed the group to make changes. Again, Cage wondered what the hell he'd gotten himself into. But he took the next turn, covering their assigned grid.

Their receiver made no noise and, block after block, Joule sat quietly until at last she said, "This whole group thing is weird."

Cage could only agree. "I have to admit, Susan is not the one I thought we would be holding back."

"That's for *sure*." His sister offered the word as though it were a grudge as she looked out the window.

After a tense discussion, the group had informed Susan that she was not allowed to bring her shotgun into the car and simply begin firing if she and Steve located the pack first. In fact, Steve had insisted she leave the gun behind, or she wouldn't be riding with him.

Each team drove the neighborhood, up and down each

main street, then turning and running the cross streets. Cage and Joule had gotten out of the car at the end of the cul de sacs and walked around with the receiver, hoping to get just close enough to catch the edge of a signal they might have otherwise missed. They did this despite the fact that the group had agreed they would not leave their cars.

All Cage could say was that they hadn't left the car *much*. They'd done it together, which was as safe as they could be. And they'd done it with weapons in hand, just in case. He wasn't sure how he would explain breaking protocol if this was what yielded the signal, but it hadn't happened. Joule was looking out the window when they did hear a noise. Only it wasn't the receiver, it was their phones.

"Kayla and Ivy have something," Joule announced and motioned for Cage to make a U-turn.

Ten minutes later, they pulled up and had Steve and Susan park behind them. Though Ivy waited at the side of her car, Kayla was walking forward, the receiver in her outstretched hand, eyes on the small display.

"Stop her!" Joule commanded, and Cage heard his voice right over his sister's.

"She's too close to the woods," Cage said, "and sometimes they walk around during the day."

"This pack... they're *big*. The ones we measured were pushing eighty pounds and they're pure muscle. These guys are bigger. I wouldn't risk getting close."

It appeared Kayla wasn't listening to them at all, and Ivy had to step forward and physically pull her back.

The group convened and made a plan, and then they headed into the woods. Again, Cage thought how strange it felt. He knew Joule had his back, but he didn't really know any of the rest of these people—only that they felt the way that he did about the night hunters.

They made it to the location that Kayla's receivers clearly marked without incidents.

Turning to his sister, Cage asked softly, "Are *we* the pack now? Are there enough of us that they see us but they won't come out?"

"Interesting. We're finally a threat. Is that it? They see numbers?" she asked, following his thought process. But he noticed then that Kayla was listening, though the other three weren't.

Still, it was Kayla, who said, "They're here. In fact, there's one receiver over this way." She pointed toward the ground on her left, having paid attention to Joule the day before when she explained about the night hunters burrowing. "And there's another over here." She pointed ninety degrees off from the first position.

"Then we need to put the trough where you're standing," Cage announced, wondering if the group would follow his instructions. He was just a kid to them. But he and Joule were also the ones who'd done this successfully before.

The group had decided that, once they knew where the hunters were, they'd feed them more rat poison.

"I don't understand why we can't just kill them now," Susan said, her irritation coming through. "We dig up some of the dirt, turn over the leaves, and shoot them where they are."

Cage tried to be gentle, but he was getting exasperated. "Because we don't know how many there are. Because we don't know if they all ate the poison. We don't even know if the ones who did eat the poison are weakened by it yet."

He struggled to make his voice reasonable. "The ones we found weren't all in one burrow, so some others could pop up behind us while we're dealing with the first group. We might walk into a full-on battle, and we're not prepared."

Well, he and Joule were, but they were prepared to not fight a whole pack by themselves.

Susan barely agreed to the answer, and in her eyes, Cage shockingly saw shades of Nate Mazur. He saw the desire for revenge over a lost loved one. It almost bothered him that he understood Susan.

Cage saw his father's legacy in this group. Nate had left something solid behind, whether he'd intended to or not. He announced his father's rules. "We stay together as a group. No one splits up. No one goes alone."

The next piece of the agenda was the trough. They had to set it up in this new location and add the meat and the rat poison. He and Joule had put it into the trunk of the car, ready for this. Only now, Cage realized with relief, there was a team of six to haul the pieces around.

As he pulled an unwieldy part of the trough from his trunk, he noticed it now had a funky smell. Would these hunters recognize the smell of the other hunters? Maybe the smell of the meat would cover it and they would eat it anyway. They'd eaten from it the night before, so he hoped it would go well. They'd just have to wait and see.

Once everything was in place, Susan stood back. "We still haven't seen one."

Suppressing a sigh, Cage pointed out, "We might have seen one and not known it. They camouflage very well."

"Tomorrow night," Joule said firmly, reminding them they had all agreed not to come back on their own, though Cage still didn't trust Susan.

Silently, they headed back to the road, climbed into their cars, and headed home. No one said anything as they all turned into different driveways, almost as though what they had done would remain a dirty secret.

Once inside, Cage looked out the window and realized they'd just made it: The day was growing late. After grabbing a quick bite to eat, he and Joule closed all the curtains against the new, bigger pack of larger canines that might be wandering their yard at night. They turned out the lights, barricaded themselves into the bedroom, and grew quiet.

He must have stared at the ceiling for an hour or more before he heard the noises of the hunters outside. No longer able to keep his eyes open, and feeling he was as safe as he could get, Cage fell into a very uneasy sleep.

78

C age felt his phone buzz in his hand. It had needed to go off several times before he felt it enough to wake up. But he felt it now.

As his eyes peeled open into the dark of night, he looked around, trying to focus on anything. There was a street lamp in the cul de sac and it let just a little light in around the curtains of the second floor window that he and Joule had not barricaded. So he noticed that she, too, was starting to squirm awake.

Her phone had been left lying on her chest on top of the covers, and the vibrations seemed to be a little slower to rouse her. Whereas they had always left the phones completely off at night, Kayla and Steve had insisted the group had to be able to communicate.

They'd stood in the street together, each setting their phone to the "vibrate only" mode. In fact, Kayla had handled each phone, competently dismantling the speakers, making sure they couldn't go off unintentionally. One by one, the group set had their screens to very, very dim light.

Surely, the hunters couldn't hear or see his phone as it went off now, Cage thought. Still, the very fact that his phone was alerting him to something made him nervous.

Blinking his eyes and his brain awake, Cage turned the phone up and looked at it. The message was brief and concerning.

Susan is missing.

"Fuck," he whispered into the night as he noticed Joule, her face now lit by her own dim screen, also reading the message. She echoed his sentiment, though her words were more creative.

He began slowly throwing off the covers, grateful now that the other thing Steve and Kayla had insisted on was sharing information early. The little band had not intended to go out at night, but at least they were ready.

He and his sister had shared their jars of carbon black powder. Both Steve and Kayla had ordered sets of their own and promised to replace the borrowed jars as soon as their shipments arrived.

Joule had showed them the black charcoal tooth whitener. Though it didn't ink them out of the night the way the carbon black powder did, it did cover their teeth and keep them from looking like Cheshire Cats in the dark. Kayla and Ivy had headed off to buy supplies, including several tubes of the stuff, volunteering to get some for Steve and Susan.

Cage explained that he and Joule had initially been rubbing their black t-shirts into the carbon powder. But after she had stabbed Cage inadvertently, they had decided the disappearing act worked too well. The group had agreed and voted to simply go in black clothing and apply the carbon on their faces and anywhere else their skin might show.

When Kayla and Ivy returned, they brought other purchases as well, including multiple boxes of black, latex-free gloves that they had found at the beauty shop. *Brilliant*, Cage thought. Having never dyed his hair, it hadn't occurred to him that black latex might exist.

Now, in the dark of the room, he pulled on the gloves as his sister came out of the bathroom, dressed in black head to toe. Her blonde curls were tucked up under a hairnet and she worked the thin black cap over that. She had already darkened her face, the skin at her wrists, and her neck.

There was no point in flashing any skin. They couldn't afford anything that might show light—that might show the night hunters where to bite. He was just texting "Ready" to the group when he got the same notice back from Steve.

"Two minutes," came from Kayla and Ivy.

With a nod to his sister and no words spoken, they slowly undid the braces across the bedroom door. The boards scraped and creaked and would have been loud had he not been working so hard to keep the sounds to a minimum.

The noise felt jarring in the night. But though he heard sounds that made him cringe, he did not hear any response of hunters. He could only hope they weren't sitting, waiting, in the hallway. But he'd not heard the windows break, or the doors get pushed in by a pack of persistent creatures. Slowly, he crept down the stairs and turned the knob of the front door, stepping forward into the dark.

As he clutched his short sword and dagger, he barely saw Joule's outline emerge from the house behind him. She carefully closed the door behind her but didn't lock it. She had her bow already over her shoulder, quiver sitting on her back, stilettos in hand.

She was not going for distance. She was ready for close fighting. If they encountered anything in the yard, that was how it would go down. So they were ready.

Though he held his own weapons, he now also wore the

crossbow, much like a backpack. It had taken a while to figure out how to rig it up so he could both wear it and get to it quickly. He'd wound up with his own quiver of short arrows on his hip, close at hand.

Cage had learned from watching Joule early on. She'd packed her quiver long ago with Kleenex and foam so the arrows didn't rattle and make noise. He'd done the same, and his weapons sat ready should he need to use the crossbow.

He turned to his sister, seeing the whites of her eyes. They'd decided against the black contact lenses. She'd grown concerned they could trap the powder under the lenses and cause damage. Or—maybe worse—they might lose the ability to see clearly in the middle of a fight.

Though they still mostly blended into the night, at least they shouldn't be running into each other anymore. With the group, that had become even more of a concern, so they were trying for the best mix of caution and protection.

They'd been learning as they went. Test, adjust, test again. *Another lesson from my parents*, Cage thought.

The pair headed slowly down the street, constantly looking over their shoulders, constantly listening for the noise of soft, padded feet coming up behind them. But they didn't hear anything.

At last, they landed in the designated meeting area, where Steve already waited. He held something up to his mouth. After a look around and a deep breath, he took his hand away.

"Is that an inhaler?" Cage asked. "Do you have asthma?" He was blinking. How on earth did Steve think he could fight if he was going to get stricken with an asthma attack? If he was already having one...

"I'm allergic to dogs," Steve told them both as he pocketed the inhaler. "It's standard albuterol, and I'm taking it now as a precaution."

"You can't fight if you can't fight!" Joule sputtered out. Though Cage heard that she was trying to hold back her exasperation, she wasn't achieving it.

The three of them turned their heads as the door on their left opened, letting Ivy and Kayla emerge slowly into the night.

"Steve's asthmatic," Joule announced by way of greeting. "I don't think he can come out with us."

Steven frowned. "I'm fine. Tell you what—just leave me behind if I have an attack."

Cage felt his face pull into his mother's famous, *Oh really?* expression. He probably looked just like her right now.

Kayla looked at Steve, then at the group. "If he says he can come, he can." Then she looked back at Steve. "We may not be able to save you, though."

"I understand. I have to do this, and I'm taking precautions."

"You're allergic to *dogs.*" Joule tossed the words to the street between them.

Steve just raised an eyebrow. "Night hunters aren't dogs."

Well fuck, Cage thought. He had that.

With a sigh that said she was dropping it, Joule asked, "Susan?"

Kayla held up her phone. The dim setting made it virtually impossible to read, but one by one, they saw the line on the map as she said, "I put a tracker on her car."

Cage found his first response was to jerk back and ask, "Did you track all of us?"

"No," Kayla said, it as though it made perfect sense. "Only Susan. She's the only one I didn't trust. And look—" She held the phone up again. "I was right to not trust her."

Sure enough, the tracked car appeared to be parked several streets over—exactly where they had parked to head into the woods to find the hunters.

Cage looked first to Joule, then to the group. He sighed, angry at the old woman for creating a mess and an unplanned outing—because he knew those were the most dangerous of all. Still, she was in no shape to be left out with the new pack, alone.

"We have to go get her."

79

Joule had needed to remove her bow and quiver to find a way to carry the additional weapons that Kayla and Ivy provided them. She'd then piled everything back on in a way that she hoped would allow her to get to each item quickly. Like almost everything tonight, the new setup was untested. That made her nervous.

They'd brought two cars, opting for Steve's and Ivy's as the largest and strongest. Again, Joule thought they still wouldn't stand up to a hunter attack. Hadn't the police tried staying in their vehicles—their fortified cars—and hadn't the hunters still come through the windows and pulled them out? She had little faith in an ordinary SUV.

She was riding in the passenger seat, sitting forward so as not to lean into the quiver on her back. The bow hung in the same direction as the quiver. But underneath it now was a bag with four flip-top water bottles. Kayla had handed out more black gloves, telling everyone, "Double up, guys. This is dangerous."

She felt heavy now, Joule thought, with water bottles

hanging off of her right hip, bow over her shoulder, stilettos in sheaths strapped on her left.

She was slow getting out of the car, mostly because she was checking her surroundings. She didn't hear or see anything, and that only added to her sense of unease. Pulling the bow off her shoulder, she grabbed for an arrow, hoping to be able to aim at something and maybe slow it down.

Looking around, she saw that Kayla and Ivy had both crawled from the car in front of them, and Steve was emerging just as slowly from the driver's seat. The three of them were ready for hand-to-hand combat. So was Cage, who had set himself up with the crossbow.

It seemed Joule and her brother were to be the first line of attack. It was their job to get out front and slow anything coming from a distance. Once the hunters got closer, they were to step back and let the hand-to-hand fighters take the front. Ivy had argued that the rear was the safest place, and it was where the children belonged.

Joule scoffed. She was used to handling both distance and the up-close fighting. She had been a child last year, but not this year.

Silently, the group looked to each other and motioned to move forward. Joule turned to head into the woods along the path, but it was Ivy who put a hand on her arm to stop her. Next, she quickly reached out and tapped Cage.

"No," she said softly, catching the eyes of all four other group members. "Kayla and I found a shorter distance, less time in the woods to the site."

Joule's eyes flicked immediately to her brother as though to ask, *is this okay?*

He offered only the faintest of shrugs, but she couldn't imagine that Kayla had missed it. *Were Kayla and Ivy right?*

It was hard to tell. But there was no way to determine

whether or not they should be trusted. There was only the logic that there was no specific reason *not* to.

The group headed down the street toward Kayla's supposedly shorter entry point.

"It's longer in general," Ivy offered in a soft whisper, "but we'll spend less time in the woods, and the woods seems to be the most dangerous place.

Speaking, too, was odd, and Joule felt it in her bones. She and Cage had gone out almost completely silently, but now there were *whisper discussions*.

It felt like too many people to coordinate—people who didn't trust each other enough to just stay quiet and follow along.

It was clear Kayla and Ivy knew each other well, as did Joule and Cage. But Steve did not have that connection with anyone else in the group. Even with two groups, they still had to communicate between themselves.

The five of them approached the woods, stepping into the yard of the third house on the right, when Joule heard the noise.

She whipped around. Though they had been checking behind them, they had still managed to miss this.

A pack of hunters had appeared in the street. And though it seemed to have not spotted the people yet, Joule knew they couldn't just sneak away.

These hunters—the bigger, bolder hunters—seemed to have learned to stay out of the streetlights. That was something their predecessor pack had not known.

Joule was asking herself if the intelligence of the leader played into it, even as she let an arrow fly. Immediately, she reached back, plucked another and notched it.

She had arrows in two of the creatures and noticed Cage had shorter crossbow pieces embedded into two others. Each missile landed with a thunk, speed driving the shaft into muscle and flesh and eliciting a grunt or howl.

At first, the hunters milled in the street, growing irritated with the attack but unable to find their attackers. But as Joule sank another arrow, the hunters either spotted the group or were moving toward the arrows. They began to approach.

The pack, it seemed, did not care about its own wounded individuals, and that made them even more dangerous. Joule let another arrow fly before the canines got close enough to become a hand-to-hand threat.

Quickly, she glanced over to see if Steve was still breathing normally. At least he appeared to be.

It was Kayla who stepped up, and Joule could have heard sworn she heard an angry, muttered, "Fuckers ate my dogs."

She remembered then that Kayla and Ivy had moved in with several pit bulls in tow. It was enough to make her wonder, at the time, if the two gentle-looking women had started a dog fighting ring on their street. Clearly, that was not the case. The pets had been beloved, and Kayla was now pissed.

She stepped forward as a huge canine jumped up at her, baring the shiny teeth in its massive jaws. Kayla began jabbing and slicing, generally fighting in a haphazard manner. She cut through air half the time, but still managed to lay deep wounds into the first attacker and then any of the hunters that got close enough to feel her blade. Her anger seemed enough of a fighting method to get her through.

Steve had moved behind Joule, closing the circle with Ivy as Kayla continued fighting the approaching hunters. Behind them, Steve and Cage were swearing blue streaks and guarding their backs.

Joule had turned to the side of the group and Cage stood directly behind her, facing the other way, the five of them forming a small circle ready to defend themselves the best they could. But Joule was pissed. They'd come out for Susan and wound up with a fight on their hands before they'd even found her.

Steve's voice was only attracting more hunters, she knew, but since the pack had already found them, she wondered if there was purpose in shutting him up. Still, she shushed him.

He nodded back at her, his fists still clenching two of his prized kitchen knives. Only Susan had carried a gun of any kind. None of them were well enough trained to hit a dog and not a person. They couldn't kill a random onlooker by accident with a sword or knife.

Her eyes tracking movement just beyond the edge of the dim streetlight, Joule watched as one of the hunters came around to flank the group. She put an arrow in its side and notched another. Shooting a second into the same hunter finally began to slow it down.

They would not get encircled, she told herself

Steve, at least, had shut up.

"Water!" Kayla called out and Joule glanced to her left where Kayla and Ivy fought as the front line.

She watched as the two women deftly plucked the water bottles they'd brought from the bag each wore at her hip. Using a single finger, each flipped the lid on a bottle and aimed them at the hunter's faces. Almost as one, they squirted the water at open, panting mouths.

Joule could only pray and wait. She pulled the bow tighter and swung to her right.

80

Cage heard the scream, but he didn't know who or what had made it. When he heard it a second time, he paid closer attention. It did sound human.

It flitted through his mind that it was probably Susan. And if it was Susan, she had brought this on herself. She'd known not to go out on her own. But a second set of thoughts followed the first. *What if it wasn't Susan?* What if it was someone else who was caught outside? What if it was a *kid*?

Steve, who was turning his head frantically looking between Cage and his sister, finally settled on Cage. As Cage watched in horror, a hunter came up behind Steve. He was pointing at it to warn the man as Steve turned back to the canine that had gotten precariously close. Even as he swung at the hunter, Steve told him "Go! We've got this. You get her."

Cage almost rebelled. Susan could take what she got. *Don't split up the group.* But like Nate, Susan had already broken that cardinal rule, and saving her meant breaking it again. Besides, Joule was already running.

Two steps behind her, he realized that if they could find Susan, they too would have a group of three. Not that Susan would be much of an advantage. But at least they could form into two groups again, instead of three.

Joule still held her bow in her hand. But as he watched, she was slinging it over her shoulder, reaching to her hip and grabbing for her stilettos, coming up with one in each grip. She didn't miss a step as she darted past him and into the woods.

He was right behind her, thinking that wasn't a bad idea. He managed to sling the crossbow over one shoulder, knowing that it would bounce, but doing it anyway. It freed his hands to reach for his short sword and his dagger. If anything, a fight in the woods would be hand-to-hand.

The twins ran blindly into the trees, staying close, picking their feet up high and trying not to trip over roots and twigs on the unfamiliar path. More than once, Cage came down on a stick, and only by sheer force of will did he keep his ankle from rolling as he crashed through it.

Periodically, he turned and looked over his shoulder. He noticed his sister was checking, too. But they pushed through the underbrush, staying on the path and heading toward where they had heard the very human sound. He had no idea if they were going the right direction. But then he heard it again. Another scream, a swear, a human grunt.

Still not certain it was Susan, he had managed to figure out it was adult and female. *Probably Susan*, he thought—but he wouldn't know until he saw her.

Joule's long legs ate up the ground. Though Cage was taller, her drive must have been stronger, and he fought to keep up.

He heard the noises again. Closer, and this time Joule must have felt it was worth the risk. "*Susan!*" she hollered out. "*Susan!*"

The woman yell back, "Over here!" quickly followed by, "Fucker!"

Clearly the last word was not aimed at the two of them.

Cage had already surmised before he could see it that the

meat with the rat poison had not killed all of the night hunters in this pack. He'd hoped it would do a thorough job, but he'd not believed. Because, even after they had baited their own pack for some time, the hunters had not all been dead. Some had still been strong enough to put up a decent fight.

That was part of the reason Susan had been stupid to come in here.

He heard it then—the blast of a shotgun and a thump as she hit something hard. Cage pulled up short behind Joule, the two of them skidding to a stop as they watched Susan swing the shotgun like a bat, catching a hunter upside the head. It tipped off to the side, legs crossing, paw over paw, as it fought to stay upright.

Susan swore at the animal, words Cage would have guessed the old woman didn't even know and certainly would have scolded him for if *he* had said them.

"On your left!" Joule called, raising her arm and throwing one of the stilettos as though it were a knife. It thumped the hunter but fell to the ground. Maybe she had caused a good bruise, or hit something vital. Still, it was probably a mistake to lose her weapon, he thought.

The blow did seem to stall the hunter though, which gave him a moment to react. Joule used her now-empty hand to deftly pull the bow off of her shoulder and he realized her change of weapon was the better decision.

Grabbing for his own crossbow, and feeling the bruise on his back where it had bounced for the whole run, he clutched the straps and swung it around. Mounting an arrow, he aimed for the hunter to Susan's right.

The silver-haired woman was staring down one that must have been right in front of her. Cage couldn't see it, but the night hunter and Susan had spotted each other. He heard the blast as the shotgun went off again and watched as the elderly woman reloaded quickly and easily.

Cage sank crossbow arrows into the sides of hunters, who paid no attention to him. He didn't know if they couldn't spot him or if they just hated Susan more, but he shot again and again and watched as several of the canines wobbled off to the side.

That was when he saw Susan's leg—shredded.

Perhaps the scream had happened when one of the hunters had grabbed her. But another one of them was coming at her, and now still another one was diving for her leg again.

Joule had run up closer, almost too close to use her bow and arrows, but she'd managed to sink several more. At least the hunters toppled and fell as she hit them—maybe the poison was helping to make them easier to fight—and Cage tried to keep up, shooting any that he could get a clear line of sight on.

He then noticed the shovel Susan had abandoned. Slinging his crossbow over his shoulder once again, he leaned down and picked the tool up in a smooth motion. He had too much adrenaline to notice if it any of it hurt.

The shovel was heavy and firm in his hands. This one was not collapsible. And when he used the metal end to hit the nearest hunter, it offered a satisfying thunk.

He felt as though he had been fighting for some time when, at last, the three of them stopped. They stood breathing heavily, but they were the last ones standing.

Susan leaned over and put her hands on her knees. Cage understood the desire. He would have done it, too, but it wasn't a safe position.

Quickly, Susan appeared to catch on and stood back up, though her breathing was still heavy. She stood now like the twins did, scanning the woods around them with the tip of her shotgun leading the way. There must have been another round left in her barrel.

Joule had changed positions, putting her back to Susan's.

Standing with one foot in front of the other, still ready to fight. She had an arrow in place, should she see anything.

But the arrow stayed notched.

Cage stepped in and became the third side of the triangle, watching for anything coming from his side. But nothing moved. It was Susan who first declared them done.

"We got them. I dug them up and killed a bunch. There's three dead ones over there." She pointed with the tip of the shotgun, and Cage tipped his head just quickly enough to catch the direction and see the turned earth she pointed at. "We got them all!"

He could hear the glee in her voice, even though she was still scanning the space with the tip of her shotgun, which showed that, although she'd declared it, she didn't quite believe it.

He heard his own breath soughing in and out of his lungs. His chest heaved and he thought, *good. It's over.*

But then he turned to his sister.

Joule's face turned to his, but her expression was anything but triumphant.

"If this is the pack—the one we baited and fed the poison to —then who's out on the street fighting Kayla and Ivy and Steve?"

81

J oule ran only a few feet before she realized that there was no way Susan could keep up. She probably couldn't keep up on a good day, and certainly not now with the gash in her leg. Joule's brain went through rapid iterations of the options.

Should she pull off one of her shirts? She had two on. The top shirt was long sleeved and would cover Susan's wound well. But the undershirt was just that. Her arms and shoulders were not covered in the carbon black powder and she would shine like a beacon in the forest. Also, to get to it, she'd have to take off all of her weapons—which wasn't safe, not out here.

But if she did it, she would have a shirt, and she could bind the old woman's wound. Would it make Susan fast enough? She thought not. Would it cover the blood and maybe stop the hunters from coming after them? Joule didn't know. The creatures didn't have a good sense of smell, so maybe it wouldn't change anything.

They hadn't brought bandages. They had a kit in the car, but they hadn't carried all the materials into the fray.

It was Susan who reached out. "Give me one of those water bottles. I'll rinse it and then I'll keep going."

"No!" Cage protested suddenly and too loudly for the woods at night. He made it clear that she could *not* have these water bottles. "We need to tie it up," he said, clearly having followed a similar train of thought to Joule's.

It was Susan who looked back and forth between the two of them. The look on her face said she was clearly disappointed in their lack of pre-planning and failure to bring a first-aid kit for her.

Well, Joule thought, *she was disappointed in most of Susan's life choices right now. So Susan could stuff it.*

After Joule just stared at her for a moment, as though to say she didn't know what to do, Susan eventually pulled off her own long sleeved sweater. At least she had come out in black. Underneath it, she wore another three quarters-sleeved black shirt. To Joule, it looked far too nice to be out in the woods in, but apparently, Susan had not thought about the quality of her garments and the filthiness of the fight before her.

Though the shirt was black on black, sequins beaded the neckline and made a pattern of flowers and leaves down the front. It was a light catcher, that was for sure. But Susan was already wrapping the black sweater around her lower leg. It stretched as she pulled at it, making it go much further than it otherwise might have. When she ran out of sleeves and knotted it, her leg was bulked to the point where it probably hindered her walking.

"Go," she said, motioning them back toward the street. "Who knows what I just tied into my leg, but go."

Her older hand, slightly gnarled at the knuckles, waved them on. But Joule had no doubt that hand could deal out what it wished. She'd certainly shown she could wield a shotgun with skill.

Joule jogged now, no longer flat out running the way she

had to get here. If she did, they would leave Susan in the dust. It was not okay to do that. The woman could not keep up and there was every possibility that there were more hunters in the woods behind them, or even in front of them.

Though Susan had declared the job done, Joule was not going to accept the answer the older woman doled out. She watched as her brother snuck around to the back of the small group, putting Susan in the middle.

"I'm fine," Susan protested.

"You're injured," Cage retorted, brooking no argument. The slower speed allowed him to walk mostly backward, thus guarding from anything coming up the trail behind them. He kept the crossbow lifted. Just in case.

Joule's thoughts churned. With Susan's leg covered, they made rapid—though not the fastest—time back toward where they had left the others. She couldn't help but wonder, if these were the hunters they had baited, then who was in the street?

Another pack? She tried to remember if she recognized any of the individuals. But she'd been fighting, moving too quickly and paying attention to other things. Her adrenaline had been too high to make any of those kinds of analyses.

Had the pack split? She didn't think so. On cursory glance —though again, she hadn't been counting, and she tried to do her best from memory—it appeared that Susan had killed enough of them to account for the whole group they'd poisoned. It didn't seem that the number they'd left behind was only half of what they'd been seeing... no, it wasn't. She was sure of it.

Fuck, Joule thought. They believed they'd cleared out the territory and made way for another stronger pack to come in. But that hadn't been it at all. What they had done had been far, far worse. They had opened an arena for the strongest to come and test themselves.

As she emerged from the woods, Joule scanned the street

up and down. Though Ivy, Kayla, and Steve, were fighting a good fight, there were still a sizeable number of the pack left. The animals appeared to be wounded and not attacking at full steam, but that didn't stop them from coming in waves and wearing down the three humans that Joule and Cage had left behind.

Ivy and Kayla fought, moving backward and forward getting attacked and pushing against the oncoming dogs. But Steve had turned into some kind of madman. He was pushing into the center of the fight, almost as though he thought he was invincible.

Shaking his head, Cage began running toward them. He must have decided that Susan could just keep up. But it was Joule who stalked the space carefully, sweeping her gaze wide. Again, taking in the street, she turned left and saw the fight.

When she turned opposite the woods, she saw the houses flanking the opposite side of the row and saw nothing. There were no hunters sneaking out between the mostly empty homes. Not that she could see. She saw nothing in the dim porch lights some of the residents offered.

But as she swung her bow and arrow to the right, she noticed a startling sight. In the light at the end of the street, another pack stood waiting, ready for the fight.

82

J oule ran toward the oncoming pack. It might be a
stupid idea, but she did it anyway. She had to get as
many arrows into them as possible before they got
close, before they really registered her darkened form
and that it was the one hurting them.

No wonder the other night hunters weren't falling when
they were shot or cut. These packs likely had no rat poison in
them at all.

But what about the water? she wondered. *Was it even working?*

She didn't have time to look and see. The new pack maybe
hadn't spotted the team in all their black carbon, but the fight
itself could not be missed. The pack was still approaching their
group, and she hadn't called out to warn them yet. Her voice
was choking as her throat was starting to clamp on her.

So she didn't yell out. Instead, Joule acted.

She had the advantage of distance. Before they got too
close, she would turn and run back to her group, to be part of
her own safety in numbers. But for now, she quietly let arrows
fly, taking a moment to aim, pull hard on the string, and sink
her arrows deep into her targets.

She did all this as the pack gained speed. She put arrow after arrow into them, and it didn't stop any of them, though she could account for many injuries.

Her hand reached back to pull another arrow from her quiver and caught only empty air. *Shit,* she thought, *she was out of ammo.* She'd never run out before.

She'd carried the arrows night after night when they went out and though she lost many during each outing, she'd stocked up, ordering an ungodly number from online stores. She'd never ordered too many from one place, as she didn't want to draw attention to all the crazy things she and her brother had been purchasing. The last thing she needed was some kind of NSA agent showing up on her doorstep. But she had plenty of arrows. Or so she'd thought.

It was suddenly time to retreat. Time to alert the others.

"Cage!" She yelled it at the top of her lungs before realizing he was no longer fighting alongside the group. He and Steve had come her direction. Though Steve stood ready with his knife in hand, Cage he took over shooting at the hunters. His darkened form stood planted as his crossbow sank short, stubby arrows into the pack members in rapid succession.

But he wasn't stopping them either. In fact, the animals were now approaching even faster.

She tugged at him and Steve as she passed by. "Go! Go!"

Joule ran back toward the relative safety of the group, hearing that Cage had followed her. With no more arrows, her bow was worthless. Tossing it aside, Joule ran on, even as she listened to it clatter to the pavement. Under that sound, she heard her brother behind her. Hopefully he had a few arrows left.

"Kayla! Ivy!" She didn't yell for Susan. Susan had stepped into the fray and was whacking at one of the hunters that was trying to get in from behind where the others were fighting.

Joule looked back to Steve to see he was running *into* the

approaching pack instead of away. Her mouth hung open in horror as he waded in, hacking at the oncomers. The carbon powder wouldn't be enough. They were dark but not invisible. She whispered, "*Oh, holy shit.*"

Watching as Cage turned, she saw his eyes go wide as the pack started to surround Steve. One bit at his arm, but Steve managed to shake it off. Another went for his leg, but again, he shook it off.

Frowning, Joule stood frozen. It was Cage who moved to help their friend, but even he pulled up to a dead stop. Suddenly, she found her voice.

"They aren't biting him!"

"Yes, they are," Cage hollered back.

"No, they are but they don't hold onto him. They attack *us*, but they're attacking Steve's *weapons*. Not *him*." She almost smacked herself. Now was not the time for scientific inquiry.

Cage was acting, grabbing at Steve and pulling him back to the group.

As she, too, darted back into the safety of their own numbers, Joule could hear the hunters running behind them. The group had to get into formation.

"Water?" she asked Steve as they reached the edge and took their places in the circle. She'd noticed he was holding a bottle.

He tossed the empty container to the side. "Wasted most of it."

"Wasted?" she asked, pulling her one remaining stiletto and letting the grip roll into her hand.

"It doesn't work."

Kayla had laced the water in the bottles with cyanide. The high doses should have killed the dogs on contact. That was why Kayla had been insistent that they all double glove. They couldn't afford to get it on themselves.

Steve moved forward, putting himself in front of her and her brother. While Joule had appreciated Kayla's know-how and Ivy's ability to make things happen, she had underappreciated Steve's management skills and willingness to fight until this moment.

This was not the first time he had stepped in front of them. She didn't know if he had kids of his own, but he clearly thought of them as children and he was protecting them.

She had to appreciate that.

Steve was aimed toward the pack that was no longer chasing them but getting into some kind of formation. She cautioned him, "Don't run into them. Let them come to us. We have to keep our backs together. Are you hurt?"

Though they'd seen the dogs bite at him, he ran as though nothing had gotten a good hit. Steve shook his head. "Probably a few punctures." But he wasn't looking at her. He was watching the hunters and crouching into a better stance. "You good?"

She nodded. That was another thing she began to appreciate about Steve. He might be trying to protect her, but he also seemed to understand that she and Cage had done this before. They had survived, so Steve listened.

She heard the shouts of concern as Kayla and Ivy must have been able to find a moment to turn their heads and see what was coming. While they gathered themselves for just seconds, Joule pressed Steve again. "The water—you have to get it into their mouths directly and squeeze the bottle. Get as much as you can. Because that's the only way it works."

Joule thought about when they'd studied cyanide in chemistry class. She would have thought it would have taken less. Maybe it did, but if the effects weren't fast and, if the night hunters were as impervious to pain as it seemed they might be, it might take a while for them to go down.

"Okay," she nodded, one stiletto in her hand. She had thrown the other, hitting a hunter with it, back in the woods, but not having gained much for the loss.

She was down to her last weapon, so she reached into the

bag on her right hip, pulled out a water bottle and flipped the top open. She aimed it toward the approaching hunters and got ready.

Steve looked at her. "I've got a spare knife. Do you want it?"

But then Joule put the pieces together. "No. I want your *inhaler!*"

83

Cage swung with everything he had. Even so, his arms reverberated as the sword connected with first flesh and then bone as the hunter leapt at him.

The dog was heavy, thick, and determined. The impact shook Cage. This pack was black, blending even more into the night than the brindle hunters had, or at least he thought so. Maybe he was just getting tired, but *tired* was not acceptable.

The hunter still came at him, momentum carrying him forward despite the series of strikes Cage had dealt. The heavy body jolted into him, but Cage wouldn't let it take him down. However, the bump made him stumble back a few feet. He slashed with the sword again, and pushed backwards with everything he had.

To his side, Steve was talking to Joule. "No, you have to shake it first."

Not understanding, but not allowing himself to get sidetracked, he focused on the hunter as it fell onto its back, yelped, and rolled over before climbing to its feet to come at him again. It didn't matter though. Cage already had a second hunter coming at him and a third.

Steve had stepped in to take some of the brunt off Cage. He carried a larger sword and he brought it down across the back of the hunter as it went airborne, leaping at Cage. Before the hunter even hit the ground, Steve swung again, two hands on the sword. He used that grip, not because it was a broadsword and carried its own weight, but to put his own might behind the swing. He turned the other way in a beautiful twist even as he felled another hunter that was aiming for Joule.

The problem was, the hunters fell, but they got back up. Even the deep gouges in their sides didn't seem to stop them. It slowed them down, sure, but they were still big, they were still heavy, and their jaws still worked.

The group of humans had all sustained bites or cuts, despite heavy clothing and their coordinated protection of each other. Despite the fact that they'd managed to wound and slow most of the hunters with arrows and shotgun pellets at a distance, before the creatures even got in range of biting. They were starting to wear thin.

Cage had already felt the sting as one set of teeth had gotten far too close to his forearm. He'd yanked his arm out, reclaiming the limb as his own, but he wasn't unscathed. He could feel the blood seeping into the long sleeve of his black T-shirt. Of course, he couldn't see the injury, but it was bad enough that he could smell it, even if the hunters couldn't.

Luckily, there was no pain to ignore. He was far too high on the fight and the need to survive. He slashed again and again and noticed that Joule had only the stiletto and the water bottle as her weapons, but she held something else, too.

"Cage!" She was shaking the thing and pushing it toward him. "Steve's inhaler. Take it!"

As the small plastic device pressed into his hand, she turned and struck at the dogs that came at her, hopefully letting them bleed out. But that was a slow game and they needed the fastest one they could find.

Cage frowned at the inhaler as Steve stepped in front of him. "Suck in a full breath! I'm covering you."

Still, Cage looked to Joule, questioning.

But she yelled back. "The wheelchair guy—Dr. Brett's list said he had asthma!"

Suddenly understanding, Cage stuck the inhaler in his mouth, and popped down the plunger. The sensation was overwhelming and it was hard to breathe in deeply. But he did it.

The dogs were only nipping at Steve. They weren't holding on. They hadn't shredded him like they had tried to do to Susan, or even like the bite on Cage's own arm. He wondered how fast the medicine would work.

With a slick sidestep, Cage let one of the hunters jump by him, missing his target. Cage hadn't wanted to be the target anyway. But he swung the dagger as the creatures passed, smacking at it even as he whirled away.

"Joule," he called out. "Take this!" He shoved the dagger into her hand. The stiletto, though very serviceable in a pair, was virtually useless here on its own. She could push it into the dogs and slide it around, but she left only a puncture wound. The dagger would kill them faster.

He'd heard what Joule and Steve had said about the water. And this time he had an idea. "Kayla! Ivy! Susan!" He pushed the inhaler at Ivy, the closest one to him and let Steve bark out the orders to take the medication.

With the short sword in one hand, and a water bottle grasped in the other, Cage faced the hunters again. He was armed with everything he could be. Waiting, he stayed still until another hunter came at him, then he swung with all his might, putting his whole upper body behind the move the way he had been taught in years of karate class. Cage was grateful now for all the repetition his instructors had put him through. It had made the move practically instinctual.

He came down hard with the sword, cutting into the side of

the hunter. Then he lunged, sidestepping as he flayed the creature's flank. But next he prayed the water would work. He followed the first arm with the second, and as he passed the open wound, he sprayed it with the cyanide water.

He heard the sharp squeal followed by a howl and watched as the hunter hit the pavement with a hard thud. It was not injured enough to warrant all of its limbs going limp, but it must have been in severe pain.

As Cage watched, the legs scrambled, but the dog struggled to rise onto his feet again. As it yowled, Cage's eyes scanned for the next hunter that came at him and he tried the move again.

This time he hit the dog on the neck, and managed to make the one-two combo more fluid. He moved in almost a full circle, his right arm arcing up and over, the blade coming down and cutting into the skin. This time, his left hand trailed so closely behind it that he was practically filling the wound with the cyanide water as he cut it.

Another scream sounded, and another hunter fell.

Cage yelled to his sister, "Slash and spray!"

Her eyes darted to his and for a moment they made contact there in the dark.

She nodded and he watched as a hunter leaped up behind her, aiming for her head.

84

Joule felt the air around her move. She must have seen the hunter from her peripheral vision, for she knew the creature that she couldn't quite fully see was leaping to her left, trying to take her down even as she looked at her brother.

She stepped quickly right, moving out of the direct attack. Turning—her left hand holding the dagger he had given her—she swung it hard. This weapon had more weight than the stilettos, and though she still had to put her own force behind it, this was enough.

She yelled with the move, just like she'd been taught in her MMA classes. She'd never expected to be fighting non-human mammals with it, but she did what she had to. Her hand ran the weapon across the hunter's face. She cut into the jaw, and she felt the blade slide along the bone guiding her cut toward its throat, and she watched as the flesh sliced wide.

Still, as she moved to deliver the water, the hunter jumped at her again, its jaws clamping onto her exposed wrist. She felt the pressure and used it to squeeze the bottle. For a moment she panicked—had she just lost her hand? Or at least the use of it?

But it didn't stop her from delivering a stream of cyanide directly into the gaping neck wound. She felt the pressure easy as she heard the sound of the hunter crying and falling, the same noise she had heard her brother achieve several times before.

As she looked down at her arm, she was surprised to see only a few small puncture wounds. The hunter hadn't bit hard. Was it the inhaler? Or had she just gotten lucky? She didn't know.

She had to be careful though, and not get the cyanide on her open cuts. She also had to keep it off of her fellow fighters. Joule pulled back a little bit.

Beside her, she saw Kayla and Ivy working as a team. They'd all taken hits off the inhaler as far as she knew, but so far no one had been bitten to test it. They fought with one of them hacking and the other sometimes turning and squirting water toward the wound, or down an open mouth. As she watched, Ivy rushed a hunter coming at her, jaws gaping wide. Holding a fresh bottle she'd pulled from her bag, Ivy used one black-gloved finger to flip it open. As the jaws came at her, she shoved the bottle into the open mouth and let the hunter's bite squeeze it down its own throat. Ivy's words indicated her satisfaction with the result.

It was Kayla who yelled, "You killed Newton!"

Joule had no idea who *Newton* was, but she watched as Kayla took her anger out on a hunter that was already off its feet. They must have already slashed it, poisoned it, both, or more.

Joule didn't know where the anger had come from, but she watched as Kayla's foot swung in an arc, catching the hunter in the ribcage and sending it flying. The brindle color swung through the air, not high and not long, too heavy for someone

Kayla's size to have had much effect, but the effect when it landed was stunning.

The hunters turned from her. The other hunters were their enemy, maybe even more than Kayla was. It was an enemy they could easily see, and that probably helped. The downed hunter was a partially defeated enemy already, and though the brindle hunter stood up and faced them down, growled even though the sound burbled, the black hunters turned on it as a pack, moving in a single unit.

In a moment of brilliant thought, Joule grabbed a water bottle and doused the brindle hunter with the cyanide water. It likely wouldn't kill him, but it could kill every one of the black hunters who took a big enough bite.

"Get another," she yelled. "Get them all!"

When one of the black hunters inadvertently came near her, she slashed at it, and slashed and slashed. She'd just emptied her water bottle and she was going to have to kill this one by sheer strength. There was no secret weapon right now except her anger. The hunters had not only killed a pit bull named Newton, but they'd also killed her Mom and her Dad. Joule felt a surge of power with that thought and she brought the short dagger down with more force than she'd known she could.

As soon as the hunter stumbled a bit, Cage leapt in. "Step back!" he hollered as he stabbed it with his own short sword.

Joule took advantage of the move, knowing her brother could handle it. The hunter was already wounded, but he was heavy. She ran the few short steps to Kayla and Ivy.

"Another! Give them all the water!" she yelled. Leaning down, she helped Ivy's two gloved hands pick up a fallen brindle hunter by its feet and sling it. Together, they tossed it into the fray as it protested.

Suck a duck, Joule thought, as the creature dropped right into the melee.

Somehow, she had managed to ignore some of the noise. It seemed Susan was bashing some of the hunters with a shotgun. Maybe they had been too close to shoot? But now that the packs had turned on each other, maybe Susan could get a step back. She seemed to be defending herself well enough, despite the damage to her leg.

Joule turned and looked at the fight in front of her, for once able to observe rather than just react. Though the black pack was fresher and clearly had an advantage, the brindles were still trying to fight back. It seemed one of the evolutionary disadvantages of the hunters was that they didn't know when to quit, when to retreat, when to regroup and come back another day or just call it a loss. But Joule and the group were going to use that to their advantage.

Susan had no such compunctions. As Joule suspected, as soon as Susan found two feet between her and the hunter, she quickly loaded shells and pumped the shotgun. She seemed to have loaded her pants pockets with a huge amount of spare shells.

The noise of her shots hung heavy in the night, though none of the hunters seemed to notice the two shots in rapid succession. As far as Joule could see, Susan peppered most of the dogs.

Though she tried to get out of the way, one bumped her, but she was ready. It turned on her, black-coated, angry, and as fresh for the fight as any of them could be. This hunter already had several gashes on his side, but Joule guessed she did, too. Like the canine in front of her, she was caught up in the fight and didn't feel them.

"Put all the water on the pack!" she yelled again, though it came out more like a grunt. Because as she watched her teammates pull out their water bottles and aim at the few still-fighting dogs, Joule watched as Cage brought the short sword down across the hunter's back. It didn't cut too deep, or create an open wound, but he clearly damaged the spine.

The hunter—in a fit of its own rage—looked up at her and howled. Joule jammed her brother's dagger through its open mouth and let the weight of it drag her arm down as it fell.

85

C age watched as what was left of the brindle pack somehow found the energy for a pointless try at defending themselves. No longer defending territory, they were probably only trying to save their own lives at this point. But it was enough. It was a distraction for the black hunters, who were no longer moving as a unit against the people.

He scanned the fight, still slicing at the occasional hunter that found Cage in the darkness and thought he was an acceptable target. But he wasn't. Pushing them off, he sent them back into the fray with fresh injuries and cyanide in the cuts.

"Get in the cars!" he yelled to the group. "Let's get out of here!"

It was Joule who looked at him, holding up her last water bottle. Kayla and Ivy behind her had caught on.

"All the water," she said again. Though Steve was clearly reluctant, and it took a minute, they pulled them out one by one, and emptied the last of the water onto the few hunters that were remaining fully in the fight.

Between Susan's shotgun and the slices from swords,

daggers and more, there were plenty of night hunters injured, and the few that still stood probably wouldn't last long. The cyanide would kill them, even if it took a few minutes.

He watched as one stumbled, fell, and burbled blood from its mouth.

Good.

Throwing the bottles on to the ground, Cage ran, grabbing his sister's arm and pulling her along. If only two of them made it to the car, it would be him and Joule. He ducked into the passenger side back seat, pushing her into the front as Steve approached from the other side.

The older man tugged on the other door handle for a moment, and Cage suffered a shock of panic that Steve had dropped the keys. They'd been monumentally stupid coming out here with only one set. But Steve pulled the door opened and quickly slid the key into the ignition, turning it as though it were any normal day.

He squealed the tires as he peeled out, even as the frenzy in the street died down. Even as the slashing bites and growls turned to tugs and whines as the fight came to a conclusion.

The six humans in the group fled the scene and headed back up the street. It was Kayla who stuck her hand out the window—not a move that Cage would have done—to motion their second car to turn into her driveway.

The second car followed her up the short drive to the brick house and watched as the white garage doors chugged their way up on two open spaces. His heart stopped. The damn doors were so slow. His consolation was that the hunters were busy. His fear was that there was another pack waiting.

But as soon as the door was maybe one inch over the roof of his car, he pushed the gas and jolted them into the spot. Next to them, Kayla pulled her car into the space in a more respectable manner, but she must have hit a button as the garage doors began closing behind them.

Cage sat frozen in the car as none of them moved, listening to what seemed like the slowest garage doors in the world. The noisy chug would have brought night hunters at any other time. If there was another pack around here, surely the grinding noise was alerting them to exactly where the people/prey were.

When the door was finally down and the cars off, they sat in silence for another moment before Kayla climbed out. Everyone followed suit as quietly as they could. She didn't shut the car doors. Despite the noisiness of the garage door closing, none of them made avoidable sounds.

Kayla and Ivy climbed the three short steps to the door connecting the garage into the house. Cage and the rest of the group followed softly. The ragtag group tumbled into the kitchen scattering around the space, worn thin and not willing to get too far from each other.

Leaning on the countertop, Cage noticed his hands had left blood smeared on the granite surface. On the floor, he could see drips that he thought probably were from Susan, but maybe were from him. He didn't know who else might be bleeding, but they all needed to be checked.

He looked around at each of them, and one by one, they looked back at him. Everyone was here, and everyone ultimately looked okay.

So they drank water that Ivy poured from a filter she kept in the fridge, and no one spoke.

They had survived.

86

C age hadn't seen any night hunters for three full days. Joule said the same, and the reports from Steve, Susan, and Kayla and Ivy were the same: no hunters —nothing on the cameras. No evidence in the yards.

Susan and Kayla and Ivy had also installed night vision cameras on their homes, giving all of them a much wider range to monitor. They could see from the back of the Mazur home to the end of the street they lived on now.

Joule had tapped a closed circuit system to all three houses and to Steve. Any of them could link into any camera or any recorded feed at any time. Steve had volunteered to get one, but it was generally agreed that being next door to Kayla and Ivy, his camera would have mostly been redundant.

Now, they had twice as many cameras to watch, but three times as many eyes. Cage would not have predicted this turn of events, but he found he liked it.

So far, no one in the group had asked after the twins' parents, even though Cage knew they had all waved to Kaya and Nate in the past. His parents hadn't known everyone on the street, but Nate had been able to name the neighbors most of the time when Cage had asked. These people had known Cage's parents, but they hadn't asked—they'd simply understood.

In fact, none of them asked the others if they had lost any family members. The one they all knew about was Susan's son, and that was only because she had volunteered the information. Ivy said Kayla had yelled that the hunters had killed Newton, but he didn't ask who Newton was. No one wanted to relive their losses, they just wanted to avenge them.

Cage had found a cut on his leg the next day, even though they'd all passed a cursory inspection at Kayla and Ivy's before going home with the daylight. Joule had been quick to point out that the wound was already partially healed when he found it. Cage figured he must have gotten it jumping out of the tree into the branches, several nights before.

He'd showered five separate times now in the small handful of days. It was an obvious attempt to wash away the carbon black powder that he had not been needing to wear any more. He wanted to look like a person, not the dulled-out version that the carbon made him look like when it was left lingering on his skin. He and his sister had been dialed down by several shades of grey for some time.

Their altered hue was an odd side-effect of the powder. The first wash left them looking only slightly dead. By now, they had washed enough that almost all of it was gone, but the faint traces of powder absorbed the light a normal human reflected, leaving them just a little less vibrant than their usual selves for days. He'd seen the same on the rest of the team.

Susan had gone to the ER for her leg that day. The staff there had stitched her up and sent her home with instructions to stay off it. She ignored that as well as the antibiotics. Cage didn't agree, but he was finding some respect for the woman.

Apparently, when the staff had asked her what happened, she'd not even said "dog bite" but only raised an eyebrow and refused more explanation. As far as Cage knew, nothing had been followed up on or reported about Susan's wound.

He and Ivy both had cuts that needed something more than a Band-aid. Like before, he had washed his injuries using soap in the shower and had done his best at home. When his biggest gash was as clean as he could get it, he held the wound together for his sister to apply their mother's superglue again. Ivy and Kayla had apparently done the same thing. The group had agreed to shower and change and regroup quickly for street clean-up.

When Cage and Joule called Dr. Brett to come check them over that morning, he'd brought them several rounds of amoxicillin again. This time, though, he'd said, "Maybe it's time you stopped gluing yourselves together. Or doing things that make you have to glue yourselves together."

Cage had laughed. "That's the idea."

Dr. Brett had introduced himself around the group, meeting all except Susan, who'd still been in the ER into the afternoon. Once Cage and Joule explained what they'd done, he'd cleared his schedule and come with a large pickup truck, tarps, body bags, and more.

Though they had found several other neighbors kicking at the carcasses the next morning, the team had shooed them away, Dr. Brett sounding official and scary. The twins watched the reactions in their neighbors. Most stood around in awe as the vet helped the team clean up the dead hunters. Dr. Brett didn't once ask what they'd done or how. He already knew enough.

Everyone was curious about the hunters, but that didn't mean they should be poking them with a stick. *What if they hadn't been dead?* Cage thought.

Trying to stay clean—since they'd all just showered—they worked to get the bodies into individual bags in the back of the truck.

"There's cyanide in the water that was on them," Ivy warned him. But since he'd already been briefed by the twins, he only answered, "I know," and continued his help hauling the bodies away. Dr. Brett had taken all of the carcasses.

Neither Cage nor his sister had asked what he was going to do with them. The group stayed silent on that one as well, as though some unspoken pact had been made.

When everything was packed up, Dr. Brett turned back to them, holding a small bag he'd grabbed from the cab of the truck.

"There's an online source for asthma inhalers written in there. And several doses of steroids. You'd have to start taking them at least in the morning before you go out, though."

While he looked at the group, he'd handed the bag to Cage. "I think you might be right about the medications. The guy in the wheelchair was taking the same inhaler." Then he waved good-bye to all of them and climbed into the truck.

Only when he was out of sight had they all turned away and headed home. Cage had showered one more time and laid on his bed in a pool of bright sunlight and warmth. It didn't stop him from falling into a deep, exhausted sleep before his sister even made it into the room.

She must have barricaded the door when she came in, and they both must have slept the sleep of the dead. Cage woke the next morning with the rising sun and headed downstairs to eat and sit in the chairs looking down the street. He'd watched the video from the night cameras before Joule came down the stairs.

"Morning!" She had on her bright pink T-shirt for the first time in ages. She looked like the high school kid she was for once, wearing shorts, sneakers, and a sheen to her face that indicated she'd managed to wash the very last of the carbon black powder away.

"Today's the day," she chirped.

Plucking at the corner of his own bright blue T-shirt to indicate he'd been paying attention, Cage nodded his reply. He hoped that he, too, had managed to wash himself back into humanity.

They gathered the two boxes of materials they had prepped and walked down the street in the sunlight. Once again, the neighborhood looked as though nothing was wrong, as though they didn't pull the curtains tight and clip them closed at night, as though they didn't sleep with barricades on the doors.

But the fact was, for three nights, there had been nothing wrong. Nothing in the front yard. Nothing in the backyard. Nothing down the street.

He didn't doubt that there were more hunters—somewhere —and he didn't doubt that more hunters would come. But now they had a plan. Kayla and Ivy had insisted they do this at their house. Steve and Susan had begged off the whole project, wanting nothing to do with this part of it, though they had agreed it was a great idea.

Once inside, Ivy had played generous hostess, offering sodas and snacks. Together, they'd covered the countertop in black plastic that Ivy had bought just for this. She taped it down around the corners and Cage and Joule—the tallest of the four—helped hang a thin, solid-color blanket behind them with the idea of creating a small studio. Their hope was to disguise the location.

Ivy clipped her phone onto a tripod that she had already set up and looked up at Kayla. "Do you want to be in this? Or do you want me to do it?"

"I think I can," Kayla told her, standing ramrod straight at the counter. Her hands were clasped, fingers interlaced, her back straight. But she made every line on precise cues and never messed it up.

Still, Cage and Joule were more fun.

They ran through it a couple of times before Ivy said they

were ready and turned on the camera. She snapped a still shot and showed them how she'd captured the countertop perfectly. How their shirts and hands showed, but not their faces. Voice would be the only thing any one had to go on, because the point was not to become famous. They were just distributing information.

They didn't mention any names. No streets. No location.

But they showed the design for the trough and did a quick demo of how to stuff and tie a steak with rat poison. Joule held up the boxes showing the two brands that seemed to have worked best. They mentioned that—once this was live on the internet—all the designs would be downloadable from the comments.

They showed the carbon black powder, mentioning the ballpark price and where they had ordered it from. They suggested crossbows, arrows, and handguns—if a person was qualified to handle them. They talked through the timeframe needed to bait, wait, and bait again. They showed off the trackers and the frequency readers, both the original and the better version, with Kayla promising that schematics for the upgrade would be downloadable.

Cage held up the inhaler. "We don't know that this works, but we have some limited evidence that some side effect of the inhaler causes the hunters to not bite, or not want to cause real damage." He went on to emphasize that it was medicine and should not be overdosed, but he'd seen it work. They showed off the bottles, cyanide water, which weapons worked best, and more.

They taught anyone watching how to eradicate a species.

E ight weeks later, Joule turned to her brother. "Did you see the comments that are showing up on our video?"

She'd been tracking the numbers. Thinking she could check it once a day to see if anyone had even watched it was a mistake. Once a day check-ins would not be enough; the post had blown up. Joule had to log in several times a day just to see most of what was going on. A conversation had started and more than one thread had spun off.

Interestingly enough, some of their comments were coming from other states. It seemed the night hunters had evolved and traveled further than they'd originally expected. But groups of fighters were forming up. People had gone online and said where they were from and asked, did anyone want to join their Black Carbon group?

Cage grinned in response to her question. "It blew up again last night. People are reporting in that it's working. We have seven groups that are now patrolling neighborhoods that have been clear for four weeks. Nine more have been clear for two weeks or less, but clear, nonetheless."

"Where did you find that?"

"Search 'Black Carbon'," he told her, and Joule filed that information away for later.

The post with the video contained comments—strings and strings of them—about how it had worked. Some people had created and posted about adaptations they had made. Some had changed the trough, or the location. One group put it in an intersection between two packs they'd located and had intentionally started a war between the hunters, letting them mostly take each other out. The humans had finished the job.

Kayla had designed a better trough that stood on a movable post, so the meat bounced and swayed in the bin, making the whole thing look like it was alive.

"Is the moving trough a better delivery system?" her brother asked.

She'd checked last light. "Preliminary results look good. I'm trying to track comments from the same commenters, to follow one group through the process. Mostly, I can do it. And it looks good. We should tell Kayla."

"If she hasn't already been following it for herself," he said. Joule was thinking he was probably right, when he asked a second question. "Did you see the troughs in the other subdivisions?"

Apparently, he'd gone out driving several times without her. At first, it was a quick hop to the grocery at the end of the street. But then they'd found that they could split up now and go different ways when they needed or wanted. The old survival rules were starting to fall away.

They weren't completely done eradicating the species, but she was watching. Joule had seen two hunters in her backyard over the course of the summer. But since they'd continued to put bait out, both times, she'd been able to use Cage's crossbow to fire preliminary shots from the upstairs window. Once the animals were down, she had used the handgun to finish them off.

Both hunters had been solitary. Surely there were a few others straggling here and there that she hadn't woken up to see. But she was sleeping at night again, and for that, she was grateful.

"Are you packed?" he asked.

Joule nodded. It was both a silly question—because he'd been packing with her—and a huge, philosophical one. She wasn't sure she ever would really be *packed*. They'd both spent the last week carefully combing through the house, one room at a time, picking out what they wanted to take with them.

Cage had chosen some of Nate's shirts, and Joule kept her father's watch and ID. She had a scarf of her mother's and a blouse that she remembered Kaya wearing when the twins had been little. Joule didn't think she'd ever wear it, but she wasn't emotionally ready to let it go. So she'd packed it.

They'd asked their grandparents to store a handful of boxes for them—things they couldn't take to school. The phone call explaining that Nate was gone had been a hard one. But the twins had fought to stay in the house, insisting that the neighborhood had been cleared of the creatures. They'd not told their grandparents that they had been the ones to eliminate the threat.

At last, they'd packed up everything they couldn't afford to lose if the house was repossessed. They stuck Nate's tools into a wheeled, red work cabinet from the garage and loaded it onto the trailer last. They set aside Kaya's most prized books, boxing them with her sewing machine they were taking for their grandmother.

It was more difficult than Joule could have anticipated, picking what stayed and what went. She could only assume that there might not be a house to come back to. The property might belong to the bank by the time they hit fall break—or at least by Christmas.

But the twins had buckled down and they had done it. They

had picked the things out and left the rest. The boxes that would go to their grandparents had been packed into the car with Joule.

They would drop those things off on their way to Stanford. They intended to loop out of their way to visit their grandparents, but neither twin was expecting a pleasant trip. They knew it was going to be hard. But they had a plan and kept the side stop to only three nights and two days for exactly that reason.

Still not quite eighteen, they couldn't sell the house themselves. Their father still hadn't been declared as deceased. Or even missing. Who would report it, if not them? His work hadn't even called.

Steve had commiserated once, saying that his office hadn't been checking on the missing, either. It was too depressing, and there was nothing they could do about it. Filing a report never found anyone. Everyone knew about the hunters. So there was nothing official to give Joule and her brother any legal claim to the property. They'd have to wait and see.

Kayla and Ivy had agreed to pick up the mail several times a week and keep an eye out for anything that looked like an important bill. Joule had given them carte blanche to open the mail. They would all stay in touch. Maybe in a few months, the twins would be able sell the place, but it couldn't happen now.

It was a seven-hour drive to their grandparents. They would leave just before noon, with Cage driving their mother's larger car with the trailer in tow. Joule would follow up behind them in what had been her dad's car. Since they were leaving their own, older car behind, she guessed her dad's car was hers now.

As the time to leave approached, her heart began to clench. She had known this day would come, but she had expected her parents to drive her and Cage to school. She'd expected to get dropped off and thoroughly expected not to have a car and certainly not to have her father's.

Even six months ago, she wouldn't have been able to foresee

today going like it would go. She'd not considered that her parents wouldn't be here to see them off. To keep the house while they were away. To simply still be here.

The night hunters had changed everything.

But she breathed in the satisfaction that she had changed everything for the hunters, too. The neighborhood was starting to flourish again. Even in just a few months, one of the houses had sold. Susan had gotten her lawn mowed and kindly sent her lawn guy down the street to take care of the Mazur yard. Who knew Susan could step up? They had all stepped up.

But Joule was out of time to reminisce. They had to hit the road. She went through the house now, locking things up. She'd showed Kayla and Ivy everything she could think of, given them keys, told them what needed to be done, who to call, that kind of thing. Now she was closing curtains against the daylight, locking the place up, and leaving everything as clean as she and Cage were able to get it.

She realized that, in just a few weeks, there would be dust everywhere, and no one to clean it off. She pulled the curtains on the wide front bay window last and watched as Kayla and Ivy walked up the driveway toward the house. Her heart caught in her throat. She'd made new friends, but she was already leaving.

Kayla and Ivy were watching the neighborhood now. Everything was under control as best it could be. Nights were safe again. Kayla had a new dog.

And her new friends had come to see Cage and Joule off.

S tanford, Spring the next year...

JOULE SAT on her dorm room bed, reading. Or at least she was trying.

Ginnifer popped the door open with no warning. Despite the bookshelf Joule had moved so the doorway didn't reveal everything in the room, the noise filtered in. Joule felt her muscles clench and reminded herself that she had only a few more months with the girl. Then the semester would be over, and next year she'd *choose* a roommate.

"I know! I *know*. Right?" Ginnifer shrieked into her phone.

Joule had no idea what the girl was going on about, or to whom, but she was pretty certain it wasn't about interplanetary travel, or green energy, or even pond algae. If Ginnifer ever spoke of anything important, Joule would be shocked. How had she even been accepted to Stanford? And this was a dorm. Had her parents bribed someone?

"Hey Joule." Ginnifer's greeting was flat as she threw her bag onto the bed. She'd long since given up asking what Joule was reading.

Joule only nodded back. Ginnifer was mad at her, and Joule kind of liked it. She was at least quieter when angry.

Cage had gotten a decent roommate, and that seemed so unfair. They got along. And Joule got Ginnifer.

It had been three days now that Ginnifer hadn't really been talking to her. She'd found Joule in their shared bathroom, checking behind the shower curtain before using the facilities. Ginnifer had laughed at her as though she were an idiot. "I mean, if you did find a serial killer in there, what would you even do?"

Motioning to the back of the toilet, Joule calmly replied, "I'd use the top of the tank against the side of his head."

Ginnifer had blinked.

Joule should have shut up, but Ginnifer was what her mother would have jokingly called a "lesson in growing as a person." Joule was not growing. "Just because you don't have a plan, doesn't mean you should assume that I don't have one."

She'd walked away, the thinly veiled insult hanging in the air. Ginnifer hadn't spoken to her in the three days since.

Still, the mild peace was bound to be broken sooner or later. By Ginnifer. Sure enough, she turned to Joule—who was still in the same place, reading—and spoke as though they were suddenly best buds. "Did you see the pictures someone's trying to pass around?"

Joule only raised an eyebrow. Ginnifer could be referring to any of a number of things.

"Down by the bay. The water keeps coming up and some of the houses have lakes right into their backyards!"

The bay was hardly a "lake," but Joule had found that correcting Ginnifer was a waste of time. She only nodded, but Ginnifer wasn't finished with her.

Tapping quickly, her roommate pulled something up and handed the tablet to Joule. "I mean, look. No one is going to believe that!"

Not mean enough to tell Ginnifer she didn't care, Joule took the tablet, intending to give the picture a cursory glance. But the photo showed a shape in the water off the porch. A fin cut the surface and the shadow was clear. Just four feet away from the house. If whoever took the photo walked down the steps, they'd be in the water with a killer.

"It's so obviously photoshopped," Ginnifer said, rolling her eyes, her hand out to get her tablet back.

But Joule was hanging onto it.

Stanford—the whole area in fact—had flooded recently. Deep enough to inspire a few students to kayak in the waters around campus. Though that water had eventually washed away, there had been warnings this week about storms coming through, about waves pushing seawater into the areas that abutted the bay. Low-lying areas were already sandbagging.

Flood watches had been issued, and the next day's classes already canceled. There was a possibility of epic flooding this weekend.

The picture in Joule's hands meant the problems were worse than high waters and strong currents. Far, far worse.

"It's not photoshopped," she told Ginnifer, still reluctant to hand the disturbing picture back.

A tap came at the window then, and Joule looked up as the first of the predicted rain hit the glass.

ABOUT THE AUTHOR

A.J.'s world is strange place where patterns jump out and catch the eye, little is missed, and most of it can be recalled with a deep breath. In this world, the smell of Florida takes three weeks to fully leave the senses and the air in Dallas is so thick that the planes "sink" to the runways rather than actually landing.

For A.J., reality is always a little bit off from the norm and something usually lurks right under the surface. As a story-teller, A.J. loves irony, the unexpected, and a puzzle where all the pieces fit and make sense. Originally a scientist and a teacher, the writer says research is always a key player in the stories. AJ's motto is "It could happen. It wouldn't. But it could."

A.J. has lived in Florida and Los Angeles among a handful of other places. Recent whims have brought the dark writer to Tennessee, where home is a deceptively normal-looking neighborhood just outside Nashville.

For more information:
www.ReadAJS.com
AJ@ReadAJS.com